Winter's Thrall

Winter's Magic Part 2.5

L. STARLA

WINTER'S THRALL

Cover illustration © Jana Hoffmann
Graphics & book design by L. Starla
Editing by Felix Staica

First edition 2022.

ISBN-13 (Paperback) 978-0-6488424-7-7
ISBN-13 (eBook) 978-0-6488424-6-0

Self-published.

Note from the Author

Trigger Warning *Winter's Thrall* is a dark paranormal romance with strong sexual content that blurs the lines of consent. It also includes graphic m/m, BDSM, and incest scenes. Feel free to skip ahead to *Winter's Mother 1*, the next main entry in the series if such matters are likely to offend or be a psychological trigger.

While this book contains scenes with dubious consent, I do not condone such behaviour.

Remember, Rape Fetish does not equal consent. BDSM scenes should *always* be sane, safe, and consensual. Establish rules, limits, and safewords before you play.

If you are a victim of sexual assault, please consider reporting the crime immediately by ringing emergency services.

For post assault support, I recommend reaching out to a professional, confidential counselling service such as:
   1800RESPECT in Australia (Ph 1800 737 732)
   RAINN in the United States (Ph 800 656 4673)
   SUPPORTLINE in the United Kingdom
   (Ph 01708 765 200)

Dedication

—This book is for fans of Brendan Winters. After falling in love with him myself, I knew he needed his own story. Happy reading!

Epigraph

"Go where the pain is, go where the pleasure is."
— Anne Rice

Playlist

"The Mystic" by Adam Jensen
"Horns" by Bryce Fox
"Flesh" by Simon Curtis
"2 Wicky" by Hooverphonic
"Undisclosed Desires" by Muse
"I Come With Knives" by IAMX
"Saptak-Samaya Mix-Solace" by DJ Cary
"Give Up" by The Beautiful Monument
"I Don't Know Why" by Imagine Dragons
"Mantra" by Bring Me The Horizon
"Complications" by Interpol
"The Crawl" by Placebo
'Bloodline" by Northlane
"Novocaine" by The Unlikely Candidates
"Animal" by Badflower
"Underground" by MISSIO
"Stranger" by Johnny Hollow
"Endless Reverie" by Azam Ali
"The Allure" by Beats Antique
"My Empire" by Windwaker
'Bed of Thorns" by Gary Numan

Playlist available on Spotify.

The Cast of Characters

<u>Pure Blood Mages</u>

Brendan Winters AKA **Jet** (Pure-mage Enchanter, Slave)

Alannah Winters (Councillor, Conjurer, Dress Maker)

Liam Winters (Councillor, Warlock, Police Officer)

Jaxon Hayes (Warlock, Police Officer), from Broken Hill

Kevin Doyle (Broken Hill District Council Head, Mayor)

High Magus O'Grady (NSW High Magus, Mayor)

Acolyte Carran (Spiritual leader), from Sydney

Other Magicals

Caleb Hawthorn AKA **Stirling** (Fae- Endarkened, Gangster)

Bridey Hawthorn AKA **Lady Violet** (Fae- Endarkened, Crime boss), Caleb's older sister

Tyler Quirke (Half-mage Warlock, Police Officer), Brendan's doppelganger

Shane Walsh (Half-mage Warlock, Police Officer), from Broken Hill

Samantha Harrison (Dark mage Abjurer), from Sydney

Levi Delaney (Half-mage, Head Slave)

Damien (Dark mage, Cult member), from Sydney

Melanie (Dark mage, Cult member), Damien's partner from Sydney

Maurus Hawthorn (Dark mage, Slave trader & Cult member), Caleb & Bridey's father

Tara Winters AKA **Lady Scarlett** (Lich, Crime Boss), Brendan's Grandmother

Jacob Bennett (Boggart, Gangster), Brendan's best mate

Cara Hughes (Half-mage Shaman, Conservationist), Alannah's best friend

Nick Patterson (Orc, Orchardist)

Ben Sanders (Weredingo, Vet Assistant)

Connor Foley (Half-mage Abjurer, Marine Biologist)

Bailey Dougherty (Half-mage Warlock, Bartender)

Bianca Oakley (Fae- Wood Nymph, Cabaret Singer)

Amy Smith (Dwarf, Metallurgist & Council Blacksmith)

Prologue

September, during the early events of Winter's Maiden 2.

Sensing him close by, Bridey surveyed the dingy country pub. The news of Daddy's thugs tracking him down had thrilled her to bits. And there he was. Grinning, she gave his group a cursory glance confirming her prediction: Caleb had befriended an assortment of magical people.

It pleased her no end that her brother instantly recognised her, even after all their years of separation. She had missed him and hated her mother for tearing their family apart. When she reached his booth, she drank in the sight of him: from his high cheekbones and chiselled jaw to his long black locks and delicious piercings. 'Hello, Brother dearest.'

'Bridey? W-what are you doing here?' Caleb's shocked reaction was not what Bridey had hoped for.

The guy sitting beside Caleb gripped her brother's shoulder in a show of support. 'Well, well, well. The wayward sister returns.'

Holy shit! When she scrutinised him, he took her breath away. She'd never seen such a fine specimen of a man. Bright green eyes glared at her from beneath dark, choppy hair. A silver ring adorned his prominent brow and a five o'clock shadow accentuated his jaw, drawing attention to luscious lips. And that was merely his outward appearance. Even the man's aura was sexy. She had to know him in every way possible. 'And you are?' The way he studied the air surrounding her intrigued Bridey. *Is he an enchanter too?*

'Brendan Winters. Perhaps you've heard of me?'

Bingo! 'Oh, indeed. The infamous enchanter of Gaeilge Shores. I didn't realise my brother had such interesting friends. Mother did such a stellar job of hiding him from me.' She looked at Caleb and smiled. 'Relax, darling. I'm not going to hurt you. I'm here on business and I'd like your help connecting with the magic community in town.'

'Just business?' Caleb asked.

'Yes, sweetheart. *Just* business. Unless you want more.' When he visibly shivered, she could not hold back the laugh. 'Oh, Caleb... you are precious. And far too much like our sweet Mother. But your friends?' Her eyes travelled around the group, settling on Brendan. 'I think your friends will be a lot of fun. And I'm all for mixing business with pleasure.'

Intense lust flickered in Brendan's aura as his lips parted.

Bridey narrowed her gaze. 'May I sit?'

He shrugged. 'It's a free country.'

When her backside perched in his lap; Brendan rewarded Bridey with the sensation of his arousal. She could not help herself as she writhed against him, drawing an odd sound from his pursed lips.

Their dry humping did not amuse Caleb and she detected a hint of jealousy on top of his disgust.

The mage with spiky hair rose. 'I'm getting another round of drinks. Who's in?' The rest of the group pushed their glasses forward.

She smiled at Spiky. 'I'll have a Purple Haze, thank you darling.'

He frowned at her. 'A what?'

'*Pur-ple Haze*. It's a cocktail. Don't tell me this backwater doesn't know about cocktails!'

'Sure, we know about cocktails. We're just not pretentious enough to care.' Spiky was also sassy.

'Oh dear. I see I'm going to have my work cut out for me with you. What's your name, handsome?'

After a moment of hesitation, he replied, 'Bailey. Bailey Dougherty.'

Remembering the sign on the door, she gasped with delight. 'As in *the* Doughertys? Owners of this fine establishment?'

'Exactly. So, I suggest you show this *backwater* more respect if you don't want piss in your fancy-schmancy drink.' Bailey turned on his heels and strode off to the bar.

'Wow. What a gem.' Bridey turned back to her brother. 'So Caleb, who else do we have here?'

He introduced the rest of his friends.

Bridey noticed how most of the other guys at the table stared at her with hungry eyes, especially the orc and werepup. If she played her cards right, she could bank on a wild night without compulsion. Taking them willingly provided a more exciting challenge, although she'd settle for using her old tricks if necessary.

Chapter One

Eleven weeks later: the day after Brendan sees Liam kiss Alannah. (This occurs prior to Alannah's showdown with Richard.)

Brendan's eyes fluttered open and landed on the dark fae enchantress in bed beside him. 'Oh Shit!' He had several regrets in life, most of which involved Tinder. But looking upon Bridey's sleeping form hit him with a compunction which trumped the lot. In a moment of weakness, he had divorced his soulmate and sold himself into the service of a woman he despised.

Feeling the call of nature, he rose from the bed and froze when he discovered metal cuffs around his ankles, tethered to long chains. He bent over to inspect his bonds. 'Cold iron. Damnit!' The material blocked magic and the locked restraints held tight. Even if he could channel a useful mana source or tune into any ley lines, there would be no escaping his shackles. At least the chains had enough length for him to reach the bathroom.

When he returned to the bedroom, Bridey — or Lady Violet in business circles — sat up and gawked at him hungrily. 'Morning, handsome. How do you feel? Has the pain gone away?'

He glared at her. 'The physical pain has.'

'Excellent. I have fulfilled my end of the bargain, now let's discuss yours.' She held out a contract. 'I honestly thought you would've learned your lesson last time you signed one of these without reading the fine print.'

Snatching the page, Brendan stared in horror at his signature, a bloody autograph beneath seven clauses:

> 1. *The subject, Brendan Winters, has agreed to enter a period of sexual servitude in service of Lady Violet.*
>
> 2. *The agreed period for this contract is one full calendar year from the date of signing.*
>
> 3. *Sexual servitude requires complete submission to Lady Violet, who invokes the right to insist upon any sexual act she desires.*

4. *Failure to submit may lead to the use of compulsion or result in punishment within Lady Violet's dungeon.*

5. *The subject will dress and act according to Lady Violet's every whim and show due respect to all other members of her household.*

6. *The subject may not leave Lady Violet's residence during the period of servitude except under her express orders.*

7. *Attempts to escape will result in punishment within Lady Violet's dungeon and may risk the wellbeing of other members of the Winters Clan.*

This is much worse than the Rhapsody production contract. The chains rattled as he slumped down beside her and tugged at them. 'Are these necessary?'

'I could hardly have my latest acquisition running off in the middle of the night, could I? When you earn my trust, I will permit you to move freely through my home. They are a precaution until such time.'

Brendan groaned. 'How am I supposed to earn your trust?'

'By doing everything I ask and not making any escape attempts when I loosen your tethers.'

'Can I at least go home first and put my affairs in order?'

Lady Violet laughed maniacally. 'Do you think I am stupid, Brendan? I will send Caleb to deal with your apartment when the time is right. For the next twelve months, this is your home, sweetcakes. And when you do step outside, you will remain by my side. Is that clear?'

His last sliver of hope disintegrated as he looked at her with frosty, dead eyes. 'Perfectly.'

'Good. Now get yourself cleaned up. I expect to see you at breakfast in twenty minutes. Levi will collect you at the appointed time.' She strode across the room and left, not bothering to dress before stepping out.

After letting out the mother of all sighs, he pulled himself up and dragged his feet along the floor. Showering challenged him, with his chains tangling several times. He usually preferred to take his time bathing, allowing himself to relax, but it was an impossible task in his current state. So, he sprayed himself with scalding water and wrapped a towel around his torso.

Stepping out of the steam cloud, he found a shirtless guy waiting for him. By all appearances, he was a half-mage; tall and slim, although well-toned, with tanned skin and a small goatee. Aside from the spiked leather collar around his neck, he wore only a pair of faded, ripped jeans.

Brendan jumped. 'The fuck, man? You startled me.'

'Sorry. Brendan, is it?'

He nodded.

'I'm Levi. Lady Violet told me you were expecting me. Here are some clothes.' He dropped the pile of clean laundry on the bed. 'I hope they're an adequate fit. I have filled your drawers with much of the same. There are also some suits and special outfits hanging in the wardrobe, but you can only wear those upon Lady Violet's request.'

Glancing over the options, Brendan observed an assortment of jeans and leather pants. 'There are no underpants or tops here.'

'She only grants such luxuries when we escort her outside.'

Brendan gaped at him. 'For real?'

'Yes. Lady Violet likes to see as much of our bodies on display as possible and she wants us ready to service her at a moment's notice. We only get pants because of her more… conservative clientele.'

He noticed the bruises on Levi's torso. 'So, you're one of her sex slaves too?'

Levi winced. 'I prefer the term *submissive*, but yes, I am essentially a slave.'

Brendan began rubbing himself dry. 'How many of us are there?'

'She likes to keep our number at seven.'

He snorted. 'What? One for each night of the week?'

Levi laughed. 'If only. No, Lady Violet has a thing about the number seven being auspicious or some shit. But I think she also likes to have a variety of men to cater to each of her different tastes. You should expect her to call upon you several times a week… possibly more, given you're her new favourite.'

Throwing the towel aside, Brendan picked up a pair of black leather pants.

As he stood upright, Levi cast an appreciative eye over Brendan's naked body, lingering a while at the sight of his Prince Albert piercing. 'I can see why Lady Violet likes you.'

Brendan was no slouch when it came to his physique, and he knew his other assets were desirable. 'No offence man, but I'm not into dudes.'

'None taken, but you should know your sexual preference means nothing to Lady Violet. If she wants you to sleep with a man, you will do it if you know what's good for you.'

His eyes bugged out. 'What happens if I refuse?'

'One of two things: either she will compel you to do it, or she will beat you to within an inch of your life.'

Brendan gulped. 'Is that what happened to you?'

Levi smiled. 'No. I actually enjoy the way she marks my flesh.'

With a cocked brow, he shot Levi a dubious look. 'Really?'

'It may come as a surprise to you at this stage, but most of us have grown quite fond of Lady Violet. So, don't get any funny ideas about running off.' With a wave of his hand, Levi released the cuffs from Brendan's ankles. 'You will only need to wear these in your room.'

Brendan slid into the tight pants that clung to every ridge and valley of his sculpted legs, emphasising the bulge between them. *May as well look the part.*

'Excellent choice,' Levi nodded his approval. 'Those pants are sure to please Lady Violet. She also insists you wear this.' He stepped forward and attached a collar resembling his own to Brendan's neck.

He brought a hand up to test the feel of the thing. The spikes were sharp, made of cold iron. Not enough to stop him channelling mana, but they would prevent him from magiporting.

'Come on, let's get some breakfast. We must not keep Lady Violet waiting.'

The moment Maurus Hawthorn walked into the dining room that morning, Caleb stiffened. He wasn't in the mood for one of his father's lectures. But when Dad planted his larger-than-life presence directly next to him, Caleb knew that's exactly what he was in for.

Maurus scowled at him. 'Put a shirt on, Son. You look like one of your sister's slaves.'

He snorted. 'I may as well be, with all the demands she makes of me.'

His dad's fist clenched on the table. 'You ought to show her more respect. Bridey adores you.'

'She has a sick and extremely twisted way of showing it.'

As if on cue, the devil herself walked into the room and smiled the moment she spotted Maurus.

'Hi Daddy!' She ran into his arms, falling into his lap as they kissed.

Ick! Caleb still couldn't deal with the level of intimacy they shared. His whole family was all sorts of messed up.

Dressed in one of her many purple corsets and black miniskirts, Bridey moved across to Caleb and straddled him. 'Morning, sweetheart.' As her skirt hitched up, his sister's slick arousal soaked into his jeans and her mouth claimed his with the hunger of a starved lioness.

Caleb detested how remarkable her lips felt pressed against his, how sweet she tasted, and most of all, how much his cock responded to her. 'I didn't realise I was on the breakfast menu.'

Bridey dabbed his nose with one of her manicured fingertips. 'Caleb, dear, you are always on my menu.' She moved to her own chair to his left and watched as servants spread the actual food on the table.

'Have you started training yet?' Dad's gruff voice pulled Caleb's attention away from Bridey's huge breasts.

'No.'

Maurus growled. 'I've been patient with you, Son, because of what your mother did, but I'm done waiting. You could be a great necromancer, Caleb. It's about time you lived up to your potential.'

'Not gonna happen. I don't wanna go dark.'

His dad chuckled. 'I've got news for you, my boy: your soul is already damned. You may as well embrace it.' Then all signs of humour fled. 'It's time to man up and start pulling your weight in this family. You have two options: either join my business or Bridey's.'

Caleb hated the idea of working for his father. From what he'd gathered, it was more of a cult than a company: one practising some of the darkest magic known to mage kind. It made Bridey's life of crime look like a teddy bear's picnic. 'Fine. I'll join the Dark Syndicate.'

Bridey gasped and clapped her hands together. 'Oh Caleb, do you honestly mean it?'

He looked at her and nodded.

She pulled him into a firm embrace. 'I love you so much! I can't wait to work together.'

A young woman in a skimpy French maid costume announced, 'Breakfast is ready.'

Bridey pulled out of Caleb's arms. 'Thank you, Isabelle. The seven may enter.'

The maid bowed, turned, and opened the door for Bridey's harem.

Caleb had been dreading this moment since the previous night.

As soon as Brendan entered—head lowered, as expected of a slave—Caleb observed how Bridey's eyes lit up. Her reaction didn't surprise him either. He had never seen a man pull off tight leather pants so well. The bastard even rocked the slave collar better than anyone else. Ironically, the whole outfit on Brendan's imposing frame made him look more Dominant than submissive.

Maurus erupted from his seat. 'Are you insane, Bridey?'

Having thought as much for ages, Caleb couldn't help the snigger.

Her jaw dropped open. 'What's wrong, Daddy?'

Dad thrust a hand toward Brendan. 'This. Him! Surely you realise your latest catch is a pure mage. Don't you think the Council will notice he's missing?'

Bridey moved across the room and encircled the shoulders of her latest prize with her arm. 'Don't be silly. Brendan here came to me willingly. Didn't you handsome?'

Brendan's gaze lifted and immediately fell upon Caleb. 'Yes, Madame.'

Pure delight registered in her expression.

Maurus shook his head. 'He must be a spy. You cannot trust him, sweetheart.'

'He is not just any pure mage. We have history. Brendan, honey, this is my dad, Maurus. Please explain the situation to him.'

Stepping forward, Brendan offered his hand to their unimpressed father, who shook it reluctantly. 'It's a pleasure to meet you, Sir. Your daughter refers to my involvement with the Dark Syndicate. I was the original source of Rhapsody.'

Caleb almost choked on his coffee. This was news to him. He hadn't realised all those previous visits had been business calls. After Bridey told him about the time she'd fucked Brendan, Caleb had assumed a more sexual relationship existed between them.

Maurus narrowed his eyes on Brendan. 'Let me see your aura.' A moment later he grinned. 'Well, I'll be damned a second time. A bloodline mage with balls enough to dabble in the dark arts.' He glared at Caleb. 'Yet my own son, born with a tainted soul, won't even practise a modicum of necromancy.'

Christ! Even my old man prefers Brendo.

Dad turned his attention back to Brendan. 'What clan are you from, son?'

'The Winters clan, Sir.'

'No shit? You're *the* Brendan Winters?'

Caleb rolled his eyes. *Trust a fellow womaniser with a track record more infamous than Dad's own to impress him.*

Maurus clapped a firm hand on Brendan's back which didn't even make him flinch. 'So, it took a minx like my baby girl to reel you in, huh?'

'Ha! You are precious, Daddy. I wasn't the woman who stole his heart, but I do get the honours of mending it after the bitch went and broke it.' Bridey took Brendan's hand and kissed it.

'Is this true?' Maurus asked Brendan.

'Yes, Sir. Alannah, my soul mate, betrayed me. Lady Violet severed the link for me.'

Caleb had seen and heard as much when Brendan's miserable arse came crawling back to Bridey. He couldn't believe Alannah would do such a thing, but Brendan had seen it with his own eyes.

The old man offered him a nod. 'Women can be vicious creatures. I've had my fair share of heartache too, son. But stick with my girl here and she'll treat ya right.'

Bile rose in Caleb's throat because Dad knew shit about women. Mum leaving was his fault. Dad had corrupted Caleb's sweet sister and turned her into the monster who, in turn, took Caleb's innocence. Mum was only trying to protect him.

'Yes, Sir,' Brendan replied.

Caleb missed the flippant Brendan he once knew. *Is this all an act of compliance to protect himself from Bridey's wrath, or has Alannah majorly damaged him?*

Everything about Maurus Hawthorn sickened Brendan. Knowing this man's history did not help, but even if it had been a true first impression, there would be nothing to recommend Maurus. The long black hair—moustache and beard—along with the biker tattoo sleeves all added to the sicko sleaze vibe. But his aura spoke extensively for him: a pure black soul covered in a thick layer of lust pulsing brightly every time he looked at his daughter. It went some way in explaining Bridey turning out the way she had.

Brendan could clearly see Caleb's hatred for his father, but the jealousy oozing from him was a mystery. *Did Bridey stick her claws into Caleb that deep?*

'Come on, handsome, I'd like to sit with you for breakfast.' Bridey tugged on his hand, pulling him onto a chair. Of course, her idea of 'sit with' meant making a seat of Brendan's lap.

His famished stomach groaned at the sight of the feast laid out on the table. He wondered how he would actually eat with a fae enchantress perched atop him. Fear prickled across his skin as he glanced at the other slaves who took positions on the floor around her feet. They were all skinny men, with pale complexions and hair that varied in length from medium to long. Brendan could see how he fitted the aesthetic, although his muscular build stood out like a tall poppy. *Does she starve these guys? Will I wither away too?*

With a heeled boot pressed into Levi's back, Bridey leaned over the table and filled her plate with an assortment of fruits and pastries. Once she had served herself, Caleb and Maurus followed suit.

After throwing a few scraps to the floor for the other guys to fight over, Bridey turned to straddle Brendan. 'Don't worry, handsome. You will all get a chance to eat the leftovers once I have finished. She handed him her plate. 'Feed me.'

His eyes widened with shock, but he smacked the metaphorical mask back on his face, remembering what Levi had told him. 'Yes, Madame.' Brendan took the dish and broke the food into smaller chunks. He brought a piece of croissant to her lips.

She grazed his fingers with her teeth as she took the pastry into her mouth. The gesture was too damn hot, and he felt himself slipping. As soon as she had swallowed her mouthful, Bridey sucked on his fingers with a lascivious gaze piercing the last of his composure.

'Fuck!' He exhaled the muttered curse.

Bridey beamed as she ground against his hardening cock. 'Later, handsome.' She opened her mouth for another bite. Brendan continued to oblige, and as he lifted a grape, she flashed him a wicked grin. 'I want to take those from your teeth.'

Oh hell! It amazed him how this woman could turn something as simple as breakfast into an act of foreplay. Gripping the fruit between his teeth, he braced himself for the contact. But nothing could have prepared him for the heat of her lips as they pressed against his. Memories of their first night together flooded his mind. Her kisses were still among the most erotic he had ever experienced. Logically, he knew she achieved this through her magical attunement to his senses and emotions, pulling the same tricks he often used to enhance the experience; but his body still responded favourably to her touch.

'Mm, delicious.' She licked her lips and eyed the plate to indicate she wanted more.

This time, she bit into the grape with her lips pressed against his, letting the juices explode into his mouth. It was the sweetest torture to have his stomach grumble while the rest of his body cried out for more of what Bridey could offer. Yet his mind and soul wanted none of it. He could not have been more conflicted if he was Parliament.

A sudden commotion broke the spell between them, and the maid appeared at their side. 'Sorry to interrupt, Madame, but Lady Scarlett is here to see you.'

Bridey tensed and swivelled around to face the girl. 'Thank you, Isabelle. Let her in.'

'Yes, Madame.'

When Isabelle stepped aside, Tara burst into the room like a storm cloud. As soon as she spotted Brendan her eyes flashed with lightning, and she unleashed her fury on Bridey. '*You stupid girl!* I warned you to keep your hands off him. Do you have any idea what you have done?'

Bridey scoffed. 'I'm sorry, Madame, but I'm not the one who broke his heart. Your precious Alannah did that without my help. No offence, but I still don't get what you see in the girl.' She leaned into him and rubbed his bare chest. 'Brendan, on the other hand... I can definitely see his potential.'

Eyeing him, Tara spoke to Brendan telepathically, '*Does she speak the truth about Alannah?*'

He opened his mind to his grandmother, letting her see for herself as he replayed the memory of Alannah leaping into Liam's lap and kissing him. The recollection emotionally traumatised him, but at least the physical pain he had felt as their souls separated had dissipated. Bridey's ritual had successfully severed their link.

Tara's wide eyes betrayed her surprise. 'Is there some way you misread the situation?' she asked aloud. 'Alannah has the entire Council looking for you, Brendan. She is worried about you. When I sensed you here, I assumed my misguided *employee* was holding you against your will.'

More doubts plagued his mind. *Why does Alannah care about me? What am I missing?*

'Shit!' Maurus cut in. 'See, sweetheart, this is why I warned you to stay away from the bloodline mages.'

'Relax, Daddy. Brendan wants to remain hidden, don't you, my dear?' Bridey's nails dug into his thigh as she smiled at him sweetly.

Shielding his thoughts from Bridey's mind reading, he nodded. 'Yes, Madame.' Addressing Tara telepathically, he admitted to selling his freedom. *'I'm one of her slaves now, please get me the hell outta here.'*

Tara gave Bridey a sidelong glance. 'If Brendan is not your prisoner, why is he wearing a slave collar?' Her own thoughts entered Brendan's mind. *'You are not ready, darling prince.'*

'A mere formality,' Bridey continued. 'We have a mutually beneficial arrangement, which I assure you he enjoys as much as I do.' She squeezed his hard nipples to emphasise her point, drawing a pleasurable moan from his throat. 'See? What I'd like to know, Lady Scarlett, is how you were able to sense him here when I have wards up strong enough to conceal this place from the Council's detection magic.'

'Not ready for what?' Brendan demanded.

'Not ready to leave here, to return to Alannah.'

'Please, Grandmother, I'm begging you. Don't leave me to rot in this place.'

Tara's arctic eyes pierced him with shards of ice. *'Enough! My word is final. Accept your fate and wait for the right time.'* She returned her attention to Bridey. 'Some magic is more powerful than anything of Earthly origin.'

Bridey sighed. 'Always so cryptic. I may not channel Aether or nether, but I know they can't be used in scrying spells. You are not soulmates, so the only other possibility is blood magic, which would require….' Her voice trailed off as her eyes flicked back and forth from Brendan to Tara.

Tara laughed drily. 'Has it taken you this long to figure it out, Violet?'

Caleb furrowed his brow. 'Wait, what's going on?'

Brendan bit his tongue.

Bridey ignored him as her eyes narrowed on Tara. 'You died.'

'A minor inconvenience for a lich, I assure you.'

'The fuck?' Caleb glared at Brendan. 'Did you know?'

He nodded. 'Kinda hard to fail in recognising one's own grandmother.'

'Was this why the Council were cagey about letting us in to watch Alannah's trial? Because they discovered the truth and wanted to cover it up?' Caleb asked.

'Alannah's relationship with me was the premise of the trial.' Tara admitted. 'They charged her with treason and the practice of illegal magic… magic I taught her.'

With eyes bulging, Caleb whistled a single note. '*D-amn*. How'd she get outta that mess?'

Tara directed her gaze toward Brendan and smiled. 'She had an excellent lawyer.'

Caleb shot him a look. 'You represented Alannah?'

Brendan nodded.

'Gods, dude. Is there anything you don't excel at?' Although light-hearted, Caleb laced his words with envious undertones.

He could think of plenty of his own flaws and failures, but he did not want to go there. Especially not in present company.

'I still do not trust you, Violet,' insisted Tara. 'As a show of good faith, you will accept Brendan's help on your next job.'

'Wait, don't I get a say in this?' Brendan demanded.

Tara grinned at him. 'Trust me, darling prince, you *will* want in on this job.'

Chapter Two

'Fuck, I swiped right accidently.' Tyler Quirke threw his phone down on the station's break room table in disgust. Like most of the Council's warlocks, he had pursued a career in law enforcement.

Jaxon Hayes dived for the discarded device. 'You aren't still wasting your time with that app, are you, Quirky?' he teased Tyler affectionately. Jaxon may have been his superior in the Council and on the force, but they had always joked around and taunted each other like best mates.

Tyler groaned as he reached out a hand. 'Piss off, Hayes. And give it back.'

'That's Inspector Hayes to you, Sergeant.' Jaxon flashed his pearly whites before looking at the girl's profile.

'You know we can't all have your luck with women, *Inspector*,' Shane pointed out as he sat down with his coffee. In a country town like Broken Hill, warlocks often stuck together, and Shane

Walsh had always been a great team player, even though his half-mage blood made him less powerful than the others.

Jaxon gazed off into the distance a moment. 'You're right. Tanya's pretty special.' He returned his attention to Tyler's phone. 'But what's wrong with Samantha? See, she's a hottie. Oh, and she likes cooking, camping, and hunting.'

Tyler snorted. 'Read on.'

'So, she has a thing for knives. What's the problem?'

'She sounds like a damn psycho, that's what.'

Jaxon slid the phone across the table and laughed. 'I dunno man, she could add some much-needed spice to your sex life.'

Tyler grabbed his phone back. 'Christ, bro! I may be into some kinky shit, but blood-play isn't my thing.'

'No? Then why did you date the v—'

Shane cleared his throat as one of the human officers entered the room.

'—ery hot chick with the teeth?' Jaxon asked.

'I told you, nothing weird happened with her.'

Jones, the human officer, approached Jaxon. 'Sorry to interrupt, Inspector, but the mayor is here to see you.'

'Thanks, Constable. Let him know I'll be there in a minute.' As soon as Jones left, Jaxon rose. 'Come on lads, this might be field work.' That was code for warlock duties, since the Mayor of Broken Hill also led the Mages Council for the Orana region.

When they reached Jaxon's office, Kevin Doyle sat in one of the visitor's chairs with a cup of tea. Jaxon settled into his own seat. 'Greetings, My Lord.'

'Councillor.' Doyle inclined his head a fraction of an inch toward Jaxon before glancing at Tyler and Shane. 'Ah good, I see you have come prepared. Hello Warlock Quirke and Warlock Walsh.'

Jaxon closed the door. 'Figured you'd have some Council business.'

'Well, you ain't wrong. The missus caught a whiff of something dodgy east of here, just out of town.' Councillor Doyle was married to Vivian, the Council member for Organic mana. If she sensed something, the chances of foul deeds were likely.

'Any particulars?' Jaxon sat in a chair, opposite Doyle.

'She said it was blood magic. Might be a vamp nest, but still worth checking out.'

Jaxon shot Tyler an impish grin. 'Might be Quirky's latest date.'

Tyler rolled his eyes.

'I don't think I want to know what you mean, Councillor. Anyway, I'd suggest getting out there while you still have plenty of sunlight, in case you are dealing with some rogue bloodsuckers.'

'Yes, of course, My Lord.' As soon as Doyle took his leave, Jaxon turned to them. 'Right, lads, gear up and meet me out the front of my house in twenty.'

The second Tyler got home, he switched out his standard issue police pistol for a blessed dagger, strapped a matching sabre to his belt, and cast a basic glamour spell to hide it from non-magical eyes. His blood was pumping with anticipation as he ran the few blocks between his and Jaxon's house. It had been a while since he had seen any decent action, both in and out of the bedroom. While combat was not his preferred rush, it still satisfied some of his darker urges.

Jaxon shook his head when Tyler arrived. 'You didn't waste any time! A tad too eager perhaps?'

'I've been chomping at the bit for a decent fight lately.'

'Easy tiger. We don't even know what we're dealing with yet.'

Tyler shrugged. 'I'm sure it will present some form of challenge.'

They jumped in Jaxon's patrol car as soon as Shane got there and headed east. Things were calm and quiet as they cruised along. Several townsfolk stopped to wave, either because they were polite law-abiders, or because they were chicks looking for another round with Tyler.

Tyler did not dislike the local girls, they simply bored him. He put it down to his restless nature and the desire to move on to a more exciting life.

Following the directions to their GPS coordinates took them along a dirt track for the second leg of the journey. Their destination was an old weatherboard shack with a rusted tin roof, which they could only see with the aid of glamour-piercing sunglasses.

Jaxon whistled as he exhaled. 'Someone didn't want the Council to see this place.'

Cocking his glasses, Tyler agreed. 'I'd love to meet the conjurer who imbued these. Damn nifty things.'

'I also hear she's a babe,' added Shane.

'And way out of both your leagues because she's a bloodline mage,' Jaxon explained.

'Typical,' Tyler huffed. He hated the stupid class system dictating who a mage could partner with. Besides, he was ninety percent: practically pure. One great-grandfather diddled the maid and fathered the bastard line of Quirkes. It was quite the scandal when Tyler's mum discovered Dad was not a pure blood. And Tyler figured himself as skilled as a bloodline warlock, so why couldn't he bone the same women?

'You boys ready?' Jaxon's voice brought Tyler back to the present situation.

'Yep,' Tyler replied.

'Yes, boss,' Shane called out from the back of the sedan.

'Walsh, you cover the rear flank, while Quirky and I suss things out,' Jaxon ordered.

'Got it.' Shane slipped away and snuck around the back.

Taking point as usual, Tyler tried the door and found it locked. Nothing his deft hands and a quality lockpick could not handle. A few minutes later they stepped into a slaughterhouse where the butcher was using a cursed blade and chanting in some cultish language as she slit open the sacrificial lamb.

The woman looked up and snarled at her intruders.

Jaxon chuckled. 'Well look at that. If it isn't Knife Girl!'

'What's the job?' Bridey's bare arse-cheeks remained firmly planted in Brendan's lap. He wondered why she even bothered with the sorry excuse for a skirt.

'Information gathering, with probable theft down the line. Oh, and it will mean relocating to Sydney,' Tara replied.

'Why would *I* want any part of this?' Brendan asked.

'Well for one thing,' Tara explained, 'if you do want to avoid Alannah, the move will put plenty of distance between you. But I also imagine the nature of the information itself will interest you.'

His eyes narrowed on her. 'Go on.'

'A tribe of Egyptian elves recently moved to New South Wales and set themselves up along the Hawkesbury River. They are a reclusive bunch, but from what my sources tell me, they have befriended a local dark cult. I want to know everything you can get on these elves; especially their secret magic.'

'When you say tribe,' inquired Brendan, 'Do you mean these elves still practise their traditional way of life?'

'To some extent, yes.'

'Shit! They could be the last living link to the Ancient Egyptians,' —whom Brendan understood to be the most powerful mages of all time.

'Now do you understand the significance of this job?'

'Hell yeah.'

Bridey leaned in, pressing her breasts against him. 'Will you work with me, handsome?'

Brendan considered his options carefully. If he refused the job, he would get more time apart from Bridey, but then he would likely die of boredom while stuck in her house. Dangerous though it might be, this work presented him with a chance to learn some fascinating magic lore, possibly new spells, and it might provide a golden opportunity for escape. He grinned at his captor. 'Yes, if it pleases you, Madame.'

After sucking in a sharp breath, Bridey kissed him fervently. When she pulled back, her heavy lids sat upon dark eyes burning with lust. 'It pleases me very much.'

'Ahem… here are the details.' Tara dropped a large envelope on the dining table.

Bridey reached her hand out and Isabelle, the maid, clambered to bring her the package.

With Bridey distracted as she flicked through the documents, Tara drew Brendan's attention as she spoke in his mind. '*Do not despair, darling prince. I have seen glimpses of your reunion in the future. There is still hope for the two of you.*'

Brendan knew exactly to whom she referred, and her words were like CPR to his soul. '*Thank you, Grandmother.*'

'Right. I will leave you to it.' Tara strode out the room.

Bridey leaped to her feet. 'This is exciting!' She turned to face Brendan. 'Come and see me as soon as you've eaten.' After pecking him on the lips, she skipped off like a schoolgirl: *a seriously hot schoolgirl.*

Blinking, Brendan dismissed the visions of Bridey in plaid skirts as he became aware of the death-stares from eight men. 'What?' He directed the question to Caleb.

'You've been her slave for a day, and you are already getting special treatment. They resent you for it and I can't say I blame them.' Caleb let his chair screech along the wood floor as he pushed it and stormed off.

'I will watch you closely, son.' Maurus's voice drew Brendan's attention. 'I hope you don't give me any reason to lose my newfound respect for you.'

'Of course not, Sir.'

The senior Hawthorn left Brendan alone with his fellow slaves, none of whom spared him a second glance as they dug into the food.

Caleb found Bridey in her suite, absorbed in work at her desk. The light rap of his knuckles against the open door got her attention, but he didn't wait for an invitation.

When he settled on the end of her bed, she spun around in her gas-lift chair and smiled. 'I love it when you come to my bed willingly.'

'Cut the crap, Bry. I want to know where I stand with this Sydney job.'

With two long strides, she crossed the room and straddled him, running a fingernail along his hairline. 'Do you still want to join the Syndicate?'

He took a deep breath before replying, 'Yes.'

'Then you have a choice. You can either stay here and hold down the fort for me, or you can join me in Sydney. Either way, I could use your help.'

Feeling rejected, he closed his eyes. 'So, you don't really want me to go with you?'

She pressed her forehead to his. 'Of course I do, sweetheart. Why would you think otherwise?'

'Because you're giving me the option to stay and… because you've got Brendan now.' He opened his eyes again.

'Oh, sweetie, I gave you the option because you deserve to make the choice. You have been good to me lately; I hoped you would want to come with me. As for Brendan….' She ran her hands along Caleb's bare chest. 'You need to understand he will never replace you. You are my first love and will always hold a special place in my heart.'

He huffed. 'I thought that was Dad's honour.'

Wide eyed, she shook her head. 'Not like that, honey. Dad touched me in a lot of ways, but he didn't fuck me before I turned eighteen. Nor did he ever steal my heart like you did.'

Caleb's breath stuck in his throat, and he whispered a curse. *Why couldn't she love me like a brother?* 'Why didn't you tell me I took your virginity?'

'I thought you'd realised. I mean there was blood on the sheets and everything.'

Thinking back to his first time, Caleb recalled how scared and clueless he'd been about the whole ordeal. It wasn't a happy memory. 'I guess I didn't think to look at the aftermath.'

'Well, now you know.'

'Why'd you do it? You could have had your pick of the boys you went to school with, so why'd ya pop your cherry by raping your twelve-year-old brother?'

Gasping, she jumped out of his lap. 'Is that all it was to you?'

He groaned. 'Come on Bry, don't sugar-coat it. You knew I was petrified, so you compelled me with magic.'

'Oh, you want to play it like that, hmm?' Narrowing her eyes, she shoved her hands against her hips, acting like the bossy brat she'd always been. 'What about those bedroom eyes you often gave me both before and after it happened? And don't think I hadn't noticed all the times you jerked off to fantasies of me. You can't tell me you didn't want me as bad as I wanted you.'

'I was a pubescent boy, Bry. I got hard for anyone with tits and arse. Didn't mean I was willing to go through with it, especially not with my sister.'

'I thought you loved me and wanted me… that's why I did it.' When her eyes watered, Caleb wished for an attunement to emotions because he would have given anything to know if she was manipulating him. 'You can be so dense, Caleb.' She spoke between sobs, slumping beside him. Grabbing his hand, she used it to wipe her tears. 'What could I possibly hope to get out of you by faking these?'

'Shit! I… I don't get it, Bry. Why me?'

'The better question is why not you?'

'I dunno, how about the fact I'm your br—'

'Shush.' She pressed a finger to his mouth. 'It was a rhetorical question, and I haven't finished. There is a lot to recommend you, Caleb. I know you don't tend to let others get close to you. You haven't had many people reinforce your worth. I count myself among one of the lucky few to know the real you and I love everything about you, sweetheart.'

Her words clawed at his heart like briars, entangling themselves in the mess of what he felt for her. He stretched out on the bed and dragged his hands down his face in frustration.

Bridey took the opportunity to mount him, pinning his arms to the bed. 'You're not a pubescent boy anymore, Caleb. And I'm not using my charms, so how do you explain this?' She thrust herself against his growing erection.

'It's exactly what you think it is. I won't deny how these days you turn me on like no other woman can, but that doesn't make it right—'

'Do I strike you as someone who cares what's right?' Her face hovered centimetres above his.

'Well, no, but—'

'Let it go, sweetheart.' She kissed him deeply, her writhing prompting him to moan into her mouth.

In that delicious moment he wanted nothing more than her.

But a knock at the door prompted her to sit up, killing the mood. 'Come in.'

'Sorry for interrupting, Madame, but you asked me to come and see you straight after breakfast.' Brendan's voice pounded the nails in that moment's coffin.

And Bridey's response buried it deep. 'Not a problem, handsome. Please take a seat.'

Flipping his head to the side, Caleb glared at Brendan, who hesitated once he'd read the situation.

'I can always come back later.'

'Don't be silly. Sit here.' She patted a patch of bed directly beside her and Caleb. 'As my two favourite men, you will see a lot more of each other anyway. In future, when one of you walks in on something involving either of you, I want the other one of you to join in. Do you understand?'

'Yes, Madame.' Brendan didn't bat an eye. Caleb knew he'd taken part in all sorts of gangbangs before—a threesome with a brother and sister probably didn't faze him.

Looking down at Caleb from the perch she made of his crotch, Bridey's eyes filled with expectation.

Caleb exhaled sharply. 'Fine. Whatever.'

She beamed. 'Splendid. Now, let's talk business.'

Brendan took his seat on Bridey's bed even though it was all kinds of awkward. She did not even move from her position atop Caleb, who at least wore his black jeans. Brendan knew it was only a matter of time until Bridey demanded the aforementioned threesome, but he still could not stomach the idea. Sharing a woman with friends was not the problem—he had done so plenty of times. But the thought of involving Caleb in the act was sickening, especially if Caleb was not consenting. Then again, glimpses of Caleb's aura and attitude recently made him wonder if the siblings' relationship dynamic had evolved.

Bridey looked at Brendan. 'Caleb has chosen to join the Syndicate, although I'm still waiting to hear if he plans to stay here or join us in Sydney.' She returned her attention to her brother.

That she gave Caleb a choice when she could have compelled him surprised Brendan.

Caleb stared at her. 'I go where you go.'

A gleeful squeal escaped her as she bent down to peck his lips. 'I'm thrilled to hear you say it. Oh, and Brendan dear, if you are going to be working with me, you will need to join the Syndicate in an official capacity too.'

Shit! I didn't think about that.

'Which brings me to my next point. You will both need codenames.'

Brendan's mouth gaped open. 'I didn't think your grunts got those.'

With a sudden click of her finger, a leash appeared in her hand. It connected to Brendan's collar, and she used it to reel him in. 'You are precious, handsome. You might be my slave on an intimate level, but when it comes to work, you will have a more elevated rank. You will both be my captains.'

Caleb stretched his arms, tucking his hands behind his neck. 'What's it mean to be a captain?'

'You must protect me, but you will also command your own teams of soldiers and associates.'

Caleb's face lit up. 'Sounds like a pretty sweet deal. So, what's my name, Bry?' He gave her a pelvic thrust, toppling her balance, and bringing her face-to-face with him.

Yup, definite change in that relationship.

She moaned. 'If you keep this up, sweetheart, I will have to take you right here and now.'

He replied with a smug grin.

'*Caleb*,' she warned.

'Hmm?'

Bridey sucked in an audible breath. With a flick of her wrist, the bedroom door slammed shut and the lock clicked into place. She tugged Brendan's tether before releasing it and letting it vanish. 'Remove your pants, slave.'

Gods no! 'Yes, Madame.' Brendan's hands trembled as he pulled at the waistband. He did not want this. *But what else can I do?* If he refused, she would either compel him or beat him. *And what's up with Caleb?*

Glancing at the bed answered his question in a literal sense when Bridey made quick work of removing her brother's jeans. 'Fetch two condoms from the nightstand, slave.' Her voice was low and breathy.

'Yes, Madame.' Once free of the tight leather garment, he reached across to the drawers and grabbed a couple of foil packets and tossed them on the bed.

Bridey opened one. 'Put the other on yourself.' With eyes fixed on Caleb, she failed to see Brendan's predicament.

For the first time in his life, Brendan was sporting a sponge dick.

Ascending upon Caleb, Bridey groaned. 'What are you waiting for, slave? Take me from behind.'

She was riding Caleb at a leisurely pace, drawing various guttural noises from him. Nothing about the scene suggested a lack of willingness.

A moment later, Bridey shot Brendan a look of displeasure. Her eyes lowered and she gasped. 'Oh dear.'

When she stopped moving, Caleb's head lolled to the side, and he sniggered. 'So, it *can* happen to the great Brendan Winters.'

Brendan's cheeks flushed from anger and humiliation. 'Shut up, bro. You're not helping.'

'Why would I want to help? Also, I'm not your damn bro.'

'*No, but you are hers!* You know… the woman you just shoved your cock inside?' he seethed, unable to contain his outrage anymore. *How do neither of them see the wrongness of the whole sordid affair?*

Caleb snorted. 'Oh, now you have a problem with fucking family members?'

Brendan saw red as he rushed at Caleb with a clenched fist.

But Bridey compelled him to halt. 'What the hell is going on with you two?'

'You're the enchantress, Bry. Why don't you tell us?' Caleb retorted.

Bridey withdrew from Caleb and stood up. 'Your jealousy is clear as day, sweetheart, but what I'd like to know is why. And what is *your* problem, Brendan? The two of you used to be friends.'

Throwing the useless condom aside, Caleb sat up and pulled a blanket across his lap. 'All the single girls in town couldn't satisfy you, could they Winters? You had to fuck with the ones who weren't yours. You're a bigger arsehole than your brother.'

Brendan's eyes narrowed on Caleb. 'You aren't just talking about Bridey, are you?'

Caleb gave him a slow clap. 'Somebody give this man a medal.'

He pulled up the desk chair and collapsed in it. 'I should have figured she got to you too.'

'That stupid *bitch*,' Bridey spat. She sat on the bed and grasped at Caleb's hands. 'What did she do to you, honey?'

'She didn't *do* anything. Not directly.'

Bridey shook her head. 'I don't understand how she could have such an effect on men without using magic.'

'It's called natural beauty, Bry. Look it up.'

Slap! Her hand struck Caleb's cheek, leaving a bright red impression.

'So now we're back to the foreplay, huh?' Caleb hissed. 'Although you might want to get some Viagra for Mr. Flaccid there.'

'Enough, Caleb! Stop acting like such a brat. Now, I suggest both of you quit pining after Alannah like she's a wonderwall and grow up.'

Ouch! Talk about a boot up the arse of reality. 'With all due respect, Madame, I am trying, but I can't easily erase her from my heart with the wave of a magic wand. What I felt for Lana was deep. I still love her as much as I hate her.' The truth of Brendan's own words came as another blow.

Bridey nodded her understanding. 'I'm sorry, handsome. I'm only trying to help. I get furious when I think of what she did to you, and to learn she sank her claws into my sweet Caleb's heart too? It's unforgivable.'

Caleb laughed derisively. 'Like you can talk, Bry.'

She shot him an angry look, but her face softened as Caleb's meaning registered. 'You really *do* love me?'

'How can you of all people not see?'

'It's a side effect of being an enchanter,' Brendan explained. 'We are blind when it comes to reading the love others feel for us.'

'Is that true?' Caleb asked.

'Yes,' Bridey replied.

Caleb exhaled through clenched teeth. 'You don't need to worry about what I felt for Alannah. You pushed those feelings aside when you came back into my life and bulldozed your way into my heart.'

She leaped into Caleb's arms, pushing him back on the bed and kissed him passionately. *Christ! Not again.* A few minutes later she came up for air. 'You are dismissed for now, slave.'

Thank the Gods!

Chapter Three

Shit! No wonder Tyler recognised the redhead in black velvet robes kneeling before them. 'Told you she was trouble.' *What was her name again? I think it started with S. Sally maybe?*

'Stop right there, miss,' Jaxon ordered. 'With the authority vested in me by the Council of Mages, I order you to drop your weapon and raise your hands slowly above your head.'

The dagger slipped out of her grip as she obeyed Jaxon's orders. Tossing her head back, she gave them a better view of her perfect lips and nose, both accentuated by piercings. As soon as her wicked gaze—lined heavily with black makeup— landed on Tyler, she gave him a lascivious grin making his cock twitch. 'Are you going to arrest me, officer?' Even her deep, husky voice sounded sexy.

Fuck! Tyler glanced around to see if he could spot the film crew.

'Damn straight we are.' Jaxon stepped forward with a pair of cold iron cuffs. 'We are taking you in under suspicion of practising illegal magic. Will you come without a fight?'

'Only if *he* takes me.' She gave a slight nod toward Tyler.

Jaxon muttered a curse under his breath as he handed the manacles to Tyler and prepared a lightning bolt in his fingers.

Tyler approached her cautiously. Grabbing her arms, he restrained her. *Or was it Sandra?*

She reversed into him and tilted her head up to look into his eyes. 'Hey, hot stuff, do you enjoy tying up girls?'

Shoving her forward, Tyler tried to ignore how incredible she felt pressed against his body. 'You are not obliged to say anything, however anything you do say can be used as evidence against you.'

'Mm. I'd love to have *you* used against me.'

'I'm sure I can arrange it… just not in the way you're hoping.' *No, not Sandra.*

After licking her lips, she shrugged. 'Your loss.'

'I doubt it.'

'If that's so, why did your dick salute me?'

Samantha. That had to be her name. Thankfully, they reached the car before he needed to reply, and

Tyler handed Knife Girl off to Shane, who sat with her in the back.

When they reached the station, Probably Samantha refused to budge.

'Step out of the vehicle miss.' Jaxon's tone was firm.

'I said I wanted Hot Stuff to take me.'

He sighed, stepping aside. 'Sorry, Quirky. She's all yours.'

Annoyed, Tyler pulled her out of the car without a word.

'Mm. I see you like to play rough too.'

Their first stop was the shielded evidence room, bringing them to the moment Tyler had both dreaded and anticipated. He frisked her robe to check for concealed weapons or magical tools.

'Are you going to strip search me now?' *Why does she have to sound excited about it?*

'Yes. We must follow standard protocol,' Jaxon replied for him.

Tyler removed her robe, freezing in awe of the art all over her body. A few occult symbols mixed with colourful, feminine imagery, and an Aquarius design took pride-of-place on her back.

Samantha glanced over her shoulder, smiling when she realised what had stolen Tyler's attention. 'Do you like my ink? I designed them all myself, although I couldn't draw the final pieces on my back for obvious reasons.'

'You're a tattoo artist?' He stepped closer and traced the design with his fingers, covering her soft skin in goose bumps.

'Uh huh.'

'*Quirky*,' Jaxon warned. 'Stop getting distracted by the pretty lady and do your job.'

Tyler placed the robe in the red evidence tub and removed her cuffs. 'Please take off your bra and underpants.

'Ooh. Are you sure you wouldn't prefer the honours?'

He smirked at her. 'Sorry, it's against the rules.'

She pouted, but complied, handing each undergarment to him in the process.

When she stood naked before him, Tyler's pulse quickened, sending blood to all the wrong parts of his body. *So very wrong.* 'Please squat and cough.' He tried to sound unaffected, but his shaky voice betrayed him.

'As you wish, officer.' Samantha crouched in front of him and coughed.

After inspecting her mouth, Tyler pulled on a pair of nitrile gloves to continue the cavity search. As his fingers brushed against her delicate folds, he wished the thin layer of rubber on his hands could do more to desensitise him, especially when her muscles clenched around him, and she moaned.

'Oh my. Straight to third base and we haven't even kissed yet.'

Hot damn! Once I'm done with work for the day, I am gonna bone the first available redhead I can find.
'All clear.' He rose, returning her underwear. 'Put these back on.'

She huffed. 'You haven't even brought me to climax yet.'

'And I never will. Now get dressed.' He handed her a set of teal prison clothes since they needed to confiscate her magic robe.

They escorted a dressed and restrained Samantha to the interrogation room.

Still standing, Jaxon set his phone to video. 'Please state your name for the record.'

'Samantha Harrison.' Her hazel eyes remained glued to Tyler as she spoke. 'What's *your* name, sexy?'

'I'm sorry, Samantha,' Jaxon explained. 'But you don't seem to understand how this works. My colleague and I ask the questions. Not you.'

Sitting back, she crossed her legs and arms and pressed her lips together.

Jaxon dropped into one of the chairs across from her. 'Now, what were you doing in the ritual circle?'

No answer.

'You were performing blood magic, weren't you?'

She remained tight-lipped and focused on Tyler who slouched against the wall.

He sighed. 'My name is Tyler.'

Samantha smiled. 'Thank you, Tyler. Are you going to ask me out on a date?'

'No.'

'That's okay. I'm cool with a casual hook up if it's all you want.'

Tyler leaned forward, pressing his palms into the Laminex between them. 'Let me get something through your thick head, sweetheart. This fantasy involving me you've got goin' on? It. Will. *Never*. Happen. I suggest you stop testing my patience, because my boss here is actually the good cop and you really don't want bad cop Tyler to come out and play.'

She gulped. Hard.

Like my cock. And unleashing his inner wolverine did not help contain his arousal. 'Now answer the boss' questions.' Sitting down to hide his evident lust, Tyler reclined into the back of the chair and crossed his arms.

'I was doing it to hide myself.'

'Hide yourself from what?' Jaxon asked.

'Don't you mean from whom? I won't answer the question unless you offer me full witness protection.'

Tyler laughed. 'You're a suspect, not a witness. We don't need to offer you shit.'

'Fine. I won't give you inside information on the biggest criminal organisation in the magic world.'

'And what organisation would that be?' he scoffed.

'I told you: protection first, then I talk.'

Jaxon sighed. 'Fine. If you tell us something useful, I promise the Council's protection.'

'You actually are the good cop, huh?'

'Yes.'

'I have one more condition.'

'For fuck's sake. What?' Tyler threw his arms up.

'When you verify my initial intel, I want a full pardon.'

He sucked in a deep breath.

But Jaxon beat him to the post. 'If your word is true, you have ours. Full protection and reprieve from anything linking you to their crimes. Now start talking.'

'Have you ever heard of the Obsidian Cult?'

Tyler's jaw hit the floor. 'Shit!'

Bridey's kiss was the ultimate contradiction: bittersweet, soft yet hard, taking Caleb to the Celestial and Stygian realms all at once. And it made him want her more, despite how much he despised the idea.

She yanked the blanket away, rendering him naked and vulnerable. 'I've got to have you now, Caleb. I need you inside me.' After rubbing against him for a moment, Bridey pushed herself onto his dick.

'Ah, fuck!' It felt even better than usual, especially when she moved against him. Until he realised why. 'Holdup, Bry! I'm bareback here.'

Grinning, she removed her corset and continued thrusting. 'I know. You feel so damn good.'

He grunted. 'So do you.' Sucking in a breath, he pressed his head firmly into the mattress.

'What's the problem, sweetheart?' Her muscles tightened around him.

'I'm not going to be able to hold back if you keep that up.'

Squashing her enormous breasts against his chest, she let her breath tickle his neck and ear as she spoke, 'I don't want you to hold back.'

His skin tingled all over. 'Are you crazy, Bry? I can't come inside you.'

'Why not?'

'You're my sister. What if—'

She cut him off with another Earth-shattering kiss. 'I told you to let it go.'

Caleb squeezed his eyes shut and tried to focus on the pleasure. But it was no use. It was like she had transported him back eight years: that first instance was the last time he had experienced unprotected sex. 'I'm trying, Bry, but I can't.' His arousal began to soften as he opened his eyes.

Anger flashed in her gaze. 'Don't you dare pull back from me.'

Like that's gonna help! 'I can't do this, Bry,' he rasped.

'You can and you will.' Her eyes flickered with violet flecks as a familiar floral fragrance invaded his senses.

Oh Gods, not again! He could feel her intruding in his mind, breaking apart his inhibitions with her intoxicating presence. His traitorous cock responded even before his willpower broke. And as soon as it did, she rode him hard like a savage beast, tearing the last of his resistance to shreds. Caleb lost himself in the ecstasy of the moment. There was nothing like sex with an enchantress employing all her magic tricks.

She wrenched a climax from Caleb, exploding a million stars in his mind.

But when he recovered his wits, the rapture turned to resentment. Silently fuming, he sat up and slipped into his jeans.

'Caleb, honey, what are you doing?'

Ignoring her, he strode out of the room and slammed the door.

Bridey raced into the hall a second later, still naked except for the ridiculous mini skirt.

'*What is your problem, Caleb?*' she screamed.

'You and your damn mind games, that's what!'

'*Excuse* me?'

He slammed her into the wall with a vice grip around her throat. 'One minute you're dangling free will in my face like a mouth-watering steak, the next you throw it to the dogs. You can't have it both ways, Sis. Either turn me into one of your mindless slaves or listen to me when I tell you to stop.'

When it appeared like she was struggling to breathe and trying to talk, he released his hold.

'Is everything okay here, Madame?' Levi's hot breath tickled the back of Caleb's neck.

Glancing over his shoulder, she nodded. 'Yes, thank you, slave. Please leave us.' She turned her attention to Caleb. 'Maybe you should stay in Adelaide.'

Her words stung like a bitch, but he figured she was manipulating him—again. 'Maybe I will.'

Tears pooled in her eyes.

'See? Two can play at that game, Bry.'

'I'm serious, Caleb. I think you should have some time alone to decide what you want because I'm not the only one playing mind games, little Brother.'

He snorted. 'Right. And in the meantime, you can get nice and cosy with Brendan.'

'This is exactly what I'm talking about, sweetheart. You harp on about how wrong it is to be fucking me—how much you hate what we have—yet you start spraying about the place like a tomcat as soon as I become genuinely interested in another guy. You don't own me, Caleb. No man ever will.'

'No. Only *you* get to own people.'

'I don't expect you to understand what I have with my slaves, but they do enjoy serving me.'

'Oh really? Is that why you compel them into preforming depraved acts no sane man would consent to?'

Bridey clenched her fists and her jaw. She never could stand it when Caleb proved her wrong. 'I only do it to free them of the shame they would feel by making the choice. They get as much pleasure out of doing that stuff as I do.'

He gaped at her in disbelief. 'Christ, Bry. Is this what you tell yourself to deal with your own guilt, or is remorse a foreign concept to you?'

She glared at him. 'You can stay in South Australia until you have cooled off. *When* you decide you can't live without me, we will discuss your move to Sydney. But don't expect me to change, Caleb. You will have to accept me for who I am and be prepared to utterly surrender yourself to me.'

'Don't you mean "*If*"?' He walked away from her, unable to bear the torture of gazing upon her glorious body while her wicked mind toyed with him. When Caleb reached the main parlour, he spotted Brendan lounging in front of the big screen television. When Brendan looked up, Caleb scowled. 'I hope you enjoy the Bridey rollercoaster.'

He stepped into the lift to the carpark, to his piece of crap Corolla, and all the way back to his nominal home. It was odd to think of it as home, given how he'd scarcely been there in the last two months.

The Obsidian Cult. Tyler had heard rumours, some of which made his skin crawl.

Jaxon shifted in his seat. 'The Cult is nothing more than folklore: urban legends to scare the kiddies.'

'That's where you're wrong, officer,' replied Samantha.

He huffed. 'And what makes you the expert?'

'I never said I was an expert, but I know they are real because they recruited me.'

Arms still crossed, Tyler stroked his chin with the thumb and forefinger of his right hand. 'How do you know they aren't some sect of dark mages with delusions of grandeur?'

She tensed, then took a few deep breaths. 'Why do you think I resorted to blood magic to try and hide from them? These guys don't want to be known for who they are. They assimilate with other gangs, hide behind corporate logos, and infiltrate governments. I had no idea who employed me at first. By the time I learned the truth, it was too late. I barely escaped with my life and now I have a great big target on my head.'

'Shit!' Tyler rose and paced the room. 'Is this why you didn't resist arrest?'

She nodded.

'What did they hire you for?'

'I'd rather not say.'

Jaxon sighed. 'You have my word that what you say will not incriminate you. We just need to understand what or whom we are dealing with.'

The look of trepidation she gave Tyler almost winded him.

'Please sit down, Quirky, you're making our witness too nervous.'

Sinking into his chair, Tyler attempted a reassuring smile. 'You have my word too, Samantha.'

After a minute of silence, she lowered her gaze, staring down at a dot on the table. 'My skill as a hunter got their attention. They sent me after wild animals and the odd rustling job at first. Then I was taking down big burly men. My employer assured me these thugs were the lowest forms of scum to walk the Earth and I was doin' society a favour. I didn't mind. I enjoyed the thrill of the chase and fed on the fear and disbelief in their eyes when they realised a chick had bested them. But when I was asked to capture innocent women and children and bring them in alive, I began to question things.'

Tyler tapped his finger on the table.

Jaxon was doing well to maintain his mask, although his left eye twitched. 'What happened to the innocents you kidnapped?'

'I don't know.' Samantha's voice trembled. 'They caught me snooping when I was looking into it. The rest is history.'

Being sexy as fuck was bad enough; why'd she have to go and strum my sympathy chords, damnit? 'So where can we get our hands on these arseholes?'

Samantha peeked up at Tyler from beneath her long lashes. 'My contact operated out of an abattoir in Mulgrave.' The look in her eyes was indecipherable, but it sure as hell turned him on.

For a moment, Tyler wished he could channel emotions. When the left side of Samantha's lip curled up in a knowing expression, he wondered if she was. *Shit! Now I'm in trouble.* 'What are your attunements, Samantha?'

'Senses and organic mana; classic abjurer. Why do you ask, Hot Stuff?'

'Because it's my job.'

This time the right side of her lip joined its friend. 'I am registered. You could've looked me up.'

'Really? I figured you for more of a rogue. Besides, abjurers heal people, not kill them.'

'I wasn't always a naughty girl. At least not in the legal sense.' She winked at him.

Captivated by her smile, Tyler propped his elbows on the table and steepled his fingers beneath his chin. 'Do you have any other attunements I should know about?'

Leaning forward, she brought her face as close to his as the table would allow. 'I don't need to channel emotions to know how hard you are for me right now, sweetheart. The lust in your eyes is plain to see.'

Tyler felt like a sailor stranded on the rocks by the siren filling his vision. And his quickened pulse thumped, mimicking the crashing winds drowning everything around him.

'Quit the flirting, Quirky.' Jaxon's distant warning cry drifted across the stormy seas.

Reclining in her chair, Samantha broke the spell and grinned smugly.

So much trouble.

Brendan dozed on the chaise longue as removalists bustled about, packing and moving Bridey's belongings. He'd given up on the mind-numbing tripe on TV hours ago. The viewing had become increasingly more difficult as the workmen continued to walk in front of the screen.

The one time he attempted a change of scenery, Levi dutifully informed Brendan of the requirement to stay indoors. Even his bathroom breaks were supervised. Sighing, Brendan sprawled out on the couch and took the opportunity to be lazy. It was still preferable to being chained to his bed.

'Why don't I get tied up in *this* room?' Brendan asked as Levi sat in the armchair next to him.

'I'm sure I could arrange it, handsome.' Bridey's voice startled him as she crept up behind the sofa. 'My purple bondage rope would look spectacular on your porcelain complexion.'

The thought of soft tethers stroking his skin while she had her way with him terrified him as much as it thrilled him. He shoved the image aside, hoping Bridey did not catch a glimpse. 'Not what I meant.'

She perched on the armrest and leaned into him. 'I know, but I think it's what you want.' Her fingers brushed his face.

Shit! He had to be more careful about letting his guard down around such a skilled mind reader.

'But to answer your question, this is my public parlour. I don't wish to alarm the clients of my more legitimate business operations with the sight of chained-up slaves. And I know you are well supervised here.' Bridey gestured toward Levi who continued to watch Brendan.

'In other words, you don't want them to know we are your hostages.'

Bridey grinned as her hand cupped his chin. 'You're not just a pretty face with a delicious body.' She repositioned directly above him, and Brendan instinctively brought his arms up to prevent her from falling. Her tongue caressed his lips before it plunged into his mouth.

He groaned as pleasure seized his body and held it for ransom. His grip around her sculpted hips tightened as she kissed him.

'Undress me,' she whispered the command in his ear, almost like a plea.

'Are you sure?' Brendan glanced around the room. 'There are still workmen here. Surely your room would be more suitable?'

'They won't mind. Some of them might even enjoy the spectacle. So, let's show them how well Brendan Winters performs.'

Oh hell. Exhibitionism with an audience was one of the few things left on his sexual bucket list and she was waving it before his raging hormones like a red flag. Brendan was beyond thinking or caring who ignited his desires.

He unzipped her corset at a leisurely pace, wanting to savour the experience, but also needing to get his breathing under control. As Bridey's chest sprang free of its fetters, Brendan thought of two young puppies let off their leashes, bounding and playful. Another jolt of lust surged through him, and he felt the sudden urge to taste them. *By the Gods!* He could have sworn he tasted the tart sweetness of stone fruit on his tongue and wouldn't have been surprised to see juice dripping from where his mouth had been.

Her head tilted back, and she let out a drawn-out moan. Looking back at him from beneath droopy lids, she brought her thumb and forefinger into her mouth and sucked on them a moment. Those moist digits clamped on to his left nipple as she prepared her other hand the same way.

Christ! He desperately needed to be free of his tight leather pants. Naturally, Bridey acted on his wishes, knowing exactly what he desired. After pulling them from his ankles, she rose and slid her skirt down in a slow, deliberate fashion. Brendan noticed the crowd of spectators who had stopped working. A few stood there aghast, but most of them were grinning either from amusement or arousal. Acknowledging their presence only enhanced the rush of excitement he experienced.

She sidled over to a locked cabinet from which she extracted some rope, making his breath hitch. As she returned, the sight of her curvaceous body moving in a gradual, provocative manner, while holding purple rope between long, slender fingers, was superheating his blood. Arriving at the edge of the lounge, she motioned for him to sit up. 'It's time we made some of your wildest fantasies come true. But first, I want to be sure this is what you truly want.'

Stunned, Brendan stared at her. *Why is she asking me for consent? Is it part of her pretence for the benefit of our audience?*

'Are you willing to surrender yourself to me here and now, Brendan?'

'Mm, yes.'

She pushed him back into the corner of the seat. 'Stretch your arms out across the backrest.'

As he followed her instructions, Brendan relished the sensation of his skin gliding over the velvet upholstery, all while keeping his gaze pinned on the woman's elven facial features: her high cheekbones and small nose with soft, silvery skin; almond eyes and high, rounded brow highlighted with dark, purple eye makeup; glossy, heart-shaped lips; and pointy ears accentuated with lines of dainty white gold studs; all framed with long, black, lustrous locks.

When she knelt to strap him down, he closed his eyes to focus on the silken texture of the braided cord and the delicate scent of violets washing over him.

'Look at me, handsome.'

The level of intoxication she had already inspired made it difficult for his eyes to open. But a look of fierce hunger rewarded Brendan for his efforts. Bridey impaled herself upon him. He inhaled sharply between clenched teeth. Everything felt extraordinary as her nails clawed his skin and she writhed against him.

'Mm. You have the most breathtaking cock, Brendan. I love the way it rips my cunt open.' Her rough voice sounded close.

'Fuck!' he rasped. He would have said more if he could, but she rendered Brendan Winters speechless.

Quickening the tempo; their bodies collided together in a symphony of panting, slapping, and squelching bringing his senses to new heights. Climbing that mountain eventually brought him to the peak of ecstasy from which he plummeted into the dark abyss of delirium.

Once partial lucidity returned, Brendan became aware of Bridey's warm body clinging to him and her relaxed breaths tickling his neck.

'Wow.' *Fucking phenomenal.*

Bridey looked into his eyes. 'See how perfect we are together? If you stick with me *and* behave, every time can be like this.'

Chapter Four

As soon as they got to Sydney, Bridey insisted on a housewarming. Of course, her idea of celebrating meant a weeklong orgy that kept Brendan run off his feet, which he actually spent little time on. In fact, they were the part of his body doing the least amount of work, with his brain a close second.

'Mm. You have incredible stamina, handsome.' Bridey collapsed beside him on the plum, silk sheets of her enormous canopy bed.

Leila, one of her endarkened guests, slept soundly on Brendan's other side despite the blaring tribal fusion beats coming through every speaker in the house. Glancing at Leila's partially uncovered breasts stirred his dick within minutes of use, making him extremely grateful Bridey had chosen to share him with all her new female acquaintances. *What had Bridey just said? Oh, right… stamina.* He rolled to face her. 'Might have something to do with how much I usually work out; not that I've had a chance to lift weights since moving in with you, Madame.'

'You raise a good point. I was going to get Caleb to pack your things and send them over, along with that sexy car of yours. But he can't do anything until you ring your family and let them know you are okay.' She stood up and walked over to her wall safe. When she returned, she was holding Brendan's phone. 'This should be entertaining.' Her eyes gleamed sadistically. 'Talk to Liam. Let him know you are fine.'

Damn it. He was hoping to call Alannah. *Of course, Bridey would never allow direct contact with her.* He would have to think of a way to send a coded rescue plea through his dense brother.

Bridey hit the call button and handed him the phone.

It took a while for Liam to answer. 'Where the hell have you been?'

'Chill, bro. What's got your knickers in a twist?' Brendan shouted, turning to Bridey and asking her to turn the music down with a hand gesture.

Liam growled. 'Are you serious right now? You disappeared for over a week without telling anyone. I half expected to find you dead in a ditch somewhere. Now I'm thinking I'll be the one to put your corpse in said ditch.'

Once the beats stopped, Brendan poured all the acrimony he could muster into his voice. 'Woah bro, that's pretty harsh, especially coming from you right now.'

'I warned you to keep your hands off her.'

Brendan laughed at the irony. 'Relax, man. It was just a fun tumble in the hay. I doubt it meant much to her, considering she has you again now.' He braced himself for the necessary lie forming part of his plan. 'And you can tell our princess it meant about as much to me too. Oh, and if she doesn't believe you, let her know I severed the link and I'm now whiling away the hours in the arms of a real woman—one who takes care of all my darkest desires.'

Bridey giggled with delight.

'If you're content in your newfound *happiness*, why call me? What the hell do you want?' Liam spat.

'I wanted to say goodbye now that I've settled into my new home beyond the state borders. Plus, I had those messages for you to deliver to Lana.' *Please deliver the damn message, bro.*

'I'm glad you left town, Brendan, because you've saved me a homicide charge.' Liam's deadly serious tone suggested he had missed the hidden meaning.

But Brendan figured only Alannah would get it.

Liam continued, 'And I mean it when I say, if I see you again, I will kill you for what you did to Lana. Good riddance, *Brother*!'

Brendan laughed nervously as Bridey took the phone and ended the call. 'You're right, that was amusing. Things will certainly get interesting the next time I see Liam.'

Bridey was rubbing his back. 'Don't worry, handsome. You don't have to see him ever again if you don't want to.'

Wouldn't that make a pleasant change? Pity it would also mean no more Lana.

'I love how you think of me as the real woman in your life. Shall we explore some more of those dark desires you mentioned?'

'What did you have in mind?'

'I was hoping you would tell me. They are your desires, after all. What's something you want to try, but never have?'

'Hmm. A toughie. I mean, what haven't I tried?'

'Has anyone ever explored this part of your body?' Reaching around, her finger pressed firmly

72

against his back passage, causing his whole body to tense up.

'No.'

Bridey's eyes widened. 'Haven't you ever been curious?'

'Not really.'

'Come on, let's try it. It is only fair given how much you take *my* arse.'

Brendan snickered. 'Yeah, but you enjoy it. A lot.'

'And what's to say you won't enjoy it if you never try?'

He sighed. 'Fine.'

She clapped gleefully. Producing some lube and a set of anal beads from the side drawer, she pointed to the bed. 'On your hands and knees, slave.'

Surprisingly, the simple order turned Brendan on. He had always fancied himself more of a Dominant. *Am I a switch?* Once in position, he practised some deep breathing exercises to relax his body. Did not help much when the lube invaded his senses. 'IImph, that tickles.'

'Does this tickle?' Her fingers were rubbing his entrance.

He sucked in a sharp breath. 'No, it feels spectacular.'

'And what about this?' The first of the beads penetrated him.

'Fuck, it hurts! But in a good way.' He screamed out in pain as she rammed the rest of the toy into him.

She eased them out, then thrust into him again. Bearing down into it, he found after a few repeats he felt more pleasure than pain. 'I think you're enjoying this,' she whispered.

'Uh huh.'

'That's great because I have plans for this gorgeous arse of yours.'

Oh hell.

Looking up from his *Candy Crush* game, Tyler watched as Jaxon entered the break room in a huff.

He pushed Tyler's feet off the table and nodded a silent greeting toward Shane. 'Still no progress from the Sydney warlocks.'

After regaining his balance, Tyler frowned at Jaxon. 'That was our damn lead! *We* should be investigating the cult. I don't give a shit about jurisdictions.'

'No, but the Council does. Unless they find evidence of a global, or at least national threat, we can't do anything.'

Violently pushing his chair back, Tyler leaped to his feet and paced the room. 'The longer they take to verify Sam's statement, the longer she is cooped up in a holding cell. It's not fair on her.'

Shane snorted. 'You only want her out so you can nail her to your bed.'

'Shut up man.' Tyler glared at him.

'Am I wrong?'

The sound of Jaxon's pager saved him from the need to confess. 'A mage magiported into town. I'm gonna check it out.'

'You need our help, boss?' asked Shane.

'No. The Council didn't detect a threat. Probably a tourist. They only need me to greet our visitor.'

Tyler sighed as Jaxon left.

'So, am I wrong?' Shane wore a smug grin Tyler wished he could wipe away with a fist.

He slumped back in his chair. 'Wouldn't *you* enjoy a bit of her southern comfort, given the chance?'

Shane chuckled. 'She might be hot as hell, but that's exactly where she'll take you.'

'Fuck! I'm halfway there already. I can't get her out of my head, Walshy. She's haunted my dreams for the last week, driving me to daily sheet changes.'

'Damn! You've got it bad. Have you tried a substitute? There are plenty of chicks on the Quirky waiting list.'

'Yeah. Once. Didn't help much.'

'Hmph.'

A moment later, Shane's phone rang. 'Hey boss … yeah of course.' He hung up and turned to Tyler. 'Gear up and meet at Jaxon's in ten.'

'On it.'

When Tyler entered Jaxon's lounge room, he blinked twice and pinched himself to be sure he was not dreaming. Sure enough, the stunning woman standing before him was real. As were her hourglass curves, showcased by a snug fitting black singlet top and short skirt. '*Hot damn!*' he muttered under his breath. *What I wouldn't give to bend her over the couch right now.*

Jaxon rolled his eyes. 'This is Alannah, and she needs our help.'

Tyler's eyes trailed upwards from her boots, taking in every glorious inch of her shapely figure, pausing a moment at her perky tits. But gazing upon her face stole the breath from his lungs. Luminous, black hair crowned her proportioned oval face. And her wide eyes fixed on him. Grinning, he rose along with his arousal, extending a hand to greet her.

'This obnoxious flirt is Tyler Quirke,' explained Jaxon.

As she went for the shake, he turned her hand over and brought her knuckles to his lips. 'It's my pleasure, Alannah.'

She laughed. 'I'm sure it is, but don't go hogging all the enjoyment.' Her deep, sensual voice could have been talking about the rain in Spain and he would have heard 'Please take me now.'

'Trust me, beautiful, I'm extremely generous in that department.'

Alannah released his hand and snorted. 'That's what they all say.'

Shane whistled through his teeth and stepped in front of her. 'Hi, Alannah. I'm Shane Walsh.'

'Hi, Shane,' she replied as she shook his hand.

'You'll have to excuse Tyler, here. He's starstruck. I mean, just the other week he was going on about how much he'd love to meet the conjurer who made those glamour-piercing glasses and here you are, in the flesh.'

Tyler gaped at her. 'You made those? Holy shit!'

Shane slapped him on the back. 'You have no effing idea, do you Quirky? Try following some relevant news for a change.'

'There's plenty of significant stuff reported on social media,' Tyler retorted.

'Oh really? When was the last time you saw the Council of Mages post on Instagram?'

Jaxon cleared his throat. 'Guys, please. As riveting a debate as this is, Alannah has an urgent matter requiring our attention.'

Tyler directed his focus on their gorgeous guest. 'Sorry, beautiful. I'm all yours.' He offered her a wink.

Returning his smile, she kept her gaze on him. 'I need help taking down Richard Lane. Do you know him?'

Terror replaced Tyler's mirth. 'Now that's a name I know all too well. Are you telling me he is in my backyard?' From what Tyler had heard, Australia's previous inquisitor was a nasty piece of work who the Council exiled for his archaic methods of interrogation.

She nodded. 'He took me and Liam hostage as part of his revenge plot. I barely got out, but Liam is still there.'

'Liam?'

'Liam Winters. My um, boyfriend.'

Everything clicked. *That's where I know her from!* Tyler felt enraged on Alannah's behalf for all she must have endured at Richard's vile hands. 'Tell me where he's at and I'll pulverise the arsehole for you.'

'Your enthusiasm is admirable, Quirky,' said Jaxon. 'But this is not the time for one-man heroics or half-cocked plans. We need to sit down and talk strategy.'

'Right, of course.' Tyler sat on the sofa. 'What do we need to know, Alannah?'

He did not expect her to sit next to him, let alone close enough for their thighs to touch. But Tyler sensed Alannah would be full of surprises.

After commandeering the jukebox to play all the tolerable metal and rock available, Caleb sank back onto his usual stool at the bar of Doyle Dougherty's, the only pub in Gaeilge Shores. 'You've gotta talk your dad into updating that piece of shit.'

Bailey glanced up from polishing glasses. 'Even if he did, it's not likely to have much to our taste on it. Another pale ale?'

'Better make it something stronger.' Caleb pulled out his e-cigarette.

'Seriously, man? You're gonna get me in trouble again if you smoke in here.'

He took one drag and put it away. 'Sorry, Bay. I needed a smidgen to take the edge off.'

Bailey pushed a bottle of Jameson's along with a chilled whiskey tumbler across the bar. 'Do you realise you've been in here every afternoon for the last week? And your mood has been spiralling each time?'

'What's your point?' He poured a measured shot over the ice and watched in fascination as it swirled around the frozen chunks of water.

'You gonna tell me what's clearly eating at you?'

'Nope.' A large swig of liquor warmed his insides.

Bailey sighed. 'Maybe you should get a job. As much as I love your constant cheerful company, the day drinking habit isn't helping.'

'I have a job. I just tend to work nights.'

His spiky-haired warlock friend stared at him. 'Really? What is it?'

'Nothing I should be telling one of the Council's pets about.'

'Oh hell. Don't tell me you've gotten mixed up in the family business.'

'Fine. I won't.' Caleb skulled the rest of his drink and poured another.

'You're lucky I don't also work for the cops.'

Caleb sniggered. 'No way in hell I'd be mates with you if you did. I can't stand the smell of bacon.'

'See, this is what I don't get about you, man. Your vegetarianism clearly isn't for your health because of how much you drink and smoke. It can't be because of ethics if you're working the unseelie circuit. Why bother?'

He glared at Bailey. 'Do I question your lifestyle choices?'

'No. But mine aren't all shit.'

Caleb groaned. 'Look, bro, I don't do anything to violate animal rights. It's the true-blue[1] reason for my diet. Besides, I never said I was happy about my job. I was given two options, so I went with the lesser evil.'

'Is this what's eating at you?'

'Partly.'

Bailey leaned toward him. 'When was the last time you got laid?'

He snorted. 'Why do you assume this has anything to do with sex?'

---

[1] Genuine

'I didn't before, but with that reaction I'm almost positive it does. I only meant to imply sex can be an effective stress reliever.'

'Unless it's the cause.'

Whistling as he exhaled, Bailey poured himself a shot from Caleb's bottle and threw it back. 'So, Bridey's up to her old tricks again?'

'You sure you're not a mind reader, Bay?'

'I wish I was sometimes. It'd make understanding you a helluva lot easier. You know you can press charges, right? The Council frown upon magic compulsion, especially when used in sex crimes.'

He slumped forward with his elbows on the bar. 'It's not that simple, Bay.'

'Why not? Way I see it, if she did you wrong, you have every right to seek justice.'

'Because I don't *want* to. I love her, man. As fucked up as it sounds.'

'It's not wrong to love your sister, even if she *is* a manipulative whore.'

Caleb scowled at Bailey. Even though he agreed, he hated hearing other guys talk derogatory shit about her. 'It *is* wrong the way I love her.'

Bailey's eyes widened. 'Christ! You don't actually enjoy what she does to you?'

'It's not always non-consensual and even when she enthrals me, she does it in a pleasurable way. I don't feel all the shame and mortification until after the fact.' Caleb downed another shot, and another. Sorrow was not the only emotion he was hoping to drown.

'Shit! You've gotta get away from her, Thornsy. She's poisoning you.'

'You think I don't know? Besides, she moved interstate last week, so there's plenty of distance between us. Problem is I fucking miss her.'

Bailey shook his head. 'You should date other people. Experience some healthy relationships, or even some meaningless hook ups if that's your thing. Anything to get your mind off her.'

'Right, 'cause it's easy to pick up in a town where everyone knows who I am.'

'You'd be surprised. Try casting your eye around the pub tonight. If you see anyone you're attracted to, make a move. If they turn you down, shrug it off and move onto your next prospect.'

'Fine. Whatever. Can we drop the subject now?' A commotion at the door did exactly that. When he turned, Caleb glimpsed his two favourite redheads entering. 'Holy shit! Jacob's back!' He hadn't been alone in Sombre Town lately: the whole friendship group felt the loss of Jacob when he'd disappeared ten days ago.

A bunch of their other friends filed in after Jacob and Cara, taking up residence in their usual booth.

Caleb joined them, directing his initial fist bump and greeting with the impish boggart. 'Hey man, it's great to see you home safe.' He noticed the bruises and gashes on Jacob's face. 'Although you don't look too sound.'

'Richard Lane kidnapped and tortured me, so I've seen better days.' Jacob pulled Cara onto his lap, freeing space for Caleb to sit next to him. 'At least I'm free, which is more than I can say for Alannah right now.'

'What?' Nick roared across the table. Along with every other guy in their group, the orc was a member of the Alannah Winters fan club and could probably become the new president with Brendan out of the picture. 'Why didn't you say something earlier? And why are we sitting here rather than getting her back?'

Jacob frowned. 'The Council have it covered. They don't want us non-mage folk interfering.'

A loud growl slipped from Ben. 'What about Bailey, Connor, and Cara?'

'If things escalate, the Council might summon them, but Richard is in New South Wales right now. They are only mobilising units over there.'

'By the Gods! Way to make us feel helpless,' replied Connor. 'Is Brendo with her? Did Richard capture him shortly after you?'

'No, he's been... wait! Did you think Brendan was missing all this time?'

Most of the group nodded.

Oh hell!

Jacob shot Caleb a look. 'Why don't you guys ask Thornsy? He knows what Brendan's been up to.'

All eyes turned on him.

Cara's dagger stare stung the most. 'What the hell? How could you?'

Chapter Five

'Because he's hurting.' Bianca offered Caleb a sympathetic smile across the table. 'He hates Brendan for what he did.' It was easy to forget how insightful the nymph could be. She didn't make a habit of flaunting her magical gifts in public.

Caleb began comparing her to Bridey. What the nymph lacked by not being attuned to senses mana, she made up for with empathy and a virtuous soul. 'It's true,' Caleb explained. 'Brendan left Alannah and ran off with my sister.'

'What?' Cara gaped. 'Don't tell me the bitch enthralled him?'

Caleb winced. 'No. I know what her magical compulsion looks like better than anyone. Brendan went with her willingly.'

'But why? Alannah was his soulmate.' Tears welled in Cara's eyes.

'Fucked if I know why Brendan does what he does. Apparently, his soul is tainted now, which could have something to do with it.' He stole another peek at Bianca.

'No! I don't believe you!' exclaimed Cara.

'It's true,' Bianca explained. 'I saw his darkened aura myself almost two months ago.'

'But why?' Cara repeated.

Jacob visibly squirmed beneath her.

Caleb didn't miss a beat. 'Damn it, Jacob! Don't tell me you were in on that racket too?'

The boggart hung his head as Cara slid off his lap, pushing Caleb down the booth, and stared at Jacob.

Bailey approached the table. 'What's this about a racket?'

'I can't say,' Jacob replied sheepishly. It was no secret to their friends Jacob worked the unseelie crime scene, but as far as they knew, he only committed petty theft, so Bailey generally turned a blind eye.

Caleb leaned forward on the table to look past Cara, directing his glare at Jacob. 'Was it your idea, or his?'

Jacob gulped and hesitated. 'Mine.'

Bailey tapped the end of the table. 'Is someone gonna fill me in here?'

Jumping up, Nick pulled Bailey aside to explain the situation while Caleb scowled at Jacob.

'So I guess I have you to thank for Brendan stealing her from me.'

'Those two nymphomaniacs didn't need any help to find each other,' Jacob replied. 'You saw the chemistry between them when she first arrived in town. I had nothing to do with that. Maybe Brendo prefers sluts who can pull the same magic tricks he does. Could explain why he kept going back to Bianca's bed.'

Cara gasped. 'Jacob! Take that back!'

Connor cleared his throat. 'If you weren't still recovering from Richard, I'd drag you outside and beat the shit out of you right now, Jacob.'

'Naw, has the little subbie finally found a pair?' Jacob scoffed.

Amy, Connor's dwarven Dom, shot Jacob a death glare.

Even as his eyes wandered in Bianca's direction again, Caleb couldn't hold back the snigger.

When Bailey and Nick returned, the tension around the table was thicker than Daddy Hawthorn's criminal record.

'Let me get this right,' Bailey interceded. 'Brendo got into something highly illegal that brought him closer to Bridey and set him on the path to dark mage wonderland. Oh, and Jacob hatched this scheme?'

Jacob's Adam's apple bobbed as he nodded.

'It doesn't take a degree in rocket science to know what you bastards have been up to.'

Most of the group looked at Bailey with inquiring eyes as Jacob paled.

'Come on guys. What was the biggest criminal news of the magic community all year?'

'The Inquisitor getting shafted?' Connor suggested.

'Rhapsody.' Everyone shot Ben a surprised look. Their weredingo friend had remained relatively quiet up to this point. 'I figured it was the drug Brendan gave me at The Vault. Trial batch?'

The wide-eyed boggart gradually bobbed his head.

'What the hell, Jacob?' The tears were trickling down Cara's face by this stage.

Someone drew up alongside Caleb. When he turned, Bianca extended a hand and smiled down at him. 'Come on, sweetheart, let's leave them to sort out their shitstorm.'

Curious to know what Bianca was proposing, he took her hand and slid away from the booth. Once outside, they walked alongside each other in silence for a few minutes. There was a gentle sea breeze in the air, and Caleb almost forgot it was the start of summer.

'Do you want to talk about it?' she eventually asked.

'About what?'

'Your feelings for Bridey. What happened with Brendan. Any of it.'

Caleb sighed. 'Not really. I need to forget her.'

'I understand.' She stopped walking and pressed herself close to him. 'I can help with that.'

His breath stuttered. If she had made the offer two or more years ago, he would have her pinned up against the nearest wall within seconds. Bianca had been one of his two biggest crushes ever since he moved to Gaeilge Shores. But they'd become good friends of late. 'I don't know, Bee. What if this messes with our friendship?'

'You know I'm capable of doing friends with bennies.' She was right. Brendan wasn't the only guy in their group she'd slept with. Nick and Ben had fucked her on several occasions. There was even a threesome with Jacob and Cara.

But Caleb's brain was wired differently. 'I don't know if I am.'

She ran her long, slender fingers through his hair. 'If you decide you want more after spending one night with me, we can cross that bridge then. But right now, I can feel how much you want me. Are you going to deny what you need?'

Looking over her shoulder, Caleb noticed they'd reached his cottage. When his attention returned to her face, he backed her into his front door, caging her in his arms. 'I prefer things rough, Bee. Sure you still wanna give me what I need?'

Bianca grinned. 'Do I look afraid to you?'

His mouth clamped down on hers as his right hand fished for keys in his pocket. Once inside the house, they undressed frantically between bursts of kissing on the way to Caleb's bedroom.

Caleb woke from his lustful haze hours later. Bianca had drifted off beside him, but his own frayed mind didn't release him from its clutches. Not as a train of thought barrelled into the station: *sex with Bianca was great and all, but it doesn't compare to what Bridey can offer. I really can't live without her.*

Peering out of the limousine window, Brendan watched as their demon driver merged with traffic on the M7. 'Explain to me: why are we traipsing across the city to meet these people in a Gods forsaken nightclub when we moved to Windsor to get close to them?'

'Two reasons, handsome. Their need for anonymity and our desire to impress. This isn't any club. It is the premier nightlife spot for the magical community, not only for the state, but the whole nation. You'll see.'

He sighed, wondering what sort of impression his black mesh top and tight leather pants would have on these dark mages. *At least I get to wear shoes.* But as they pulled up outside the Darlinghurst club forty minutes later, Brendan understood why Bridey had chosen the outfit. All manner of magical races were filing into the place, but their dress code was the one thing they all had in common: sexually provocative.

Bypassing the queue thanks to Bridey's VIP status, they stepped inside. Deafening tribal fusion beats assaulted Brendan's ears. The genre had become flavour of the month because of Sydney's latest elvish immigrants. He did not mind the music, but it could have lost some decibels.

Bridey encircled him in her arms and pressed her lips against his ear. 'I can see a few Council mages around. I'm going to cast selective glamour to conceal us from them.'

'Good thinking,' Brendan agreed.

As the shimmering spell enveloped their bodies, she pulled him up some stairs and stopped at a VIP booth. 'Get me a Purple Haze, will you handsome?' Bridey slipped a wad of cash into his hand and sat down.

'Yes, Madame.' As he made his way across the mezzanine, Brendan caught sight of someone who made his heart stop for a split second.

She sat alone in a booth directly below, watching the dancefloor until three guys joined her. They were all mages, although Brendan did not know any of them. More importantly, there was no sign of Liam anywhere.

His heart was pounding. *Shit! Did Alannah understand my message? Is she here to find me? To free me?* He was pushing through the crowds towards her when a hand grabbed his arm.

'Where are you going, handsome? I hope you're not trying to escape?' Bridey gestured toward his collar, reminding him of the invisible tether binding Brendan to his master.

Panic seized him for a moment. 'Uh, no. I'm heading for the bar.'

Bridey eyed him suspiciously. 'There's one up here, over there.' She pointed to their nearest drinks counter.

'Right, of course.' He smiled and ordered their drinks.

When he returned to their table, the dark mages had joined her. Bridey presented him using his Syndicate codename: 'This is my partner, Jet. Jet, this is Damien, and Melanie.'

He shook each of their hands as Bridey introduced them. When they sat down, Brendan tried his best to engage in the small talk, but he was restless, with eyes constantly shifting to Alannah. When he saw her move onto the floor, he decided to try his luck and offered Bridey his award-winning smile. 'Shall we dance?'

'A wonderful idea, hon. What do you guys say?' She directed her question to their guests.

'I'd love to,' the blonde bimbo known as Melanie beamed.

'Well, I'd hate to disappoint such a beautiful lady,' replied Damien, nodding with his head full of hair gel while taking Melanie's hand.

Brendan led them to a prime position where he could observe Alannah without alerting Bridey to her presence. Their proximity allowed him to see how close she was dancing to her male companion. *Too damn close*. Brendan pressed up against his own partner and let her grind against him while he tuned into Alannah's conversation with heightened hearing.

The guy's lips pressed against her ear. 'Fuck! This is like the sweetest form of torture.'

'Uh huh.' Alannah's voice slurred a fraction. *She must've drunk a bit.*

'I've been hard for you ever since seeing the way you handled yourself in combat. Harder still when you plunged a blade deep into Richard's heart.'

What the hell? Did that sleaze infer she'd killed Richard?

Alannah sighed. 'Sounds like something he would have said.'

'So, this other guy I remind you of, is he like your ex or something?'

Shit! Were they talking about me? Upon closer inspection, Brendan noticed the guy's uncanny resemblance to himself.

Alannah took a deep breath. 'Yeah. An ex who didn't just break my heart but shattered it into millions of tiny pieces.'

Her words pierced his soul with regret. *Gods, Lana! What have I done?*

'I'm sorry to hear that. What about me reminds you of him?'

She's clearly not over me if she's slow dancing with my stunt double. He was on the verge of cutting in and showing Alannah how sorry he was.

But her response stopped him. 'You're overtly flirting even though my heart belongs to someone else. But also, you could easily pass as his twin.'

Her heart belongs to someone else. Is she talking about Liam? A fresh jolt of pain seized his chest. But he questioned the logic. *Why is Lana out with this guy rather than Arse Face?*

His clone's hand moved to Alannah's backside. 'Is he attractive?'

'Extremely.'

'Then I'll take it as a compliment, Alannah.'

'Please, call me Lana.' She pressed her head against his chest.

No way! There were only two people in the world she liked using that name. Brendan was not about to let some impersonator take his place. He broke free of Bridey's grip and moved towards Alannah.

'Where do you think you're going?' Bridey had crept up behind him. She tugged on his collar with a short leash that would have been invisible to onlookers. Spying the source of Brendan's interest, she laughed. 'Do you honestly think she is going to take you back? She's clearly enjoying another man's company.'

Brendan scowled at his captor and turned back to Alannah. Dread filled his gut as he watched her kiss his double. The savage, ferocious kiss reminded him of the passion they had shared.

'Although,' Bridey continued, 'that guy does look a lot like you. Maybe she never stopped loving you after all.' She paused as if to let it sink in as her arms slithered their way around his waist.

And boy, did it sink in!

'Not that it matters now. You broke her heart and all faith she ever had in you by severing your soul link. Not to mention your debt to me. I still own you, Brendan, so don't even think about running off with another woman.'

Bugger what they say about fate. Bridey Hawthorn is the cruellest mistress.

She dragged him back to their booth, releasing the tether a moment before Damien and Melanie came into view. 'It's time for business. So, get your head out of the clouds and focus.'

Brendan huffed as she slammed him down in his seat and straddled him.

He could hear Damien titter. 'I hope we aren't interrupting.'

'Not at all,' Bridey drawled in her deepest, most seductive voice. 'Why don't you join us?'

Melanie giggled. 'Sounds delightfully naughty.'

Fighting the urge to roll his eyes, Brendan shut them instead. A moment later, their booth became a heated make-out session. But he tuned it all out, unaware who was touching or kissing him most of the time. All he thought about was his desire to be free so he could return to Alannah.

'Would you like to come back to our place?' Bridey's voice drifted through the fog.

'Mm, yes please.' Melanie, groggy with lust, sounded close.

When awareness returned to Brendan, the dark mage chick was in his lap. Realising his fingers probed her insides did not even shock him, but his instinctive channelling of emotions and senses concurrently did. *When did I start doing that? Was it because I was thinking of Lana?*

'Nothing would please me more,' replied Damien.

As they made their way to the exit, Brendan pulled Bridey back out of Damien's earshot to query her, 'I thought we were supposed to be working, not fucking around?'

'Oh, you are precious. We *are* working.'

A sickening understanding struck him. 'Is this what you've been doing for the last week? Working the scene by fucking all our contacts?'

'It's what *we've* been doing, handsome. Don't tell me you haven't been taking the opportunity to gain intel from their vulnerable minds? I certainly have.'

'Uh, no. I thought we were just having fun. You didn't tell me they were leads. In fact, you've told me shit. This is not how a business relationship works, *Violet*,' he spat.

She growled. 'That's *Lady* Violet to you, *Jet*. And don't forget I am still your boss when I'm not your Mistress. I'm the one giving the orders.'

Bitch! 'What will Lady Scarlett say when she hears you've been keeping me in the dark?'

Bridey laughed. 'She won't be hearing much of anything anymore.'

He halted and someone ploughed into his back.

'*Watch it, mate!*'

Brendan spun and glared at the goblin who gulped and backed away. Turning back to look at Bridey, he ignored her scowl. 'What do you mean Lady Scarlett won't hear much anymore?'

'Exactly what it sounds like. She's dead.'

Shaking his head in disbelief, he pulled Bridey in close. 'Are you sure she's gone this time?'

'Yes. They destroyed her soul crystal first.'

'But how?'

Bridey grinned malevolently. 'This is the best bit, actually. It was none other than your beloved Alannah who killed her.'

He was utterly gobsmacked. 'That can't be right.'

'Well, I can't imagine the official Council reports getting it wrong. Now, hurry along. We can't keep our guests waiting.'

Brendan resumed walking, masking the grief threatening to burst through its dam. He swallowed against the lump pinching his vocal cords. 'So… who's running the Syndicate now?'

'We are yet to decide. It's customary to allow a week of mourning before the upper echelons gather at a summit to vote in the next Boss.'

Interesting. 'I presume that includes captains.'

Bridey sighed. 'Usually.'

'I want to go.' *This could be a convenient opportunity to undermine her.*

'I suppose I can arrange it. They will expect to see you and I could use your vote anyway.'

'Good.' With newfound enthusiasm for his work, Brendan pushed forward and caught up with

Damien and Melanie, slipping an arm over each of their shoulders. 'Sorry to keep you waiting. The missus and I bumped into an old friend.'

'Not a problem,' Damien smiled.

Grinning, Brendan opened the limo door for them.

Bridey cocked a brow at him on her approach. 'What's your angle, Jet?'

He narrowed his eyes. 'Just doing my job, Madame.' The brutal kiss he savaged her with left her moaning for more. *Yup, I still got it.*

Chapter Six

As soon as Alannah and Liam left, Tyler collapsed onto the couch of the Darlinghurst hotel with a big dumb grin painted across his face. 'Mm. Best night of my life.' He replayed the highlights in his mind. Like the way Alannah clawed at his back when he nailed her in missionary, or the sight of her chest bouncing as she rode him. *Fuck!* The memories alone aroused him.

Shane pushed Tyler's legs aside and joined him. 'Pity she has a boyfriend.'

'Don't be such a buzz kill, man.'

Jaxon took one of the armchairs. 'You're damn lucky Liam didn't kick your arse.'

He shrugged. 'At least I would have died happy.'

Sipping on his coffee, Shane studied Tyler across the steam wafting from his cup. 'Does this mean you're finally over Samantha?'

'Ha!' He had not thought about the firecracker dark mage with red hair since meeting Alannah. 'I guess Lana did *me* a service too.'

Jaxon picked up the room service menu from the coffee table. 'I'm almost afraid to ask, but what are you talking about?'

Alannah had opened her heart to Tyler and told her whole tragic love story over the course of the night. Sex was not the only therapy he had provided her, and he explained it all to the guys.

Shane shook his head. 'Wow. Brendan sounds like a real jerk. To think I used to idolise the guy for all the no-strings pussy he could reel in without repercussions.'

Jaxon sighed.

'What?' Shane jerked his head toward Jaxon.

'Could you be any cruder, Walshy?'

Shane smirked. 'Probably, but that's more Quirky's department.'

Jaxon's phone filled the hotel suite with the sound of Ed Sheeran singing 'Shape of You', so he took the call to his room.

'Hmm.' Shane looked at Tyler thoughtfully.

He lolled his head to the side dreamily. 'What?'

'It looks like you've gone from a ridiculous obsession to an impossible one.'

'She'd consume your thoughts too if she'd rocked your world half as well as she did mine. Lana reminds me of wild strawberries. You wanna know why?'

'Go on.' Shane loved hearing about other people having sex almost as much as he loved watching it.

'She smells and even tastes like strawberries. And she becomes a ferocious animal in bed.'

Shane shifted to accommodate his own obvious arousal. 'Yeah, I heard her through the walls.'

Tyler closed his eyes, allowing flashbacks to occupy his mind. 'I haven't even told you the best part.'

'Oh hell. I'm gonna need a cold shower in a minute.'

'You're not alone. I'll never forget the red marks I left on her soft, milky skin. Lana is a serious masochist.'

'Shit, man. She sounds like the perfect yin to your yang. It's unfortunate she's a bloodline mage, not to mention taken.'

He could not hide the wicked grin creeping across his face. 'I reckon she'll be back for more.'

'Why?'

'She told me a secret about her relationship with Liam. Suffice to say, they are not the most compatible pair. I'll happily sit on the sidelines if it means I'm the one who gets to bring her immense pleasure.'

Shane punched him in the arm. 'You dirty little homewrecker.'

Tugging his arm back, Tyler feigned injury. He leaped at Shane and tackled him to the ground.

They were still grappling when Jaxon returned. 'I don't know if I've walked onto the set of a gay porno or the WWE.'

Pinning Shane's chest to the floor in a Half Nelson, Tyler looked up and grinned. 'You're in time to see my boom boom boom.'

'Please spare me. Besides, we have Council work to discuss.'

Clambering off his opponent, Tyler returned to the couch. 'I'm all ears.'

After stretching out a crick in his neck, Shane joined them. 'After that beat-down I'd say you're all muscle,' he whinged.

'I don't usually hear any complaints about this bod from the ladies.' Tyler returned his attention to Jaxon. 'What's the job, boss?'

'The Council confirmed Samantha's intel. They have approved her release and protective custody on the condition I organise it.'

'That's great news,' Tyler replied.

Jaxon sat in quiet contemplation for a moment. 'After last night, I guess Quirky won't be interested in working with Samantha anymore.'

His ears pricked up. 'Ah, what?'

'High Magus O'Grady suggested we provide the protective detail and use our position to continue gathering information.'

'How so?'

'Moving to the City for one thing. But we would also have to live with Samantha.'

Tyler thought back to his brief encounters with the fiery redhead. Residing in such proximity to her would be dangerous yet exhilarating. He prayed for the fortitude to withstand the inevitable heat. 'Count me in.'

Having seen her guests out, Bridey returned to her bedroom. She was glad to be rid of the dark mage couple and the stench of their cigarette smoke, not to mention the girl's irritating giggle. A change of clothes would be essential. She went straight to the large mahogany wardrobe to select her outfit. *Which*

shade of purple today? Turning, she threw the thistle-coloured corset on the bedroom bench and jumped. 'Shit! You startled me, handsome. I didn't realise you were still in here.'

Brendan's naked body was sitting on her bed and his muscular arms bulged as they rested upon bent knees. *He truly is picture-perfect sex appeal.* The left side of his lip curled in unison with his pierced brow. 'You never gave me the order to leave.'

The expedience of his obedience is impressive. As she knelt against the edge of the mattress, her silk robe gaped open, and he devoured the view she offered with hungry eyes. *How does he reduce me to a quivering teenage girl just with a look?* Feeling the need to recover her sanity, Bridey glanced at the door and waved dismissively. 'You may leave, slave.'

But he did not move. 'I thought you might like to hear what I learned from reading Melanie's mind.'

Adolescent brain instantly transformed to criminal mastermind as Bridey's attention jerked back. 'And what, pray tell, did you garner from that minute head of hers?'

'I'll tell you on one condition.'

After sliding across the soft sheets, she pushed Brendan's knees down and straddled him.

She combed her fingernails through his thick, black hair. 'Are you trying to negotiate with me, slave? I could compel the information from you.'

'Or you could tell me what you got from Damien. I want to help with this mission, but to be effective, I need to know everything you've learned about these people.'

Moving her hand to his chest, she forced him back against the bed. 'I'm the only one who gets to do the pushing.' Lust-filled intent replaced his smirk, and she felt his arousal growing. 'Mm, I love how easy it is to turn you on.'

He thrust against her. 'I could say the same about you, Madame. You're dripping all over me.'

Parting her lips, Bridey tried to catch her breath and reel in her pulse, but both had long since bolted. Control was slipping from her grasp, and she hated it. She brought her palm firmly across Brendan's cheek, leaving a bright red handprint.

Brendan did not flinch. In fact, he replied with a shit-eating grin as he prodded at her opening again.

She slapped his other cheek with greater force before lunging on his cock and taking him with all the frenzy of a possessed woman.

Five glorious orgasms later, she pulled back, depriving him of his own climax.

He glared at her. 'Why doth you leave me so unsatisfied?'

'Because I'm the boss and you will tell me what you know if you want more.'

The insolent bastard shrugged and wrapped a large hand around his erection. Maintaining eye contact, he stroked his shaft, and swirled his thumb through the glistening drop that had formed on the tip.

Bridey's eyes kept flicking between his gaze and the sight of his desire. *And damn—but it looks incredibly hot. He must know he's playing with fire. For every inch of power he attempts to wrest from me, I'll yank back more.* Wrenching his hand away, she restrained his wrist along with its partner, using the manacles fixed to her bed. 'Try coming without me now.'

A low growl sounded from deep in his diaphragm.

'Tell me.'

'Melanie observed my tainted soul and thought about the reward she'd get for recruiting me, a bloodline mage, into the Cult.'

She rose and stamped her foot. 'Damn it! How did she know who you were?' Her eyes narrowed on him. 'You didn't tell them, did you?'

Brendan's expression was incredulous. 'No. But if she could read my aura, she would have seen how strong my magic is. It's not hard to pick the partials from the pures when you know what to look for. We could work this in our favour. I could be your inside man.'

Her eyes travelled over his arousal as she licked her lips. Bridey had to admit his idea was brilliant. 'Would you like to be inside?' She offered him a suggestive look.

'I'll penetrate anything if it pleases you, Madame.'

Oh hell. There I go, turning to mush again. With one swift movement, she mounted him. This time Bridey did not stop until she milked him for every last drop, tearing a guttural cry from him.

With her face pressed against his chest, she listened to the sound of his beating heart: erratic at first, but it gradually settled.

'What did you learn from Damien?'

Tilting her head up, she peered into his big green eyes. 'You mean other than how useless he is at pleasuring a woman? Not much. I bet you ruined Melanie for him.'

A satisfied smile appeared on his face. 'Good.'

'Don't tell me you actually enjoyed fucking that bimbo?'

'Gods no! But *she* had a wonderful time which makes my job easier.' His eyes gleamed wickedly.

Sitting up and still astride him, Bridey brushed her fingers over his skin, starting from his shackled wrists, down his arms and across his torso. Goosebumps prickled his flesh and he bucked against the restraints. 'I think I'm really going to enjoy plotting and scheming with you, Brendan Winters.'

Something about Samantha's wide-eyed awe stirred more than Tyler's hormones. He studied her as she took in the luxury of her new Darlinghurst house. *Our new home*. The hallway opened into a dining room furnished with a solid ebony table and six high-backed, black leather chairs.

Walking through the dining room brought them to the living room and back to the front of the house. Suede couches, a Persian rug, and a large, wall-mounted television were the main features of this space. 'This place is astounding,' she rasped.

'You've only seen two rooms so far.'

She nodded. 'And their combined floorspace already is bigger than my poky flat in The Rocks.' When they moved into the galley kitchen, her jaw dropped.

The modern interior of white granite and black timber contrasted starkly with the terrace's Federation façade. *The Council must have renovated the place recently.* 'Come on, I'll show you to your room.'

After climbing the first flight of stairs, Samantha paused at the landing, glanced down the hall, and back at Tyler as he ascended to the top floor. 'What are all those rooms?'

'This is Jaxon, Tanya, and Shane's floor. We are up here.'

'Oh?' She dragged her tongue across her bottom lip as desire filled her eyes.

Tyler had hoped his time with Alannah would have helped him build some resistance to Samantha's charms. *Alas no.* Gulping, he spun around and jogged up the stairs.

'Who's Tanya?'

'Jaxon's woman. She's an abjurer like you, but bloodline.' Walking along the upper corridor, he tapped against a closed door. 'This is my room.' He continued to the end. 'And here is yours.'

Brushing past him with deliberate contact, Samantha beelined for the bed and sat on the crisp white linens. She leaned back on her elbows and smiled at him. 'Are the separate rooms necessary, Hot Stuff? This big ol' bed is too much for just me.'

He cursed under his breath as his dick twitched. 'They are... essential.'

'I give it a week, tops.'

'What do you give a week?'

'You. Before you stop resisting the urge to keep me warm at night.' She winked at him.

Tyler strode across the room. Raising his right leg, his foot rested on the end of her bed. 'Only a week, huh? I'm offended you have so little faith in my willpower.'

'On the contrary—a week is much more than I'd give most men.'

'You're rather sure of yourself.'

'You don't believe me?' She crawled across the bed toward him with a cocky grin.

'No.' He should have pulled back, but his more stubborn, defiant side won out and he stood his ground. Instant regret surged through him as her hand ran along his leg and up his thigh.

'Tell me, hottie, why did you take the room next to mine?'

'It's where Jaxon put me.'

'Did you disagree with him over it?'

His jaw clenched as he fought the temptation to lie for the sake of argument. 'No.'

'Curious.' Her hand moved to his waistband and tugged at the zip of his blue uniform pants. The proximity of her face and his crotch had not escaped his attention either.

A throat cleared from the doorway, and he cussed below his breath while jumping back. Jaxon glared with stern disapproval. 'I hope I don't have to pull you off this case, Quirky. Miss Harrison is an official informant now. All intimate contact with her is strictly out of the question.'

'Won't be a problem boss, but how can Samantha be an informant when she is in protective custody?'

'To begin with, she will talk us through the details of every hunt she went on. If we need more, we can disguise her.'

She went pale with fear. 'I... I can't go back to them.'

Jaxon stepped inside the room and crossed his arms in a stoic pose. 'Don't worry, Miss Harrison, we do not intend to put you in dangerous situations. If we take you out in the field, we'll surround you with warlocks.'

Tyler shook his head. 'I can't believe you would consider any form of fieldwork for Sam. It's too risky.'

'We will assess the risks when the time comes. For now, I suggest you both freshen up, then join me in the living room so we can get to work.' Jaxon left them alone again.

Samantha smiled warmly as she rose. 'I think I'm growing on you, Tyler.'

'What gives you that impression?'

She drew close and placed her hands on his chest. 'Well for one, you're worried about me.'

'Concern for your safety is in my job description.'

Her lips curled into a smirk. 'What about giving informants nicknames? You called me Sam before. Only my friends use that name.'

He feigned a gasp. 'My Gods! You have friends?'

'Deflection and denial won't hide the truth from me, sweetheart. I look forward to breaking down all your defences and inhibitions.' She sauntered past him and into the bathroom.

Desperate for release from the tension mounting in his balls, Tyler headed straight for his room. After stripping out of his uniform, he collapsed on the bed and closed his eyes. Calling upon memories of Alannah, he bolted toward the climax.

'Mm, quite a show.'

Tyler jack-knifed and grabbed a pillow to cover his lap. 'How long have you been standing there?'

The sight of Samantha in the doorway in a towel was wreaking havoc with his determination. 'About a minute. I came to let you know the shower is free.' She gave him a wicked grin. 'Were you thinking about me?'

'No.'

She shrugged. 'Perhaps you need more inspiration.' Letting her towel drop, she strolled forward. Her brightly inked, curved body was magnificent. Her tits were not exactly large, but they were firm and perky. A tattoo adorned her left side: a heart within a circle of flames with fiery tendrils sprawling across her skin and setting the rest of her chest ablaze.

The enchanting fragrance of coconut wafted across the room and surrounded him. He could feel a lump forming in his throat, making swallowing difficult. 'I think we need to establish some share-housing rules and boundaries.'

'What's the point? I don't follow rules anyway,' Samantha grinned.

'Figures. Even so, I want you to know my bedroom is off limits.'

Samantha reached the end of his bed, standing before him in all her naked glory. 'Then put a lock on the door.'

'Fine, if that's what it takes. Now please excuse me.' He bolted from her intoxicating presence and sealed himself in the bathroom. But his new surrounds did little to break her spell. The odour of a tropical paradise filled his senses. When he stepped into the shower, he found her coconut body wash and banana haircare products. *No wonder she smells edible. Oh Gods! I am in serious trouble.*

Except for the floorplan, Bridey's new house was essentially the same as her previous den. Caleb took in the sights as he entered. All the same purple velvet and black leather furnishings; the same old-style décor and lighting making the place look like a brothel. He knew this was intentional because business for his sister generally involved the art of seduction. And she'd made it perfectly clear she wouldn't be changing for him, putting the onus on him. *That's fine, sweetheart. You want a new me, you'll get a new me.*

A wolf-whistle greeted him the moment he stepped into the parlour. Levi followed up the praise by blatantly checking him out. 'Looking sexy, My Lord.'

I guess I can pull off leather too. He'd worried about overdoing it with the leather trench coat, leather pants, and tight, black mesh top. But Bridey did love the material. *Speaking of Bridey....* 'Tell me, slave, where is my sister?'

'Lady Violet is in her chambers. Third on your left down there.'

Descending the stairs, he followed Levi's directions and found a closed door. Banging, screaming, and moaning permeated through the walls. He considered finding his own room and sneaking in a nap before dinner.

Then Bridey's cries stopped him in his tracks. *'Fuck me harder, Brendan! Tear me open with your massive cock!'*

Jealousy reared its ugly head and all sense of propriety fled as Caleb barged into the room. But he didn't achieve the grand entrance he'd hoped for. They were both facing away from him and the noise they made drowned his booted footfalls. Feeling awkward, he wondered how he should announce himself. In the end, Caleb slammed the door shut and leaned against it with arms crossed.

'The fuck?' Brendan glanced over his shoulder. His jaw dropped at the sight of Caleb.

'What now?' Bridey grumbled as she pulled away from Brendan and turned to face the door. Kneeling naked on the bed, she gasped. 'Caleb?'

He took a moment to appreciate the view and gave her a sly grin. 'Surprise, Sister dearest.' Warm tingles spread across his body as she scanned him with hungry eyes.

'To what do I owe this honour?' Bridey employed her deepest, most seductive voice.

Pushing off against the door, he crossed the room and stood before her, paying no heed to Brendan. 'I decided I couldn't live without you, Bry.'

Her eyes lit up as she ran her hands along his jacket seams. Tugging it off, she let the heavy garment drop with a thud on the wooden floor.

Manicured nails touched his nipple rings a second later, teasing them through the thin veil of mesh fabric. The result was immediate, and Caleb's knees sank to the mattress as pleasure shot through him. He pulled her into his arms and kissed her savagely.

Pivoting, Bridey pushed him onto his back. 'Remove Caleb's boots, slave.'

At first, he thought it weird to have a slave remove his shoes, but this was Brendan. Caleb also felt some perverse pleasure in the way Bridey ordered Brendan to degrade himself on Caleb's behalf.

'Yes, Madame.' Brendan's voice betrayed a hint of reluctance.

If Bridey noticed, she ignored it as she continued kissing Caleb. Her tongue toyed with each of his three lip piercings with renewed interest. It plunged into his mouth and circled around his tongue ring. 'Mm, have I told you how much I love all these?'

Caleb met her gaze and smiled with smug satisfaction. 'Once or twice.'

At the sound of his second boot hitting the floor, Bridey commenced removing Caleb's pants, freeing him from their restrictive hold. As she lowered herself onto him, she eyed him intently.

He knew she was testing him because she hadn't bothered with protection. Caleb maintained the eye contact, refusing to flinch or succumb to any of his misgivings.

She moved gently at first, her breasts quivering in the undulating motion. Moans slipped out each time he entered her.

The doubts still crept in. *This is your sister, you sick bastard!* But he focussed on the blissful expression on her beautiful face. *Let it go, Caleb.*

'Join us, slave,' she rasped, still with her attention on Caleb.

'I'm sorry, Madame, but I can't,' Brendan replied.

With a sigh, she turned to face Brendan. 'That was an order, slave. Do I need to compel you?'

'Probably. I'm not gonna be able to perform without some magical assistance.'

Caleb rolled his eyes. *Here we go again.*

'Why?' Bridey asked. 'You are normally insatiable.'

'It's the whole incest thing. Big turn off, I'm afraid.'

The distraction brought Bridey's movements to a stop, impacting on Caleb's desire. But he was determined to stick with it this time, so he thrust into her.

A loud groan escaped her. 'If Caleb can get over it, why can't you?'

His next thrust made her collapse against his chest. 'Forget Brendan. Let me ravish you.'

'But I want you both at the same time.' She sounded like a whiney brat rather than a grown arse woman. 'I have an idea. Brendan, lie down next to Caleb.'

Brendan hesitated but eventually obeyed her.

Bridey climbed off Caleb and retrieved a blindfold from her bedside drawers which she placed over Brendan's eyes. Next came the leather cuffs around his wrists. 'I want you to forget Caleb's presence. Focus on me.' She spoke into Caleb's mind. *'Once you can see him getting into it, take me from behind.'*

Why doesn't she compel him like with all the other slaves? The thought brought a few insecurities to the surface of his mind as he watched Bridey pleasure Brendan back to a heightened state.

By the time the two of them were going at it, Caleb lost all desire to join in; he was too green with envy. Rolling out of bed, he grabbed his pants, and snuck out of the room. He leaned against the wall to dress. Reclining his head, he winced and shut his eyes as the sounds of Bridey's orgasms washed over him.

'Wow. Things must be getting serious between them if she's even shutting you out.' Levi's voice prompted his eyes to flick open.

'What do you mean?'

'The rest of us slaves have had bugger all time with Lady Violet since moving here. She doesn't just favour Brendan, she has him in her bed all night, every night and then some.'

'Shit! Really?'

Levi nodded.

Things were worse than Caleb thought.

Brendan is going to be a problem if I don't do something about him.

Chapter Seven

When Tyler had cooled off, he made his way to the living room. But the efforts he had gone to with the cold shower were all in vain when he beheld the scene before him. Again, he found himself checking for cameras before returning his gaze to the fox lying on the floor. Denim short shorts barely covered her arse cheeks and her legs swung like scissors as she read her magazine. 'Is there something wrong with the couch?' Tyler asked.

Rolling onto her back, she faced him with impish eyes. 'I'm sure it's fine, but I feel more at home on hard surfaces.'

He tried to control his breathing, but her transparent white singlet top did not help, especially since it revealed her obvious lack of bra. Thoughts of ruining the rug along with his sanity and career filled his mind. For once, he was thankful for the cockblocker in the room.

Jaxon shook his head in disapproval of Tyler's obvious affliction. 'Sit down, Quirky. We have work to get on with.'

Tyler took the sofa, at which point Samantha decided the plush seat next to him was suitable after all.

'Let's start with the details of the first time you killed a person,' Jaxon suggested.

'What do you want to know?'

'Everything.'

Samantha gulped and looked at Tyler with wide eyes.

He attempted a reassuring smile as he nodded for her to spit it out.

'It started about two years ago now. I was almost seventeen at the time.' Clutching Tyler's hand, she curled up against him.

Tyler's heart ached for her. To be a hardened criminal by seventeen suggested the girl had lost her innocence at a young age. He wondered what her youth had been like.

'I was delivering my latest game to Mr. Black at the abattoir:

> *After paying me in cash, he handed me a manilla folder. 'This is your next assignment.'*

I gasped at the file. 'What you are suggesting is murder.'

'Read the man's bio and you'll see how you're doing the world a favour.'

A second glance showed my target was a felon with several charges of assault, drug trafficking, and even rape. His real name was Andrew Short, but he was a notorious gang leader better known by the alias Sharp Knuckles.

Tyler exchanged a glance with Jaxon. They both remembered the name, but the media reports claimed he had died of a drug overdose.

'What does this man have to do with you?' I asked.

'Let's just say he is a spanner in the cogs of business.'

If Mr. Black had dealings with Mr. Short, I didn't want to know the specifics, so I took the job description and left.

According to my briefing, I was required to make his death look like an overdose, which meant getting close and personal. I shuddered at the thought. But I was uniquely adept at illusionary magic for

an abjurer and as far as I knew, Mr. Sharp
was only human. So, I organised a meeting
through my old gang contacts.

Jaxon was engrossed in her tale, leaning forward like an attentive child listening to his favourite story. 'Old gang?'

'Nothing as organised as the Knuckle Heads. We were a bunch of magical street kids who stuck together. Most were unseelie, but a few of us were otherwise.' Samantha continued her story:

When I met Sharp Knuckles, he
warmed to me straight away. Too warm if
you ask me. The guy was an absolute sleaze
who couldn't keep his hands to himself. But I
didn't let it deter me, instead using it to my
advantage. I played the drug-running angle,
starting small to build trust. Eventually, I
got my hands on a shitload of
methamphetamine.

The night before I was scheduled to
make my first meth run, Knuckles invited me
to party with him in his room. Seizing the
opportunity, I went prepared with two
preloaded syringes. One a placebo, the other a
lethal dose of ice.

Things started out much as I had envisioned. We shared a couple of whiskeys while listening to shitty RnB, all with his arm draped over my shoulders. When he begged me for a striptease, I figured there was no harm in it if he kept his own clothes on, so I complied. It took a lot of restraint on my part to hold back the bile when he began jerking off to my performance.

Then came the moment of truth. He approached me with hungry eyes and grabby hands. 'I gotta fuck you, baby.'

I smiled sweetly. 'Yeah, okay, but why don't we make it feel fantastic?' Pulling out the needles, I held them up. "You can deduct these from my cut."

Knuckles laughed heartily for a full minute. 'Come on, sweetheart. You and I both know you don't need to use drugs to enhance the experience. Let's cut the crap and both agree to use our attunements to heighten each other's sense of touch.'

I gaped at him in wide-eyed wonder.

He feigned shock. 'Wait? Didn't you know I'm magical too?' Dropping his extremely powerful glamour, he revealed himself as a dark elf. He sauntered forward.

'Um, I think I should go.' I tried backing away, but my legs hit the bed.

'There's no way you're gonna leave this room tonight, baby. Not after getting me all hot and hard.' He pounced on me, pinning me to the bed with his muscular frame.

When I screamed, he muffled my cries with his vile mouth. But common sense, or perhaps it was my survival instinct, kicked in and I realised it was in my best interest to play along. Letting him think I was enjoying the way he defiled my body would ensure my freedom afterwards.

That was exactly how it played out, and as he dozed beside me in bed, I stuck him with the needle. I used my organic attunements to increase the rate of uptake. As soon as I was sure of his demise, I dressed and slipped away.

The story horrified Tyler. Knowing the lengths she had gone to churned his nauseous gut. 'Did you end up using sex to get to the other guys you assassinated?'

'A few, but not the majority.'

Jaxon's furrowed brow suggested equal displeasure. 'Did your employer know Mr. Short was a dark elf?'

'He denied all knowledge, but I suspect he, or at least someone in the Cult knew.'

'What makes you think that?'

A smug grin took over Samantha's visage. 'Because every other man I killed was a magical disguising themselves as human.'

Feeling parched and famished from hours of sex, Brendan made his way to the kitchen. After turning on the light, he dashed for the fridge and grabbed the orange juice. When he spun toward the breakfast bar, he didn't expect to see anyone sitting at it. 'Christ! What the hell man?'

Caleb sat alone, sipping from a whiskey glass, and glaring at Brendan.

'Why are you drinking alone in the dark?'

'Why are you always banging my sister?'

He chugged a mouthful of juice from the carton and slammed it on the bench. 'Is that what this is all about? A pity party because you can no longer have your own sick way with her whenever you want? I don't get you, man. Since when did you go from being Bridey's biggest hater to the president of her goddamn fan club?'

Caleb rose and faced off against him. 'Shut your mouth, Winters. You have no idea what you're talking about.'

'No? So, you're not jealous because I get to fuck Bridey more than you?'

Seething rage boiled in Caleb's features. '*I. Said. Shut. Up!*' He attempted to shove Brendan back. But the effect was almost comical given their size difference. The scrawny goth had nothing on Brendan's build of pure muscle. Caleb did not appear to care.

Brendan was getting sick of Caleb's attitude, especially since it wasn't like Brendan had a lot of choice when it came to Bridey. 'Or what? You'll hit me? Go for it, Thornsy. Take your best shot, you filthy sister-fucker.'

Caleb's right fist collided with Brendan's left cheek, immediately followed by a left hook to the jaw.

Brendan staggered, shocked at the force behind Caleb's punch. Slamming into his opponent, he decked Caleb and followed up by pinning him to the floor. 'Why did you follow her, Thornsy? You had your chance at freedom and squandered it.' He became vaguely aware of footsteps running throughout the house.

'You don't get it, do you?' Caleb spat. 'I was never her slave. I sought Bridey out willingly. I don't just love my sister. I'm in love with her.'

A gasp drew Brendan's attention to the doorway and a shocked Bridey. 'Step back, slave.' As soon as he rose, she ran to Caleb and pulled him up and into her arms. 'Oh Gods, are you okay, sweetie?' She studied Caleb's black eye. 'Levi, get Marcus.'

Levi's gentle reply of 'Yes, Madame,' came from the hall as he retreated.

Bridey turned a lethal gaze on Brendan. 'What the hell is wrong with you?'

'Your brother's attitude problem, that's what.'

'Have you forgotten your place, slave? You must never raise a hand against me or mine.'

Caleb wore a satisfied smirk for all of one second before Bridey turned back to him—then he gave her an apologetic expression. 'I'm sorry, Bry. I lost my shit when he called me a *filthy sister-fucker*.'

Again, she turned the stink eye on Brendan. 'Did you really insult my dear boy with such putrid language?'

This was ridiculous. He felt like he was back in primary school. 'Yes.'

'Yes what?'

'Yes, Madame.'

Marcus rushed into the room a moment later and got to work on healing Caleb's injuries.

'So, you provoked him?'

Brendan threw up his hands in a defensive stance. 'Oh, you want to play the blame game? Caleb's unhinged because of you and I'm at the end of my own damn tether because of Alannah. It all comes back to you bitches.'

She stormed across the room and slapped him hard across the bruised cheek.

It hurt like hell, but Brendan was beyond caring.

'Levi, lock Brendan in the dungeon for the rest of the night.' Her eyes narrowed on Brendan. 'Perhaps some solitary confinement will help you cool off.'

A set of large hands grabbed Brendan and led him away. He did not worry at first because he expected to see more of a BDSM playroom. While he was not wrong about the room's intended purpose, there was more of a medieval torture chamber aesthetic to the place. Numerous sets of cold iron chains dangled from the stone walls, a steel spanking bench sat to the right, and a wooden cross to the left. There were no soft furnishings or silken ropes in sight. *Bridey likes to play extremely rough. No surprises there.* He turned to face Levi, who was tying him to the St. Andrew's Cross. 'Is this where she flogs you?'

'In theory. She hasn't touched me since we moved here.'

'Don't tell me you're envious too?'

Levi scowled at him. 'Do you realise she hasn't spent time with any of us lately? Lady Violet has focussed one-hundred percent of her attention on you.'

'That's not true. She's been working.'

'With *you*.'

Brendan bit his lip. There was no point arguing.

'At first I thought I'd outgrown my use because her sadistic streak had gone. But now it seems you'll replace me there too.'

His pulse was racing, and a cold sweat dripped from his brow. 'What do you mean?'

Levi ignored him as he continued securing the bonds. He walked to the exit, pausing to look over his shoulder. 'Enjoy your flogging, Brendan.' He flipped the light switch and closed the door.

The room plunged into complete darkness. Brendan had never experienced pure pitch black before. Not even living in the country, away from the light pollution of the city, had prepared him for this. At least there had been the moon and stars back then. This sealed underground chamber did not allow a crack of light to enter from the rest of the house, too dim even for a single shadow. Every creak and groan in the building's foundations stole his breath. Each sound toyed with his wild imagination. Living in a world of magic—knowing ghosts, ghouls, and demons were real—only enhanced his fear during the bleak solitude. Pushing anxiety aside, he calmed his breathing and attempted sleep.

As with any night when he closed his eyes, his thoughts returned to Alannah. He missed her more than ever, craving the feel of her soft skin, her strawberry-scented hair, the sound of her laugh, and the look of desire in her eyes. Not to mention her sweet, musky taste. He loved the way she tingled on his tongue. *If I ever get the chance again, I swear to the Gods I will feast upon you, Lana.*

Memories of all the intimate times they had shared came flooding back, making him stiff as a board with no means of relief. Ironic how Bridey was not the instigator of his true torture.

With a grunt, Tyler startled himself awake. 'Shit! I must have dozed off. Sorry guys.'

'Sleep well?' Samantha's voice sounded close. Too close.

As awareness of his position set in, he realised where his subconscious had decided to rest his head. *Those soft things aren't cushions, are they?* Jolting upright on the couch, he blinked and gave her a sheepish smile. 'Sorry.'

'Trust me, sweetness, if it bothered me, I would have moved.' She brought her thumb up to his chin and wiped at something. 'You were drooling.'

A brief inspection revealed a wet patch on her top turning the white fabric even more transparent. Mesmerised, the crick in Tyler's neck ceased to worry him, no longer the stiffest part of his body.

'Oh good, Quirky's awake.' Jaxon entered the room with a coffee in hand.

'I'm gonna grab myself one of those.' He dashed into the kitchen and took his time fixing a drink. Glancing at his watch, he noticed it was 3AM. *Have they been up working all this time?*

After a few deep breaths, Tyler returned to the living room. 'Woah!' The number of police files littering the floor had more than doubled since he nodded off.

'Walshy printed out the last one.' Jaxon placed the profile at the end of the bottom row.

'Where is he now?'

'Turned in for the night. Unlike some members of the team, he's been awake this whole time.'

Tyler gave Jaxon a guilty grin. 'Did he do a stat analysis for us first?'

'Here.' Jaxon shoved the report in his face.

He took it and sat on an armchair to maintain necessary distance from Samantha. Sipping on his coffee, Tyler flicked through the summary. *Christ!* She had killed fifteen men in two years: two dark elves, seven endarkened, two goblins, two ogres, one dark mage, and a gorgon. But no obvious patterns. 'A gorgon? Wow, I didn't think we had many of those in Sydney.'

'You'd be surprised,' replied Samantha.

'Please tell me you didn't sleep with'—he checked the gorgon's name—'Mr. Ambrose.'

She bit her lip, telling him all he needed to know.

Images of her blindfolded and tied up in a dark dungeon filled his mind. 'Fuck!'

Samantha laughed. 'Don't worry. It was actually a pretty wild night.' When her gaze met his, her eyes widened and her mouth formed an 'O.' 'You weren't worried, were you?'

Holding his breath, he shook his head.

'Oh my. I knew there was a reason I felt drawn to you.'

'Quirky!' Jaxon broke their heated stare. 'Get over here.' He handed Tyler a marker. 'Make yourself useful.'

'Ouch, boss.'

Jaxon ignored his comment as he moved between the files. 'What do all these guys have in common? Why did the cult target them?'

'You mean aside from them all being magical?'

'There has to be more to it, but you may as well list it.'

Tyler stepped up to the large whiteboard mounted on the wall and wrote MAGICAL in big bold letters, along with the other obvious factor: MALES. 'Well, they're all criminals.'

'Uh huh.' Jaxon's gaze drifted far away.

'I guess by extension they would all be dark. The two goblins are the only possible anomaly there, but if they were crooks—'

'Samantha, do you know if those goblins had black souls?' Jaxon cut Tyler off.

She shrugged. 'I don't know for sure, but they were scumbags, so I wouldn't put it past them.'

Tyler added MALEVOLENT and MURKY SOULS to the list. 'Sam, you mentioned these guys were all disguised as humans. What exactly did you mean?'

'Well, they used strong glamour, making it hard for other magicals to detect their true nature. They weren't registered with the Council either.'

MASKED and MISCREANTS.

'Ho-ly shit!' Jaxon exclaimed as he rushed from one file to the next.

'What is it, boss?'

Jaxon fell silent while he continued checking the facts. When the Inspector looked up, his expression cried Eureka! 'They were all suspects for murders committed shortly before Samantha killed them.' His focus shifted to Samantha. 'You might have been the clean-up crew.'

Tyler wrote MURDER SUSPECTS, pleased he was able to use another M word.

When Jaxon looked at the board, he rolled his eyes. 'On that note, I'm gonna call it a night. Quirky, I want you to pull up everything in the system on the murder cases these guys were linked to. Tomorrow we will compile and compare the data.'

'Sure thing.' Tyler followed Jaxon upstairs, veering right to enter the office.

As he sat down at the computer desk, Samantha drew close, placing her hands on his shoulders. 'What can I do to help?' She began to massage him.

Tyler sucked in a deep breath. 'As enjoyable as that feels, Sam, it's a serious distraction.'

'Um… sorry.' She sat on the chair next to him with an expectant look.

'Maybe you should get some sleep. You must be exhausted.'

'Nah, I'm good.'

'Okay, fine. You can take notes for me. Fire up that laptop and open a new spreadsheet. Title the columns: name, age, race, gender, home, and cause of death.'

Samantha gave him a blank look.

'What?'

'I uh, don't know how to do any of that.'

'Seriously?' He felt his mouth gaping open.

'I dropped out of school at the age of thirteen. I haven't used a computer since year seven, and even then, I sucked at it.'

'Oh. Can you write with a pen?'

'Yeah.'

He grabbed a notebook and drew the table up for her. 'Here, jot the notes on this.'

'Thanks.'

He grabbed the summary file and entered the first name into the police database, which linked directly to a murder case. 'Jannette Dawson, sixteen-year-old human girl from Surry Hills. Cause of death was exsanguination resulting from sharp force trauma to the carotid artery.'

'Ah, what does that mean?'

Tyler sighed, gaining a new appreciation for his competent colleagues. 'Blood loss, neck wound.'

'Okay, got it.'

He eyed her sceptically before glancing at the page. Surprisingly, her writing was neat, and all the information was there, although she had used the astrological gender symbol, and the cause of death was a drawing of a neck with blood dripping from it.

'Artist, remember?'

His gaze shifted to the ink on her chest before meeting her eyes. 'How could I forget?'

She grinned knowingly.

Tearing his eyes away from her, Tyler returned his attention to the screen. After hitting PRINT on the case file, he punched in the name of the

141

next suspect. 'This time we have Sarah Woods, another human girl, aged fourteen, from Parramatta. Same cause of death.'

As they continued compiling the details, the link became obvious. 'They're all teenage girls who died in the same way. Tying them all to different suspects is what kept the human police from calling it a serial killing. I wonder why the Cult picked these girls.'

'Seems obvious to me.' Samantha was leaning back with her bare feet propped up on the desk. 'They were used for blood magic and if I were to hazard a guess, I'd put money on their virgin status. Human virgin blood is a lot more potent than lamb's blood.'

Hot damn! Her smarts made him ache for her even more. 'Question is, were those men trying to hide like you, or were they performing a ritual for the Cult?'

Bright light washed over Brendan, forcing him to squint. After blinking a few times, his eyes adjusted to the new luminescence.

'Tsk, tsk. You've been fantasising about her again. You ought to stop tormenting yourself.' Bridey stood before him holding a cat o' nine tails.

Shit! Levi had been right. 'Are you going to beat me now, Madame?'

Stepping close, she stripped him, freeing the erection from the confines of his pants and gripping it firmly. 'Would you like a flogging, slave?'

He sucked in a sharp breath, savouring the way she enveloped his dick in her warmth. 'W… what kind of a question is that?'

'A simple one. Would you like to meet the cat?' She moved back, releasing her hold of him.

Brendan's eyes widened as he shook his head adamantly. 'No, Madame.'

'No? What a shame.' With a sudden flick of her wrist, she struck him across the chest.

'*Ah, fuck!*' His skin burned from the whip's sting.

Bridey's grin turned malicious, reminding him of all the reasons he despised her. 'I thought you enjoyed receiving pain as much as you loved giving it.'

'Not *that* much pain,' he rasped.

'You know the deal, handsome.' Her hand returned to squeezing him. 'Sink into it.'

Her behaviour would disgust Brendan's kinkster friends. There was nothing sane, safe, or consensual about Bridey. The woman was a deviant who subscribed to the old libertine way of life, and she gave the Marquis de Sade a run for his money. *Was it any wonder the original sadist was also endarkened?*

Crack! Another blow, this time to his stomach.

A guttural cry escaped him. This time Brendan closed his eyes to regulate his breathing. His arousal was waning, but Bridey's hand brought it back with a vengeance mere seconds before punishing his left thigh. *At least the pain is more tolerable this time.* As Bridey oscillated between hurting and pleasuring him, the sensations merged, and he felt himself slipping into a euphoric trance.

When lucidity returned, Marcus was dressing the wounds left by the lashings. A quick glimpse of his surroundings told him they were on his own bed. Bridey sat on the edge of the mattress, half a metre from him, looking pleased with herself. The rest of the slaves stood around the room like silent sentinels mocking his stupidity.

Caleb was there too, front and centre with a smirk showing how much he was revelling in Brendan's humiliation. 'It doesn't pay to anger my sister.'

The left side of his lip curled up. 'Depends who you ask. I think I understand what Levi sees in her now. And it looks like I found another way to please my mistress.'

'Fuck you, Winters!' Caleb charged at him, pinning his throat in a choke hold.

'*Caleb!*' Bridey screamed. 'Stop it.'

He pulled his hand back, but Caleb still towered over Brendan with a menacing glare.

Once Marcus finished, Bridey drew closer. 'This feud needs to end. Right. Now.'

'Like it's that easy, Bry.' Caleb gave her an incredulous look.

'Sure it is. The two of you used to be friends. You need to kiss and make up.'

Oh hell.

'What are you suggesting?' Caleb asked.

Bridey sat back and crossed her arms with wicked intent in her eyes.

Caleb paled. 'You didn't mean literally, did you?'

She nodded. 'You are both harbouring a lot of aggression and animosity for one another. I want to see the pair of you fuck the hostility out of each other.'

'No way.' Caleb began backing away from the bed.

'Don't make me compel you sweetie.'

'Are you going to compel him too?' His arm flung toward Brendan. 'Because I doubt he wants this either.'

Bridey stood in front of Caleb. 'I don't need to because, unlike you, Brendan submits to *all* my requests.'

Caleb hissed but stood his ground.

Mounting Brendan, Bridey kissed him, flooding his senses with her strong, feminine power. She paused. 'Slaves, don't let Caleb leave.'

Brendan peeked over Bridey's shoulder and saw Caleb attempting an escape. But Bridey claimed his mouth again, stealing all his attention. The way she devoured him while her fingers toyed with all the sensitive parts of his body drove him to distraction.

A moment later he was inside her and she employed the reverse cowgirl position. 'Come to me, Caleb.'

When Caleb wavered, Levi pushed him forward. He reluctantly crossed the remaining distance.

'Strip for me please, sweetheart.' Bridey spoke with a soft, pleading tone as she continued to grind against Brendan.

Much to Brendan's surprise, Caleb complied, removing his black mesh top, and inching off the leather pants.

'Now kiss me.'

This time there was no hesitation when Caleb straddled Brendan's thighs to reach Bridey.

Brendan closed his eyes to avoid watching the siblings sucking face. Instead, he focused on probing Bridey's welcoming depths. He felt disappointed when she retreated. But the weight of a warm body filled the void and soft lips crashed against his. They could have belonged to a woman's mouth except the piercings gave their owner's identity away. His eyes shot open in shock and met with Caleb's.

Pure desire sizzled in Caleb's aura. 'Can we please get this over with? And don't get any funny ideas, 'cause I'm only doing this for Bridey.'

'Fine.' He closed his eyes and let Caleb kiss him again. Without thinking, Brendan channelled his attunements, heightening what they felt.

Before long they were both moaning as they writhed together. The noise was like an alarm sounding in Brendan's brain as realisation hit him. The experience was a huge turn on, and upon inspection, it fuelled Caleb's lust too.

'Turn over so I can fuck you.' Caleb issued the order in a breathy voice.

Why did that have to sound so damn hot? Brendan obeyed without a second thought. The next surprise came when he discovered surrendering to Caleb's sodomy felt better than sex with Bridey.

Chapter Eight

The room was peaceful, dimly lit by the afternoon sun peeking around the velvet curtains. The only movements were the rise and fall of two breathing chests; the only sounds were the breaths escaping their mouths. Brendan felt grateful Bridey had chosen to give the guys some privacy in the end. Shifting onto his side, he took a moment to gaze upon Caleb, who had closed his eyes. 'Hey, are you sleeping?' He kept his voice to a low whisper.

'No,' Caleb replied without opening his eyes.

'Do you still hate me?'

Caleb sighed, pausing before he answered, 'No. Do you? Hate me, I mean?'

Well, I'll be damned. Bridey's insane plan worked. 'No.'

His eyes fluttered open, and his head turned to face Brendan. 'So what… does this mean we're friends again?'

'If you want. I never had a problem with *you*. It was your attitude getting on my nerves.'

'Fair point.' Caleb snorted. 'I dunno about being friends after that, though. Every time you talk, I'm gonna remember your girly pleas for me to go harder.'

Brendan punched him playfully in the arm. 'Come on, man. You loved it as much as I did.'

'Shut up, Winters.'

He could not hold back the chuckle. 'Not until you admit how much you love my arse.'

'Not gonna happen.' Caleb wore a smirk big enough to cover his naked body.

A body Brendan felt strangely attracted to. *Men didn't turn me on before. Why now? What's changed?* He leaped at Caleb and tackled him.

They both laughed as they grappled each other. Inevitably, Brendan won their wrestling match, pinning Caleb to the mattress. As he looked down upon his goth friend, the humour between them escalated to heated desire. The bright red lust flickering in Caleb's aura was beckoning him. *Is this really what I want?* Typically, he let his hard dick answer as his lips pressed against Caleb's.

When his arousal turned into a savage need, Brendan growled into Caleb's ear before asserting himself in a gruff voice. 'Now it's my turn on top.'

Caleb's eyes shot wide open, but he nodded. 'Please go easy on me. I've never… you know?'

Gods! Caleb is an anal virgin, yet he is offering himself to me! The thought alone drove Brendan wild. 'I understand. Let me know if you need me to stop at any stage.'

'Will do.'

Brendan sat back, allowing Caleb to move into position as he grabbed the lube. When his attention returned to the naked man before him, the resemblance between Caleb and Bridey's bodies astounded Brendan. *Especially from this vantage point.* With long black hair cascading down the silvery skin of his narrow shoulders and back, even his arse was small like hers; although it had a firmer, more masculine shape to it. 'Gosh, you look pretty, Thornsy.'

'Shut up and fuck me already.' His body trembled.

Floored by Caleb's nerves combined with willing desire, Brendan pressed his chest against Caleb's back, embracing him from behind. He trailed kisses up Caleb's right shoulder blade before sinking his teeth into the shoulder itself.

Caleb groaned as his body bucked against Brendan.

Fire ignited between Brendan's legs, prompting him to pop the cap on the tube he was holding. He lathered the stuff liberally along his shaft and over Caleb's tight little hole, before testing the waters with a single finger.

Caleb moaned.

'How does this feel?'

'Awesome. Truly fucking awesome.'

He continued working Caleb up to the moment of truth. Reaching around, he gripped Caleb's cock before plunging his own deep inside him. 'Does it still feel good?'

'Gods yes!'

Confident Caleb was not about to cry out in pain, Brendan let himself get lost in the pleasure until their bodies collapsed together.

Once he had caught his breath, Caleb cracked up laughing.

Brendan smiled, trying to stifle his own laugh. 'What?'

'I doubt Bridey banked on this.'

'This?'

'Us. Enjoying the sex. I wonder if it screws with her plans.'

'You know, I suspect we are right where she wants us. Think about the times she pushed for a threesome with us. Plus, there's the way she's been grooming me for anal.'

Caleb snuggled up against Brendan's side and eyed him warily. 'Are you telling me you'll only want more sex with me if it's on *her* terms?'

'No, but….' His arm instinctively came up to encircle Caleb's back and his fingers entwined with his long locks. 'You know I don't have a lot of say with your sister. I'm still her slave.'

'See, I think you're wrong. Officially, you might be her slave, but you are the only member of The Seven who chose servitude. And you're one of few men she has seduced without using magic. In fact, she hasn't *ever* compelled you.'

Pressing his hand against Caleb's back, Brendan froze. 'Shit! It can't be true, surely? What about….'

'Ben and Nick? She admitted to using magic to charm them before telling me you were… special.'

The jealousy Caleb had exuded began making more sense to Brendan. 'Special?'

'Yeah. I think she has genuine feelings for you. Given that, I bet you have more power in your relationship with her than you realise.'

'I never thought of it like that.' Grinning, Brendan contemplated the ways he could use those feelings to his advantage.

153

Samantha had gone back to haunting Tyler's dreams again. Vivid images of the fiery redhead submitting to him filled his mind even as he woke in a searing, sticky haze. He failed at all attempts to throw back the bedding until he was cognizant enough to realise his legs had tangled in the sheets.

The Sydney sun blazed through the sheer white curtains, but it did not bother him half as much as the humidity. The stifling atmosphere already made him miss Broken Hill's hot, dry summers. After flicking on the air conditioner, he slipped on his thinnest robe and headed to the bathroom.

Still in a bit of daze, he locked the door behind him and let the robe fall to the floor before pulling back the shower curtain. *Christ! Am I still dreaming?*

Her naked body stood before him with droplets of water trickling down her chest and beading on her strawberry buds. 'If I knew you were planning to join me, I would have waited. Although, I don't mind showering again if it means getting wet with you.' Samantha's deep, husky voice broke his trance.

'Shit! Sorry. I didn't know you were in here.' Tyler stepped back, reaching for a towel.

But she charged into him, wrapping her arms around him, and bringing her bare skin flush against his. 'Honestly, Tyler? When are you going to stop denying the chemistry between us?'

Storm clouds gathered in and around his head as he glared at her. 'I'm not denying anything, Samantha. I'm just not acting on my desires.'

'Why not? Can't you see how much I want you?' One of her hands travelled down his back and cupped his left arse cheek.

The breath he released through his clenched teeth sounded like a snake hissing. 'You know why. Or have you forgotten the boss' rules? If anything happens between us, they'll take me off this case. My job is also at risk.'

A finger on her other hand skimmed along his waist, covering his flesh in goosebumps. 'Only if we get caught. I'm an expert at evading the authorities when I want to.' Stepping back, she tugged at his hand before retreating into the tiled alcove. 'Come on, Tyler. Stop agonising over the rules and take what you want for a change.' She turned the water back on, all while keeping her eyes locked on him.

He should have seized the opportunity to get the hell out of there. But there was something mesmerising about the sight of the water gushing down over her. *You need to leave, you idiot. Like. Right. Now.*

'What are you waiting for, sweetness?'
He went to turn away.

…

But he did not.

…

Because his feet, along with the rest of his body, betrayed him. He crashed into her, pinning her to the wall with his bodyweight as his mouth devoured her. The kiss was brutal, as were the rough hands gripping her tightly. Even more savage was the way he thrust his cock into her.

She yielded to his touch, gripping him with her tight walls and moaning.

As he came, Tyler unleashed all his pent-up frustration and rage into her. It was the first time he'd experienced angry sex. And as he came down from the high, he felt dirty and ashamed. After a quick rinse under the water, he scowled at Samantha, who was still revelling in her afterglow. 'Happy now?' Grabbing a towel, he made his escape, slamming the door behind him.

Samantha barged into his room. 'What the hell is wrong with you, Tyler?'

I must remember to put a lock on that thing. Tyler huffed. 'What's wrong with *me*? You're the one who seduced me, despite my warnings.'

'Don't project your bullshit on me, sweetheart. You wanted it as much as I did. I'm not an enchantress, Tyler. You exercised free will. Along with some extremely hot muscles, I might add.' She smirked at him.

'You don't even care what this could do to me, to us?'

'I care. I'm just not worried.'

He collapsed on the bed, combing his fingers through his hair. 'I lost control back there, Sam. Didn't I scare you?'

She sat beside him, her hair dripping all over them and the quilt. 'Not at all. I loved it. I'm not a fragile cupcake. I can take everything you dish out and then some. More importantly, I want to.'

'Fuck! Do you understand what you're suggesting?'

'Of course. I can sense darkness deep inside you, Tyler. You don't need to hide your true self from me. Give me all your violence, let me be an outlet for your aggression.' She climbed into his lap.

He stared at her in wide-eyed amazement. 'What if I really hurt you?'

Samantha smiled. 'Kinda the point, hun.'

'No. I mean like serious bodily harm.'

She shrugged. 'I can heal myself with magic. You don't need to worry about boundaries with me. Imagine how liberating it will be.'

He closed his eyes to think carefully about her proposal. It posed a higher risk than the possibility of getting caught with his dick inside her. Yet he could not suppress the urges clawing at his insides, fighting for their chance at freedom. Tyler looked into her eyes. 'Do you honestly want to submit to me with no limits?'

'Yes.' There was no hesitation or doubt in her reply.

Instantly hard, Tyler's eyes narrowed on her. 'I want you to drop to your knees before me.'

And she did.

The way Brendan held him—playing with his hair and caressing his skin—made Caleb feel vulnerable. He didn't like being defenceless, especially with someone who changed partners more often than underwear. But that's how Brendan was with women. *Perhaps he'll treat a man differently, treat* me *differently. Gods! Why am I thinking like this? It was just sex. So what if it was mind-altering and out of this world? It was still just sex.*

Was it though? Caleb couldn't help but wonder why Brendan continued to hug him well after the fact. He tried reminding himself they'd both done this for Bridey: she was the priority here. But it was useless to continue denying the feelings he'd harboured for Brendan all this time.

'Oh hell, Thornsy! Have you honestly been crushing on me for years?'

His breathing quickened as he tried to pull away, but Brendan's strong arms stopped him from moving. Unable to escape, Caleb conceded, wrapping his arms around Brendan. 'Have you been reading my mind this whole time?'

'Hard not to when you're thinking so damn loud. And for the record, I didn't drop every woman I slept with.'

'No? Name one.'

'Alannah.'

'Really? 'Cause from where I was sitting, it looked like you ghosted her big time.'

Brendan's grip on his hair tightened and he tugged at Caleb's scalp producing a delicious sting. 'That's not fair, and you know it. I left because she couldn't keep her hands off Liam. I thought she was the one, Thornsy. Hence the soul link; not that I knew we were making the ultimate commitment at the time, but when I did know, I was all in. I even made attempts to start a family with her during *and* after Beltane.'

'Shit, man! I'm sorry. I had no idea you'd fallen so hard and deep with her.' Caleb relaxed back into Brendan's embrace.

'It doesn't matter now, does it?' The sorrow in Brendan's voice came across loud and clear.

'What if you tried talking to her?'

'I can't. Bridey won't let me contact her. Besides, I made my Gods forsaken bed. Now I gotta lie in it.'

Resenting the implied rejection, Caleb shifted and looked down into Brendan's bright green eyes. 'Are you saying you don't want to be here?'

'Honestly? I didn't at first. But things are more complicated now.'

'Complicated how?'

'Well, there's the job I took on, for one thing. I've become invested in pursuing the secret knowledge Tara was referring to. And now there's you.'

Caleb's heart skipped a beat. 'Don't toy with me, Winters.'

'I'm not. You weren't the only one blown away by the experience we shared, Thornsy. It's been a real eye-opener for me. I've never fancied a dude before. Yet here we are, and I don't feel the least bit uncomfortable. I don't know if it means I've been so deep in the damn closet I got lost in Narnia, or if it's something I only feel with you. Like maybe you're a refuge in the sea of Bridey's madness. Whatever the case may be, I'm thankful for your company.'

He nodded and resumed resting his head on Brendan's chest. A snigger escaped him a second later. 'You think Bridey's crazy?'

'Come on, man, you know her better than anyone. Don't tell me you disagree.'

'I don't. I've always kinda thought it. You don't like her much, do you?'

Brendan took a deep breath and held it in his lungs.

'Don't worry. The truth won't offend me and I sure as hell won't tell her.'

He exhaled audibly. 'Sorry, bro, but I despise the bitch.'

'If that's the case, why do you do everything she asks without her compelling you?'

'I'm terrified of what she'll do to me and those I care about.'

Caleb sighed. 'I'm sorry.'

'What for? It's not like you have any control over her behaviour.'

'I know. But she's still family and I can't help but feel partially responsible. I'm also sorry for my irrational jealousy.'

Brendan's hand went back to playing with his hair and stroking his back. 'Don't sweat it, Thornsy. It wasn't irrational when you thought things were serious between me and her, or when you thought I was acting with complete free will. What is illogical is what you feel for her. Are you seriously in love with the whack job?'

'I know it's absurd, but yeah. She got under my skin when I was young. I never told you the full story of my childhood, or the relationship I shared with Bridey. The two of us were extremely tight before Mum took me away. Things weren't always sexual, either. But when my wet dreams and fantasies started, she was the object of every one of them.'

He froze. 'Christ! Are you saying you wanted her to rape you?'

'Yes and no. When she tried to seduce me, I was petrified; not of her, but of what I felt for her and the wrongness of it all. That's why she compelled me. I still hadn't come to terms with my feelings at the time and resented her for forcing herself on me.'

'Understandable.' His petting continued.

'I didn't get over the incest factor until the recent period of separation from her, when I had time to think. Honestly, I'm now more bothered by the fact she keeps sex slaves.'

'Well, the slavery thing *is* pretty disturbing. Is there anything you can do to set them free?'

'Believe me, I've tried talking her into letting them go. But she wouldn't budge on the issue. I even threatened to aid in their escape, but she only laughed at me, claiming she'd find a new Seven after Dad's thugs hunted down and killed the others.'

'Oh hell!'

'My thoughts exactly. So, in the interest of their safety and my own sanity, I leave well enough alone on the topic.'

'I'm almost afraid to ask, but what fate befell my predecessor?'

'Oh, she's still around, she just doesn't get counted among The Seven anymore.'

Brendan surged upright, resting against the headboard. 'She? Do you mean the maid?'

'Yeah. Isabelle was her first slave. She was a gift from Dad whose company deals in people trafficking, among other horrors.' Feeling the urge to kiss Brendan's gaping jaw, Caleb straddled him and claimed his mouth.

A familiar laugh sounded from the doorway. 'Are the two of you still going at it? I guess it's fair to assume you have resolved your issues with each other, yes?' Bridey stepped up beside the bed and placed a hand on Caleb's shoulder. 'I hate to interrupt such fun. In fact, I wish I could join in, but we have an important dinner meeting. I need both of you to shower and suit up.'

Caleb groaned. 'Suits? Seriously? What sort of meeting is it?'

'Syndicate business. And I need both of my captains looking sharp.' She left the room.

Reluctantly, he tore himself away from Brendan and rose to his feet.

Brendan followed, making his way to the ensuite bathroom. Pausing at the door, he turned and grinned lasciviously. 'Wanna join me in the shower?'

Joy mixed with desire rushed through every one of Caleb's blood vessels. 'Hell yes.'

Dressed in black Armani, walking alongside Caleb who wore the same, Brendan felt like he had stepped off the set of a *Men in Black* film.

Caleb's mind wandered elsewhere though, as he kept stealing glances. *'Why does he have to look so fucking sexy in that suit?'*

Brendan grinned at his new lover and spoke telepathically. *'Would you rather I wear nothing?'*

'I'm trying to focus on business, Winters!'

'Hey, I can't help it if I'm too sexy for my clothes.' Brendan smiled to himself. *Damn, it feels good to joke around and flirt again.*

Caleb groaned. *'If I soil this suit, I'll make you clean it by hand.'*

Brendan laughed as they entered the dining room, but his humour faded as soon as he spotted their guests.

Bridey remained seated at the table. 'Ah, Jet, I assume you remember Damien and Melanie?'

Rising from her chair, Melanie beamed at the sight of him. 'Hi, handsome.'

After closing the distance, Brendan took her hand and kissed her knuckles. 'It is a pleasure to see you again, My Lady.'

And... cue the giggles. 'Oh, please Jet, you don't need to act formal when I know what an animal you are in bed.'

Caleb choked on his snigger.

All eyes cut to him.

'Oh dear, sweetheart. Are you okay?' Bridey approached her brother.

'Yes, sorry Madame. Something got stuck in my throat.'

With her arm around Caleb, Bridey glanced back to the pair of dark mages. 'I'd like to introduce Stirling, another of my captains.'

Damien stood to shake Caleb's hand. 'Any relation to Lady Violet here? You look alike.'

'Yes we're—'

'Cousins.' Bridey broke in. 'First cousins on my mother's side.'

Interesting. Why is she concealing their true relationship?

Brendan exchanged a look with Caleb who answered with his thoughts: '*She probably intends to jump my bones in front of them.*'

Something did not add up though. '*I can't imagine incest turning these guys off. They're as deviant as Bridey, possibly more,*' Brendan replied telepathically.

Melanie took Caleb's hand and batted her eyelashes at him. 'It is a pleasure to meet you, Lord Stirling.'

'Ick, Winters, I can't believe you fucked this chick.'

'You make it sound like I had a choice.'

They all settled in for drinks and appetisers, with Brendan and Caleb flanking Bridey.

Damien watched Isabelle with a lecherous eye as she delivered dishes to the table. 'Your hospitality is exceptional, Lady Violet. I do hope you have another wild night of debauchery planned for us this evening.'

'It's certainly on the cards, but I thought we should discuss business first.'

Licking his lips, Damien reluctantly returned his attention to Bridey. 'Oh? What did you have in mind?'

'I represent an organisation that wants to connect with yours.'

Damien's brows bounced off his hairline. 'You work in the meat industry?'

Bridey laughed. 'Don't play coy with me, sweetheart. I'm not talking about your corporate front. I refer to your dark mage cult.'

A stern frown crept across Damien's features. 'I don't know what you're talking about.'

'Plausible deniability—I get it. But you forget we run in the same circles, Damien. Plus, my father is also a Cult member.' The sound of her biting into a carrot stick filled the ensuing silence.

'What's your father's name?' Damien eventually asked.

'Maurus Hawthorn.'

Damien's eyes bugged out. 'You're Lord Hawthorn's daughter?'

Bridey's eyes gleamed wickedly. 'That's what I said, yes.'

'I thought his kids were dark mages too. I didn't realise the old cad bedded an elf.'

'Daddy prefers to keep his family life private, so it's no wonder you didn't have your facts straight.'

Caleb coughed again.

She shot him a warning look. 'Isabelle, darling. Would you get Sterling some water?'

'Certainly, Madame.' The maid poured Caleb a drink from a crystal decanter.

'Do you understand I'll need a show of good faith before we forge any sort of allegiance?' Damien continued.

'Of course. I will also require something of you.'

'Such as?'

'Jet here wants someone to school him in the dark arts. It would give me immense pleasure if you would take my beloved under your wing.'

'The fuck?' Caleb's thought screamed at Brendan.

Damien looked extremely pleased by the prospect. 'Is that so, Jet?'

'Yes, sir. I've only had a chance to dabble thus far and now I have a thirst for more.'

'He speaks the truth, honey,' explained Melanie. 'I have glimpsed his tainted soul.'

'Very well. I am willing to bring Jet into the fold. But I also have a job for you, Lady Violet.'

'Go on.' Bridey gestured with her delicate fingers before daintily bringing an hors d'oeuvre to her lips.

Unless they knew her like I did, most people would have a hard time imagining the brutal force those hands were capable of.

'A client of mine requires an artifact that is currently locked up tight in the Ancient Egyptian collection of The Australian Museum. I want you to retrieve this item for me.'

'And what is this treasure you seek?'

'A lazurite scarab. You are welcome to anything else you find in the collection.'

Bridey leaned over the table, letting her breasts fall free from their cage of corsetry. 'A generous offer. Consider the job done.'

Damien's eyes glued themselves to her chest as he sipped his sherry. The way he fell for her feminine charms was almost laughable, but Brendan remembered being in the same boat when he had first met the enchantress. Damien tipped his glass to her. 'I am pleased to hear it, My Lady. When can I expect my delivery?'

'I will require some time to plan a job this big. And my organisation is having a leadership conference in a few days. I'll need at least two weeks to pull it off, possibly three.'

The letch licked his lips. 'Marvellous. I look forward to working more *closely* with you.' He turned to face Brendan. 'As I'm sure my wife looks forward to working with you, Jet.'

Brendan employed his most charming smile. 'Indeed, sir. When can I start my training?'

'Tomorrow night if Lady Violet can spare you for a few hours.'

Bridey leaned into her brother and ran her hand along his arm. 'It's true I'll miss him, but I'm sure Sterling will happily keep me company in Jet's absence.'

'I'm sure he will.' Damien winked at Caleb.

After several courses and a lot of dull small talk, the meal was wrapping up. Isabelle was collecting the empty plates. As she reached for Damien's, he groped her arse. Shock registered in her expression, but she hid her surprise well and kept a firm grip of the crockery.

'Isabelle, darling, why don't you leave those for now and show our guests to their room?' Bridey grinned knowingly at Damien. 'Please make yourselves quite at home and my captains and I will join you shortly.'

'Thank you, Madame.' Damien rose, along with Melanie, and eagerly followed the maid.

As soon as the dark mages were out of earshot, Caleb turned to Brendan and chided him in a hushed voice, 'Are you insane, Winters? Do you have any idea what you're signing up for with those guys?'

'Relax, Thornsy. This is our best way to get someone on the inside. I know what I'm doing,' replied Brendan in a whisper.

Bridey placed a reassuring hand on Caleb's shoulder. 'He's right, sweetheart. Brendan is smart. You don't need to worry about him.'

Caleb looked sternly at Brendan. '*I hope you don't do irreparable damage to your soul.*'

Chapter Nine

Awareness of someone beside him woke Brendan from his slumber. The silk sheets caressed his bare skin as he stirred, and he savoured the comfort of his soft bed. *I could get used to such luxuries.* He opened his eyes, hoping for the brother, but the sister greeted him.

'So? How'd last night go?' Bridey asked in a shrill voice he might have expected from a cheerleader but not from his criminal mistress.

He groaned. 'What time is it?'

'Nine.'

'Christ! I haven't even had six hours of sleep yet and you're already hounding me about work?'

Her hand slid down his bare torso. 'Would you rather play first?'

'As a general rule, I always prefer playtime.'

With a delighted laugh, Bridey pulled back the covers and grabbed his morning wood. 'Give me the cliff notes and I'll make it worth your while.'

With a sigh, Brendan cast his mind back to his training session with Melanie and Damien. 'Not much to report. It was mostly an initiation ceremony where I got to meet a few other cultists. They were all pleasantly surprised to see me there.'

'Initiation? Already?'

'Of course. They needed to open me up to the Stygian element before I could start my practical training.'

'I figured they'd start with theory.'

He shook his head. 'They use a congruent approach.'

'Curious.' Bridey lurched forward and sat astride him. 'That's enough business for now, don't you think?'

It often amazed Brendan how a woman he detested could bring him such incredible pleasure. *I must be even better at compartmentalising my emotions these days, and there's no denying her beauty.* Especially not as she rocked back and forth in a slow, gentle rhythm, her chest bouncing. Or with the look of pure joy painted on her face as she took him deep inside, surrounding him with her soft, silky warmth.

As their mutual desire mounted, the most erotic moaning noises escaped her throat. 'Enchant me, handsome. I want to feel your magic.'

Brendan froze. He did not use his magic on Bridey because he did not want her to channel him at the same time. The last time he did so with a woman had ended in disaster.

'Relax, sweetheart. I promise I won't go linking our souls. I want to know what it feels like to be on the receiving end for a change.'

'Okay, fine.' Flipping Bridey onto her back, he took charge. He needed full sensory awareness, which he could only achieve when he was in control. Brendan commenced with touch, tuning into the feel of her soft skin beneath his fingertips. As he tapped into the power, he amplified the sensation.

'Oh my.' Her breathing became heavier, her moans raspier.

'I've only just started, Madame.' Sound and sight came next. He focussed on the orgasmic grunts and whimpers escaping her throat and the way her gorgeous body jolted as he thrust his fingers inside her, letting the magic flow through him and into her.

Welcoming her natural, floral aroma in his nostrils, he dove between her legs and tasted her tangy juices. *Gods! I could get addicted to this flavour.* Brendan feasted on her, bringing forth countless waves of her ecstasy and lapping them up like a thirsty dog.

Finally, he channelled her emotions: lust and… *Oh shit! No way! Surely she's projecting what she feels for Thornsy.* Pushing the bombshell aside, he concentrated on her carnal hunger, letting it fuel his own arousal as he drove himself into her.

A bright flash behind his eyes blinded him as they exploded together, then darkness took him into a semi-conscious state of euphoria.

Bridey wrapped herself around Brendan when he stirred. 'You were spectacular, handsome.' She looked down into his eyes with a peculiar expression.

'What? Why are you looking at me like that?'

She bit her lip and smiled. 'You came back.'

Confused, he looked at her blankly.

'You left the confines of my house without supervision, and you came back to me. You didn't even try to escape.'

Fuck! It did not even occur to Brendan she was not keeping tabs on him when he was out.

'I've become extremely fond of you, Brendan, and I suspect I'm growing on you too.'

No! Please, Gods, no! When Caleb spoke of genuine feelings, Brendan did not think he had meant serious sentiments. He shrugged. 'Perhaps. The sex *is* out of this world.'

'Mm. You're not wrong.' She claimed his lips in a passionate kiss. 'If you keep up this good behaviour, I might end your contract of servitude early.'

Hope surged through him. 'Really?' She nodded. But then suspicion took root. 'Why?'

'Because I think you and I would be great together... as equal partners.'

Brendan's heart sank. She was not talking about true freedom. Not from her.

'I'd even go so far as to put money on the fact that by the time I remove this,' Bridey carefully touched the spikes of his collar, 'you will choose to stay with me.'

Oh hell! You may as well add delusional *to her list of crazy, right alongside* psychopathic. 'You seem sure of yourself, Madame.'

'You doubt my ability to show true affection, don't you?'

'Not as much as my own heart's ability to feel much of anything anymore.' The truth of his own words slapped him hard across the face.

Bridey smiled sympathetically. 'If that's the case, handsome, I'm already halfway there.'

Samantha smiled as she gazed at Tyler dozing beside her. One of his strong, masculine arms draped across her chest, almost pinning her down. In a few hours he would make his exit, usually leaving once she'd drifted off. She understood why he couldn't spend the whole night in her bed—the risk was too high—but waking up alone still sucked.

I'll just make the most of this moment. He was easily the best-looking man she'd ever seduced. *And the sex is unreal!* The last four nights had been the wildest ride of her life, which was saying something for a kinky submissive with her wealth of experience. Their chemistry was off the charts and their relationship had genuine potential, which saddened Samantha because she should *not* fall for this guy.

As her eyelids drooped, Samantha sighed. Staying awake to watch her lover sleep wasn't the only reason she held the Sandman at bay for as long as possible. Her dreams had always disturbed her and ever since she started working for *him*, she dreaded her nightly visions.

But the riptide of fatigue pulled her under, and Samantha soon found herself washed up among some reeds on the banks of the Nile. Kek's intimidating form appeared, greeting her with a rictus grin showing his sharpened teeth. *'Good evening, Samantha. How are things progressing?'*

'I have the warlocks busy following your false leads.'

'Excellent. And the doppelganger? Is he ready?'

'I have unleashed his dark side, as requested.'

The dark elf brought his hand up to her cheek and devoured her with his hungry eyes. *'I have felt much of what he has done to your body, and it has given me great pleasure. You've done exceptionally well, my dear. But do you think he is ready for the next step?'*

The worst thing about dreamscape telepathy? Not being able to lie or suppress one's thoughts from the oneiromancer. She desperately wanted to tell him 'no,' to buy more time. *'Yes. They are already talking about sending someone in undercover.'*

'Good, because we have already recruited the Original. Make sure they send the doppelganger.'

'Yes, sir.'

His arm snaked along Samantha's waist, spinning her around and pressing his body against her back. *'Now get on your hands and knees for me.'* He whispered the order harshly in her ear.

'I don't want to, sir.'

'Oh? So, you want to play that old favourite, hmm?'

Damn it! Why did I ever tell him about those fantasies? 'No. I'm not in the mood.'

'Well too bad, Samantha.' He pushed her to the ground.

Her once-clothed body was instantly naked and clambering in the mud of the riverbank.

Kek grabbed a handful of reeds and bundled them into a makeshift whip to flog her.

The blood-curdling cry spewing from her mouth only encouraged him further.

'Sam? Please wake up!'

Samantha crashed back to reality; heart racing and sweat pouring off her as she sat up in bed.

Tyler pulled her into his arms. 'Christ! You worried me with all the screaming and thrashing about. Are you okay, baby?'

'Yeah. It was just a nightmare.'

'Your subconscious sure did a number on you. Fuck! You're still shaking.'

She was. But as he held her close and comforted her, the gravity of her situation sunk in. For the first time since childhood, Samantha cried. Big, hideous sobs broke free from her as the tears streamed down her face.

Lifting her chin, he peered deep into her eyes. 'Hey, sweetheart, what's wrong?'

'I think I'm in love with you, Tyler.'

Stepping from the boat, Brendan gaped in awe of his weekend lodgings: a private island resort. White, luxury apartments lined the curved beach, with a large conference centre to the north and an entertainment complex to the south. The Syndicate spared no expense when it came to their comfort. When he glanced back at his companions, the setting sun captivated him as it painted the crystal-clear ocean with vibrant shades of red, pink, and orange.

Laughing, Bridey linked her arm with his. 'These summits are as much an excuse to party as they are business. Naturally, we have exclusive use of the place. There won't be any humans to worry about.'

'What about the staff?' asked Caleb.

'All unseelie. The Syndicate owns the entire island.'

''Course they do.'

She took Caleb's arm. 'Don't you mean *we* do? You are a part of this too now, sweetness.'

'I know, but it hasn't sunk in for me yet. Maybe if you gave me more responsibilities and more actual work.'

Bridey motioned for them to continue walking. 'Well, I could use more help with this museum job. Why don't the pair of you look over my plans and give me some advice? When we get home, that is.'

'Yeah, fine.' Caleb sounded unenthusiastic. So yeah, he sounded like Caleb.

The seed of a plan planted itself in Brendan's brain. 'What if you let us oversee the whole operation? We are captains, after all. Let us command our teams.'

Wide-eyed-panic struck Caleb's visage. *'What the hell, Winters?'*

'Roll with it, Thornsy.'

Bridey stopped to consider his suggestion. 'Okay.'

Adrenaline surged through him. 'So, you'll let us run this job?'

'Yes, but I want you to give me a full run-down of your plan before you put anything into action. I need to feel confident you won't botch things.'

Brendan smiled. 'Of course.'

'Now let's go have some fun.' Bridey urged them towards the southern end of the island. She led them through crowds of fae and dark mages who mingled in the casino, introducing them to all the important folk as they went.

'I didn't realise Australia had so many Syndicate leaders,' Brendan commented as they moved across to the restaurant. He noticed the complex also housed a nightclub, movie theatre, and games arcade.

'They aren't only Australian, handsome. This is the entire Oceania branch of the Syndicate.'

Their evening meal dragged. Sure, the gourmet food was exquisite, but Brendan had seen kiddie pools deeper than the boot lickers and toffee-nosed arseholes hovering around Bridey. Syndicate politics put him in mind of high school cliques, and he'd never had the patience for such bullshit.

Glancing around the table, his eyes fell on Caleb, who concentrated on the plate in front of him. Caleb had barely spoken to him since their intimate encounter three days ago and Brendan suspected it was an avoidance tactic. When he probed Caleb's mind, he found it locked up tight. *Yup, definitely evading me! But why? Was it something I said? I know I rocked his world, so….* He tried to humour Caleb telepathically. *'Thrilling dinner conversation, hey Thornsy?'*

That got him a look, or more of glare. *'I'm sure it is, if you find supply and demand curves sexy.'*

Brendan laughed silently. *'Come on, man, the only curves I found sexy in Year Twelve economics were Miss Harper's.'*

'You're such a pig, Winters.' The bitter tone of Caleb's thought fell short of the intended insult thanks to the grin tugging at his delicate lips.

'Yeah, you remember that hottie, too.' Ice-breaking mission success.

Moving into the cocktail lounge, Bridey encircled her two captains in her arms. 'Why don't you boys go have some drinks and unwind while I mingle for a bit?' She left them both with a peck on the cheek before disappearing in the crowd.

Brendan followed Caleb, who beelined for the bar where they both ordered straight whiskey. Spotting a quiet table in the corner with a couple of free seats, he gestured for Caleb to follow. When Caleb refused to budge, Brendan grabbed his arm and dragged him across the room.

'What the hell, man?'

Plucking the drink from Caleb's hand, Brendan put both their glasses on the table. He pushed Caleb up against the wall, caging the man between his arms. 'I wanna know what's going on inside that pretty head of yours, Thornsy. Why have you been avoiding me?'

Quick, shallow breaths slipped through Caleb's soft, kissable lips.

Brendan narrowed his eyes. 'You know, I thought you would have snuck into my room at least once in the last few nights.'

'I figured you were busy.'

'Bullshit.' He pressed his body hard up against Caleb's and fixed his gaze on the silver-lined mouth a moment before meeting the dark-brown eyes staring coolly back at him.

'Back off, Winters.'

'Oh, we're back to your antagonistic tripe, now are we? I honestly thought we'd moved past that after fucking each other stupid.'

Caleb sighed. 'It's not that.'

Unable to control the urge to touch, Brendan brought his fingers up to Caleb's face, caressing the soft, glimmering skin covering his well-defined cheekbone. 'What is it?'

His sinfully gorgeous eyes closed. 'I can't do this with you.'

Brendan's messed-up heart slammed against the walls of his chest. *I've only just discovered these feelings for Caleb and he's already slipping through my fingers.* 'Why? Did Bridey tell you to stay away from me? Because she didn't say anything about this,' he waved at the small amount of air between them, 'to me.'

'No.'

'Then what?'

Caleb filled his lungs with a deep breath and opened his eyes. 'I don't think we should be intimate again.' A hint of salty sadness brimmed his eyes.

Brendan's pulse was hammering by this point. 'I hear your words, Thornsy, but they don't make any sense. I thought you wanted me?'

'I did.' The past tense punched Brendan in the gut.

'But you don't want me anymore, huh?' Brendan pulled away to grab his drink and knock it back in one mouthful. His attention returned to Caleb, but this time he kept his distance. 'Nah, I get it. You were bicurious right? One day of mind-blowing sex with me was enough to satisfy your little crush. Now you can go back to your incestuous obsession with a psychotic bitch.' He slammed his glass down hard enough for a shard of ice to leap out and plummet to its death. Storming across the room, he returned to the bar for another shot of Ireland's best medicine.

'Trouble in paradise?' A rich, feminine voice startled him.

Turning around with a fresh refill in hand, Brendan beheld the most buxom blonde he had ever seen. Golden hair fell in loose curls around the plunging neckline of a light-orange cocktail dress. Looking her up and down, he tried to keep his tone polite despite the surge of desire he felt. 'Excuse me, Madame?'

'I could not help but notice the spat you had with your lover over there.' She gestured toward Caleb, who sat alone at the corner table, looking at his phone.

'Oh. He's not my lover.' *But hot damn, you could be.* 'Can I get you a drink, Lady….'

'Amber. They call me Lady Amber.' She reached her hand out, not to shake, but as though she expected him to kiss it.

Brendan accepted her invitation willingly, even though she gave off haughty snob vibes. If Bridey had taught him anything, it was how he did not need to like a woman to appreciate her beauty. And Amber projected beauty in spades. 'And they call me Lord Jet.'

'I would love a martini, thank you, Jet.'

After getting her drink, they moved to a nearby couch where Brendan sat as close to Amber as respectfully possible.

'Tell me, Jet, are you vying for the top spot?'

He snorted. 'Ah, no.'

'Why not?'

'Well, I'm pretty new to the Syndicate for one. And I'm only a Captain.'

When she smiled, her brilliant green eyes lit up the room. 'Your current rank shouldn't matter. Bloodline ties to the previous Boss, however, would count in your favour.'

Surprised, Brendan felt his eyes widen. 'You know who I am?'

'Yes, I do. I make it my job to know all the big names in the magic world, but I also have a particular interest in your clan.'

Okay, that's a tad creepy, but I'm not gonna complain about having such a sexy stalker.

'I think you have a valid claim.'

He shrugged. 'Politics isn't my thing. I detest the idea of brown-nosing and selling myself.'

'Is it just the campaigning, or do you dislike having authority?'

Brendan scanned the room for Bridey and spotted her hanging all over some endarkened man in a flashy pinstripe suit. She remained oblivious to his conversation. When his focus returned to Amber, her ample cleavage caught his eye. *Oh, the things I could do to that rack!* Licking his lips, he threw his right arm across her backrest and leaned in closer. 'Don't get me wrong, My Lady. I love power and control as much as the next dark mage, but I'm more of a doer.'

'Curious.' She appeared lost in thought for a moment before turning to face him. 'If you are not planning to make a bid for the position, would you consider voting for me?'

Hell yes! She's gotta be a better option than Bridey. He placed his left hand on her knee and gave her his best bedroom eyes. 'I might be persuaded.'

'I think I am too old for you, sweetheart.'

'What's a few years? I'm honestly not bothered.'

'Trust me, Jet, the age gap is much bigger than you realise.'

He studied her carefully. 'You must be using some serious mojo to glamour yourself, because you don't look a day over twenty-five.'

Amber laughed. 'More than you know. Your offer is both gratifying and tempting, but I must decline your advances.'

Brendan did not bother to hide his disappointment or remove his hand from her. 'Is there any way I can change your mind?'

'Trust me when I say you will thank me later for resisting your charms. Besides, I think your friend is getting jealous.'

Following her line of sight, Brendan's eyes locked with Caleb's. While schooling his poker face, he failed to conceal the murky-green aura from Brendan's prying gaze.

'I tell you what. If you vote for me and I win the election, I will make it worth your while.' She was grinning when he turned back to face her.

He could not say no to such a gorgeous smile. 'We have a deal, My Lady.'

Amber rose to her feet. 'I am glad we have reached an understanding. Please excuse me, My Lord, but I have some *brown-nosing* to do.' With a wink, she walked into the crowd.

He sighed as she disappeared. Closing his eyes, Brendan reclined his head. *Two rejections in one night? I must be losing my touch.*

A shadow moved in front of him, blocking some of the light filtering through his eyelids. 'Was she like the first woman ever you couldn't seduce the panties off?'

Brendan growled as his eyes flicked open to glower at Caleb. 'Either fuck me, or fuck off, Thornsy.'

'Wow! You sure know how to flatter a guy. Don't tell me you—'

'Hmm,' he cut Caleb off before the damn fairy could spew forth anymore attitude. 'You're still here, which means you're either deaf or begging to be my bitch tonight. I'll give you five seconds to start walking away.'

That shut Caleb's trap, but he did not move.

'Five.'

Intense dark eyes stared back at him.

'Four.'

A wisp of hair fell across his brow as his head inclined.

'Three.'

Caleb's lips parted. *Those damned lips.*

'Two.'

Brendan jumped to his feet, ready to take what he wanted. But Caleb remained still.

'One.'

Seizing Caleb's ponytail with one hand as he slid the other around his waist, Brendan pulled Caleb's body flush against his. 'Time's up, Thornsy. Now you're mine.'

Chapter Ten

Dumbstruck, Tyler stared at Samantha in shock. Her confession of love was the last thing he expected from her. Like, ever. Her emotional state compounded the strangeness of her words. 'Ah....' *Nope. Still no words.*

She blinked her big, brown eyes, red and puffy with tears that continued to flow.

'But how? I mean, we've only known each other a couple of weeks.' *Not even enough time to make sense of my own feelings.*

Pulling out of his grip, she turned away. 'I... I'm sorry. It slipped out. Forget I said anything.' Her tone did not carry resentment; nothing but remorse and anguish.

'Hey.' He closed the gap between their bare bodies, enfolding her with his arms. 'It's okay. I'm surprised and confused. I....'

'It's not okay, Tyler. I'm the last person on Earth you should be with. We shouldn't be doing this.'

The cause for her concern started to make sense. His lack of reciprocation was not what upset her. Tyler placed a comforting hand on her arm. 'I know I worried about delving into the forbidden before, but I've moved past those fears. I honestly don't care if I lose my job over this, if it means I can be with you.' He did not know if it was love yet, but those were some strong feelings. 'You've grown on me, Sam. What I feel for you is deeper than—'

'Stop it!' she cried. 'You don't understand. I'm toxic, Tyler. This has nothing to do with *your* boss.'

Alarm bells rang out and dread festered in his gut. 'What do you mean?'

'I… I can't tell you.'

'Sam, please,' he pleaded with everything he had.

'I mean I… lit… rally can't… ss-say. Just… please don't… under the covers.'

Holy. Shit. 'Non-disclosure spell?'

She blinked at him. Twice. It was all he needed to confirm his suspicions.

'Fuck!' Tyler leaped out of the bed and paced the room. Millions of questions formed in his mind, but there was no point asking her any of them. 'I gotta find a way to break the spell.' He paused midstride and spun to face her. 'Would you stop me from lifting it?'

Her head hesitantly shook as if testing her limits. 'No,' she whispered.

Complete ignorance with dispelling such magic became the main problem. 'I need some time alone to think.'

Samantha nodded her understanding with eyes full of sorrow.

After slipping into his jeans, not bothering with the rest of his clothes, Tyler shut himself away in his own room and collapsed on his bed. *I ought to tell Jaxon about this, but that will mean admitting to my relationship with Sam. Not to mention the shit it would land her in.* Being honest with himself, he realised that despite her betrayal, he still cared for Samantha. *Gods, I am messed up!*

But if I can't turn to the Council for advice, then who? After racking his brains for several hours, the sun began to rise, and the answer came as his phone sprang to life with a text from Alannah: HEY, ARE YOU AWAKE YET?

Not bothering with a written reply, he hit the call button. 'Hi, beautiful. What's up?'

'Me. I couldn't sleep last night.'

'Thinking about him?' Tyler was not sure if she wanted to hear the jerk's name, so he played it safe.

'Yeah. It feels wrong to burden Liam with this. I hope you don't mind?'

'I don't mind, Lana. Not at all. What were you thinking about?'

'How much I miss everything about him. I don't understand why he left me.' Her voice cracked.

'Neither do I, gorgeous. There's no way I would have.'

'I was sort of wondering if…,' her voice trailed off.

Tyler's heart skipped a beat. 'Did you want to see me again?'

'Uh huh.'

His blood surged with the unspoken meaning. Tyler figured he must be an emotional masochist because what he wanted from Alannah was more than she could offer, but he would take what he could get. 'Tell me a time and place and I'll be there.'

'Really? I mean, are you honestly okay with this?'

Tyler sighed, smiling to himself. 'Yes, Lana. You're a phenomenal woman and I'd have to be crazy to say no to any intimate contact with you. But more than that, I know you need a good friend right now. And frankly, so do I.'

'Shit! I'm such a selfish bitch. I didn't even ask how you were. I'm sorry, Ty.' The way she shortened his name did not escape his attention. And Gods help him, but he loved it.

'It's okay, beautiful. I know you're going through a rough patch, and I want to be here for you.'

'Thank you. What's been bothering you?'

'Christ! I don't even know where to start.'

'Are your troubles work related, or something more personal?'

Closing his eyes, he thought about how to broach the topic before giving up on the idea of sugar-coating things. 'Both. I've managed to mess everything up big time. All because I couldn't keep my pants on.'

Alannah made that adorable snort of hers. 'Tell me about it.'

Tyler loved how well she understood him. So, he told her all about Samantha, from the way he had met her in Broken Hill right up to the two big bombshells she had dropped. And his new best friend listened attentively, giving him endearing noises of acknowledgement and words of encouragement as he went.

'Wow. That's huge, Ty. How do you feel about her?'

'I like her a lot. I was on the verge of entertaining the idea of a serious relationship, but when she admitted to her deception, I instantly forced my heart to apply the brakes. Now I'm confused. I thought we were having a bit of fun, then she tells me all that. Before I can do much else, I need to break the non-disclosure spell. You don't happen to know much about dispelling mind control magic, do you?'

'I imagine it's like nullifying any other spells. I don't have a lot of experience with this stuff, but I'm guessing one could use nether, like how Richard negated your attacks.'

Tyler sat up surprised. 'That was nether?' He paused for thought. 'Wait, how did you know?'

'Promise not to freak out?'

'Might be too late.' *Is Alannah dabbling in dark magic?*

'I'm attuned to nether, but it's not as sinister as you might think. I don't use it for nefarious purposes, and I have a safe way to channel it.'

'What if it taints your soul, Lana?'

'I guarantee it doesn't. If you like, I could have a go at dispelling whatever magic is holding Sam's tongue.'

'Are you sure it's safe?'

'Yes, Ty. It's perfectly safe.'

'Then, yes please and thank you.'

Half a laugh slipped from her. 'Hey, it's the least I can do, considering what I'm asking of you.'

'Believe me, gorgeous, that has its own rewards. Speaking of which, you haven't named a time and place yet.'

'I was thinking of meeting you at the hotel in Sydney. I'm sure you know the one I mean.'

Memories of his wild night with Alannah flooded his mind. 'Mhmm. When?'

'In two hours? Text me with the room number once you've checked in. You can introduce me to Samantha tomorrow.'

'Will do. I'll see you soon, okay Lana?'

'Okay. And thank you, Ty.'

Tyler was like a tornado, rushing to shower and get ready. On his way out of the house, he knocked on Shane's door.

Shane took one look at him and grinned. 'Hot date?'

'Damn straight. Would you mind keeping an extra eye on our charge today?'

'No probs, man.' Shane bumped fists with him. As Tyler turned to leave, he called after him, 'Oh, and Quirky?'

'Yeah?'

'If you're meeting who I think you are, please be careful.'

'Of course.'

Walking the few blocks needed to reach their hotel room gave Tyler time to think about the two chicks at the centre of his life. *Of all the women I take to bed, why do I have to fall for the ones I can't or shouldn't have?* There was no way he was going to admit it to Alannah, but he was already drowning in the depths of what he felt for her. Problem was, she only wanted him as a best friend with totally messed up benefits.

As for Samantha? Knowing there was a chance Alannah could help break the non-disclosure spell gave him hope. Pending what his Firecracker had to say, he was prepared to forgive her. Not only were the last few nights with Samantha the best in his life, but Tyler felt a genuine connection with her. Smiling, he thought about Samantha the rest of the way to the hotel.

Now you're mine. Brendan's words resonated in Caleb's damned, filthy soul, pushing aside all his fears, and arousing him more than he thought possible. The way Brendan's lips savagely crashed into his own burned hotter than hellfire.

Wasting no time, Brendan dragged him out of the cocktail lounge and straight for their suite, kicking open his bedroom door with a terrifying force that excited Caleb. He threw Caleb down on the bed and literally ripped the clothes from his body.

Whether Caleb was born with his submissive nature, or if his sister had cultivated the tendency, he would never know. But he was certain Bridey had shown him how much he needed the pain, the humiliation, and most importantly, the loss of control. These were all things he knew Brendan could've given him once, but in the last two weeks he had seen circumstances—along with two certain women—crush Brendan's soul, leaving Caleb to wonder if those fires of passion had fizzled. That night, he saw the spark of dominance rekindle Brendan's flame.

The heat blazed. The physicality felt brutal. Unlike the first time, Brendan didn't go easy on him, which made the night perfect. *His* Brendan— the man whom Caleb had fallen for before any women had ruined him—was back. Not only that, but this time he was making Caleb's wildest fantasies come true.

With their carnal needs satisfied, Brendan's nurturing side returned as he held Caleb in his arms and toyed with the tangled tendrils of hair falling around his shoulders. 'Don't ever pull away from me again, Thornsy.'

'I'm sorry. I kinda freaked out.'

'Why?'

'Several reasons, but if I had to narrow it down, I'd say your inevitable rejection scared me.'

Pursing his lips, Brendan exhaled sharply, whistling as he did. 'You're already writing me off? How about giving me a chance to show you I can be serious?'

'I said I'm sorry, okay. I honestly didn't think you wanted more than sex. Not that I'm complaining about that. *Especially* this time. But—'

'Wait up. What do you mean *especially* this time?'

Sprawling his arm across Brendan's chest and entwining their legs, Caleb yielded further to the embrace. 'It was exactly what I needed, what I desired. The violence, the complete surrender.'

'Oh? You prefer it rough, huh?'

'Gods yes!'

'Good to know. Extremely good to know. Now, go on.'

'Given I'm the first and only man you've fucked, I figured *you* were the bicurious one. I thought I was some passing phase and as soon as you were free of Bridey, you'd dump me and go back to being straight.'

Brendan sighed. 'Does it matter if you're the only guy I'm attracted to? The point is I *am* into you.' His face transformed with a wicked grin as he leaned closer to Caleb's ear. '*Really* deep into you.' The gruffness of his voice sent Caleb's mind reeling as goosebumps covered his body.

'Brendan,' he warned.

A hand clamped down on his mouth as Brendan straddled him. 'Shoosh, Thornsy. Neither of us know what the future holds. Let's make the most of our time together now. I want you, okay? And not just for that pretty little arse of yours.'

His eyes widened in surprise for the briefest of moments.

Claiming every inch of his body, Brendan ravished him again. And again.

Winters sure does have some stamina. 'What else do you want me for, if not just my arse?' Caleb asked as they collapsed hours later.

'You, Thornsy. I want all of you. I get enough meaningless sex from your sister. The woman's a relentless nymphomaniac.'

Caleb laughed. 'I couldn't agree more. What was the deal with the blonde broad in the orange dress? Were you trying to make me jealous?'

'So, you *were* envious of her, huh?' Mischief glimmered in his eyes. The same look had attracted Caleb the first time they'd met:

> *Caleb followed Locky to the courtyard where they claimed one of the lunch tables. They had clicked the moment they sat beside each other in homeroom and stuck together for the rest of the morning, helping each other survive their first day of high school. Where the goblin had grown up in the town, Caleb had recently moved there with his mum, so he didn't know any of the kids in the area.*
>
> *The moment he planted his arse on a bench, a foul stench emerged from behind, followed by a deep, taunting voice, 'Hey freaks, you're in our spot!'*
>
> *Turning to face the troll, Caleb gulped at the sight of the guy's enormous tusks. Still he wasn't about to let a bunch of bullies push him around. He made a show of sniffing the*

table. 'Funny. I can't smell your scent here. I guess it's been a while since you last marked your territory and since there aren't any reserved signs, I'm thinking it's fair game.'

The troll lifted Caleb up by his collar, exhaling putrid fumes that made him feel dizzy. 'Listen up faggot! I know ya new in town, so I'll give you one last warning. Take your green boyfriend and fuck off outta my spot!'

'Yo, Chad! It's time you and your buddies took a hike back to Hicksville.'

Looking over his shoulder, Caleb spotted two guys. Judging by their auras they were both magical, although the shorter one oozed so much power that he could only be a pure mage.

'What the fuck do you want Winters?' Chad dropped Caleb and he scrambled to regain his footing.

Winters… where have I heard that name before?

'You hard of hearing old man?' asked Winters. 'I told you to get lost, scram, beat it, piss off. This spot now belongs to me and my friends. Oh, and next time I hear you spouting homophobic nonsense, I'll make you

and your mates all fall in love with each other so hard you won't be able to resist fucking each other to death.'

The troll gaped at him. 'You wouldn't dare? The Council frowns on that shit.'

Winters grinned slyly, and something twinkled in his emerald eyes, stealing Caleb's breath in the process. 'Screw the Council. Besides, who would they believe? One of their own, or a bunch of low life trolls?'

Chad huffed and marched away with his friends in tow.

Sitting at the table, Winters stretched out across the bench, looking like a fucking sex god with his long limbs sprawled out and his beaming smile. 'Ignore those wankers. They think anyone who doesn't conform to their drab sense of fashion is gay. I swear to the gods they are more conservative than the Council. Just don't let 'em get you alone off campus, yeah?'

'Cheers man.' Caleb sat opposite Winters. 'I wasn't too worried about Chad. I can hold my own in a fight, but you probably saved me from getting detention on my first day.'

Winters snorted and glanced at Locky over Caleb's shoulder. 'Hey Munroe, you gonna take a seat, or do you plan to hover about behind the new kid like his shadow?'

'You do realise Caleb and I are unseelie, right?' Locky asked timidly.

'Dude, my best mate here is cursed.' Winters gestured to the guy with long black hair who was now sitting beside him. 'Does it look like I give a fuck what race you are?'

Upon closer inspection, Caleb realised that the guy with long hair also had luminescent eyes. Like a vampire. Hot damn. If those guys are lovers, I really hope they let me in on some of that action. Locky slumped into the chair next to him and Caleb sensed him fidgeting. Is he just as turned on by them as me?

'So, Caleb, right?' Winters' silken voice brought him back to the moment and he nodded. 'I'm Brendan Winters, and this surly fucker is Austin Pearce.'

Caleb's thoughts returned to the present and he considered Brendan's question of jealousy. 'Maybe a tad. Although, I'd be a hypocrite to expect exclusivity.'

'Right! It'd be impossible with Bridey around.'

'Exactly. But you're evading my question, Winters. Come on man, she was hot *as*. Were you genuinely flirting with her?'

'Of course I was. Although I think she only wanted me for my vote rather than my mad skills in the bedroom.'

Caleb sat up. 'Wait, what? She's running for the boss' job?'

'Yup.'

'So, how are you intending to vote?'

'I….' Brendan bit his lip to hold his tongue, worry evident on his face.

He caressed Brendan's designer stubble, loving the masculine feel of it against his skin. 'It's okay. I won't tell her. But you'd better prepare for the fallout when Bridey doesn't find your name among the list of people voting for her.'

'Shit! It's not a blind ballot?'

'Not exactly. The votes are cast with magic. The candidates will only know if you selected them.'

Brendan closed his eyes as he considered Caleb's words. When they opened again, something devious flickered in his dark, sinister expression.

'Voting isn't compulsory, right? I can tell her I refused to vote.'

'It's an option, but she'll still crack a fit. Personally, I'd rather not risk her wrath, so I'll be voting for her.'

'Yeah, but you're in love with Bridey. It makes sense you'd want to back her.'

If only things were so simple. 'Honestly, I'd rather she didn't take on the Boss' job. It'd mean less time to spend with her and more pressure on all of us.'

'I didn't consider that. I've got enough on my plate with the Cult. Yet another reason to vote against her.'

Caleb shook his head. 'You're a braver man than me, Brendo.'

Brendan huffed. 'Hardly.' The room fell silent as they both lost themselves in thought. After what might have been half an hour, possibly more, Brendan propped himself up and looked down into Caleb's eyes. 'Humour me, here, Thornsy. And please don't freak out or take this question the wrong way. But hypothetically speaking, if you had to choose between me or Bridey, who would you stay with? Like if I were to leave your sister's service next week, or even next month, for example, and you were forced to make the decision.'

Oh hell. How could I not take it the wrong way? 'Brendan,' he whispered, 'I don't think I can make a choice.'

A smile tugged at Brendan's lips. 'Does that mean you love *me* as much as you do Bridey?'

The sly bastard! I gotta hand it to him though. 'Yeah, it does.'

Tyler felt like he was living in a fantasy role-playing game when he awoke well-rested. He rarely slept soundly; less so when worries plagued his mind, and he had plenty of those. But holding Alannah Winters and talking to her between bouts of passion compounded with sex-induced fatigue produced a full-night's sleep.

The dark-haired angel stirred in his arms, opened her eyes, and smiled at him. 'Morning.'

'Afternoon, gorgeous.'

Alannah groaned. 'Already? Damnit. I'm not ready for reality yet.'

Tyler sat astride her, hovering close to her face. 'I'm happy to keep pretending. What if we run away to some remote island paradise together?'

Her arms encircled his waist. 'Sounds tremendously tempting, but I have a boyfriend back home who would miss me.' She sighed. 'And I'd feel guilty pulling a *Brendan* on him. Not to mention all my other responsibilities. Besides, you have Samantha to worry about. I want to help the pair of you.'

Leaning in closer, he kissed the soft patch of skin beneath her ear. 'You're an extraordinary woman, Lana.'

She quivered in response to his light touch. 'Okay, maybe once more.' Her voice became breathy as her fingernails dug into the firm muscles of his backside.

Pulling back a hair's breadth, Tyler gave her a serious look. Things felt more real in that moment, as though she was seeing *him* rather than her ex. 'Are you sure?'

'Yes, Tyler. I'm sure.'

Tyler's heart soared at the sound of his name on her lips. He wasted no time tearing open the foil packet and preparing himself to sink into her.

Once Alannah caught her breath, she laughed. 'Gods, I think I'm addicted to sex with you, Ty.'

His wide grin failed to hide the thrill her words gave him. 'Well I'm not gonna complain, although your boyfriend might.'

When she rolled on to her side to look at him, there was an impish gleam in her eyes. 'What he doesn't know won't hurt him.'

Tyler's eyes shot open wide with shock. 'Liam doesn't know you're with me?'

'Hell no! He'd lose his shit. The first time was okay because things were still in a state of flux. But I doubt he would be so cool about it now.'

'Fuck! So, where does he think you are?' This was indisputable cheating and Tyler was complicit. Yet the fear of Liam's wrath was much stronger than any hint of guilt.

'He thinks I'm visiting my old Melbourne friends.'

'If Liam catches us….'

'He won't. It's why I came to Sydney. Please don't worry about him, or me.' She left the bed and walked toward the bathroom. 'Let's shower and go deal with your girlfriend.'

'She's not my girlfriend, Lana.'

When she reached the door, Alannah paused as she gripped the handle. Glancing over her shoulder, she offered a spectacular view of her perfect porcelain skin and the womanly curves of her hips and backside. 'Not yet, she's not.'

After checking out of the hotel, Tyler took Alannah to the safehouse in Darlinghurst. He was relieved to learn Jaxon was out with Tanya.

Shane's eyes remained glued to his game of *Overwatch* when they entered the living room.

Tyler laced his fingers with Alannah's and squeezed her hand as he approached Shane. 'Where's Samantha?'

'Moping in her room.' The brief distraction proved lethal to his game's avatar. He flung his controller onto the coffee table in a huff and looked up at them. 'Holy. Shit! Alannah?' He leaped to his feet and pulled her into a bear hug. 'It's great to see you again.'

She laughed. 'You too, Walshy.'

'What are you doing here?'

'I'm about to make Tyler's threesome fantasies come true.' She winked.

Tyler spluttered. 'Shit! How'd you know about those?'

Alannah linked her arm with his and grinned. 'Oh, come on, you're nothing if not predictable, Ty.'

Shane's jaw hit the floor. 'Can I watch?'

This could make for a convenient cover story. Tyler turned and called over his shoulder as he guided Alannah towards the stairs, 'Maybe next time, Walshy.'

Canned laughter permeated Samantha's closed door, so he pounded his fist against the timber.

'Come in.'

Tyler felt his cheeks flush at the sight of Samantha sprawled out on her bed in a pair of blue satin boxershorts and matching camisole.

Her focus shifted from the television to the woman standing beside Tyler, and she visibly tensed.

Closing the door behind him, Tyler approached her cautiously, unsure if she was about to strike out like a cornered animal. 'Sam, this is Alannah. She's here to lift the spell.'

Samantha's eyes darted between Tyler and Alannah several times before settling on him. 'A bloodline mage? Are you for real?'

'It's okay, Sam, you can trust Lana. She's not exactly on speaking terms with most of the Council right now.'

Alannah smiled. 'Hi Samantha. Tyler's right. I don't play by the rules. I can see you're a dark mage and it doesn't bother me. I want to help you.'

Samantha eyed her sceptically. 'Why?'

'Because I care about Tyler, and he cares about you.'

Her eyes drifted back to Tyler. 'Really?'

'Yes.' He closed the rest of the distance between them and sat on the bed. Up close, he saw evidence of prolonged crying in her bloodshot eyes. His heart melted for Samantha, prompting him to bring a hand up and tuck several strands of vibrant red hair behind her ear. 'I'm not going anywhere, Sam, but I need to hear what they've roped you into.'

'Okay. What should I do?'

Tyler directed a questioning gaze toward Alannah.

'Sit cross-legged on the bed for me.' Alannah retrieved a large white crystal from her handbag. She sat in front of Samantha, mirroring her stance with their knees touching, and placed the crystal in her lap. 'Lean forward and close your eyes.'

Samantha obeyed without question. Tyler was not prepared for what came next and almost embarrassed himself when Alannah grabbed Samantha's neck, pulling her face in close to her own. At first, he thought they were about to kiss, but Alannah simply pressed her forehead to Samantha's. *Wishful thinking, I guess.* They still looked incredibly hot together and Tyler's imagination was running wild.

Several minutes later, Alannah leaned back and looked at Tyler. 'I think it worked. Ask her a couple of test questions.'

'Sam, have you been working with the Cult even after coming into our protective custody?'

Remorse showed in her eyes as they met his. 'Yes.'

'But we blocked all of your telecommunication channels and heavily warded the house. How are you in contact with them?'

'Through dream telepathy.'

'I….' Tyler stammered. 'I didn't know that was even a thing.'

'It's definitely a thing. The nightmare you woke me from was one such dream.'

He glanced at Alannah. 'Have you ever heard of dream telepathy?'

'No.'

'It's dark elf magic,' Samantha explained. 'And something unique to those of the Cult. They like to guard their secrets well.'

'Are they actually the Obsidian Cult?' Tyler noticed Alannah jerk back in surprise. *I guess I left that detail out of the briefing.*

'Yes, although it's a name they created to inspire fear in the wider magic community while hiding their true identity.'

'Who are they?'

Samantha shrugged. 'I don't know. Only first tier members are privileged to that information. My master is one such elf, but I am only second tier, which is as far as mages can advance. The inner circle restricts access to pure blood dark elves who are born into the ranks.' Her eyes moved to Alannah. 'Like with Council mages.'

'Are they also misogynistic arseholes, like the Council?' Alannah's question made both Tyler and Sam chuckle, easing the tension in the air.

'No. The Cult has as many women as men.'

Tyler took a deep breath before asking the big one: 'What do the Cult want with me?'

Samantha's hand slipped into his and squeezed it hard. 'They want to recruit you and corrupt your soul.'

A single laugh burst forth from Tyler. 'Right, how do they expect to achieve that?'

'By using me to get to you; to make you think you are going undercover to expose them. Once they have you, they can use mind control to trick you into performing dark magic.'

'Christ!' Tyler stared at her in shock. 'Why me?'

'Because you're a doppelganger.'

The Dark Syndicate sure knew how to party, and they did it hard. Lots of sex, substance abuse, and loud music. All day and all night. By the time Sunday afternoon rolled around, Brendan felt wrecked. He had done well to avoid the politics and make the most of the fun times. Problem was, the situation at hand called for intellect and strategy.

It was time to vote. They all assembled in the conference centre where the three candidates sat on the stage awaiting the results. Lady Violet, Lady Amber, and Lord Slate were their options. The administrators mandated complete silence. A large wall clock marked the seconds, filling the auditorium with a merciless ticking, reverberating with an eerie echo.

As soon as Bridey shifted her gaze from Brendan's general direction, he withdrew the enchanted parchment and quill pen given to him upon entry. After sharing a look with Caleb, who sat beside him, he pierced his thumb with the nib. An unfortunate aspect of being a Syndicate member was the need to participate in blood magic, but it was the only way to cast his vote. He wrote LADY AMBER on the paper, watching as the writing disappeared from the page. He popped them in his pocket and turned an anxious eye to the timepiece counting down the last few minutes until the deadline.

A bell chimed at 6PM and the returning officer, a short, grey-haired dark mage, rose from his seat on the stage. 'All votes have been cast. You have chosen our new leader.' He produced three old-fashioned scrolls and eased each one apart, keeping the room in suspense longer than necessary. After comparing the results, he looked up at the crowd. 'Your new elected official is Lady Amber.'

As Brendan breathed a sigh of relief, Bridey gasped, grabbing for the scrolls. 'Give me those.'

Frowning, the old man pulled back. 'Lady Violet, please. Show the respect and decorum expected of someone with your title.' He handed her the one scroll she could see and gave the others to their respective owners.

'The stage is yours, Lady Amber.'

'Thank you, my Lord.' The knockout blonde rose and took the microphone. 'I am honoured most of you continue to put your trust in my family. My sister was an excellent leader before me, and with the help of my great nephew, I promise we will do our best to fill the shoes of a powerful woman.' She gestured toward Brendan.

What. The. Actual. Fuck?

'So, without further ado, I would like to introduce my Second in Command, Lord Jet.'

All eyes turned on him, but none of them worried him more than Bridey's lethal glare.

Chapter Eleven

'A what now?' Tyler knew the term, but not the significance.

'A doppelganger,' Samantha repeated without explanation.

'Okay, babe, pretend for a moment I have no idea what you're talking about.'

'You are the non-related, identical twin of another. Humans use the term frivolously, but in our world, there is magical significance to such phenomena.'

'Shit! I never even stopped to think about the reason you look like him.' Alannah jumped up from the bed and grabbed her bag.

Samantha gasped. 'Alannah knows the Original?'

'Now I'm insulted. What makes you think I'm not the Original and that jerk's the copy?'

Alannah returned to them a moment later with her phone in hand.

'Trust me, Hot Stuff,' Samantha explained as she grasped his hand, 'this is not something to take offence over. The Original is usually the first of the doppelganger twins to fall into darkness. In your case, the other guy's soul was tainted first. But if he is a pure mage, it's unlikely he carries the doppelganger gene.'

'I don't know why I never thought to show you this before.' Alannah thrust her phone under Tyler's nose.

When he looked at the image on the screen, he needed to blink several times to be sure his eyes were not playing tricks on him. He wondered if Alannah had taken a candid photo of him. But that could not be it. This had to be a picture of Brendan because the hairstyle differed to his own and the man sported an eyebrow piercing. 'Damn, this is creepy. I can see why you found comfort in my arms, Lana.'

Samantha squeezed his shoulder. 'Wait, what am I missing here?'

He handed her the phone. 'He is Alannah's ex-boyfriend, Brendan Winters.'

'Ex-soulmate,' Alannah corrected. 'We made the ultimate commitment, then he up and left me without saying a word. I thought he had been the victim of a violent crime at first, but he rang his brother to gloat about running off with another woman. I was still grieving my loss when I met Tyler.' She bit her lip.

'And slept with him because he looked like the man you love?' Samantha finished for her.

'Yeah.' Alannah avoided eye contact with Samantha.

Talk about awkward!

Thankfully, Samantha acted cool, despite knowing he had also been intimate with the other woman in the room. 'Winters, huh? It makes sense Tyler's double would belong to such an infamous clan. I mean, look at who his grandmother was. From what I've heard, there is usually at least one who turns dark in every generation.'

'Gee, thanks,' Alannah huffed.

When Samantha looked perplexed, Tyler jumped in, 'Alannah is also a Winters. She's Brendan's cousin.'

Samantha mouthed a silent 'Oh', and her expression softened. 'I wasn't trying to offend, Alannah. I know you view dark mages in a negative light, but don't forget what I am.'

'I uh….' Alannah clamped her mouth shut.

'It's okay. I'm used to it. I was born and raised a dark mage, and like my parents, I've been able to keep my sense of humanity by moderating my behaviour. But I've seen how far down the rabbit hole some go. The darkness consumes them in their quest for power and they lose their sense of morality and empathy, if they even had any to begin with. My master, however, is pure evil, like most of his dark elf kindred.' She turned to look deeply into Tyler's eyes. 'I'm afraid of what will happen if they give you a taste of power. Your innate goodness is one of the things I love most about you.'

There she goes strumming at my heartstrings! Without any thought to his surrounds, Tyler pulled Samantha in for a deep kiss. Before long he was pinning her to the bed as their passion intensified.

After clearing her throat, Alannah spoke: 'I'll take that as my cue to leave you to it.'

Samantha broke away from Tyler's lips and grinned at Alannah. 'You could always join us.'

Hot damn! His fiery redhead was pushing all the right buttons.

The sound of Alannah's footsteps approached the bed. 'Is it what the two of you really want?'

Sitting back on Samantha, he turned a lascivious gaze toward Alannah. 'That didn't sound like a refusal. I think it goes without saying how keen I am to have you both at once. But what do *you* want here, Lana?'

Alannah kneeled behind him, straddling Samantha's legs as she slid her hands down his back. She yanked his t-shirt over his head. 'I want to bring you immense pleasure, Ty. It's the least I can do considering….'

'Fuck!' He leaned back into her and groaned as Samantha's hand trailed down his front. 'I thought you were joking before, Lana. To cover up what we had planned.' A second later, Tyler's arousal sprang free of his jeans, finding a new home in Samantha's tight grip. He sucked in a deep breath.

'With Shane you mean?' Alannah's husky voice asked in his ear. 'Yeah, I was joking then. But does *this*,' reaching around, her fingers found his nipples, 'feel like a joke now, babe?'

Tyler melted. At the mercy of the two sexiest women he had ever known, he lost himself in the intense sensuality of the moment. Somewhere deep in his mind he knew there were more important things to worry about, but there was no way in hell he was letting reality spoil his fun.

His fellow Syndicate members applauded as Lady Amber beckoned Brendan to the stage. But he remained frozen by the bitter rage pouring from Bridey.

Caleb leaned his head on Brendan's shoulder. 'Oh hell, Jet, you are in serious shit with our mistress.'

'Yeah, no kidding. I swear I had no idea who Lady Amber was, or what she had planned for me.'

'Hardly matters now. You may as well embrace your moment of glory. We'll deal with my sister later.'

He shot Caleb a look. 'We?'

'Of course, man. I'm hardly gonna leave you to fend for yourself. Now go, show these people how badass you are.'

Hesitantly, Brendan rose and walked up to the stage. His legs faltered as he ascended the three steps to the raised platform. But he kept all his nerves bundled deep inside, mastering his passive mask.

Thankfully, he did not need to address the crowd. Lady Amber took care of that as he stood beside her. 'Consider me the Syndicate's public face. I grant Lord Jet the same decision-making powers I hold in this position. When dealing directly with him, I expect all of you to treat him as my equal.'

By the Gods! How did my life change so drastically? I'm a big deal crime boss! If only Jacob could see me now.

Once the formalities finished and most people had dispersed, Brendan remained standing with two scary-as-fuck women flanking him. He could also see Caleb hovering in the wings.

Bridey strode up to Lady Amber, pulled Brendan into her arms, and stared up at the tall blonde with a ferocious snarl. 'I don't know who you think you are, or what you're playing at, but Jet here is mine, not just in Syndicate business either. You see, he is under contractual obligation to remain in my service for an agreed time, making it next to impossible for him to be at your beck and call.'

Amber let out a haughty laugh. 'You are under the mistaken impression you have any say in this matter. I am your Boss, Violet. And now, so is Jet. He will no longer be taking orders from you. I could not care less about your contract. It is now,' she paused to close her eyes and click her fingers, 'officially null and void.' The abhorrent agreement appeared before their eyes, hovering in the air as it disintegrated into speckles of white dust. 'You should have known better than to mess with the Winters clan. My sister expected you to work with him as an equal partner, but she did not trust you to comply with her request. Do not think, for one second, I am unaware of everything going on behind your closed doors.' She glanced at Brendan. 'Meet me in my rooms once you have resolved anything you need to with this woman.'

Stunned and wide-eyed, Brendan simply nodded.

Satisfied by his response, Amber turned and marched away with a graceful yet determined manner.

As soon as they were alone, Bridey grabbed Caleb in a chokehold and glared at Brendan. While it did not look like she was restricting his airways, Caleb yelped hoarsely in a show of distress. 'You may have won your freedom, Jet, but don't forget I still have the one person you care about. If you wish to continue seeing my brother, you will reside under my roof and follow my rules.'

'What? So, now he's your slave because I'm not?'

Her visage took on a malicious grin. 'No, Jet, I don't need to make him my slave.' The hand gripping Caleb's throat gradually slid down his front and into the waistband of his pants. 'This man loves me unconditionally. He always was and always will be *mine*. I am willing to share him with you, but only if you continue with our former living arrangements.'

Caleb's neck arched against her shoulder, and he groaned as Bridey's hand wrapped around his growing arousal.

Brendan shook his head in disbelief. 'I can't believe how fucked up the pair of you are.'

Two pairs of dark eyes scowled back at him, and Caleb's adopted a wicked gleam. 'And you're as sordid as we are, so don't pretend like this doesn't turn you on.'

Damn him for having a wise mouth Brendan desperately wanted to kiss the shit out of. Damn him for looking hot as hell with Bridey's hand down his tailored suit pants. And damn him for being right. He felt his jaw clenching as he considered their words. 'I need time to think about it.'

Bridey inched forward with Caleb still between them.

While tempted to act upon the tension both in the air and in his trousers, Brendan had too many questions that needed answering, so he stepped back. 'If you'll excuse me, I have an important business meeting.' He turned to leave the stage.

'Oh, one last thing, handsome.'

He peered back over his shoulder. 'What?'

'To sweeten the deal, I will provide you with full protection from the authorities when you are working. But if you contact Alannah, our arrangement is off.'

He could not understand her Alannah-induced paranoia, but since Brendan had no intention to open old wounds, Bridey's deal suited him for the time being. 'Fine. But I only wear the collar in the bedroom, and you will grant me the freedom to come and go as I please. Outside of your home, *I* am *your* boss.'

She smiled victoriously. 'Of course, My Lord.'

Waking up between two gorgeous naked women, Tyler pinched himself multiple times, but reality did not sink in until he looked at the clock. *Shit! It's Sunday morning already.* He feared Jaxon had looked in on Samantha and found their limbs entwined. Although, he had bigger problems to worry about.

Samantha stirred and smiled at him. 'Hey, Hot Stuff.'

'Morning, Firecracker.'

She giggled. 'Nice nickname.'

'That's what I thought. I'm gonna grab us some coffees. Be right back.' He leaped out of bed and slipped into his jeans. Ducking out of the room, he took the stairs two at a time.

When he reached the kitchen, Jaxon was sitting at the breakfast bar. He looked up from his newspaper and glared at Tyler. 'Are you out of your mind, Quirky? I told you no fucking the informant.'

Well, that answers my previous concerns. 'Too bad I don't give a damn about those stupid rules.' He turned on the coffee machine, effectively ending the conversation with its spluttering.

Jumping in as soon as Tyler finished making the espressos, Jaxon persisted, 'Well I hope it was worth it and you made the most of your night with Miss Harrison, because it will be your last time with her.'

Tyler put the drinks down and stood directly in front of Jaxon. 'Yeah, I don't think so, boss. You see, because of my intimate involvement with Samantha, I've been able to crack this case wide open in ways you can't even begin to imagine. If you promise to keep your mouth shut, I will fill you in this afternoon; otherwise, I'll be taking Samantha with me when I leave.'

'You're playing with fire—you know that, right?'

'Yeah, well maybe I like getting burnt.' He grabbed the three beverages and carefully took them into Samantha's bedroom.

Both girls were sitting up, giving him the best sight to behold: their bare chests on display. Alannah's eyes lit up when she spotted the steaming coffee mugs. 'You are a legend, Ty.'

'Speak for yourself, beautiful.' With the drinks distributed, Tyler sat between them in the same spot he had woken up in. After imbibing several mouthfuls of caffeinated delight, he focussed his attention on Samantha. 'Tell me everything you know about doppelgangers.'

'The Egyptians call you *altaw'am alsihriu*, which means magic twin. The term doppelganger is of German origin. From what I understand, *you* are the descendent of an Egyptian god or goddess. I'm not sure which one—the Cult guards that secret. But thanks to your magical ancestry, certain traits, like your physical appearance, mystically replicated those of another magic user upon the moment of your conception.'

'Hmm. I guess I have my great-grandfather to thank. He had an affair with his half-mage maid and diluted the Quirke bloodline. I'm guessing my great-grandmother was a doppelganger and I wonder if old gramps knew anything about it.'

Samantha shook her head. 'Unlikely. I doubt *she* even knew. The Cult like to keep this knowledge under wraps and it is rare for doppelgangers to live in the same country as their Original, let alone meet them. But when the opportunity arises for the Cult to bring you together with your Original, they jump on it. You are the reason a number of inner circle members recently moved to Sydney.'

Alannah leaned forward to peer at Samantha across Tyler. 'What do you mean, "bring them together"?'

She sighed. 'I'm sorry, Alannah, but the Cult already have Brendan. If they recruit Tyler and tempt him, it will set him on the dark path. Once they taint his soul, they will be able to bring the pair together to practise dark rituals of immense power… the sort with catastrophic results.'

When he looked at Alannah, Tyler saw several tears trickling down her pale cheeks. He wiped a few of them away with his thumb. 'I'm sorry, beautiful. I know this must be hard news to swallow. But I promise I won't go anywhere near this cult. I won't let them use me and Brendan against you or anyone you love.'

All she could manage was a slight nod.

He brought his arm around Alannah's shoulders to comfort her, then turned back to Samantha. 'How did you get mixed up in all this?'

'My parents groomed me for the Cult, but until the inner circle moved to Sydney, I only worked on the outskirts. But Kek, my new master, took an interest in me and brought me into the second tier through mind control and… other manipulations.' She did not need to say more for Tyler to understand the implications. Samantha trembled.

With his free arm, Tyler pulled her close to his chest. 'Hey. It'll be okay.'

'I'm legitimately in danger now, Tyler. The next time Kek contacts me, he will detect my betrayal.'

'Lana?'

'Hmm?' Her head was also resting against him as she snuggled into his side.

'Are you able to block the Cult's access to Samantha's mind?'

'I don't know. Possibly. It would be easier to keep such shields in place if Samantha was able to channel the Stygian element too.'

Samantha huffed. 'Fortunately, my dark mage initiation opened me to nether.'

Sitting up, Alannah dried her eyes and forced a smile. 'I guess I'd better shower and dress now 'cause it looks like we're in for a long day.'

Tyler's eyes remained fixed on the sight of Alannah's arse until she disappeared into the hallway.

Once the door closed, Samantha whispered to him, 'You're in love with her, aren't you?'

He gazed into her hazel eyes. 'She's not the only woman I'm in love with.'

A boggart with copper-coloured hair guarded the room Brendan needed to visit. 'Greetings, Lord Jet. I am Lady Amber's captain. You can call me Rusty.'

'Thank you, Rusty.' He wondered if Rusty was any relation to Jacob, although most boggarts looked the same to him. It was unusual to see one in the upper ranks of the Syndicate, but not unheard of. Unlike the seelie fae who rank their folk according to race, the unseelie earned their positions through merit. Given how boggarts were one of the least magical fae, they needed to prove themselves through their wit and cunning in the criminal world.

'My Lady is expecting you, please head straight in.'

Brendan nodded and entered through the door Rusty opened for him, finding Amber sitting on an elegant chaise longue.

'Please make yourself at home,' she insisted with a nod toward one of the matching armchairs.

Sitting on the antique, he realised her deliberate choice of words had not included 'comfortable' with good reason. This furniture was the next best thing to medieval torture devices.

'I imagine you have a few questions?'

He snorted. 'To put it mildly.'

'Give me a moment.' Closing her eyes, she cast a series of spells, the last of which popped Brendan's ears. 'I have warded the room so we can speak freely. Ask away.'

'Are you really my great aunt?'

Amber dropped her glamour, revealing herself for the lich she was: hair and eyes both faded to white, and ribs showing through the semi-transparent skin of her chest. Yet her face remained vibrant and firm. 'Yes, Brendan. I am Dana, Tara's sister.'

Feeling nauseated by the memory of his own seduction attempts, he shifted his focus to a spot on the wall to ground himself. 'Why didn't you tell me before the vote?'

'Because it was not safe. The enemy has spies everywhere, even among the most irreputable organisations.'

'I don't understand.'

'It is too soon to explain the nature of our enemy, but I want you to understand the Syndicate is your grandmother's legacy, an asset for you to use in your quest for knowledge and power. But also, a means of protection and disguise. She intended for you and Alannah to take the reins together, but I heard the two of you had a falling out.'

Gobsmacked, he did not even register Dana's last comment about his relationship with Alannah. 'Wait, are you saying Tara built this organisation for me and Lana?'

'More like rebuilt it, but yes. When she could not use her previous role as Queen of the Cursed to control Alannah, she realised there was more to gain by elevating the girl to her full potential. She also discovered… things. *Your* role in this is critical, but perhaps you can both conduct your own research separately until the pair of you reunite.'

Brendan scoffed. 'Any form of amicable reunion is unlikely at this stage. Her actions destroyed me, and I reacted drastically, hurting her just as much.'

'Oh, the young and foolish heart. Do you still love her, though?'

He closed his eyes to search his soul. 'Yeah, I do. But I hate her too.'

'Do you care about her enough to want what is best for her?'

'Yes.' He did not even need to think about it. Despite how much she had broken his heart, he would always care about Alannah.

'Then running the Syndicate and using it the way Tara intended will provide an opportunity for you to help Alannah, even if only at a distance for now.'

He nodded his agreement, mulling over Dana's words. 'What do you mean run the Syndicate? I thought that was your job and I am your 2IC?'

'I have my hands full as leader of the cursed and this is your Syndicate, not mine. I only intend to be the face because you dislike politics. You are the true leader, at least until you are ready to bring Alannah on board.'

Brendan combed both hands through his hair. 'I have no idea how to lead these people.'

She offered him a sympathetic smile. 'I am here to help with your transition. But, before we get to the ins and outs of upper-level management, I would like to hear about your progress with the Egyptian elves.'

He cocked a brow in surprise. 'You knew about that job?'

Dana laughed. 'Of course. I was Tara's wing-woman. She kept me abreast of all her work and vice versa. Until I took over as the Queen, I was the one working from the shadows, gathering intel, and making secret deals on her behalf. She used her defeat at Alannah's hands as an opportunity to trade places and keep her identity hidden.'

'I assume you refer to her first defeat. From what I hear, Tara's true death was also Lana's doing. But I honestly don't understand why. I thought Alannah was on Tara's side?'

A conspiratorial grin crossed his great aunt's face. 'That is what Alannah wanted the world to think. Richard was the one who murdered my sister and Alannah avenged Tara's death.'

Brendan wished he had been there to see Alannah finish the arsehole.

'So, about these elves?'

'Oh right.' He forced his mind away from the woman who had turned his world upside down. 'Violet used her contacts to become acquainted with some Egyptian elves and their local dark mage associates. The closest we got is my joining a cult.'

Dana's eyes widened with surprise. 'Did the cult initiate you?'

'Yup. But it's all I've done so far.'

She leaped up from her chair and grabbed a book from her suitcase. After handing it to him, she returned to the couch. 'Have a look through this book and tell me if any of those sigilla match the one used by the cult who recruited you.'

Flicking through the book, Brendan noticed it was a handwritten research log of dark mage practitioners. 'Did you compile this?'

'Yes.'

Returning his gaze to the journal, he paid closer attention to the magic symbols until he was certain he had found the applicable motif. After reading the name of the associated cult, his eyes bugged out. 'Holy. Shit.'

'You found it? Let me see.'

He handed her the book with the page open to a hieroglyphic sigil.

Dana's brows rose as she glanced back at him. 'Are you sure this is the one?'

'Yup.'

'In that case, your job got a whole lot more interesting and significantly more dangerous.'

Chapter Twelve

When Brendan found Caleb alone in his room, anxiety radiated from Caleb's aura in plumes of burgundy smoke as he sat cross-legged on his bed, vaping his lungs out. One of these days he was going to have to teach Caleb how to conceal his aura. But it could wait until things were less strained between them. He approached from behind and placed a comforting hand on Caleb's shoulder. 'You're not the only one feeling nervous.'

Leaning back against Brendan, Caleb's free hand found his. 'I still can't believe you volunteered to organise this shit-show. You weren't even the boss man at the time.'

In the week since the vote, Brendan had dedicated most of his time to planning the crime they were about to commit. A grunt slipped from his lips as the weight of Caleb's head pressing against his crotch stirred his arousal. But it was not the time to give in to his carnal desires, so he dropped to the bed beside Caleb. 'I'm gonna be honest with you, 'cause I think you deserve to know. When I first suggested taking on this job, I had an ulterior motive, though it's no longer relevant.'

Caleb's jaw dropped. 'Shit! You were gonna try to escape, weren't you?'

He nodded.

'So that's it: you were gonna leave me, like you left Alannah?'

Feeling ashamed, he lowered his gaze to his hands. 'If you weren't in love with your sister, I would have taken you with me. But I know you can't live without her. Doesn't matter now that I'm free.'

'It *does* matter to me, 'cause of how much I love *you*, Brendan.' Tears trickled down Caleb's silver cheeks. 'You didn't care enough to stay.'

'Hey,' Brendan wiped away the droplets of anguish, 'don't forget, even as a free man, I chose to stay here.'

Bitterness filled Caleb's eyes as he glared at Brendan. 'Only because Bridey offered you protection.'

'Icing on the cake, Thornsy. *You* are the real reason I'm still in this house.' Brendan claimed his mouth in a fervent kiss, then jerked back, before things escalated to the sort of all-consuming passion that can last the whole night. 'Come on, we'd better get to work.'

Caleb's voice turned breathy. 'Yeah.'

Dressed all in black, Brendan drove Caleb and Levi to their rendezvous point in Kings Cross. It was gratifying to get behind the wheel of his Jag again after what seemed like months. In reality, a trifling shy of four weeks had transpired since he walked out of Alannah's life.

They pulled into the unmarked warehouse and let the roller-door close before getting out of the car. Climbing the steep ladder in gloomy darkness brought them to a cramped office in the loft space. Three other guys and two girls sat around the table, talking in hushed voices while they waited.

Brendan retrieved the tablet from his pocket and pulled up his notes. 'Hey everyone. Have you all reviewed the schematics and schedule?'

The chorus of 'Yes, sir' felt oddly formal, but Brendan knew he would need to get used to it.

He turned to the newly recruited endarkened guy. 'Kyle, did you manage to get a police radio scanner and Council comms interceptor for the getaway car?'

'Yes, sir.'

'Excellent. Any questions before we start?' His eyes scanned the group.

'Yes, actually,' replied Kyle. 'I was wondering how we are all gonna fit in my car?'

'Well, Zach will be staying here, and Mason is taking his motorbike.'

'Still makes six of us.'

Sierra, the four-foot-tall pixie stood and approached Caleb. 'Do you think I could ride in your lap, sugar?'

When Caleb cautiously glanced at him, Brendan was grinning. Caleb was gorgeous, but he was not accustomed to being hit on. Caleb smiled at Sierra. 'Um, yeah, sure.'

'Right,' continued Brendan, 'with Erin up front, the rest of us should fit easily in the back. Come on, time's a-wasting.' He led them all downstairs to the black Subaru WRX Kyle had recently modified with bulletproof, tinted windows.

They all stopped beside the vehicle, allowing Zach, their illusionist, to cast strong glamour spells on each of them. The idea was for them to be invisible to the untrained eye. It would take an extremely powerful mage to pierce through such a strong veil and there were not many of those around. But they all knew the spell would only last an hour, which made Caleb's role as timekeeper critical.

As the initial team member to gain concealment, Brendan would lose his cover first. But he was their enchanter, so he ought to be able to get himself out of trouble if it came to it. Caleb set the master timer going, while each person set their own watches as soon as Zach cloaked them.

Things were cosy in the back seat, but Brendan did not mind pressing himself up against Caleb and the sexy pixie who snuggled into them. Levi did not even blink an eye at the apparent intimacy the guys shared. After all, the other members of Bridey's household knew all about their sexual relationship.

The Australian Museum came into view within record time thanks to Kyle's driving skills and his souped-up Subie[2]. They parked at the bus stop outside, waiting for Sierra to perform her magic. With her attunement to nether, it was her job to bypass any wards protecting the building.

During this time, Erin got to work on the human security systems using her hacking skills. Being half elf, her magic abilities were limited, but she made up for it with her smarts. 'I'm in,' she announced, even before Sierra had finished.

'And?' Brendan asked.

---

[2] Subaru

'The alarms are disabled, and I looped the camera feed.'

'Good.'

A steel gate opened, granting them access to the business entry and Kyle moved the car behind the large stone wall. Mason arrived on his bike a minute later. The orc was their hired muscle and with any luck, they would not need him. But it always paid to prepare.

With a sigh, Sierra leaned back into Caleb's arms. 'Those were some strong wards, but I got 'em all.'

Brendan gave her a seductive smile. 'Great work, sweetie. Let's go, guys.' Except for Kyle, they all piled out of the car, meeting Mason at the door.

Brendan planted a quick kiss on Caleb's cheek before sending him to his lookout post by the gate. While Levi made use of his magic lockpicking skills, Brendan tested his telepathic comms. *'Can everyone hear me, over?'*

The replies came in their designated order starting with Caleb, *'Stirling reading you, over.'*

'Erin reading you, over.'

Kyle, Levi, Mason, and Sierra checked in. The door opened for them as soon as Brendan had finished confirming a connection with all his present team members.

Being the spell breaker, Sierra took point, followed by Levi, Erin, Brendan, and Mason. She followed the map on her iPad, leading them past a series of locked offices, up the stairs, and directly to the Ancient Egyptian collection. A few pieces of art on plinths surrounded the central exhibit—a large black sarcophagus containing 'The Black Mummy.' Glass cases lined the walls, displaying an assortment of artifacts from earthenware pots to gold statues of the gods. The shiny blue beetle was easy enough to find alongside some other magic jewellery. *'This display case is warded.'* Closing her eyes, Sierra channelled the stygian element to dispel the protections.

After a quick scan using one of her electronic gadgets, Erin smiled as her thoughts filled Brendan's mind. *'No further electronic systems.'*

As soon as Sierra gave him the all-clear, Brendan nodded toward Levi, who made quick work of the lock. Brendan grabbed the scarab and two other items catching his eye: a shimmering gold ankh pendant on a chain, and a lazurite cartouche. He let the others each select their own treasure as part of their cut. They knew the extra item he took was for Caleb and Levi claimed the loot for Kyle and Zach.

Kyle's voice boomed in Brendan's head. *'Council en route, over.'*

Shit! 'We've gotta go, now!'

Mason was still choosing his prize and Sierra pouted at Brendan. *'I haven't got mine yet!'*

Brendan wanted to groan, but he held back, not willing to risk making a sound and alerting the guards. *'Fucking hurry! We've got unwanted company coming.'*

With everything out in the open, it was a relief for Tyler to be able to hold Samantha in his arms whilst watching television in the living room. Jaxon did not exactly like it, but he was not going to stop them. Aside from playful hints of jealousy, Shane did not care.

Samantha had redeemed herself by giving them all the real intel she could. Of course, striking the Cult at their core was going to be a big undertaking, one that would take time to plan. In the meantime, Tyler was going to enjoy every moment he got with his Firecracker.

As she laughed at the sitcom, Tyler's gaze focussed on Samantha. With a glance, she caught him looking at her. 'What?'

Tucking a strand of hair behind her ear, Tyler smiled. 'Just admiring the woman I love.'

Her eyes bugged out. 'I didn't know Tyler Quirke could be so cheesy.'

He laughed. 'I was going for sweet and romantic. But hey, if you're not into hearts and flowers, I could stick to wildly inappropriate.'

After biting her lip for a second, she grinned. 'I love your wild side, but I can handle romance so long as you don't lock your beast away when in the bedroom.'

'Ah hell, I don't think that's even possible with you.'

'Glad to hear it.' She leaned in to claim his lips in a fierce kiss.

But Jaxon's voice killed their moment. 'Gear up Quirky, we've got an urgent job to attend.'

Tyler whipped his head around to face Jaxon. 'What?'

'Probable Cult-related robbery going on in the city. We have to move *now*.'

He rose to his feet. 'But what about Sam?'

'Shane and Tanya will stay here to watch her.'

'Why can't Shane go with you instead?'

'Because I need *you*.' Jaxon swapped over his guns for a bunch of imbued blades.

Samantha jumped up from the couch. 'But what if this is a trap to capture Tyler?'

Jaxon scowled at her. 'Your concern is endearing, really. But Quirky is more than capable of holding his own in a fight.'

Pulling her into his arms, Tyler kissed Samantha on the forehead. 'He's right, babe: I'll be fine. Stay close to Shane and don't let anyone in while I'm gone, okay?'

She nodded and pressed her lips to his fleetingly.

Having armed himself, Tyler followed Jaxon outside. 'So, what's going on here?'

'I got a call from the High Magus. The wards at the Australian Museum went down, which can only mean one thing.'

Puzzled, Tyler looked at him blankly.

'Someone is going after the artifacts the Council stored there for safekeeping.'

'How do we know this is Cult business? Surely the City's regular warlocks can handle this?'

'Well for one thing, most dark mages wouldn't have the means to break into this place. Plus, those artifacts they are after are Egyptian— Ancient to be precise.'

'Shit! Sam said her master was Egyptian.'

Jaxon glanced at him with an arched brow.
'Exactly.'

They magiported to the station and Jaxon
jumped behind the wheel of his patrol car. It did not
take them long to negotiate traffic with the sirens
blaring. When they arrived, Tyler could not see
anyone.

Jaxon grabbed his glamour-piercing glasses
from the console and put them on. 'Christ! Put
yours on too, Quirky.'

As the lenses slipped in front of his eyes, the
scene came into focus. A group of people wearing
balaclavas were running from the opposite side of
the building toward a black Subaru, while two more
guys approached their patrol unit. Tyler jumped out
of the car, along with Jaxon who sent a kinetic
shockwave designed to knock their opponents to
the ground.

But the guy in front put up an Aether shield
in time to deflect the blow, causing it to rebound.

Despite bracing himself for the impact, the
spell pushed Tyler back a couple of feet. 'These two
guys are the distraction, boss. We gotta get the rest
of 'em.'

'On it. Keep these folks busy.'

Retrieving a sword from its hilt, Tyler
advanced on the front man. It was curious how they

had put the skinny guy up front when the man behind him was clearly stronger and the only one drawing a weapon. Skinny Guy appeared frozen in place with his gaze locked on Tyler. *What the hell? Why isn't he preparing to fight?*

'*Fuck!*' Jaxon cried as his second attack rebounded off the shield and he fell on his arse.

The transitory distraction allowed Muscle Man to run at Tyler, almost catching him off guard. But Tyler parried at the last second. *Damn it! These guys know exactly what they're doing. I need to take out the man attuned to Aether if we are gonna have any hope of getting attacks through.* With that in mind, Tyler shifted the sword fight toward his target.

As the sound of swords clashing filled the night air, Tyler ducked and wove until he was in arm's reach of the other man. Lunging, Tyler pulled Skinny Guy up to his chest and pressed the sharp edge of his blade against the silvery skin of his throat. 'Drop your weapon,' he demanded of Muscle Man, 'or your friend will lose his head.'

'*Stirling! No!*' The pained cry pierced the night, and it came from one of the men who had reached the getaway car. It sounded like the distressed call of someone who deeply cared.

A brother? Or maybe a lover? Tyler was not about to shift his attention from the man wielding a sword to see who it was, though. He applied a touch more pressure, letting blood trickle down his captive's throat. 'I said drop. Your. Weapon.'

His opponent obeyed this time, letting the sword fall noisily to the concrete.

'Hands in the air where I can see them.'

The guy's sleeves slipped back over his wrists, and his biceps bulged as he extended his arms upward. The olive-coloured skin showing through and the horns protruding through the ski mask suggested the man was an orc.

Odd to see them siding with the bad guys. He must be a mercenary. 'Surrender now and I will put in a good word for you.'

He nodded his thanks and let Tyler handcuff him to Skinny Guy. Without the threat of immediate danger, Tyler looked at the other group and noticed them trying to pull one of the guys into the car. The one who hesitated exchanged a look with Tyler's prisoners as Jaxon approached the car with a fireball forming in his hand. Seconds later, the other man let his associate drag him away and the car sped off into the distance.

Jaxon lobbed his fireball, but it did not reach them in time. '*Damn it!* Come on Quirky, we may as well see what we can get out of these arseholes.' He stormed off toward the car and opened the back door.

Tyler clamped separate pairs of cold iron cuffs on each of the robbers and removed their masks, confirming that Skinny Guy was endarkened. *Sam didn't mention the Cult was recruiting them too*. Not that it mattered. He had always considered them to be the scum of the Earth. With no care for the unseelie man's comfort, he pushed him into the back of the car, along with the Orc, and climbed in next to Jaxon.

The warlock manhandling Caleb could've been his lover's twin. Combining the disconcerting resemblance with the rough treatment evoked a similar response in Caleb's body to when Brendan touched him. It almost didn't matter that this guy's intentions were anything but sexual.

When they reached the evidence room, the Brendan lookalike released the cuffs on his hands. 'Lose the clothes.'

This must be the infamous warlock strip-search I've heard so much about. It was embarrassing how much his dick twitched at the thought. Remembering the reality of his predicament helped to subdue his arousal as he slipped out of the plain black clothes, leaving his jeans and underpants until last.

While the sexy warlock explored Caleb's depths, the other one snickered.

'What the hell are you laughing at, Hayes?'

'I think he likes that a bit too much, Quirky.'

When Quirky—or whatever the hell his name was—looked between Caleb's legs, he swore. Jerking his hand back, he shoved Caleb, knocking him to his hands and knees. 'Get dressed.'

It was a relief to reclaim his clothes and sit with a table between him and Quirky. But when Caleb realised he was in an interrogation room, panic seized his heart in a vice.

The blond warlock set his phone to film their conversation, sat back and stared at Caleb a moment. 'I am Warlock Jaxon Hayes, and this is Tyler Quirke. Please state your name for the records.'

Caleb remained silent.

Jaxon sighed and retrieved the evidence bag containing Caleb's wallet. After snapping on a pair of blue nitrile gloves, he retrieved several cards from it. 'Are you Caleb Hawthorn?'

He nodded.

Tyler sniggered. 'What's wrong, faggot? Cat got your tongue? Oh wait, you probably don't put that thing near pussies.'

With a sneer, Caleb replied, 'Listen, you homophobic arsehole: just 'cause I like fucking men, doesn't mean I don't love women too.'

'Hey, I don't have a problem with gays, or bi people. It's criminal trash like you I detest.'

'Quirky, please,' Jaxon reprimanded his partner before turning his attention back to Caleb. 'What were you doing at the museum?'

'I was on a school excursion. What the fuck do you think I was doing there?'

'Do you admit to being party to the theft of several magic artifacts?'

Caleb shrugged. 'Maybe we were borrowing them.'

'Right, because unseelie scum like you are known for returning the shit you take.' Vitriol oozed from Tyler's tone.

'Oh, on top of being sexist, you're a racist bigot too?' Caleb challenged him.

'Don't make me shut that smart mouth of yours.'

A grin crossed Caleb's lips as he pressed them tightly together.

'Shit! We want him to talk, Quirky.' Jaxon raked his hands through his hair with a frustrated huff. 'Who were you working for tonight, Caleb?'

'A friend.' As much as he tried to avoid it, Caleb couldn't help casting lustful eyes at Tyler. *He looks so much like Brendan. Those deep-set emerald eyes, the perfect fucking jawline with enough stubble to graze my skin....*

'Can you be more specific?' Jaxon continued the questioning while Tyler glared at Caleb.

'No.'

'Why not?'

'I don't wanna.'

Tyler squirmed. 'Why the hell do you keep looking at me with bedroom eyes?'

Caleb couldn't keep the wicked grin from his face. 'You look like someone I know.'

With wide eyes, Tyler snatched the evidence bag with the loose contents of Caleb's wallet. 'South Australian licence,' he mumbled. 'Do you know Brendan Winters?'

His lips continued curling upwards. 'You might say I know him *very well*.'

Tyler paled, and his mouth fell agape when the implication hit home. 'Do you have a sister named Bridey?'

Taken aback by the leftfield question, Caleb's expression turned serious. 'Why do you ask?'

'Answer the damn question.'

'Yeah, I do.'

Rising from his seat, Tyler tossed Caleb's stuff on the table. 'These guys are Dark Syndicate.'

'Yeah but remember what your friend said about Brendan?' replied Jaxon. He turned back to Caleb. 'Have you or your sister joined any cults recently?'

'Hell no. We don't touch that shit.'

Tyler scowled maliciously. 'And what about your beloved Brendan?'

He tensed. 'What about him?'

'Has *he* joined any cults?'

Hiding his trembling hands under the table, Caleb steadied his breathing. 'I don't know, you'll have to ask him.'

'I guess I will. You gonna tell me where I can find him?'

'Is the Arch Mage a woman?' Caleb scoffed.

'You know, we could call Brendan or Bridey from your phone and trace the call,' Tyler explained.

Caleb laughed, knowing they wouldn't be able to find those numbers in his contacts. 'Yeah, good luck.'

Tyler dropped Caleb's phone on the table. 'I guess you'll have to take us home to meet the family.'

'Not gonna happen.'

'Oh, you don't want to go home? Let's see if you still feel that way after a few days in the lockup.' Tyler pulled him out of the chair and dragged him down to the basement of the cop shop. After shoving him into a cell, he removed the cuffs and locked the cage-like door with a big-arse smirk. 'Be sure to let the guards know when you are ready to post bail.'

Flying through the front door, Brendan did not even stop to don his collar as he sought out Bridey. He flung the bedroom door open and found her riding Damien like a rodeo bull.

'Jet, sweetheart, what's going on?' Bridey's voice betrayed her apprehension.

He tossed the scarab on the bed. 'There's your damn beetle, now please leave us, Damien.'

Bridey sat back on the bed to let Damien gather his things and get dressed.

Damien inspected the artifact and smiled. 'Thank you, Lord Jet. I'll be in touch,' stopping once more to shake Brendan's hand on the way out.

He watched to be sure Damien was out of earshot before turning back to Bridey. This time, he did not hold back the emotion in his voice. 'They got him, Bry. The Council got Caleb!'

'Oh Gods. What happened?' The fear in her eyes was plain to see.

'A couple of warlocks rocked up as we were leaving.' Brendan gulped back the lump forming in his throat. 'One of them grabbed him and held him at sword point and forced Mason to disarm. I wanted to go after him, but Levi and the others held me back.'

'He was doing his job protecting us,' Levi explained from the doorway. 'You knew there was a risk of this happening.'

'Doesn't make it any easier to deal with. I'm so fucking sorry, Bry.' The tears sprang free.

Leaping from the bed, Bridey embraced him. 'Please give us some privacy, slave.'

'Yes, Madame.' Levi closed the door, leaving Brendan alone in Bridey's arms.

'It's not your fault, handsome.'

'Yes, it is. You heard Levi. Caleb got caught trying to protect me. And it was my goddamn plan. I screwed up and—'

'Shh.' Bridey pressed a finger to his lips. 'I reviewed the plan with you, and it was flawless.

Obviously, the Council has magic technology beyond our understanding.'

'Shit!' Brendan lifted his head to look into her eyes. 'They were wearing glasses. Must have been how they saw through our glamour.'

'Interesting. Sounds like the work of a powerful conjurer.'

'How can you be calm about this? Aren't you worried about Caleb?'

'Of course I am,' Bridey sighed. 'I'm trying to be strong for you, handsome.'

The raw truth in her eyes floored him. This woman was hurting as much, if not more than Brendan, but she was putting his needs first. It threw all his previous opinions of her out the window. He pulled her against him, holding her tight.

'I have a few contacts I can call tomorrow. With any luck I should be able to get him out of there.'

'Fuck, I hope so.' He dug his fingers into her shoulder blades.

She ran soothing strokes along his back. 'Trust me, sweetie, Caleb's gonna be okay.' With a tug of her arms on his, Bridey drew Brendan down into her bed where she wrapped herself around him. She continued to comfort him with her gentle touch, helping him drift off to sleep. It was the first time he had shared Bridey's bed without her demanding sexual gratification. And for once, he got a proper feel for the real Bridey Hawthorn.

Chapter Thirteen

It came as a surprise to Brendan when his waking thoughts were of the beautiful woman in his arms. And they were not unpleasant like the usual kneejerk reaction he got to finding himself in bed with her after the sexual frenzy wore off. He had come to understand why her inner aura was not pitch-black. The sensitive violet patches of her soul had made themselves known. *Is that why she's obsessed with the colour purple?* These thoughts filled his mind as he admired her sleeping form.

She must have sensed him looking at her, or perhaps he moved too much, and before long she stirred and opened her eyes. Speaking with a gruff voice, she slid a hand down his bare back. 'Morning, handsome.'

At some point during the night, Brendan had stripped away the clothes obstructing his comfort, always preferring to sleep naked. He glanced at the clock before smiling at her. 'Afternoon, beautiful.'

She sucked in a breath as a grin curled her lips. Seconds later, she jack-knifed. 'Shit! I need to make those calls for Caleb.'

When she began to rise from the bed, Brendan pulled her back. 'Wait a sec.' Gathering her into his lap, he kissed her lips; not with the usual ferocity they shared, but a slow, sensual kiss. He heard a soft moan escape from her as he drew back. 'Thank you for last night, Bry.'

Pressing her forehead to his, she whistled through pursed lips. 'No one has ever kissed me like that,' she whispered. The confession painted her in a vulnerable light and broke through a crack in the shield he had erected around his heart; one of many hairline fractures her brother had made when chipping away.

'Not even Caleb?'

'No. My relationship with him is beyond complicated.'

'I can see that. How many times have you been in love before, Bry? I get the impression you've had your heart broken as severely as I have.'

She closed her eyes a moment, as though she was holding back the threat of tears. When they fluttered open again, she took a deep breath. 'Before you, Brendan, there was only ever Caleb. He's the one who broke my heart.'

'How so?' He kept his voice soft and encouraging.

'When we were younger and our relationship turned sexual, he kept pushing me away even though I could read his mind and his emotions enough to see how much he wanted me. Eventually he told our mother I had raped him, prompting Mum to run away and hide him from me.'

'I guess it would be devastating. You know he loves you now, right?'

'I know he loved me even then. But sometimes love isn't enough to overcome our fears.'

It was the crux of Caleb's problem. He had been afraid of what it would mean to allow himself the pleasure of his sister's affections. 'I'm guessing your mum is where he got his strong moral compass from?'

She adopted a lop-sided grin. 'We both did, but Dad skewed mine a lot over the years.'

'How did such a pure-hearted elf end up with your old man?'

'It wasn't her choice. My dad works in the slave trade, and she was one such victim. He took a liking to her and kept her for himself.'

'Fuck! That's heavy.' Brendan paused to let it sink in. 'Are all of your other slaves from him?'

'Yeah, they are,' she admitted. This was the side of Bridey he did not get.

'You've gotta set them free, Bry.'

Tension started to lock her up and she pulled away.

But Brendan was not about to let her true self escape. He grabbed her shoulders and looked deep into her eyes. 'Listen to me, beautiful. I know you still have some good left in your soul. You proved it to me last night. This woman, the real Bridey Hawthorn, she is the one I can feel myself falling for and she is probably the one Caleb loves. I want to see more of her and less of the persona you created for your father.'

Bridey's eyes widened as droplets trickled from them.

'Do you really love me?' he asked.

'Yes, but Dad—'

'Your old man isn't here. You can be your own woman now. Please, will you free those slaves? For me?' He pleaded with everything he had; magic tricks included.

'Okay.'

Smiling, Brendan kissed her deeply again before letting her go. 'Thank you. Now, let's get Caleb out of prison.'

As Samantha's fork slipped out from between her lips and she bit into her piece of ravioli, Tyler realised he was a captive audience. No one made eating look as sexy as she did. But the sound of Jaxon's phone ringing broke his trance.

Jaxon glanced at the caller's name. 'It's High Magus O'Grady.' He picked up the device and answered the call. 'Hello, Your Honour … *What?* … Did you try to stop them? … I see … Were you able to get his current address? … Understood. Thanks for letting me know. Bye.'

Tyler looked at him expectantly as he hung up.

'The Council dropped the charges on Caleb Hawthorn and let him go.'

'*The fuck?* Why would they do that?'

'The call came from above O'Grady. He couldn't stop them. As for why, he couldn't say.'

'Are you telling me we lost our best lead on tracking down Brendan Winters?'

'Afraid so.'

'*Damn it!*' Having lost his appetite, Tyler pushed his dinner plate into the middle of the table, standing to pace the room. 'So, we're back to square one?'

'Not exactly. We still have Samantha's intel,' Shane suggested.

'Right, because poking the wasps' nest is such a smart plan.'

'What if you follow the wasps from the nest?'

'What the hell are you talking about, Walshy?'

'He means a stakeout, Quirky,' Jaxon explained. 'If we watch their HQ, we can track the people coming and going, learn who lives where. We could pick them off one by one. Who knows, we might even spot Brendan in the process.'

Tyler flopped back onto his chair, letting Samantha soothe his nerves with a gentle caress of his thigh. 'Sounds like a slow process, but I guess it's our best shot now. It's frustrating when we almost had the guy in our grasp.'

After scraping up the last of his pasta and swallowing his hefty mouthful, Shane let his cutlery clatter onto his plate. 'What's important about catching this Brendan guy anyway?'

'You're kidding right?' Tyler asked. 'Did you not hear what Sam said about me being his doppelganger and what the Cult plan to do with us?'

'Sure I did. But how does catching Brendan, as opposed to any of the other cult members, help us?'

'Because if they don't have Brendan, they can't use *me*. Without him, it's a lot safer for *me* to enter their premises and help take them down.'

Returning from a short trip to the kitchen, Shane popped the top off his second beer. 'So what? You kill him to eliminate the threat?'

Tyler huffed. 'I wouldn't mind after what he did to Lana.'

'Quirky, you know we can't. We have to operate within the law,' Jaxon reminded him.

He put his hands up in a surrendering gesture. 'I know, boss. I was kidding. We only need to keep Brendan locked away and out of their reach when we attack. After the museum job, he's up for some hefty criminal charges anyway. Should be enough to put him away for several years.'

Shane laughed. 'Those larceny charges won't worry him as much as the whole drug operation he started back in SA. He's looking at life for that alone.'

'Excellent point.'

Jaxon gave up on his own dinner and sighed. 'If the powers that be don't let him off like they did his boyfriend.'

Shane shot Jaxon a surprised look. 'His *boyfriend*?'

Samantha and Tanya also looked on with intrigued expressions.

'I guess we forgot to mention those juicy details. Apparently, Brendan bats for the other team now, or possibly both. Oh, and that Caleb guy we arrested was his lover. We worked it out when he kept giving Tyler bedroom eyes while confessing to knowing Brendan,' Jaxon paused to add air quotes, '"very well."'

Tyler shivered. 'It was totally disturbing. Not to mention his reaction to the strip search.'

Samantha cracked up laughing. Once she calmed down, she bit her lip for a few seconds. 'I'm sorry, babe, but that was too funny.'

He groaned. 'I'm glad you find it amusing.'

She grinned. 'First Alannah, then Caleb. I wonder who your doppelganger charms will work on next?'

Shane prodded Tyler's arm. 'Ah hell Quirky, you better be careful if you visit Brendan's hometown. I heard he was a bigger slut than you.'

'Speaking of which, Liam invited us to their family's Solstice dinner on Friday night,' Jaxon informed them.

'Really?' Tyler paused for thought before continuing, 'What about Sam?'

'I asked him if you could take a plus one and he said it's fine. Honestly I think he's relieved your attention diverted from his woman.'

Swallowing a lump of guilt, Tyler chose not to remind them of his recent liaison with Alannah. 'Fair enough, but is it safe to take her?'

'Safer than leaving her. Besides, the dinner is at his parents' house and the place has even more protection than this apartment. Apparently, those wards kept Tara out when she threatened Alannah.'

Tyler breathed a sigh of relief. 'Good to know.'

Grabbing Tyler's arm, Samantha squeezed it and smiled up at him. 'It'll be nice to get out of this place for a change of scenery.'

'Are you sure?'

'Yeah, it's safe if we magiport straight there. Plus, I'd like to see Alannah again too.' A sly grin formed on her face, hinting at their shared memories.

'I guess it's a date.'

'Don't mention anything to Alannah about the dinner if you chat with her on social media before Friday night. Liam wants it to be a surprise.'

'Noted.' Having curbed his initial irritation, Tyler sat down at the table and resumed his meal.

When Bridey's demon driver dropped Caleb home, his first thoughts turned to ensuring Brendan's safety. Not having a friendly face to meet him at the police station sucked, but he understood the risks such an appearance presented to both Bridey and Brendan.

Neither Levi nor Isabelle greeted Caleb when he walked through the hall, much to his surprise. Voices drew him to the parlour, where Brendan sat extremely close to Bridey as they studied some paperwork together. Lifting their eyes to spot him, both of his lovers leaped to their feet, letting papers fall to the floor as they rushed to embrace him.

'Are you okay, sweetheart?' Bridey scanned his body. 'Do you need a healer?'

'I'm fine, Bry. They healed my battle injuries in prison.'

Brendan's fingers gingerly touched Caleb's neck as he inspected his throat. Seemingly satisfied the gash from Tyler's sword had vanished, Brendan pulled him closer and kissed him deeply. The greeting made his heart flutter and his toes curl.

'I take it you're okay?' Caleb asked him with a breathless voice.

'A hell of a lot better now you're home,' Brendan admitted.

Knowing Brendan cherished him brought a smile to Caleb's lips. The men hugged again, and Caleb doubted he'd ever get enough of feeling Brendan's body against his own.

Bridey pressed herself into Caleb's back, placing her hands on his shoulders as she peppered kisses along his neck and whispered, 'Welcome back my love.'

Pivoting to face Bridey, Caleb devoured her lips. Coming up for air, he glanced over Bridey's shoulder, and the pages on the floor caught his attention. 'What were the pair of you working on?'

'Looking at some resumés of potential household staff,' she replied.

He gave her a puzzled look. 'Why?'

Her beautiful, dark eyes lit up. 'I freed the slaves, so now I need some legit servants.'

Caleb's mouth gaped open. He threw his arms around Bridey and squeezed her tight. 'I'm damn proud of you, Bry. What brought you to that decision?'

'Brendan helped me come to my senses,' she explained.

Leaning back into Brendan, Caleb peered up at him. 'You never cease to amaze me, Winters.'

Brendan's eyes gleamed with wicked intent. 'Mm, you can thank me later, Thornsy.'

Bridey and Brendan flanking him spiked Caleb's arousal. He loved the contrast between her soft curves and his hard muscles. 'Why wait?' He felt thankful for the opportunity he'd had to shower at the decoy house on the way home because he could not wait to rip his clothes off.

Bridey stepped back. 'Mind if I watch?'

Having something else in mind, Caleb grabbed her arm and reeled her back in. 'I'd rather you join us.'

'Brendan?' Bridey asked, likely seeking reassurance because the three of them had not attempted another threesome since their earlier disasters.

'Don't worry, Bry, I have zero inhibitions left,' rasped Brendan as he pressed his arousal against Caleb's backside.

What happened in my absence? The way they squashed Caleb between them, kissing passionately over his shoulder, suggested something significant. Four weeks ago, the sight of them sucking face had stirred some different emotions, but there was no longer room for jealousy or trepidation between any of them.

As Brendan withdrew from the kiss, his hands found the hem of Caleb's t-shirt and he removed the garment. His fingers trailed down

Caleb's back while feathering kisses along his neck. A frenzy of undressing followed amidst moments of passion as they stumbled into the guestroom.

When Caleb's gaze fell upon the bed, he found Bridey adopting a submissive position for the first time in the history of their relationship. *Things are definitely about to get interesting.*

The afternoon sun was peeking through the blinds of the guestroom when Brendan awoke. The previous night had been incredible, and he found himself cursing the former hang-ups that had prevented him from enjoying both Hawthorn siblings together in the past. Hours of pure erotic delight with the three of them taking turns in the middle had made for one of the most sexually satisfying nights of his life.

Rolling on to his side, he found Caleb sleeping soundly, but no sign of Bridey. *She must be working.* Brendan figured he should be doing likewise, but he could not draw himself away from the breathtaking sight before him. Caleb looked like a dark angel, or what Brendan imagined such beings would look like if they existed.

'Are you being a creeper, Winters?' Caleb's lips curled as he spoke with a gravelly morning voice.

Brendan laughed. 'Depends on whether you were actually sleeping.'

His eyes shot open, and the grin widened. 'I'm sure I was at some point, but that's beside the point if you thought I slept while you were watching me.'

'What can I say? I've grown fond of your pretty face, Thornsy.' Leaning in, he crashed his lips into Caleb's. Brendan broke away from the kiss before he lost his last sliver of willpower. There would be plenty of time to give in to such desires in the near future, but he needed to say something while he had Caleb alone.

Cupping Caleb's silvery cheek in his hand, Brendan looked deeply into his lover's eyes. 'You freaked me out, Thornsy. Getting yourself captured… I feared the worst. The thought of them taking you from me before… before I could tell you.'

Caleb's expression turned serious with concern. 'Tell me what?'

He hated how hard it had become to talk about his true feelings. *Damn you, Lana!* Brendan gulped. 'You've worked your way into my heart in a way I thought would be impossible with how broken it was.'

Caleb's eyes widened.

Moving directly on top of him, Brendan pinned Caleb down as a way of bracing himself for the words that followed. 'I'm... in love... with you, Caleb.'

A sharp breath slipped through Caleb's lips a moment before he pulled Brendan down for another sensual kiss. As their passion intensified, the feel of Caleb's tongue ring brought back memories of other ways he had stimulated Brendan with the tiny barbell. And it was not long before they made new memories.

Brendan caught his breath. 'I fucking love your tongue, Thornsy. I'm thinking of getting my own venom piercing so you know how superb it feels.'

'Christ! I already fall apart when you go down on me. You don't need to improve on anything there.'

'Really?'

'Absolutely. How the hell did you get them expert skills without any experience before me?'

Brendan shrugged as he smirked. 'Natural talent, I suppose.'

Caleb's fist bumped Brendan's arm. 'Smug bastard.'

His smile grew. 'Oh, but you love me all the same, right?'

This time Caleb mounted him. 'Yeah, I do, Brendan. I love you.'

They spent the rest of the afternoon expressing their love for each other in every possible way.

There was a time when Brendan looked forward to the Summer Solstice. As he walked the empty halls of the inner-city office block, he imagined the smell of his mum's cooking wafting through the building. Spending the holiday alone made him realise how much he missed his mother. *Next chance I get, I'm gonna give Mum a call.*

He could have joined the Hawthorn family, but it would have meant returning to Adelaide and he was not ready. Nor did he fancy seeing their scumbag father again. Besides, with most of the magic community busy celebrating, it was the perfect time for Brendan to catch up on some Cult reading.

Turning one last corner brought him to the library. He swiped his key card against the security panel and sent a silent thank you to Erin when the door unlocked. *Hacker girl is a damn genius.*

By the Gods! The place was huge. Thankfully, the Cult organised books logically, so it did not take him long to find what he was looking for. Most of the books were in Arabic, but he had come prepared with a translation app on his phone.

He pulled out one volume entitled *Magical Artifacts of Ancient Egypt* and continued scanning the shelves until he found several leatherbound works with unlabelled spines. He grabbed the first of them and discovered he was holding an Egyptian book of Shadows belonging to the Arafa clan. Grabbing more of them revealed a whole collection of spell tomes from all the major mage clans of Egypt. *Talk about the fucking jackpot!*

Brendan took them all to the photocopier near the reading desks and got to work on his reproductions. He would have taken them, but he knew the wards would alert the inner circle if any of their precious books left the room.

Unfortunately, the mindless task gave him time to reminisce on better times and to imagine what would be happening at Cailleach Estate in his absence. He knew his parents would decorate the house in bright, warm colours symbolic of the sun and Mum would be baking her traditional pumpernickel bread while Dad roasted meats on the Weber. *Who would be there this year?* They usually invited a couple of friends, but never the same people.

A noise from down the hall broke his reverie and prompted him to take cover. He smacked the off switch on the photocopier and ducked behind one of the solid oak desks along the wall. Turning off his torch plunged the room into darkness. Minutes later, a security guard walked into the room and casually strolled through the bookshelves, checking each row with his own torch.

Brendan's heart was pounding fast, and he could feel his grip on the pile of books slipping.

Having inspected the shelves, the man moved to the reading area.

Shit! I forgot my copies. Please don't look at the photocopier.

As the half-mage guard approached the machine, the top book on Brendan's stack toppled onto the floor, diverting the man's attention in his direction.

Fuck! Thinking quickly, Brendan intruded on the guard's mind, pushing past the mind shield, and convincing him the sound came from another room down the hall. He breathed a sigh of relief as soon as the guard left. *That got too damn close.*

After waiting for the guard to move on to a different floor, Brendan hurried the last of his copying and shoved the books back in their place. He put his duplicates in a large box and hauled them out to his car.

In the comfort of his own office, he flicked through the book on artifacts, finding the two treasures he had taken from the museum and worked on translating the Arabic text.

The ancients imbued the agate ankh with the power of healing. Anyone with magical blood can use the charm to heal their wounds without needing to channel mana or cast any spells.

Glad he had chosen the shiny piece of bling, he moved on to the next entry.

Scholars believe the Cartouche of Set was used to summon the God as part of a dark mating ritual. But along with the artifact itself, the magic world lost this knowledge centuries ago.

Brendan furrowed his brow. *How did the Cult not realise it was right under their nose? Surely they scoped out the contents of the case before arranging the job?* He turned several more pages, looking for the final item of interest. When he found it, he got his answer:

> *The Lazurite Scarab provides a direct connection to all Celestial beings and the Egyptians may have used it in the original immortality rituals.*

His mouth dropped open. *With the beetle, they don't need the cartouche.* The significance of the second part of the entry also struck him. *Are they planning to become liches?*

Brendan's mind was spinning when he left his office the next day and drove home. When he checked Caleb's room, he found it empty. Looking in Bridey's quarters, he saw them both wrapped in each other's arms, sleeping soundly. He smiled at the sight. *They make such a cute couple.*

Not wanting to disturb them, he eased the door shut and headed to his bathroom. What he needed more than anything was a scalding shower to soothe his aching muscles. Scorching water poured down around him when Brendan sensed someone. Opening his eyes, he turned toward the intruder.

'Hey, handsome. Mind if I join you?' Bridey stood naked at the entrance to the shower cubicle.

'Mm, not at all.' He reached out to grasp one of her hands, pulling her in close and kissing her. Closing his eyes, Brendan pushed aside all the dark secrets he had learned to focus on Bridey. *She feels incredible in my arms and against my lips.* He slipped his fingers inside her, bringing forth a deep groan vibrating against his mouth as he continued to kiss her.

She whipped her head back. 'Oh Gods! Fuck me, Brendan. Fuck me *now*.'

Backing her up against the tiled wall, he leaned in close to her ear. 'No.' Stepping back an inch, he observed her reaction.

Gobsmacked, she stared at him in disbelief.

With a wicked grin, he pumped his fingers twice more before removing them. He pressed his arousal against the entrance to her quivering core. 'I'm not gonna fuck you this time Bry. Do you wanna know why?'

'Yes,' she rasped.

'Because I want to make love to you. Do you know why?'

With wide eyes, she replied by shaking her head.

'Because I love you.' He eased himself into her and let his instincts take over.

As they came together, Bridey collapsed against him. Brendan rinsed them both before turning off the taps. He wrapped her in a towel and carried her into his bedroom. Snuggling with him on the bed, Bridey smiled sweetly. 'Another astonishing first, thanks to you.'

'Christ! You've never made love or had gentle sex before?'

'No.'

He was beginning to understand Bridey. She was a broken woman, the product of a horrid upbringing where she never learned how to love. *Question is, am I too late to fix her?*

'What about you, Brendan? With your love of kink, I can't imagine you doing that much.'

'My tastes have nothing to do with it. I believe a loving relationship requires a balance of tender and kinky moments. I reserve sex like that for people I love, Bry, and there have only been two such other people.'

She sat up surprised. 'Two? I assume *she* was one of them, but the other?'

'Is Caleb.'

Bridey grinned widely. 'I am thrilled to hear it, handsome. You've been good for him, for both of us.'

He laughed. 'And you've been strangely good for me. In a dark and twisted kinda way.'

'Hmm. Speaking of dark and twisted, how did your work go last night?'

'Brilliant actually.' He told her about the scarab but kept the rest to himself. 'I think I have all I need from the Cult. Now I need to work on my exit strategy.'

'Exit strategy?'

'A way out of the Cult. I don't want to get messed up with anymore of their shit.'

'Why can't you tell them you're leaving?'

Brendan sighed heavily. 'Because they made me sign a blood oath, swearing lifetime service.'

Chapter Fourteen

'This is one hell of a way to spend Christmas Eve,' Tyler complained as he settled in alongside Jaxon in the front of their stakeout vehicle—a black SUV with tinted windows. *Totally not suss at all.*

'Why do you care about Christmas? You're not even human, let alone Christian.'

'I know, but I love capitalism.' He paused to sip his steaming coffee. 'And those cheesy movies. I was hoping to watch *Home Alone* with Sam tonight.'

Jaxon sighed, reaching into the backseat to produce a large cardboard box. 'Here, Merry Christmas. I hope this makes up for it.'

Tyler looked at the Krispy Kreme logo and smiled. 'You bloody legend!' He grabbed one of the cream-filled delights and handed the box back to Jaxon. 'Mm, yum,' he spoke with his mouth still half full of caramel.

After rolling his eyes, Jaxon returned his attention to the office building Samantha had told them was the Obsidian Cult's Australian headquarters. 'So, I've been meaning to ask. Will you be my best man?'

Licking the cream from his fingers, Tyler stared at him stunned for a moment. 'Ah, hell yeah.'

Jaxon announced his engagement to Tanya two nights ago at the Solstice dinner Alannah's family had hosted. 'Don't look surprised, Quirky. You're easily my best mate, so it stands to reason I'd ask you.'

'What about Walshy?'

'Why do you think I always take you on missions and leave him to watch Samantha?'

'I dunno. I figured you wanted to keep me away from Sam as much as possible.'

Jaxon laughed. 'No, you idiot. It's because I trust *you* with my life, more than I can Walshy. You're a skilled warlock and a loyal friend.'

'Hmph.' Tyler gave Jaxon's words some thought. 'That's cool. Speaking of weddings, do you think Liam will propose to Lana?'

'Given she's pregnant, you mean? Seems likely to me. Liam's nothing if not traditional when it comes to family values. Do you think she'll accept?'

A dejected sigh slipped from Tyler's mouth. 'Most likely. I know she loves him, and he provides her with much needed stability. Especially now she has a baby on the way.'

'You sound disappointed. I thought you were over her. And what about Samantha?'

'I love them both, Jax. I kinda hoped I could've had two women. Like a ménage à trois, you know? But at the same time, I need to stop kidding myself because I know what she does with me relates to her unresolved feelings for Brendan.'

'Yeah, it's pretty messed up.'

'That jerk *did* mess with Lana something awful.'

'Shit!' Jaxon's attention shifted back to the task at hand. 'Pass me those binoculars, Quirky.' He took them from Tyler's hand and looked at a shadowy figure in the distance. 'He's the same dark mage we saw the other night. I think we should follow him.'

Tyler grabbed the spying aid and confirmed what Jaxon had seen. The man with dark slicked-back hair was getting into a black convertible. 'Yeah, it's him alright. Let's go.'

Jaxon trailed the dark mage carefully, keeping a few cars behind to avoid detection. Their drive came to a stop outside an old house in Windsor. 'Call Walshy and get the lowdown on this place.'

Bringing up his contacts, he rang Shane.

The sound of gunfire blasted across the phoneline until Shane muted the television. 'Hey man, what's up?'

'I need you to run a property search.'

'No probs. Text me the address and I'll send you the deets.'

Shane's reply came within ten minutes, and Tyler read it out to Jaxon, 'The title and deed belong to a Finn Ryan, who obtained ownership in 1954. Walshy is looking up this man now.'

'That would mean the owner is approaching ninety at least. I doubt this dark mage is Finn, but I suppose they could be relatives.'

'Maybe.' Tyler chowed down on another doughnut while they waited.

Tyler's message tone sounded an hour later. 'Holy. Shit. Check this out. It can't be a coincidence.' He handed his phone to Jaxon.

'Indeed. Looks like we have our new lead.'

Brendan's idea of festive tradition involved Christmas themed horror movies. While some things would never change, everything was different this year. Rather than holding Alannah in his arms, he was embracing Caleb whilst watching

Eyes Wide Shut. Even their entertainment was more thriller than horror. At least he could send his hands exploring during the more titillating scenes.

'Things are getting a bit hot, Winters.'

'Mm, is that so, Thornsy?' He breathed heavily into the crook of Caleb's neck. 'Are you talking about the flick or what I'm doing?' To emphasise his question, Brendan plunged his hand inside Caleb's pants.

Caleb sucked in a sharp breath. 'The combination. *Ah Gods*!'

Pleasuring his lover without *needing* magic gave Brendan immense satisfaction. The thought alone drove him to maximise Caleb's gratification.

As the film ended, Caleb tilted his head, diverting his attention. 'Listen. It sounds like Bridey has company.'

Grabbing the remote, Brendan muted the volume, revealing the tell-tale sounds of sex emanating up from Bridey's room. 'Curious how she didn't invite either of us to join the fun.'

'Maybe she thought we could use the alone time.'

'Since when has *our* privacy been a concern of hers? No, I'm guessing it's one of her *business meetings*. And if this is Syndicate business, I'd like to know who she is entertaining.' Brendan dropped the controller on the coffee table and made his way downstairs to Bridey's bedroom door. Pushing it open a crack, he peered inside and groaned at the scene.

Bridey was making a show of riding Damien, clearly faking her pleasure; it would take either an enchanter, or someone with intimate knowledge of her, to read the signs, however. Luckily Brendan was both and he knew the dark mage would not be a significant threat to his own relationship with Bridey.

He was about to turn and leave when Damien caught his eye. 'Hello Lord Jet, why don't you join us?'

Bridey's head turned in surprise, her eyes wide with panic.

'It's okay, I didn't mean to intrude. I'll just—'

'No, please, I *insist*.' Damien's voice carried a commanding tone Brendan felt would be foolish to ignore.

He stepped into the room, closing the door behind him, but he did not move any closer.

Keeping his eyes fixed on Brendan, Damien reached up to stroke the side of Bridey's face. 'Your woman is exquisite. It's kind of you to lend her to me.

Brendan snorted. 'Violet is her own woman, and she does as she pleases.'

'Are you not her boss now?'

'Only in matters of business. In the bedroom she is free to fuck whoever she wants.'

Damien looked up at Bridey. 'Is that so?'

She put on one of her seductive smiles. 'Yes, Damien.' Thrusting her hips against him, she reminded him what they were in the middle of.

Ignoring her, Damien returned his gaze to Brendan. 'I want you to watch Lady Violet fuck me. I want you to stand there, knowing I am the one making her come and you may *not* touch her while she is with me.'

Is this guy for real? Brendan leaned against the closed door and crossed his arms. 'Go on. Make her come.'

They resumed their ridiculous charade, and each time Bridey faked an orgasm, Damien turned to smile smugly at Brendan. *What a wanker.* All were relieved, for their own reasons, when Damien climaxed.

After cleaning himself, Damien sat on the edge of the bed and glowered at Brendan. 'Lady Violet tells me you plan to leave the Cult.'

Feeling hurt and betrayed, Brendan shot Bridey a death glare. 'Did she now?'

'Have you forgotten your initiation oath, Lord Jet? The only way a member leaves the Cult is on their deathbed. For your sake, I hope you are not considering deserting us.'

'Of course not, Damien. I don't know where my *subordinate* got such a ridiculous idea.' He infused as much bitterness as he could into both the words and the scowl he directed her way.

'I'm glad. We will expect to see you at the next new moon ritual.'

'Don't worry. I'll be there.' With a few long strides, Brendan was out the door, slamming it behind him. He hurried up the stairs, craving the fresh night air to cool off.

Tyler took his phone back and read through the genealogy stuff Shane had dug up.

'That means Finn Ryan is Brendan's great-grandfather, right?' Jaxon asked.

'Correct. Apparently, Finn arranged the marriage of Brady Ryan and Tara Winters without the pair ever knowing each other. He shipped Brady off to Adelaide in 1979 to marry Tara a week after her eighteenth birthday. Brady brought his wife back here for family holidays every year until his mysterious death at age thirty-four in 1989.'

Jaxon huffed. 'Mysterious indeed. I bet the crazy bitch killed him. Is old man Finn still alive?'

'There are no death records, but he disappeared. It looks like Tara took over managing the property on his behalf, renting it out for years.'

'Until her grandson shows up in town,' Jaxon concluded.

'I wonder how many other skeletons there are in the Winters family closet,' Tyler mused. 'They make my own family's secrets look as innocent as an episode of *My Little Pony*.'

'I dunno, man… some of those got pretty wild. Besides, learning the maid your great-grandfather had an affair with was of Ancient Egyptian descent, and that she carried this doppelganger gene is a pretty big deal.'

'True. I'd love to dedicate some time to researching my own family history. See if I can learn more about this gene and doppelgangers in general.'

'Which God do you suppose that line descends from?'

Tyler pulled up some recent searches on his phone. 'Well, Geb and Nut were the father and mother of Egyptian mages, so it's unlikely to be them. Bes and Ptah were the fathers of dwarves, Osiris was the father of orcs, Babi among a few others fathered the giants, and Kek was the father of gorgons. If you exclude the various nature gods responsible for creating elves, fae, and other beasts, that leaves Isis, Horus, and possibly Set because I don't know where he fits in. I'm sure there's a bunch of minor deities I'm missing, but that narrows it down a bit.'

'Isis being the Goddess of magic makes sense if the link you share with your Original, or whatever Samantha called Brendan, is magic. Also consider the fact you enhance the potency of each other's magic.'

'Interesting theory. Could it mean our own Dagda[3] has fathered a race of Celtic doppelgangers?'

Jaxon shrugged. 'Maybe, but we don't know if he has ever fathered any demigods and it's not like we can ask him.' Movement ahead got his attention, and he lifted the binoculars to his eyes. 'Shit! Does that look like Brendan to you?'

Grabbing the binoculars from him, Tyler watched as his mirror image walked along the front path leading from the house, stepped out onto the street, and headed in the opposite direction. 'Tell

---

[3] The Dagda is the Celtic Father God of fertility, agriculture, strength, as well as magic, druidry and wisdom.

yes! I'm gonna grab him.' Without awaiting further instruction, he jumped out of the car and ran after Brendan.

As Tyler approached, Brendan glanced behind, but Tyler was not about to give him a chance to fight back. The instant their eyes locked; he sent a kinetic blast pushing Brendan to the ground. He immediately followed up with a lightning bolt strong enough to knock Brendan unconscious. Whipping out a set of cold iron cuffs, he secured Brendan's wrists and dragged him back to the car.

'Christ, Quirky!' exclaimed Jaxon. 'I hope you haven't fried all his braincells. Could make it hard to question him.'

He threw Brendan in the backseat and slammed the door. 'This is me giving zero fucks. The arsehole deserves a world of pain.'

As soon as Damien left, Bridey ran into the living room where she found Caleb dozing on the couch. No sign of Brendan. She darted through the house, searching every other room to no avail. *Shit!* An inspection of the garage showed his car was still there. *He must be going for a walk.* She sighed and tried calling him.

'Hi, this is the voicemail of Darth Jet. I'm currently plotting to take over the galaxy, so you'll need to leave a message after the tone….'

After trying a few more times for good measure, she gave up. *Brendan must be royally pissed with me.*

Returning to the living room, she sat beside her brother and nudged him. 'Caleb, sweetie?'

He groaned as he stirred. As his eyes opened, he sat upright. 'What's wrong, Bry?'

'I messed up.' Her voice trembled and her hands shook like a tuning fork resonating with the song of trepidation in her heart.

Caleb surveyed the room. 'Where's Brendan?'

'He, uh, left.' She tried to inhale deeply, sputtering in the process.

Every muscle in Caleb's body appeared to tense. 'What do you mean, he left?'

'I don't know exactly. He might have gone for a walk. But he is upset with me and won't answer my calls.'

'What did you do?'

She could not hold back the tears any longer. 'I had no choice. Damien forced the truth out of me and confronted Brendan with it.'

Caleb pulled her into his arms and softened his voice. 'What truth, Bry? What's going on?'

He can be such a sweet boy. 'Brendan broke into the Cult's library on the night of the Solstice. I don't know everything he learned from his knowledge quest, but he did discover the significance of the scarab you guys stole for Damien. He also told me he wanted to find a way to sever ties with the Cult.' She choked back a sob.

With one hand caressing her back, Caleb pressed a soft kiss on her forehead. 'Hey, it's okay. Take your time.'

After a few deep breaths, she continued, 'Damien must have heard about the break-in because he came here tonight to question me, and he was able to use magic to force the truth out. Oddly, Brendan leaving the Cult concerned Damien more than the stolen secrets. Apparently, Brendan signed a blood oath tying him to the Cult for life.'

'Oh Gods, Bry! This is bad, real bad. If they force Brendan down the dark mage path, there is a high chance he could spiral out of control. He wasn't born into a life of dark magic like us. One taste of the power they can offer, and he could get hooked, like a drug addict. From what I've heard, bloodline mages are the most susceptible to corruption.'

Terror gripped her heart, sending it into a rhythmic fit to rival hardcore drumming. 'Crap! I didn't even think of the possibility.' She squeezed Caleb tight as she let the tears flow. 'What if it's already too late? What if we've lost him and it's all my fault?'

'Hey, look at me.' Caleb pulled back and peered deep into her eyes. 'This is *not* your fault, Bry. And Brendan's not about to turn dark overnight. It is not too late. We just need to find him. If he felt betrayed by you, doubtless he is screening his calls. Let me try.'

She nodded and sat back, watching as Caleb dialled Brendan with his own phone.

But Caleb frowned almost as soon as he tried. 'Straight to voicemail. I'll send him a text.' After typing out a message, he put his phone down and pulled Bridey back into his arms.

'I really do love him, Caleb.'

'I know, Bry. So do I.'

Chapter Fifteen

Everything was dark, a chill seeped into his bones, and for one dreadful moment Brendan thought he was dead. But a splash of icy water over his head restored the final sliver of consciousness eluding him. Startled by the bright fluorescent light, it took him a few minutes to register his surroundings. Then he wished he were dead.

Cold iron bars lined the walls of the interrogation room. The only other person present was a blond warlock who towered over him with a scowl. 'About time you woke up.' He moved across the room and pressed a button on the intercom. 'Hey Quirky, our suspect has come to.'

The muffled sounds of the police station filtered in through the speaker box. 'I'll be right there.'

'What the hell's going on?' Brendan demanded. 'Am I under arrest?'

'Not yet. I brought you in for questioning. But given the shit on your criminal record, I don't hold out much hope for your freedom.'

Talk about the proverbial fucking frying pan fire.

A dark-haired man who looked strangely familiar walked through the door. 'Sorry if I missed anything, boss.' Distracted by his phone, he did not even look at Brendan.

'I haven't really started yet. I was explaining how we haven't yet arrested him.'

The new guy sat in a chair across the table, still looking at his phone. 'Right, let's begin.'

'Wait a minute,' Brendan interrupted, 'if I'm not in custody, I'm free to walk out of here and refuse to answer your questions, right?'

The man affectionately known as Quirky glanced up and snorted. 'Right, that'll sure help your cause. We'll subpoena your arse faster than your first fuck.' But as soon as his eyes fell on Brendan, his indifference turned into a bitter scowl.

'What my friend here is trying to say,' explained the other guy, 'is you can either cooperate now, or face the full force of the Council later.'

Brendan glared at Blondie. 'I know what a fucking subpoena is.'

'Good, I'm glad we have an understanding. So, what's your choice?'

Heaving out a sigh, Brendan reclined in his seat. 'What do you want to know?'

Blondie set his phone on the table and opened a voice recording app. 'I am Warlock Jaxon Hayes, and this is Tyler Quirke. Let's start with your name.'

'Brendan Winters.'

'Oh hell,' Hayes muttered as Tyler flew across the room and slammed a fist into Brendan's left eye.

'*That's from Lana, you piece of shit!*' Tyler screamed. 'And these are from me.' He pushed Brendan to the floor and continued to pummel him.

Tyler stunned Brendan, not only with the near-concussive blows to his head.

'*Quirky, stop it!*' Hayes cried out as he attempted to pull ninety kilos of solid warlock from Brendan. '*Get a hold of yourself before I take you off this case.*' With Tyler restrained, Hayes glared at Brendan. 'Get. Up.'

Brendan clambered to his feet.

'Sit. Down.'

Sensing Hayes was nearing the threshold where he flipped from good cop to bad cop, Brendan complied.

Hayes turned to Tyler. 'Are we going to have a problem here, Quirky? I can't have anything compromising the integrity of this case.'

'No, Sir. Let me have a few words, then we can move on.'

'Fine. Make it quick.' Hayes stopped the recording.

Tyler braced his palms on the table. 'Do you realise how much you broke Lana? Or was it your intention, you piece of dark mage scum?'

Who was this guy and why was he using the diminutive of her name? 'You don't know shit about my relationship with Lana, so shut the fuck up.'

'Oh? So, you didn't steal her away from your brother, and talk her into making the ultimate commitment right before running off into the sunset with some endarkened whore and severing the soul link?'

He gaped at Tyler, the brutal truth rendering him speechless.

'That's right. She confided everything to me. I knew her for less than twenty-four hours before she told me. Why do you think she would have poured her heart out to me when I was practically a stranger?'

Bewildered, Brendan shook his head.

Tyler leaned forward. 'Have you looked in a mirror lately? If not, I'm sure my face will do.'

Brendan's eyes widened with realisation. Tyler was the guy from the nightclub.

'I dunno if I should thank you or hate you for what followed because it was the best damn sex of my life. Problem was, she wasn't really fucking *me*.'

Shit!

'She'll never forgive you. I hope you realise that.'

Every muscle in Brendan's body tensed. 'Lana made her choice. She has Liam now.'

Tyler laughed drily. 'Right. And I'm sure she'll forget all about you when she marries him.'

Brendan shot him a look of surprise mingled with fear. *Did he seriously drop the M word?*

'It's inevitable. So, I hope you're happy with your whore and her brother, 'cause they're your lot now. That's if we don't throw your arse in gaol.'

The last of Brendan's hope pulled a vanishing act more impressive than David Copperfield.

Hayes sighed. 'Wrap this up please, Quirky. As much as I hate Brendan for what he did to Alannah, we have a job to get on with.'

'Yes, Sir,' Tyler replied with hesitation.

Brendan shifted his gaze to Hayes. 'Can I ask one thing?'

'What?' he clipped.

'How do you guys know Lana?'

'We helped her put Richard Lane and Tara Winters in the ground.'

Gods, I wish I'd been there to see her put a blade through the sadistic bastard's heart. 'Did she really kill Tara? I mean it wouldn't be the first time she tried.'

'Yep. I saw it with my own eyes.' Hayes smiled as he remembered. 'Blessed dagger in the heart, shattered soul crystal against the wall. It was glorious.'

Hmm, sounds like Lana pulled off a convincing act.

'Not as hot as when she took down Richard though,' Tyler added.

They both looked like a pair of lovesick puppies. *Yup, sounds like the Lana I remember. Breaking hearts wherever she goes.*

Hayes cleared his throat as he resumed the recording. 'Anyway, getting back to the issue at hand. Are you a member of the Obsidian Cult, or one of their contractors?'

'Shit! You know who those guys are?'

Tyler rose and leaned across the table, invading Brendan's personal space. 'Need I remind you; *we* ask the questions here?' He grabbed Brendan's throat in a choke hold. 'What's the extent of your association with the Cult?'

'Sit down, Quirky.' The other warlock spoke calmly.

When Tyler returned to his chair, he resumed glaring at Brendan.

'I'm a recent initiate.'

'Christ!' Tyler gritted his teeth. 'Do you know who those bastards are?'

He grinned. 'Yup. More than you do, I'd warrant.'

'What are you talking about?' asked Hayes.

'If you want to know more, you'll have to turn off your recording devices.'

His interrogators exchanged a look. Hayes nodded and turned off his phone.

Brendan looked at Tyler. 'And yours.'

Tyler's eyes widened. 'How?'

Brendan tapped the side of his head. 'Mind reader.'

'But this room is magic proof,' Tyler protested.

'Spooky.' Brendan leaned back and crossed his ankles. If these idiots did not know how enchanters worked, he was not about to enlighten them.

'We are his mana source,' explained Hayes, spoiling Brendan's fun.

He watched carefully as Tyler removed the digital recording device from his pocket and turned it off. When both sets of eyes returned to him, he cast the soundproofing ward he had recently learned from Dana. 'Between us, I may be a member for the Cult, but I don't work for them. I only joined them to gain access to their secrets.'

'Right. I almost forgot. You work for that Dark Syndicate slut,' Tyler scoffed.

A snigger slipped out. 'Puh-lease. I *own* the Dark Syndicate, in Australia anyway. But I don't represent their interests either.' Brendan hoped he could trust these guys since they were friends with Alannah.

Hayes narrowed his eyes, one of them twitching in the process. 'Whose interests do you serve?'

'The Winters clan.'

Pure hate poured from Tyler's aura like murky swamp mud. 'Like hell you do. How is abandoning your family in their best interest?'

'I don't expect you to understand the intricacies of my family's dynamics. One night of intimacy with Lana doesn't give you the right to judge us, and I sure as hell doubt it was enough to get the full story.'

This time Tyler leaned back and smirked. 'What makes you think it was only one night?'

'Well good for you, Tyler.' Brendan returned the smug expression. 'I'm glad Lana isn't restricting herself to my impotent brother. If you were hoping to get a rise out of me with that news, you clearly don't understand the Winters clan at all. There is only one man who could achieve such a result.'

Confusion spread across Tyler's visage in a series of fine wrinkles.

'He's talking about Liam,' explained Hayes.

'I wonder, Tyler,' Brendan went on, 'did Lana tell you how close she grew to Tara this year? Did you know Grandma was training the two of us in the art of deception as well as other… magics?'

Tyler shook his head in stunned silence.

'I didn't think so. There are few people she would trust with the knowledge. Certainly not the Council's pets.'

'So why are *you* telling us?' Tyler spat with bitter vitriol.

'Because I believe you both care about her. Am I wrong?'

'Yes, I care,' replied Hayes.

'I care about her a lot more than you do.'
Tyler barely contained his rage at this point.

'Fuck off, Tyler. You've known her for what?
A few months? I've been in love with the woman all
my life. Don't mistake my emotional response to
heartbreak as a lack of concern for her. I would still
lay down my life to protect hers. Would you?'

Tyler's jaw hit the floor.

'I would,' confirmed Hayes.

'Of course I would.' Tyler's honesty was
plain to see within the bright swirling sunset of his
aura.

Brendan narrowed his eyes on Tyler. 'Even if
it meant going against the Council?'

'Yes.'

He glanced at Hayes, who was carefully
thinking about his reply.

'I would protect her from the authorities to
the best of my abilities, but I would not taint my
soul, nor risk my own woman's life.'

'I can respect that.' Brendan sat forward and
leaned on the table. 'Lana needs allies on the inside.'

Tyler mirrored Brendan's stance. 'Why, what
is she planning?'

'At this stage she is watching and learning.
But according to Tara, knowledge is a dangerous

asset in our world. There will come a time when Alannah knows too much for her own good.'

Tyler shook his head with a puzzled expression. 'So why seek such knowledge?'

'Because someone needs to uncover the truth. Speaking of which, did you know the inner circle of the Obsidian Cult refer to themselves as the Sons of Set?'

The warlocks exchanged a look and Jaxon leaned forward. 'Does that mean they are—'

'Direct descendants of the God? Yup. They are a different race of elves. You can call them dark elves since their souls are completely black.'

'I don't suppose you came across anything about doppelgangers in your Cult research?' Tyler queried.

'No, but I haven't finished translating everything. Why do you ask?'

'Why do you think we look like twins?'

'I can't say I've given much thought to your appearance, Tyler. You're not my type. Fucking you would be too much like masturbation.'

'Well maybe you should think about it, because you and I are the reason the Sons of Set are in town.'

Curiosity was getting the better of Brendan as he sat up. 'What do you mean?'

'I'm your doppelganger, or magic twin as they call us. I don't know the full story, but apparently, I descend from an Egyptian God, one who is not a progenitor of mages or any other common magic race, and I carry a gene that created a magic link between us. Aside from looking alike, we are amplifiers for each other's magic.'

'Colour me intrigued. What's your date of birth, Tyler?'

'Fourteenth of August 2002. Why?'

Brendan remained silent for a moment. 'I was wondering if we shared a birthday.'

'And do we?' Tyler sat on the edge of his seat.

'No, I'm a week older. Same star sign, though. I don't know if that bears significance on this doppelganger stuff. What I do find intriguing is the fact you share a birthday with someone else we know.'

Tyler's eyes bugged out. 'Do you mean Lana?'

'Yup.'

After an hour of waiting, Caleb felt restless. 'I'm going for a walk to see if I can find him.'

'On your own? Are you sure it's a smart idea?' Bridey sprang to her feet and grabbed his hand.

'Yes, on my own. What's wrong with that?'

'It's the middle of the night in a rough neighbourhood, sweetie.'

Caleb smiled as he pulled her in for a hug. 'I may not have Brendan's bulk, but I do know how to fight and look after myself. Worst case, I can run or magiport. I'll be careful, Bry. Call me if you hear anything, okay?'

'Okay.' She squeezed him tight.

Stepping outside, the first thing Caleb noticed was the warmth of the night air. With the way Bridey kept the house chilled, it was easy to forget the heat of the Australian summer, especially when he rarely did go outside. There were few people around, likely due to the Christian holiday. When he reached the local park, there was a gang of human kids all dressed in black hoodies who were vandalising some play equipment.

'Hey guys, check out the goth freak!'

They all laughed as they turned to stare at him.

Morons have no idea who they're messing with. He simply flashed the unloaded Glock on his belt as he grabbed his knife and twirled it in his fingers.

The pistol was only ever a prop. Couldn't be too careful around magic users, after all: anyone attuned to the elements or matter could ignite the gunpowder of an opponent's firearm.

He continued walking and the thugs backed off when they saw he had no intention to fight. *Almost a pity. I could have used an excuse to blow off steam.* Despite what he'd said to reassure Bridey, the possibility of losing Brendan was getting to him. *Ironic how the woman who brought us together was the one to drive us apart.*

Spotting a payphone, he decided to try his luck as an unknown caller. *Not likely to work, but worth a shot.* It went straight to voicemail, again. Caleb slammed the phone down, an idea forming as he returned home.

Bridey ran to the door, looking crestfallen when she saw he was alone.

'I could try scrying?' he suggested.

'You can do that?' Bridey gawked at him in amazement.

With a shrug, he strode toward the ritual room. 'I'm attuned to cosmic and organic mana. How hard can it be?'

'So, you've never tried it before?'

'Not exactly. But I have been reading up on it, so I know what's needed.' When they reached the cellar, Caleb unlocked a chest of magic supplies and withdrew a set of maps and a bright green moldavite crystal on a silver chain. 'I need some of Brendan's hair. Would you mind retrieving a few strands from his brush?'

Nodding, she ran upstairs, giving him some much-needed peace and quiet to prepare. By the time she returned, Caleb had memorised the ritual steps and had everything else set up. He called the elements, cast the circle, and kneeled at the altar.

Not being a regular practitioner, it took several excruciating minutes to focus his mind. Eventually the mana flowed through him, and the crystal moved. The first map confirmed Brendan was still in New South Wales. Next, he narrowed it down to the metropolitan area. Finally, the crystal stabbed the page, pinpointing an exact location: The Darlinghurst Police Station. 'Fuck!' That was a place Caleb hoped he'd never have to return to.

Peeking over his shoulder, Bridey noticed where the moldavite had landed. 'Oh dear. Well at least he isn't with the Cult.'

Slicing his athame over the circle, Caleb jumped to his feet. 'How can you say that, Bry? You know how much shit Brendan is in with the Council? Those drug charges alone could be enough to get him a life sentence.'

Bridey reached out and drew him into her arms. 'I'll make some phone calls. I meant it when I promised him protection from the authorities. The Council can't touch us, sweetie, and I'm gonna make sure that applies to Brendan too.'

He gazed down upon her with narrowed eyes. 'How exactly?'

'Best if you don't know.'

'Quite the coincidence.' Tyler could not wait to share this detail with Alannah. He even smiled at the possibility of partying with her.

Brendan cleared his throat. 'What exactly do the Cult want with us?'

'They want to use us together in their dark magic rituals.'

An obnoxiously loud laugh burst from Brendan. 'I'm sorry, but the thought of a goodie-two-shoes like you getting mixed up with those arseholes is one of the funniest things I've heard in ages. I don't think you need to worry, Tyler.'

He groaned with irritation. Brendan's arrogance was getting on his nerves. 'I guess it might surprise you to know they came dangerously close to succeeding. According to my source, they have some cunning ways of tricking mages into joining them.'

The humour faded from Brendan's expression. 'How close? You didn't sign anything did you?'

'No. They haven't been able to recruit me yet, but I almost went undercover to investigate them which would have meant joining.'

Brendan sat back and sighed. For several long seconds he stared at the table, apparently lost in thought. 'If you want to take these guys out, I'm willing to help, but only on two conditions.'

'We don't make deals with scumbags like you,' Tyler scoffed.

'Quirky, please,' Jaxon warned. 'What are your conditions, Mr. Winters?'

'First of all, I want the Council to wipe my criminal record clean.'

'You have got to be kidding me!' Tyler was keen to lock the bastard away for life — an easy enough feat if they pegged him for the Rhapsody drug charges.

'I guess you guys are on your own with the Cult.' Brendan sat back and crossed his arms again.

'And what is your second condition?' Jaxon asked without blinking an eye.

A wide grin formed on Brendan's face as he turned his attention from Tyler to the real negotiator in the room. 'You can't arrest the inner circle. You need to kill them. All of them. This is critical because I guarantee no bars will hold them.'

'I can't make any promises, but I'll see what I can do.'

Tyler slammed a fist on the table. 'Seriously, Jax. What—'

'Shut it, Quirky!' Jaxon moved to the door. 'See this? It's a door you can walk through if you don't start towing the line.'

With a huff he sat back in his chair. 'Fine!'

Jaxon leaned against the door, crossing his arms. 'You need to put your personal qualms aside and focus on the bigger picture, Warlock Quirke.'

Shit! Official titles mean Jaxon is serious. Or pissed. Maybe both?

After an excruciating silence, Jaxon approached the table again. 'What exactly can you do to help us, Mr. Winters?'

'I can provide intel and access.'

'Keep talking.'

'I'll need a show of good faith first.'

Jaxon sighed. 'Give me a few minutes.' He grabbed his phone and headed for the door where he paused and pinned Tyler with a severe look. 'Behave yourself, Quirky.'

'Yes, Sir.'

Jaxon left the room, shutting Tyler in with the man he despised most in the world.

He turned an evil eye on Brendan. 'Why did you do it?'

'Do what?'

'Leave Lana without a word.'

An animalistic growl slipped from Brendan's throat. 'Have you ever been in love before, Tyler? I'm not talking about some crush or the butterflies you get at the start of a new fling. I mean real, all-consuming love where that person becomes your world.'

'I am now.'

'Christ! For your sake, I hope you're not talking about Lana.'

'No, not exactly. I have strong feels for her, don't get me wrong. But I was talking about my girlfriend.'

'Right. Now imagine you are essentially married to the woman, newlyweds at that, and she hooks up with her ex, someone you happen to despise. You don't simply hear about it but see it with your own eyes. Can you imagine how painful it would feel?'

'Yes but—'

'No buts, Tyler. Take a moment to think about how you would *feel*.'

Deciding to humour Brendan, Tyler closed his eyes and gave it some thought. Samantha's Cult master sounded like a nasty piece of work and seeing her choose to return to him would be pretty devastating.

'If someone gave you the option to instantly erase the pain, but you needed to take immediate action, would you?'

'I suppose I would,' Tyler agreed.

'Ah, but it turns out there's a catch you didn't think about because you weren't in your right mind. You've essentially sold both your soul and your freedom. So, you can't even talk through whatever issue there was between you and your woman. She is lost to you forever.'

Understanding was beginning to sink in for Tyler. He hated to admit it, but he almost felt sorry for Brendan. 'What did you see?'

'Lana was making out with Liam in the back of my parents' garden mere minutes after we had announced our soul link to the family.'

Tyler scratched his head. 'But she was in love with you. Why would she do that?'

Brendan let out a brief sardonic laugh. 'You know, I keep asking myself the same question.'

'Surely there was some misunderstanding?'

'Possibly, but it's too late now. The damage is done, and I can't contact her anyway.'

'Why?'

'That's classified.'

It was such a frustrating situation and he wished he had a magic band-aid to fix their relationship.

'So, what's the deal with you and the Hawthorns? Lana told me you ran off with Bridey, but I got the impression from Caleb you and he have a thing.'

Brendan's pierced brow arched. '*You're* the warlock who arrested him?'

'Yeah, along with Jaxon.'

'Curious how he didn't mention meeting my double.' He chuckled a moment. 'I bet he gave you hell. The man's got a major attitude.'

'One to rival yours, even.'

He nodded with a wistful smile. 'To answer your question, my relationship with Bridey is more complicated than astrophysics. But Caleb and I are very much in love—something that took me by surprise, considering I've never had any gay or bi tendencies before. We had been mates since starting high school together and I recently found out he'd had a crush on me all this time. Just when you think you know someone.' Brendan shook his head. 'I didn't even realise he was bi.'

Jaxon returned the next second holding a laptop. 'It took some serious string-pulling, but here.' He directed the screen towards Brendan. 'No record, no pending charges, and no open cases linked to your name.'

'Sweet. Thank you.'

'Now tell us everything you know about the Obsidian Cult.'

Slumping into the leather office chair, Brendan put his feet up on the solid oak desk and sipped on the expensive whiskey Tara had left behind. Dana had explained how his grandmother had owned this office building and she had left it to her two favourite grandchildren. While most of the spaces had tenancies, the tenth floor had been her headquarters and it was where he conducted his business as the new Boss of the Dark Syndicate.

He was thankful for the inner-city retreat and for Tara's exceptional taste in liquor, especially since he did not feel like going home yet. *What is it*

with the women I love betraying me? Am I wearing a sign inviting them to crush my heart into lifeless pulp?
With a sigh, he picked up his phone, being careful not to disconnect it from the charger, and powered it on. A bunch of missed calls registered, mostly from Bridey, but there were a few from Caleb, along with a message: DON'T YOU DARE SKIP TOWN BEFORE GIVING HER A CHANCE TO EXPLAIN HERSELF. WE BOTH LOVE YOU.

Fuck! Even if Bridey is a deceitful whore, I still have Thornsy and I can't leave him. While he did not have any plans to leave before fulfilling his end of the bargain with Tyler and Jaxon, the thought of moving to another city had crossed his mind. *I guess I may as well confront the bitch.*

After knocking back the last of his drink, Brendan strode out of the office and hailed a taxi. The middle-aged driver attempted some small talk at first, but soon learned Brendan was not in the mood for chatting. As soon as they pulled into the Windsor driveway, he threw a bunch of hundred-dollar notes at the driver and didn't bother waiting for change.

The front door slammed into the wall from the force of Brendan's entrance, alerting the Hawthorns to his arrival. They raced into the parlour from the rear living area. Bridey's face lit up at seeing him. 'Oh Gods, Brendan, I'm—'

'Shut. Up.' Brendan was fuming as he approached her.

She must have sensed his foul mood because she began to retreat.

He rushed at her, pinning her against the wall and caging her with his arms.

'Brendan, please—' Caleb pleaded.

'Stay out of it, Thornsy. This is between me and your sister.' He glared at her a moment. 'Does love and loyalty mean nothing to you?'

'I'm sorry. I didn't want to tell him, but he pulled the truth from me with magic.'

'You expect me to believe a half-wit like Damien could break through your mind shields when I can't?'

Bridey's eyes widened with a mixture of fear and surprise. 'I... He must've had help from the inner circle.'

'Stop lying to me.' Brendan was seething.

'I'm not, I swear.'

'How did they break through your defences?'

She gazed at her feet with a shameful expression and tears trickled from her eyes.

'Damien threatened Caleb's life if I didn't let him in my head.'

'What the hell, Bry.' Caleb drew closer.

But Brendan turned and raised a hand to stop Caleb before resuming his position with Bridey. He could not blame her for protecting her brother, the man they both loved. 'Look at me, Bry,' he demanded with a softer tone. As soon as her eyes met his, Brendan's mouth crashed with hers and he kissed her violently. Clutching her arms with a vice grip, he pulled back. 'Thank you for looking after our Caleb.'

He spun away from her and grabbed Caleb, pulling him into a loving embrace and a deep kiss that made Caleb moan into Brendan's mouth. Those sexy little noises were driving him to distraction and before long, he dragged Caleb to the couch. He stripped him bare, taking a moment to appreciate his lover's slim build, soft, silvery skin, and dark eyes full of emotion. 'I'm so damn in love with you, Thornsy.' Brendan bent Caleb over the sofa and let his own body emphasise his point.

Chapter Sixteen

Brendan's eyes were starting to glaze over as he read the latest management reports. This was the sort of dull shit he despised most about his new job. It was Friday and he was almost counting down the hours to the weekend. *Why can't the Syndicate take the week between Christmas and New Year's off, like most legit businesses?*

He welcomed the buzzing sound of his intercom, followed by his secretary's soft, feminine voice as it came through the speaker. 'Lord Stirling is here to see you, sir.'

A smile took over his face. *My final meeting for the week and the perfect distraction.* 'Let him in.' Reclining in his chair as the door opened, Brendan drank in the sight of Caleb dressed in a business suit tailored to perfection. As soon as the door closed, a whistle escaped his pursed lips.

Caleb offered him a lopsided grin. 'You wanted to see me, sir?'

'I always want to see you, and right now I'm dying to bend you naked over my desk.'

Ambling forward, Caleb unclasped the buttons of his jacket. 'Not that I'm complaining, but did you really call me into your office for sex?'

A short laugh slipped from Brendan's mouth. 'Well no. I have a sensitive matter to discuss, but now you're here and dressed like that, I find myself extremely tempted.'

He dropped the jacket over the back of a visitor's chair and moved around to Brendan, perching on the edge of the desk directly in front of him.

Springing from his seat, Brendan kissed Caleb passionately. But he pulled back before letting himself get carried away. With a sigh he sat down. 'As much as I'd love to see my fantasy become a reality, I still have a mountain of paperwork to get through before heading home tonight. I never realised running a criminal organisation would be like managing a legit company. Being a captain was a lot more exciting.'

'Indeed,' Caleb smirked. 'What can I *do you* for, Boss?'

Damn, it sounds and feels satisfying to hear him address me like that. All sorts of roleplay ideas filled his mind, but he gave himself a mental slap across the back of his head. 'I have an assignment for you. I know it's not exactly kosher for me to be calling on someone else's captain for a job like this, but I am banging your boss and I doubt she'll mind me borrowing you.' His lips curled up as the unspoken understanding passed between them. 'Besides, you're the only person I can entrust with the task and I'm hoping you won't mind the trip.'

'You need me to travel? Where to?'

'Gaeilge Shores.'

Caleb's eyes bugged out. 'Why?'

'I want to promote Jacob to be my captain and spymaster there. While I'm communicating most of the promotions in other towns via demon couriers, I feel this one deserves a more personal approach. I'm sure you can appreciate why.'

'Yes, of course.'

'I don't know if Jacob knows I'm Lord Jet. If he doesn't, please don't fill in the blanks for him. Let my identity remain a mystery for the time being.'

'And if he asks how he got promoted?'

'Tell him I went with your recommendation. Jacob is smart and skilled at what he does. I'm pretty sure the Syndicate only overlooked him before because he lacked connections. You can pretend your move to Sydney and position as

Violet's captain brought you into my inner circle or some shit.'

'Yeah, I can work with that.'

Brendan grabbed the brown paper parcel he had warded with a tamper alert spell and placed it on the desk next to Caleb. 'This is his induction pack. Please see he gets it and no one else but Jacob opens it.'

'Will do. When do you want me to go?'

'Sunday.'

'But that's New Year's Eve,' Caleb pleaded.

'I know. Promoting Jacob isn't the only task I have for you. I would like you to attend the Council's party at the Sailing Club. The folks in those circles know you well enough, so visiting your mother and spending the night with your old friends won't arouse suspicions.'

Caleb took a deep breath. 'What do you want me to do?'

'Keep your ear to the ground and tell me all the gossip and rumours circulating around town. I'll get Jacob to do this in future, but I need you to bring me the latest news.'

'Sure this isn't a ploy to keep me from my sister's New Year's Party?' Caleb gave him a devious smile.

'Maybe.' Brendan gazed upon him. He was not ready for Bridey to introduce Caleb to her party scene, and he had made his sentiments on the matter known to both of the Hawthorn siblings. As much as he could, Brendan wanted to shield his precious Caleb from the worst of the Syndicate lifestyle. It was probably a fruitless endeavour with Bridey pulling most of Caleb's strings, but Brendan would still do what he could.

Caleb sighed. 'Fine. I'll go on Sunday and have a boring New Year's Eve. But you'll owe me big time for this.'

Sliding his hands up along Caleb's thighs, Brendan rose and pressed his mouth to Caleb's ear. 'Between Bridey and myself, I'm sure we have all your kinks covered. Perhaps we could spend tonight exploring them all with you.'

A shiver ran through Caleb's body and goosebumps rose on his neck. 'Mm, yes please.'

Brendan drew back and grinned at his lover. 'Great. I'm glad we could come to an understanding. I will, of course, compensate you for your work in the usual business manner as well. Just don't forget to keep your receipts.'

Wanting to catch Jacob before the party, Caleb arrived in town late Sunday afternoon and headed straight for the boggart's cottage house. He knocked on the decorative glass panel beside the door. Apparently, the house had been in the Federation style, but someone lacking in taste renovated the interior during the fifties and as a rental tenant, Jacob could not do much about the hideous 'retro' design.

Jacob's jaw dropped when he opened the door. 'Thornsy?'

'In the flesh,' he deadpanned.

'What brings you to your old neck of the woods?'

'Business, mostly. Can I come in?'

'Yeah, sure.' He stepped aside to let Caleb in. Jacob closed the door and lead him along the hallway and into the loungeroom. 'Have a seat. Can I get you a drink?'

'Got any cold beers?'

Half a grin touched Jacob's lips. 'Always.' He dashed out of the room and returned momentarily with a couple of pale ales. After handing one to Caleb, he sat across the small room. 'So, what can I do you for?'

'I assume you are aware of the recent Syndicate leadership elections?'

He nodded his head. 'Some guy known as Lord Jet now runs the show.'

Well, that answers my first question. 'He sure does. Lady Violet, my sister, is a part of his inner circle, which means I am too. She made me her captain by the way, so you should call me Stirling when other Syndicate members are around.'

'Christ, Thornsy! I never thought I'd see the day you followed in your father's footsteps.'

A growl escaped before Caleb could repress it. 'Trust me when I say the Syndicate is like charity work compared to what my father does. He gave me a choice: join his business or my sister's. The choice was easy.'

Jacob nodded his understanding.

'Anyway, Lord Jet asked me to deliver the news in person.'

'What news?'

'Well with the changing of the guard, he is hiring new spymaster captains and he wants you to be his man in this town.'

The redhead stared at him in amazement. 'Why me?'

'He wanted my recommendation, so naturally I suggested you. We may have had our differences recently, but you are still one of the best

Syndicate members around these parts and I have to respect you for that.'

'Um… I don't know what to say.'

'Thanks will do,' Caleb replied drily.

'Yeah, ah thank you. So, what's my codename?'

'Red. He also asked me to give you this induction pack.' He withdrew the parcel from his satchel and gave it to Jacob.

'Cheers, man. Are you in town for long?'

'A couple of days. Figured I'd catch up with Mum while I'm here.'

'Most of the magical community are going to the Sailing Club tonight. You in the mood for a party?'

'Sounds good. I'd love to catch up with the rest of the gang.'

'Yeah, about that. I'm kinda on the outs with most of them now. They didn't take kindly to my corrupting influence on Brendo. Alannah is still friendly, and Ben tolerates me, but I tend to hang out with other unseelie these days.'

'Ah shit, man. I'm sorry.'

'Hey, it's not your fault. The truth was bound to come out eventually, since Richard told Liam and Alannah when he took them hostage.'

'Cara?'

'Left me.'

'Well damn. She was a decent woman. You seeing anyone else?'

'Nope. I'm flying solo for a bit. We could check out an unseelie club in the city tomorrow night if you're interested. Party together like old times?'

Caleb's instinct was to decline because he was already in two relationships, but it wasn't like either of his lovers expected him to remain exclusive when they weren't. He gave Jacob a mischievous grin. 'Yeah, okay. Dull party tonight, real one tomorrow.'

'That's the spirit.'

'Did you get in trouble with the Council?'

'The High Magus wanted to charge me, but Liam convinced Kieran to pardon me on the grounds I helped save him and Alannah.'

'Wow. The Council absolved you and proclaimed you a hero, yet Cara couldn't forgive you? What a bitch.'

Jacob shrugged. 'The betrayal was more personal for her and the other guys. Funny thing is Alannah doesn't blame me at all, and my fuck up affected her the most. Then again, she knew all about the drug trade back when she was in trouble with the Council and even helped Brendan get out of the business when they hooked up.'

This time Caleb was gobsmacked. 'Alannah knew? Brendan never mentioned.'

'Do you see Brendo often?'

Caleb tried to hide the warm smile threatening to show. 'You could say that. I do live with him.'

'Oh right, of course. He lives with your sister, and you moved there to work for her. Makes sense you would live with them too. How is he and how are things between the two of you? Last time we spoke, he wasn't exactly your favourite person.'

Caleb took a moment to approach his reply carefully. 'I smoothed things over with Brendan. And he is doing okay, all things considered.'

'Hmm, well at least he is okay. Come on, let's get ready for tonight.'

Caleb hadn't been wrong in his assumption regarding the Council's festivities. A bunch of food trucks, carnival rides, and sideshow games might have appealed to him when he was a kid, but it was entirely too wholesome for his matured tastes. The jazz band playing in the gazebo didn't do much for him either—not without Bridey present. She loved the chaotic excuse for music and would've pulled him onto the dancefloor. While he would have outwardly cringed and complained, secretly he would have loved dancing with her.

But Caleb wasn't there to have fun, so he did his best to catch up with all his old school friends and even mingled with his mother and some of her acquaintances to learn as much as possible.

Cara caught his attention as he wandered through the crowd inside the clubrooms. 'Hey, Caleb. How've you been?'

'Great, thanks. You?'

'I've been better. I suppose you heard about my breakup with Jacob?'

Unsure what to say, he simply nodded.

'You're living in Sydney with your sister now, right?'

'Yeah.'

'And Brendan?'

He could see where she was going with this, so he sighed. 'What do you want to know, Cara?'

'Why did he leave Alannah?'

A commotion on the stage saved him from an awkward conversation. Jessica Ó Máille was holding a microphone. 'Excuse me ladies and gentlemen. Alannah and Liam Winters have an important announcement to make. Get up here, you two.' She beckoned them with excited hand gestures.

Alannah took the microphone from her. 'This is awkward, but you would probably hear it on the rumour mill anyway. I am pregnant.'

Caleb's first thoughts went to Brendan. He stepped forward in the crowd to call out, 'So, which cousin is the baby daddy?'

After a visible shiver, Liam grabbed the microphone. 'Tradition forbids us from asking who the biological father is because Alannah is carrying a baby conceived at Beltane.' Turning to face her, he spurted forth a bunch of mushy words that sickened Caleb. Dropping to one knee in front of Alannah, Liam pulled a ring from his pocket. 'I adore you, Alannah Winters, and if you would do me the honour of becoming my wife, I promise to devote the rest of my life to keeping you safe and happy.' There was a moment of silence between them. 'Lana, baby, will you marry me?'

Tears streaked Alannah's cheeks as she replied, 'Yes. Very yes.'

Bugger me! Brendan will lose his shit when he hears about this. As Liam slipped the ring on her finger, Caleb disappeared into the night. He needed to call Bridey about the situation.

She picked up after a couple of attempts. 'Hey sweetie, what's up?'

'Alannah Winters is pregnant.'

'Shit! Is the child Brendan's?'

'Yeah. Beltane baby.' He knew Brendan had been her only partner that night because he confided as much to Caleb.

'Damn it. If he finds out, there won't be any stopping his return to her. You can't tell him Alannah's pregnant. And you should advise Jacob to keep the news under wraps too.'

Caleb squeezed his eyes shut. He hated the idea of keeping such tremendous news from Brendan, but he understood it was for the best. 'I'll have a word with Jacob.'

'Thanks, hun.'

With a warm afterglow on his face, Jacob woke late on the second day of January, and made his way into the kitchen as recollections of the previous night played through his mind. When he reached the table, he found a note with Caleb's messy scrawl:

Thanks for a great night and for letting me crash in your bed ;-)

Sorry to love and leave you, but I had to get going and didn't want to wake you. You look too cute when you sleep. Until next

*time, try not to do anything I wouldn't do,
LOL.*

> *Regards,*
> *Caleb.*

Jacob smiled as he read it. *After last night, I'm
not sure there is much Thornsy wouldn't do.* The
unseelie club had been entertaining, but the
afterparty they brought home with them was when
the real fun began. Letting out a satisfied sigh, he
went about brewing some coffee. He sat down in
the loungeroom, letting the steam dissipate from his
drink as he picked up the parcel Caleb had given
him.

Ripping aside the brown paper, he found a
small envelope affixed to a manilla folder which sat
atop another wrapped package. A quick flick
through the contents of the folder showed a bunch
of induction papers and forms, all standard
Syndicate stuff. But when he opened the envelope,
he found a handwritten letter:

> *Hey man, sorry it took ages to get
> back in touch. Things have been crazy for me
> of late.*

Jacob paused as the familiar tone of the writing struck him. *Is this Brendo?*

> *I bet you've already figured out who I am, yeah? See, this is one of the reasons I asked Stirling to promote you. You are hell smart, and the Syndicate should've made you captain long ago. Ah well, their loss is my gain. I also need an ally on my side. It is hard to know who I can trust these days. And as much as I'd like to think Stirling is among the select few, our relationship has grown rather intimate of late, and love complicates things. Especially when it comes to the matter I am entrusting you with.*

Jacob laughed. *Well shit! Brendo and Thornsy? I didn't see that one coming.*

> *I have made a deal with my other lover preventing me from contacting Alannah, so I need you to deliver the contents of the inner package to her. Do not, under any circumstances, let her know they came from me. She needs to believe this stuff came from her great aunt. It will give her enough context to understand their significance. The*

same will go for all future parcels I send you, most of which will arrive by demon post.

It pains me more than you'd know to keep this distance from her. I still love her, and I will forever regret the impulsive reaction that broke us apart and landed me in this mess. But for her safety, as well as my own, it is best we both move on with our lives. I hope you understand this and forgive me for what you must have perceived to be a real dick move on my part.

Are things okay for you and your woman? I'd ask you to send her my regards, but she probably hates me for what I did. And for what ought to be obvious reasons, you can't tell her I have contacted you to explain the situation. So just know my well wishes extend to you both.

Until next time, take care.
PS. Please burn this letter.

A pang of grief struck at Jacob's heart when he thought about Cara. *I guess Caleb will fill Brendo in.* A moment later, the implications of the letter struck him. *Brendan is Lord Jet, which means he has become the leader of the Oceania branch of the Syndicate.* Jacob did not know whether to cheer or cry for Brendan. *But Christ, Brendo! Being a Dark Syndicate Boss puts you directly at odds with the Council and the rest of your family.*

Jacob wondered if there would ever be any redemption for Brendan. *Will he remain estranged forever?*

Chapter Seventeen

Eager for the news, Brendan gave Caleb a quick welcome home kiss before pulling him into their room and shutting the door.

Caleb laughed as Brendan shoved him onto the bed. 'Can't wait to have your way with me, huh?'

There was no way of hiding the tent situation in his pants from Caleb. 'True, but I will wait long enough to hear your rundown.' He sat beside Caleb and looked at him expectantly.

'Well Jacob didn't know you and Lord Jet are one and the same. The promotion surprised him, but I stuck to the plan, and he didn't get suspicious. He and Cara split, by the way.'

'What? Why?'

'She was upset to learn about his involvement in the Rhapsody business and she blamed him for corrupting you. So, she left him.'

'Christ! Did he look broken up about it?'

'Hard to say. I think he is avoiding grief by hitting the party scene hard. Speaking of which….'

Brendan's pulse picked up when Caleb's words trailed off. 'What?'

'Jacob and I took a couple of chicks back to his place last night and had our own orgy. Nothing like what you and Bry would've got up to on Sunday night, but it was still pretty hot.'

Thinking back to the number of chicks and dudes he had fucked on New Year's Eve; Brendan could hardly blame Caleb for getting some on the side. An impish grin formed on his face. 'I want the graphic details later.'

'Mm, thought you might.'

'What other news of home?'

Caleb told him all the small-town gossip— some of which was amusing, most made him yawn—and none of it related to Alannah.

'Anything else to report?'

'Nothing good.'

He took a deep breath, attempting but failing to calm his racing heart. 'Go on.'

'I'm sorry, Brendan, but they're getting married. Liam proposed to her on New Year's Eve.'

'Shit! He didn't waste much time, did he? I guess he realised his mistake.'

Caleb's hand squeezed his thigh. 'You aren't only talking about Liam's mistake, are you?'

'No. But she made her choice and now I have even less reason to go back.' Brendan pushed Caleb back on the bed, pinned him down, and grinned wickedly. 'And you keep giving me more reasons to stay here.' He ravished every part of Caleb's sweet body.

As the postcoital haze wore off, Caleb snuggled into Brendan's arms. 'Mm, I love this.'

'Me too, Thornsy.'

With a contented sigh, Caleb stared at the ceiling. 'When I was crushing on you hard back in our school years, I never once imagined I would end up in your bed, let alone getting to share you with Bridey.'

His fingers caressed Caleb's arm as thoughts raced through his mind. 'Curiosity is getting the better of me, Thornsy.'

Caleb stared into Brendan's eyes. 'How so?'

'Have you fancied any guys other than me?'

'Of course I have,' he snorted. 'I'm not as sexually repressed as you.'

'Piss off.' Brendan's fist playfully punched Caleb's arm. 'Any of the guys we went to school with?'

'Yeah, there were a few who got me hot under the collar, although never as much as you did. I even fooled around with one of them.'

Intrigued, Brendan propped himself up with one arm. 'Now you've piqued my interest. Care to share?'

'Well, it's not like he's gonna mind me telling you now. I had a casual thing going with Locky.'

'Ah hell. No wonder you took his passing so hard. I'm sorry, man.' As Brendan cast his mind back to their goofy goblin friend who had lost his life in the showdown with Tara, he tried to recall if there were any signs he might have missed but came up blank.

Caleb waved his hand in a dismissive gesture. 'It's okay. It was years ago and it's not like I was in love with Locky. Sure, I miss him, but no more than you or any of the other guys do. He was a decent bloke and a great friend.'

'Yup, he sure was. Did the two of you have anal sex?'

'Yeah, but I always topped.' That explained his initial instinct to top Brendan, despite his obvious preference for the reverse.

'So why didn't you ever give him a taste of your sweet arse?'

He shrugged. 'I dunno. We found a dynamic that worked for us and never thought to switch things up. We were still extremely new to the whole experience.'

'Fair enough. So, who else did you have the hots for?'

Caleb laughed. 'Are we still talking about guys here, or do you want the full list, including girls?'

'Let's start with the guys.'

'Okay, well from our old group there was Ben and Austin.'

Brendan nodded. 'Yeah, I can see it. They were both attractive men with luscious long hair.' Leaning in closer, Brendan tucked some of Caleb's own lustrous locks behind his ear.

Caleb listed a few non-magical guys before pausing to bite his lip.

'Oh Gods, who?' Brendan prompted, fearing the worst.

'Your cousin, Steve Maher.'

A half-laugh, half-sigh of relief burst from him. 'Seriously? That tosser?'

'Hey, I never said I liked the man, but he was sexy. Plus, he also had the hair thing going for him.'

'Okay, what about the chicks?'

'Oh hell, Winters. I was hard for half the girls in our year level.'

'Come on, Thornsy, I want specifics.'

'Fine. All the ones you fucked.'

Brendan twirled a strand of Caleb's hair around his fingers as his gaze heated. 'Were you keeping track of my sex life?'

'You might say I was living vicariously through it.'

'Well damn. So, which of my many conquests were you most attracted to?'

Tension visibly formed in Caleb's jaw. 'Do you have to ask?'

With a sigh, Brendan pressed a brief kiss to his lips. 'I mean aside from Lana.'

'In that case, I would have to say Bianca.'

Fond memories of simpler times flooded Brendan's mind when he thought of the cute little nymph he used to hook up with in high school. It had always been no-strings fun with her. 'Mm, would have been an incredible threesome.'

'You know I used to think the exact same thing.'

'Damn. There's a missed opportunity. Did you ever sleep with her?' Brendan asked. 'I heard she hooked up with some of the guys in our group, but I never pried.'

'I did actually. Only once though and it was immediately before I followed you and Bridey here. I wanted to forget the pair of you, but she made me realise what I was missing.'

'Christ! I didn't think she was that bad in bed.'

Caleb sniggered. 'I never said she was. It was just the sex felt so… shallow and empty. The experience didn't compare to what I'd recently shared with Bridey.'

'I know what you mean. Meaningless sex can be fun, but it is nothing compared to being intimate with someone you love.' Brendan ran his fingers along Caleb's smooth skin, evoking a rapid recovery for them both. When their eyes locked together, there was no denying the raw emotions flowing between them.

A knock sounded at the door and Bridey approached the bed. 'Room for one more?'

Caleb smiled at her lovingly. 'For you, there is.'

After throwing her clothes aside, Bridey climbed in to face Caleb, flanking him with Brendan pressing against Caleb's back. Three bodies entwined as they spent the rest of the night losing themselves in each other.

The musty old bookstore was a curious place to meet. A small bell jingled above the door as Brendan entered, alerting the old man who stood behind the counter. The geezer's inner aura was silver, and his Celtic knot pendant bore the symbol of Lugh, father of mages: signs suggesting a spiritual leader.

He eyed Brendan in amazement. 'Fascinating. You actually do look like his twin.'

'Don't you mean he looks like me? I'm the eldest.' Brendan smirked, offering his hand. 'Brendan Winters. You are an acolyte, yes?'

With a firm handshake, the mage nodded. 'Acolyte Carran. The others are waiting for you out the back.'

'Thank you, Your Holiness.' Without further ado, Brendan strode behind the counter and through a door labelled STAFF ONLY.

The warlocks did not look pleased. 'You're late,' Hayes commented, while Tyler glared at him.

'Apologies. I'm still not used to how ghastly Sydney traffic can be.' Brendan was not sorry, not when magnificent morning sex had been the real reason for his tardiness; but they did not need to know, nor did he care what they thought. He took a seat at the cheap Laminex table in the poky kitchenette. 'So, what's the plan?'

'Simple, really,' Tyler explained, 'I walk into HQ pretending to be you on a day when they are meeting in the boardroom and take them all out.'

Brendan burst out laughing. After catching his breath, a full minute later, he slapped his hand on the table. 'I'm sorry, but there is no way that will work.'

'Do you doubt my ability to impersonate you?' Tyler asked.

'Maybe, but it's beside the point. If it was easy to walk in on them, don't you think someone would have tried by now? They keep the place locked up tight.'

'Which is why we intend to hack their security system and forge ourselves an all-access pass with your name on it,' replied Hayes. 'Did you bring your key?'

'Here.' He gave them the plastic ID card on the black lanyard. 'But they have other security measures.'

Hayes snapped a few photos of the card, along with one of Brendan, and handed back the key card. 'Figured they would, which is why we need to take impressions of fingerprints and scan your retinas.' Pulling out a high-tech device, he connected it to a laptop and waved it in front of Brendan's eyes.

'The Council are more tech-savvy in these parts. I wonder, is it to compensate for anything?'

'Hardly,' Tyler scoffed, 'I haven't received any complaints yet and I don't even need to resort to magic to please the ladies.'

Hayes rolled his eyes. 'I don't think Brendan was referring to dick sizes, Quirky. And no, we are not lacking in power here, we reserve our energy for what technology can't do.' Next, he produced two slabs of putty. 'Press your thumbs and fingers into these.' After taking Brendan's print impressions, he placed the fresh moulds in the freezer.

An uneasy feeling came over Brendan as he gave up pieces of his identity. 'Promise me you'll destroy my fake biometrics once you've dealt with these arseholes?'

'Of course,' Hayes assured him. 'We are not crooks, and we have no interest in misappropriating these items.'

He turned his attention to Tyler in an attempt to shake off his apprehension. 'Say you get all the way to the boardroom; how do you intend to take them all out before they strike back with magic more powerful than that of any warlock?'

'The element of surprise should give me enough time to hit them all with a single chain-lightning attack.'

'Are you for real? That's like twenty guys. Do you know how much mana you would burn to hit that many targets at once? How much power you would need to channel? You could kill yourself.'

Tyler gave him a smug grin. 'I've been training for something like this all my life. I can easily manage twenty people.'

Not even Liam could pull it off. Brendan felt a newfound respect for Tyler. 'Well, fuck! I'd love to see you put my brother to shame in a duel one day.'

Pride beamed from Tyler. 'You think I'm more powerful than Liam Winters?'

'If you can pull off a chain attack of twenty or more, then yeah, easily. The most targets I ever saw him hit was like five.'

'It's true, most warlocks can't pull off a stunt like this,' Hayes explained, 'but Tyler has specialised where the rest of us tend to diversify our skill sets. Plus, I think the fact he is not a bloodline mage has driven him to prove he can fight like the best of us.'

Brendan stared at Tyler in wide-eyed astonishment. 'You're not a pure blood? Your aura is as strong as Jaxon's.'

'No, I'm only ninety percent. My great-grandfather had a bastard child with his maid who was not pure. She would be where the doppelganger gene came from.'

'Interesting.' Brendan gave it some thought for a moment. 'You said doppelganger genes came from one of the other Gods, right? Possibly a God of magic?'

'Yeah, why?'

'What if descending from these two different Gods makes you more powerful despite the slight dilution of your blood? Like with the enlightened and endarkened fae.'

'You know, I never thought of it that way,' Tyler admitted.

'Right, well we've got all we need from you for now.' Hayes rose to his feet. 'I'll call you on the burner phone when we are ready for stage two.'

'Okay. See you then.' Brendan took his leave, walking back through the bookstore and waving to the acolyte on his way out. Rounding the corner to the carpark, something moved in his peripheral vision, and he spotted a dark figure bolting down the street. *What the hell?* It was hard to make out any details, but Brendan did not need to see the man's face—he could recognise that arse anywhere. *Why the fuck is Thornsy spying on me?*

Drawing the curtain aside to look through her window, Samantha sighed as she watched Tyler leave. She hated spending time without him. Not only did she love and miss Tyler, but he was the most powerful warlock of the three, and thus more adept at protecting her.

Movement on the balcony beneath drew her eye and she noticed Tanya step out and sit on one of the deckchairs. The two of them had not had much chance to connect in the time they'd lived together, and it was not like Samantha had any issues with her. Seizing the opportunity, she joined Tanya. The gentle breeze tickled her skin when she stepped outside with a coffee in her hand. 'Mind if I join you?'

Tanya looked up and smiled. 'Please do.'

Glancing at the laptop on the small round table, Samantha saw the open Pinterest results for pagan weddings. Sitting beside Tanya, she gestured toward the computer. 'How goes the planning?'

'Good. I've been compiling an inspiration board to collect ideas.'

'Neat. I've never been to a wedding before and now it looks like I'll be attending two this year.'

'Yeah, it's pretty exciting. I'm thrilled to hear about Alannah and Liam.'

Samantha could not share her enthusiasm, not when she knew the truth about Alannah's broken heart; all she could do was nod and shrug a silent reply.

'You're not pleased about the news,' Tanya observed.

'Hmph. I never was great at faking emotions. Honestly, I don't think Liam's a suitable match for Alannah.'

Tanya furrowed her brow. 'Would you rather see her raise the kid alone?'

'No. It's just….' She bit her lip to prevent the truth spilling out.

Tanya eyed Samantha suspiciously a moment, then her eyes widened as realisation dawned. 'You've got the hots for her too, don't you?'

A nervous laugh slipped out. 'Maybe.'

Tanya shook her head with amazement. 'That woman's ability to charm the pants off men,'—she cast her eyes over Samantha—'and some women, apparently… is uncanny. Especially when you consider she's not even an enchantress.

Look, Sam, you know she's a pureblood, right? Even if she wanted to live with you and Tyler, her uncle would never stand for it.'

'I know.' Feeling dejected, Samantha stared into the distance. Alannah's situation contained bucketloads of unfair.

Distracted by her inner musings, she did not notice the black clad figure dropping onto the balcony from above until it was too late. He pressed a knife to Tanya's throat and clamped a hand over the woman's mouth.

'Not a sound,' the familiar voice spoke behind her, and Samantha's skin crawled off her bones and nose-dived from the balcony.

She spun around to face Kek, cursing herself for forgetting the wards did not extend beyond the walls of the house.

'Or your friend's blood will decorate this lovely balcony,' Kek continued. 'You've been a naughty girl, *Samantha*,' pronouncing her name with a thick Arabic accent, 'and you know what I do to disobedient girls, don't you?'

Is it a rhetorical question? She never could tell with him, so she gave him a curt nod.

'Your current assignment ends now. You will come home with me this instant. And if you cooperate, we will let the healer live.'

She looked over her shoulder at Tanya whose eyes pleaded with her, but Samantha could not tell if Tanya wanted her to stay or go. Not that it mattered—there was no way she would risk the woman's life. Samantha may have been a hunter and a killer, but there were already too many innocent lives weighing on her conscience. She mouthed her final words, *'Tell Tyler I love him.'* Slipping her hand in Kek's, she let him magiport her back to hell on Earth.

When Bridey asked Caleb to spy on Brendan, she assured him it was for Brendan's protection. But as he followed Brendan to the old bookshop in Darlinghurst, he wondered if she had been upfront with him. *What are you doing here, Winters?*

As he peered through the window using binoculars, he noticed the shopkeeper was an old mage of some sort. *Is he a dark mage?* For the bazillionth time in his life, Caleb found himself wishing he could read auras like an enchanter.

After a short greeting, Brendan disappeared into the back of the shop. There was no way to get a visual from this side of the building, so he moved around the back. *Damn it!* The only window was small and frosted, suggesting the room beyond housed a toilet. Settling on making do with audio alone, he snuck into some bushes alongside the carpark. At least the minute microphone he had planted in Brendan's wallet worked well enough.

The voices of the men he spoke to sounded familiar, but he could not place them. *And who are they plotting against?* At the first mention of the Council, Caleb's blood chilled, despite the warm summer sun. *That's where I know these guys from! What the actual fuck, Winters?*

As the man he loved continued to scheme with the Council's warlocks, Caleb felt his trust in Brendan dwindling. Mention of doppelgangers pricked his ears up, literally in his case. He had heard the term doppelganger used loosely before and it was fitting when applied to Brendan and Warlock Quirke, but knowing there was some magical significance tied to the Gods? *I'll have to investigate that.*

Thanks to his wandering mind, Caleb almost missed Brendan's exit. He made a mad dash for the street, racing toward his silver Corolla. It was imperative he got out of there before Brendan recognised his car. Taking the next left turn, he wove through some side streets and sped off along a highway.

After travelling a safe distance, he told his phone to call Bridey.

'Hey sweetie.'

'Hey Bry, I have some disturbing news. I caught Brendan collaborating with a couple of Council warlocks. They are planning something big. I don't know what, but it involves using Brendan's identification.'

'Hmm.' Bridey did not sound happy. 'Did you record their conversation?'

'Of course. I'll upload it to your secure drive on the cloud.'

'Thanks, hun. Which warlocks did he meet?'

'Hayes and Quirke. The same two who arrested me. Something else came up. Do you know anything about the magical significance of doppelgangers?'

'No. Why?'

'I think it's what Brendan and Quirke are, what with them looking like twins. Quirke mentioned something about having the doppelganger gene. I don't know what it means, but I'd like to.'

'I can look into it. Given your discovery, I think it would be prudent to keep an eye on Brendan at his office. Can you do that for me?'

'Sure.' Changing into the left lane, Caleb took the next exit and turned toward the city centre.

'Oh, and Caleb?'

'Yeah?'

'Please watch your back. I'm worried Damien has his eye on you.'

'Will do. Love you, Bry.'

'Love you too, Caleb.' She ended the call.

When he got to Brendan's office, he parked a safe distance down the street and watched as Brendan's Jag pulled into the parking lot beneath the building. Tuning in to the device he had planted, Caleb heard Brendan cursing under his breath as he rode the lift. As soon as he was in his office, the speaker crackled an awful lot. 'Fuck's sake. He's even bugged the office.'

Caleb's heart stuttered. *Shit! Winters is on to me! Did he see me at the bookshop?* A loud pop sounded through the speaker, startling him.

Brendan's voice spoke sternly, 'If you ever want to see me again, you will get your arse up here right now, Thornsy.'

Chapter Eighteen

Brendan waited impatiently for Caleb to appear, tapping his fingers manically against the oak desk he had perched himself on. As soon as the door opened, Brendan flew at Caleb, grabbing him and thrusting the door closed by slamming Caleb into it. 'Why the hell are you spying on me like this?' He produced one of the listening devices, shoving it in Caleb's face.

Caleb replied with a defiant glare.

'Do you want me to hurt you?'

The left side of Caleb's lips began to curl upward, but he kept his mouth shut.

Damn masochist! Brendan released Caleb and stepped back.

'I'm serious, Caleb. I want answers. *Now.*'

They became locked in a silent stare down and Brendan erected fresh walls around his heart. Stone cold granite walls. 'If this is how you want to play it, you can get the hell out of my face. I'm done with you and Bridey.'

The smirk vanished immediately from Caleb's expression. 'I was doing Bridey's bidding. I don't know what her reasons are, but she's had me keeping tabs on you since she first appeared in Gaeilge Shores. Could be for business, or… a more personal matter. How about you tell me why you are having secret meetings with a Council warlock? If you're planning to betray us—'

'*Hell no!* There's no way I'd betray you. Do you seriously doubt my love for you? After everything I've done to prove myself?' The tension building in Brendan's skull was giving him a headache. He rubbed his palm against the side of his face, trying to relieve the pain. 'I mostly kept you and Bridey out of the loop with this to protect you, but also to maintain the integrity of the mission. The less Damien can pull from your minds the better.' After striding across the room, he slumped into his chair. The stress ball on his desk called to him, so he grabbed it and imagined he was squeezing the life out of Damien.

Lowering his gaze, Caleb fell silent.

Brendan dropped the ball on his desk and rose. *Screw this, I need a drink.* He grabbed the whiskey decanter, poured them both a shot, and threw his back in one go before refilling his glass.

Caleb ignored his drink as he mumbled, 'I'm sorry for doubting you. I guess Bridey got in my head. The prospect of your betrayal hurt, and I didn't think. I'm really fucking sorry.'

'Ah hell, Thornsy. I'm sorry for snapping at you. Come 'ere.'

Caleb obeyed the request, taking up residence in Brendan's lap. As Brendan's arms encircled his waist, Caleb pressed his forehead to Brendan's. 'I can't think straight when it comes to you, Winters. You make me crazy.'

Brendan snorted, knowing exactly what that felt like. 'Love makes us all crazy. It's the one emotion that can turn even the most sensible and logical of men into babbling fools.' He pulled Caleb's lips down to his, kissing him gently.

Hesitantly, Caleb pulled back and looked reverently into Brendan's eyes. 'What's a doppelganger?'

Panic surged through Brendan. 'Shit! You heard my conversation?'

With a sheepish look, Caleb nodded.

'You need to get the hell out of dodge. I can get you a mind shield to keep Damien out of your head, but that won't stop him torturing you, or worse….'

Caleb shook his head. 'I can't leave you to fight those arseholes. And I'm not some feeble thing you need to protect. I can hold my own.'

'I'm not saying you're weak, but these guys are more powerful than any of us. What worries me most is the possibility of them using you to manipulate me. If they get me and Tyler in a room together and they have enough leverage, there is no stopping the unspeakable evils they could unleash on the world.'

'Is this to do with the doppelganger thing?'

'Yup. Tyler is like my magic twin, born with a mystic connection to me that enhances the magic we perform together. We don't know how much, but the Cult are hellbent on finding out. It's why the inner circle came to town.'

'Then we both leave,' said Caleb. 'Let's get out of Sydney. Go someplace they can't find us.'

'Not an option. They'll find us with scrying magic.'

'But if we use wards—'

'They are attuned to nether, Thornsy. They'll break the wards.'

'Not if we get a powerful abjurer to put them up.'

'And where are we supposed to find one of those? In case you've forgotten, I'm not exactly in favour with the Council at large, even if I'm secretly working with a couple of their warlocks.'

'What about your dad?'

'*No!*' Brendan shocked himself with the force behind his response.

Even Caleb visibly cringed.

After a gentle caress of Caleb's cheek, Brendan adopted a softer tone. 'Look, I'm not gonna spend my life running. We need to put a stop to these bastards once and for all.'

'If they are as formidable as you suggest, why not send the full force of the Council against them? Why is this task falling on the shoulders of two warlocks and an outcast enchanter?'

'Bah! The Council are too busy tripping over their own red tape these days. Without hard evidence, they won't initialise outright war. Tyler and Jaxon were their best chance of finding proof, but the whole doppelganger thing has complicated matters.'

Caleb sighed. 'Bunch of wankers, the lot of 'em. Surely you've got something to take to the Council after breaking into the Cult's library.'

'So far, I've got jack. I'm still working on translating most of it.'

'What about the stuff you stole from the museum?'

'There's nothing tying them to the robbery, Thornsy. That's why they got us to do their dirty work.'

'Yeah, but aren't you technically a Cult member now?'

Brendan's eyes widened with a lightbulb moment. Sliding Caleb off his lap as he rose, Brendan planted a big kiss on Caleb's lips. 'You are brilliant, my love.'

After deleting the audio file on her laptop, Bridey sat back and closed her eyes. *Why does Caleb have to be such an effective spy? Nothing good can come of this revelation.* She never wanted to know the truth, but it was too late.

As if on cue, her phone rang with Damien's name popping up on the screen. 'Hello, Lady Violet. Do you have anything to report?'

She desperately wanted to lie. 'Yes.'

'That's excellent news. I will get there soon.'

As the line went dead, Bridey considered her options for leaving the state, or possibly even the country. She would have to get her men first, which meant a trip to Brendan's office. Pressing her hand against the back panel of her wardrobe, she opened the secret compartment where she had stashed her emergency bag. With critical supplies in hand, she ran out to her brand-new purple Ferrari and threw the duffel in the boot.

'You aren't thinking of escaping, are you?'

Bridey's heart skipped a beat and chills crawled up her back, leaving a trail of goosebumps in their wake. She turned gradually, adopting a sweet smile before coming face to face with Damien. 'Of course not. I was preparing for a leisurely cruise, which I plan to take after we finish our meeting.'

Suspicion filled Damien's eyes. 'Is that so?'

'Indeed. I'm excited to take my new wheels for a spin. Do you like her?'

Damien cast a bored glance at the Ferrari. 'It's adequate, I suppose.' He grabbed her arm and dragged her across to his limo.

She tried to pull her arm free, but he gripped her tighter. 'Where are you taking me?'

'To the office, for the meeting you were about to skip out on.'

'Ow, you're hurting me.'

'I promise a lot more pain if you don't cooperate.' Damien opened a car door and shoved her into the back seat, climbing in to join her soon after.

'Why can't we stay here?'

'Because the Boss wants to meet you.'

A new wave of icy terror gripped Bridey's spine. 'You mean….'

'The inner circle, yes.'

'But why?'

Damien turned a severe gaze on her. 'No one questions their motives, and you would do well to remember that.' His expression softened, if only slightly. 'You know, we have a bit of a drive. Why don't we make the most of our time together?' He unzipped his fly. 'Come and ride me like the expert whore you are.'

Bile filled her throat. 'My services don't come free, Damien.'

'Always such a mercantile woman. How about you rock my world, and I won't tell the Boss about your escape plan.'

'No deal. He will get inside my head and uncover all my secrets anyway.'

'I suppose he will. Fine, name your price. And before you get any ideas, cancelling this meeting is not on the table.'

'I want to know all about doppelgangers.'

His lips curled up as he leaned in closer. 'Well, well. You have been a busy little spy. What have you learned thus far?'

'I know Warlock Quirke carries the doppelganger gene, which is why he looks like Brendan. And I'm guessing the pair of them are the reason your Boss is in town. But that's about all.'

'Well, your intel is spot on. I don't know everything about doppelgangers. The inner circle like to keep their secrets. But I do know Brendan and Quirke are like mystical twins who enhance each other's magic. That's why the Cult want them.'

The implications horrified Bridey. 'What makes a doppelganger?'

'Their bloodline. Quirke has different magical ancestry to most mages. In addition to descending from a creator God, he also comes from a God of magic.'

Fascinated, Bridey stared at Damien with wide eyes. 'So, Quirke is like an uber mage?'

'Pretty much. And the havoc he could wreak with Brendan at his side would be phenomenal.'

'What is the Cult planning to do with them if they succeed in getting their hands on Quirke?'

'That's inner circle business. I've told you all I know, now get over here.'

Resisting the urge to sigh, or throw up, Bridey slid across the seat and straddled Damien's lap. 'What do you want?'

Two large hands lifted her skirt and gripped the bare cheeks of her backside. 'I want to fill all of your holes with my seed. And I want you to enhance the experience with magic.'

'I'm not sure we'll have time to bring you to orgasm three times.'

He wore a disgusting smirk. 'Fair point. I have too much sexual stamina. Fine. I'll take your arse. It's not like you ever get off with me anyway.'

Shit! I guess my acting skills need some work.

'But I want you to start working me up with your mouth.'

As she dropped to her knees in the foot well of the limo's backseat, Bridey felt tempted to bite Damien's dick. The thought alone was far from professional, and it was the first time she had felt such ill will toward a client, but she couldn't help it. Everything about Damien repulsed her, the least of which being his filthy-tasting cock. When she shifted to give him access to her arse, she did not bother prepping herself. She wanted to feel something, and since pleasure was unlikely with Damien, she resorted to pain.

The sting of his entrance was intense, and Bridey screamed out.

Damien laughed. 'That didn't sound fake. Will I finally succeed in making you come?'

'Don't mistake my pain for anything more,' Bridey retorted.

His arms held her tight as he moved a hand between her legs. 'I made a mistake assuming you were a Dominant when, in reality, you are much more of a submissive.' Damien's fingers pressed against her sensitive core as he continued to rip her open with his thrusting. With lips brushing her ear, he whispered, 'Don't forget, I've been inside your head. I know all your dirty secrets. Your pussy salivates when Caleb challenges your authority. You love how Brendan flipped the balance of power in your relationship. You want those men to control you, to make you feel the way your father did. But the thought alone scares you, doesn't it Violet? You don't want others to see your weaknesses. Fear not, your secret's safe with me. But you're not.'

The moment he dug the nails of his other hand into her throat, Bridey unravelled in Damien's arms. He had found and pushed every one of her buttons. Only one other man had done that for her, and he was an enchanter.

When they reached the corporate headquarters in the wealthy part of Sydney's city centre, Damien led Bridey into a large office on the top floor.

The elf stepping out from behind the large mahogany desk grinned, showing off brilliant white teeth as sharp as a tiger's. His skin was as dark as night and a bald head emphasised his pointy ears.

She gulped as he stood before her. Bridey was tall, especially for a woman, but this man towered over her.

'Good day, Lady Violet. I am Grand Master Kek.'

With the board meeting taking place that afternoon, the warlocks had no time to waste. Tyler grabbed his comb and styling gel and moved into the bathroom where he had access to a mirror. He styled his fringe to resemble Brendan's and changed into the suit Jaxon had given him. Apparently, it was the same label Brendan wore when conducting business.

When he returned to the bookshop's kitchen, Jaxon was making the fingerprint overlays by pouring gelatine into the chilled mould. The fake ID sat waiting for Tyler on the table, already clipped to a black lanyard.

'Do I want to know where you learned to become a master in the art of forgery?' Tyler put the black strap around his neck.

'I assure you; my training was all above-board.'

'Oh, I'm sure,' Tyler winked for effect.

Jaxon rolled his eyes and returned the putty to the freezer. No longer distracted by high-tech espionage tasks, he took a moment to look at Tyler. 'Christ! Dressed like that and with the hair, you are the spitting image of Brendan.'

'Good. Should make this job easier.'

'Aside from the fingerprints, which need a couple more minutes, are you ready?'

'Yes, I think so. I have my real mana rings in my pockets. These are fakes but should do the trick.' Tyler held out his hands to show Jaxon the rings on his index fingers mimicking Botswana agate and blue lace agate, the two crystals used by enchanters.

'They look real enough to me. And your phones?'

'Both off. I'll leave my main mobile here to prevent the risk of tracking.'

'Great thinking. I'll do the same. Now *please* don't hesitate to call me if you need help. I hate sending you in alone to do this.'

'I know the drill. Don't worry.'

'Sit down and place your hands face up on the table,' Jaxon instructed as he retrieved Brendan's fake fingerprints.

Tyler watched in awe as Jaxon adhered the thin, rubbery coatings to his fingertips. Once they were all in place, he gave the glue a few minutes to dry before heading out to the car. They reached Australia's Obsidian Cult HQ, better known as Mara Holdings Pty Ltd. After learning the name's meaning in Arabic[4], he had snickered at the irony.

Jaxon pulled into the public parking garage across the street. 'Good luck.'

'Cheers, boss.' Tyler hated to think of this as a final farewell, despite the risks. Drawing things out would only further the impression, so he left the car without looking back.

The first security checkpoint was a breeze: all he needed was the swipe card and his award-winning smile.

The human guard gave him a polite nod. 'Greetings, Lord Jet.' The formality of the man's tone made Tyler feel like royalty.

Is this what it feels like to live in Brendan's world? He beelined for the elevator where he hit the button for the 40th floor. Studies of the building's

---

[4] Mara means joy in Arabic.

schematics, combined with Brendan's intel, told him that while the Cult had multiple meeting rooms, the inner circle only ever held their board meetings on the top floor. Access to this level required fingerprint ID. Tyler took a deep breath and pressed his thumb to the touchscreen. When the red light turned green, he exhaled his relief.

The final checkpoint before the boardroom was a pretty, blonde receptionist. 'I'm sorry, sir, but you can't go in there. The board are having a meeting.'

Tyler turned on his charms. 'It's okay, they are expecting me. Perhaps Grand Master Kek forgot to tell you he summoned me?'

The blonde blushed. 'Certainly. Please go right ahead.'

Pausing at the door, Tyler was thankful for the wards surrounding the room. *The measures you use to prevent people eavesdropping on your thoughts and conversations go both ways and they are about to be your downfall.*

He drew on all his strength, all his power, as sparks tingled through his fingers. Stepping into the room, he let the chain lighting jump from his hands and strike everyone sitting at the table.

It all happened too fast. Tyler barely had time to catch Samantha's eyes at the head of the table before she fell to the floor with nineteen other bodies. 'Oh Gods!' He ran to her in a panic.

When he knelt beside Samantha to check her pulse, the door opened, and Tyler looked up to see a tall dark elf clapping his hands in deliberate mockery.

'Such a wonderful display of power Mr. Quirke. I can't wait to start working with you.'

Brendan's burner phone lit up. He put aside the book he was studying to read Tyler's message: STAGE 1 SUCCESSFUL, PROCEED TO STAGE 2. He rose and moved around to Caleb's side of the desk. 'I gotta go.'

'Why? What's going on?' Caleb stood upright, gravitating toward Brendan.

'The warlocks need me to carry out my part of the plan.'

'Which is?'

'To grab all the important books from the library.'

Caleb shook his head. 'You can't go into the place while Tyler's there.'

'It's okay. Tyler has taken down the inner circle. Only the plebs remain, and they don't know about all the doppelganger stuff.'

Relief washed over Caleb's face. 'Can I help? I imagine there are a lot of books to carry.'

'Sure. I could certainly use an extra set of hands and a pleasant view while I work.' The smirk on Caleb's face was as sexy as hell and it took all of Brendan's willpower to focus on the task at hand. 'Let's go now, before I forget what I need to do.'

It was a short walk to the Mara building from his own office block, which was just as well considering the summer sun's bite. They both carried large briefcases with them and for all intents and purposes, they looked like a pair of typical businessmen. No one would suspect them of carrying books full of ancient mystical secrets in those cases.

Brendan knew something was wrong the moment he stepped into the lobby and spied Damien sitting on one of the couches. The arsehole looked at him with a smug grin, raising the hairs on the back of Brendan's neck. 'Fuck! *Run Caleb!*' Brendan cried out as he turned to flee the building, but one of the security guards grabbed him before he got far.

Caleb froze.

Dread filled Brendan's gut like lead weights. *'I said, Go! Run!'*

Snapping out of his panicked daze, Caleb nodded and dashed outside before the other guard could catch him.

Damien sauntered over to Brendan. 'You didn't honestly think it would be that easy to take down the world's oldest and largest syndicate now, did you? I thought you were smarter than this. I'm disappointed in you, Jet—or should I call you Brendan?'

'Well at least I never disappoint a woman in bed. Did you know Violet faked every orgasm with you, or are *you* really that dumb?'

The biggest shit-eating grin filled Damien's face. 'Oh, I knew. I also know the orgasm I gave her in the back of my limo today was real *and* intense. You see, I discovered a secret about your woman, Brendan. I unlocked her hidden desires and now I have her tied up in the basement, begging for more. Would you like to see her?'

Brendan stood paralysed by fear. *If Damien has Bridey, he clearly intends to use her as leverage.*

'What's the matter, Jet? Cat got your tongue?' Damien turned and strode toward the lift. 'Come along, Harvey.'

The guard pushed Brendan forward and they followed Damien into the elevator. It was a brief descent to the basement. Brendan's eyes took a moment to adjust to the dim lighting of the underground space and when they did, he wished he could have stayed ignorant of his surroundings.

The room reminded him of the ritual cellar in his parent's house, only much grimier. There were also a lot more blood stains on the floor. But the semi-circle of St. Andrew's crosses sent his heart into frenzied palpitations. The wooden crosses bore naked women, all of whom were unconscious. His eyes scanned across the group, bulging from their sockets when they landed on Bridey's limp form. A red mist filled his vision. 'If you've hurt her!' He tried to rush toward Bridey, but Harvey held him back.

'Relax,' replied Damien. 'I gave her a mild sedative. She should wake in time to enjoy her front row seat to the dark magic show you will put on.' His hand gestured across the room to where two other men stood.

Brendan recognised Tyler, and the tall dark man fitted Melanie's description of Grand Master Kek. *The fuck? Was Tyler playing me all this time?*

'I can't say the same for Warlock Quirke's girl though,' Damien continued as he moved up to a woman with red hair and traced a finger along her face. 'I hear that lightning bolt packed quite a punch. Luckily, he didn't use lethal force, else we might have had less sway with him.'

Well, that explains it. Brendan cast his eyes over Tyler's girlfriend, surprised to see one of the Council's pets had been dating a dark mage. Another glance at Tyler showed the cold iron cuffs binding his wrists.

'Do you want to know the best part of our plan?' Damien crossed his arms and stood upright in a cloud of his own stinking arrogance.

'What?' Brendan asked impatiently.

'The best part is our backup plan: you see, in the off chance you let us kill Violet and Samantha, we have one of our men in Gaeilge Shores ready to assassinate the woman you *both* love. Pure genius. I love the synergy you doppelgangers bring to this circle.'

Brendan's whole body tensed. *How the hell did they know about Lana?*

'We make it our business to learn secrets,' Damien explained as though he had read Brendan's mind. 'Oh, and in case you think I'm bluffing....' He turned on a security monitor mounted to the far wall. It showed a live camera feed of someone watching Alannah.

'Shit!' It was the first thing Tyler had said since Brendan entered the room.

So, Tyler is in love with Lana too. The thought made Brendan feel sympathy for the guy.

'Here's how this is going to work,' Damien explained. 'The pair of you will participate in this ritual and we'll spare the lives of all four women.'

'Four?' Brendan glanced across the group of women, but no other faces were familiar. Sure it would be tragic if their innocent lives were sacrificed, but it was hardly leverage.

Tyler jerked his head toward the brunette between Samantha and Bridey. 'He's talking about Tanya, Jaxon's fiancé.'

'Indeed.' Damien stepped over to Bridey and stroked the side of her breast. 'Perform the ritual, the women live, and we will set them free. After they perform their part, of course.'

A sick feeling stirred in Brendan's stomach. 'What is the ritual?'

'A summoning.'

Brendan huffed. 'Neither Tyler nor I have the attunements for such magic.'

'Oh, but you do, Brendan. I made sure of it as part of your initiation. You see, our Dark Lord was banished to the Underworld. You will be channelling the stygian element to bring him forth, and Tyler here will enhance your magic to ensure you are capable of such a feat.'

Recalling what he had read about Set's dark mating rituals, the nausea intensified as Brendan realised what the Cult intended to do with the naked women in the room. 'Tyler won't be much use in those mana blocking shackles.'

Damien turned his attention to Brendan. 'We will release him once you invite him into the circle. If he tries anything, Harvey and I won't hesitate to hit the numbers we have on speed dial.' He nodded toward the security monitor for effect. 'Now, let's get this party started!'

Chapter Nineteen

He was running faster than ever before; running like his life depended upon it—because it did. If Caleb didn't escape the Cult's clutches, he was as good as dead because there was no way he would let them use him as leverage. *The Cult won't force Brendan to perform unspeakable evils on my account.*

Brendan's office was his first stop. He needed to pick the lock, since Brendan had secured everything before heading over to Cult central. Caleb grabbed the books they'd been reading, along with the translation notes and the blue cartouche. Too impatient to wait for the lift, he descended the stairs two at a time.

A quick peek out into the street assured him the coast was clear, so he made a dash for his car. *Now what?* Caleb glanced at the books on the seat beside him and sighed. Taking the only option remaining, he drove through the city and across the Harbour Bridge into North Sydney. After giving up on a legitimate spot, he parked in a loading zone and stormed into the Council Chambers.

The petite half-mage receptionist jumped at the sound of Caleb's brief case hitting the counter.

'I need to see High Magus O'Grady, *immediately*.'

'I'm sorry, but the High Magus is busy at the moment. You will need to make an appointment.'

'I don't give a rat's arse what his Lordship is doing. If he values his life and that of everyone else in this damn state, he will make time to see me *now*.'

'Are you threating us, sir? Because the High Magus does not take kindly to threats, nor do we appreciate interruptions by unseelie riff raff.'

Caleb laughed drily. 'Trust me, woman, I am the least of your worries right now. If you don't get the High Magus for me pronto, a cult of dark mages over in the CBD will bring hell to Earth and you can die knowing you had a chance to stop it, but let your prejudice get in the way.'

Gaping at him, she picked up her phone. 'Sorry to interrupt Your Honour, but there is a man out the front with an urgent matter. Something about a dark mage cult … Yes, Your Honour.' Dropping the handset in its cradle, she looked up at Caleb. 'He will see you now.'

Picking up his suitcase, Caleb marched on through the security gate, up the stairs, and onto the second floor of the Council's ivory tower.

High Magus O'Grady waited for Caleb at the door to his office. As soon as he glimpsed his visitor, he frowned. 'I did not expect to see one of the endarkened coming to me about this. What is your involvement with dark mage cults?'

He pushed past the High Magus into the office. 'My boyfriend went undercover to investigate one of them and now they have him in captivity.'

'And you expect me to drop everything to go rescue some unseelie?' O'Grady closed the door.

Caleb scowled at the High Magus. 'Firstly, my boyfriend is not unseelie. He is a pure mage. Secondly, the cult in question is one your own pets have been investigating and I believe they also captured Warlock Quirke.' He threw his briefcase on O'Grady's desk and flipped open the latches. 'Here is the evidence you need to mount an outright attack on the Cult's headquarters. I suggest doing so pretty soon because they have what they were looking for and are probably casting the ritual circle about now.'

O'Grady looked through the books and papers. 'How is this evidence? I can't even read most of it.'

'Those books are copies taken directly from the Cult's secret library.' He drew closer to the desk, handed O'Grady the cartouche, and flicked through the pages to where Brendan had made notes on the relic. 'This ancient artifact belonged to the Cult. But they don't need it anymore because now they have this.' Caleb skipped to the page about the lazurite scarab. 'This is what the Cult stole from the museum.'

Minutes passed in painful silence as O'Grady read Brendan's notes. He looked up with a furrowed brow. 'I still don't understand the significance of all this.'

Caleb rolled his eyes. *How could such a dumb fuck have become High Magus?* 'Did you miss the page explaining how the Obsidian Cult also call themselves the Sons of Set? They are dark elves born of an evil Egyptian God. Who do you think they want to summon with the Lazurite Scarab? I seriously doubt they are looking to invite Lugh around for tea and scones.'

With wide eyes O'Grady's attention returned to reading the page about the cartouche and the

Sons of Set. 'Apparently they used to use this trinket in a dark mating ritual. Does that mean—'

'They want more dark elf babies? Yep. I can't imagine the women they are using in the ritual are willing volunteers either. I bet Set would be keen to stay a while once he comes to town since I doubt it's much fun for him in the Underworld.' Caleb had no idea if the Cult were intending to summon Set, but it made as much sense as any of the theories he'd toyed with, and it was the most ominous story to tell the High Magus.

'You can't be serious. It would take immense power to break Set's shackles and pull him from the Underworld.'

'With Brendan and Tyler as his doppelganger, they have all the power they need. Sorry, did I forget to mention that part?'

Brendan cast the circle much like he had done for years as a regular mage, only the Cult had inverted the pentagram he stepped around. Instead of calling upon the element of Aether at the apex, he lit a purple candle at the base to call upon nether, the stygian element. With Damien and Harvey watching from the sidelines, both with phones in hand, Brendan gulped before continuing. He invited Kek, along with two other dark elves, plus Tyler, into the ritual space, asking them, 'How do you enter the circle?'

They each responded, 'With a hunger for power.'

Once the others were kneeling, Brendan took his place at the altar where he touched the Lazurite Scarab as he read the prescribed invocation:

'Set, God of Chaos, we praise you in all of your forms. You are the dark that balances the light, the violence in our hearts, and the Divine Outcast. We present you with offerings and you are free to take those of your choosing. We ask only that you honour us and bless us with power.' He felt queasy as he spoke the words of offering.

Lifting his arms, he began chanting. 'We invoke thee Set: accept our offerings and live among us.' As the words left his lips, Brendan visualised Set in the fiery pits of the Underworld and imagined the God breaking free of his prison.

The rest of the group repeated the mantra with him and after a few minutes, Brendan felt energy surging through him, giving him an incredible rush. But the air changed in the room and his heart thumped wildly as a dark form materialised in the middle of the circle.

Breath rushed out of Brendan's lungs at the sight of the red ochre-skinned man with the head and tail of a beast. Set was easily seven foot tall. *Holy. Shit. An actual God stands before me.* He experienced true awe in the face of such terrifying beauty and unbridled power.

Set leered at the women strung up around the room, all of whom had awoken and were attempting to scream, but their gags muffled their cries. He said something in Arabic before approaching Brendan.

Unsure if he wanted Set's blessing—*or is it a damning?*—but too afraid to move, Brendan remained frozen in place, allowing Set's hand to rest upon his head.

A commanding voice filled his mind. '*You have done well, my servant. As a reward, I shall strengthen your conduits.*' Power flowed into Brendan, and it felt as though he was growing. But after Set's words, he understood his capacity to channel mana was expanding. Set moved around the circle, empowering the other participants.

As Set approached the women, Brendan's stomach lurched. The first victim was a buxom blonde dark mage. No one Brendan knew, but that did not diminish the horror he felt at the sight of her thrashing about when the seven-foot-tall beast of a man forced himself upon her.

Unable to watch the whole scene unfold, Brendan turned his gaze toward Bridey, who was the eighth and last in line, assuming Set planned to follow a linear path. Her expression betrayed anguish and dread as she watched the mating ritual unfold, knowing the same fate awaited her. When her eyes met Brendan's, they pleaded with him for clemency, for release from her bindings.

Tears slipped from Brendan's eyes as he projected his thoughts into Bridey's mind. *'Would that I could, but my own hands are metaphorically tied. I'm sorry, Bry.'*

She nodded her understanding and drooped her head in resignation. It was enough to shatter Brendan's heart and he hung his head in shame.

While Set took his time with each of the women, he did not need a recovery period. *He truly is a God*, Brendan thought bitterly.

As Set drew close to Samantha, Tyler jumped up and shouted, 'No! Not her!'

Set paused and turned to face Tyler with a look of disdain.

Kek snarled at him. 'How dare you disrespect our Dark Lord! Would you prefer to see her throat slit?'

'It would be more merciful than subjecting her to *him*!' He pointed angrily at Set.

Samantha nodded her agreement.

'Shall I contact our assassin, Master?' Damien pointed to the screen on the wall behind the women.

Brendan's heart skipped a beat.

Tyler paled and dropped to his knees. 'I'm sorry, Sam.' He tried to lower his head, but Damien, who knelt beside him, leaned over and yanked Tyler's head up, forcing him to watch as Set defiled one of the women he loved in exchange for saving the life of another.

Talk about a seriously fucked up trolley problem.

As Set finished with Samantha, the basement door burst open.

Brendan had never been so happy to see such a large bunch of Council warlocks. As they filed in, he spotted Hayes and pointed toward Damien and Harvey.

Hayes did not hesitate to lob two fireballs, dropping both douchebags to the floor in a pile of ash and bone.

Although surprised at first by the extreme force used, Brendan felt a perverse sense of satisfaction at seeing Damien toasted.

With the threat of Alannah's death out of the way, Tyler rose and sent a chain lightning attack at the three dark elves and their God. 'That's for Samantha, you arseholes!' The shock threw the elves back, either dead or unconscious.

But the bolt of electricity merely annoyed Set, who sauntered toward Tyler with a menacing scowl. A few warlocks tried to stop him, but he grabbed and flung them across the room, smashing their heads against the wall.

The remaining warlocks backed down like a bunch of cowards; all except Jaxon, who silently assessed the situation.

How does one stop an angry, rampaging God of chaos? That chapter was missing from all the mage textbooks.

With nowhere to run, Tyler visibly trembled as Set moved in for the kill.

Not willing to let the God of jerkdom crush Tyler, Brendan drew on his powers of persuasion as he leaped in front of Set. 'Hey Set, buddy, old pal. Why waste your time with these idiots, when there is a whole world out there waiting for you? Think of all the lovely ladies who are ripe for the taking.' He moved up and placed a friendly arm around Set's back, since he could not reach the giant's shoulders comfortably. 'I'm what they call an expert in the art of seduction. Why don't I take you out prowling for women?'

Set looked at him doubtfully. 'You are a powerful enchanter. Why do you bother with seduction when you can take them?'

Brendan grinned. 'Because there is more excitement in the chase when they are willing. But that's my preference and quite beside the point. I know a great place to find some magic babes far more worthy than these offerings. Would you like me to show you?'

Caleb chose that moment to appear, distracting Set, and blocking the door as he stood frozen in abject horror.

'Oh look, it's my friend Caleb. He knows how to party too,' Brendan added. 'The two of us could take you out on the town and show you a good time.'

'Mm, I am hungry for more women. Although I have not finished tasting the last of my offerings.'

Brendan waved a hand through the air. 'Bah. You don't want 'em. That one,' he pointed to Tanya, 'is as bland and boring as they come. She's only ever been with one man in her life. I mean come on;

she has vanilla written all over her. And her,' he pointed to Bridey, 'trust me when I say you ain't missing much. I've been there, done that, along with most of the men in this city.'

Bridey's eyes bugged out at Brendan's blatant insult.

That's gonna take some apologising when I get home. 'Surely you want excitement from the women you take. I know I do.'

'You make a fair point.' Set let out a hearty laugh, eroding the mountain of tension in the room. 'Very well. I trust you know this world better than I do now. Show me where to find the beautiful women.'

'Okay, but first, you'll need some glamour, so the humans don't run screaming.'

'But I like the sound of humans screaming,' Set insisted.

With a chuckle, Brendan slapped Set on the arm. 'A man after my own heart. Seriously though, you don't want the humans to see you in this form or they will send their soldiers to attack you. Trust me when I say human warfare has advanced a lot since you left. Some of the weapons they use are more powerful than anything magical.'

A wide grin formed on Set's face. 'I like the sound of these modern humans and their weapons. Will you show me some?'

'Of course. But glamour first.'

'Okay,' Set agreed.

Brendan cast a basic glamour spell making Set's head appear human, hiding the tail, changing his skin to more of a chocolate colour instead of dark red, and applying a black suit in place of the skimpy loin cloth. 'Okay, all set. Ah hell, I did not intend that pun, I swear.'

'It is okay. I liked your pun,' replied Set.

'Christ! Remind me never to introduce you to my brother.' Brendan seized Set's arm and led him out of the basement, grabbing Caleb with his other arm on the way out.

'Does your brother enjoy wordplays?'

'Much too much. They are the only form of humour he attempts, and he does a pretty lousy job.' Brendan slipped his burner phone subtly into Caleb's pocket and spoke to him telepathically. *'Message Jaxon. Tell him to prepare a space for a ritual sending and to find an acolyte or hierophant who knows how to send Set back to hell. Once he has it sorted, he should message us with a time and location.'*

'I get the sense you do not like your brother much,' Set continued.

'Ha! That's an understatement. The bastard stole the love of my life. Oh, and he always had it too good.'

'I understand envy and hatred towards one's brother.'

Brendan recalled his knowledge of Egyptian history. 'Do you mean Osiris?'

'Yes. He was always the family favourite.'

'I hear you man. Liam could do no wrong and always got everything he wanted.'

'What form of vengeance have you enacted upon your brother?'

'Are you kidding me? Liam is a powerful warlock and pretty much untouchable.'

'Have you thought about killing him?' Set asked.

'Trust me, Set, I've dreamt of all the ways I could end him.'

'Perhaps I could help. I love enacting vengeance.'

'Hmm… maybe once you've finished with this City, we could go back to my hometown?' Brendan suggested.

Set nodded, pausing to take in his surroundings as they stepped outside the building. 'My word, humans have made some considerable advances in technology.'

'With unsolicited help from their magic friends of course,' Brendan pointed out. 'When was the last time you came to earth, Set?'

'I believe the year was 1038.'

A whistle slipped through Brendan's lips. 'The Middle Ages. That's over nine hundred years ago. You've got a lot to catch up on. For one thing, you see those machines moving on the road?'

'Yes.'

'They are cars and they have replaced horses as the main mode of road transport.'

'Indeed.'

'Also, this country we are in? This is Australia: a large island nation in the southern hemisphere. Most of the human world did not know of its existence back then.' Brendan started leading them toward a nearby unseelie club as he went on about the ways of the modern world, all with a view to keeping Set distracted from Caleb's texting. 'Oh, and dragons were driven to extinction.'

Set's brows rose. 'Really? How?'

'Humans literally hunted them to death. They would have done the same to us mages and the other magical races if we hadn't started using glamour. Most humans began subscribing to monotheistic religion and persecuted anyone practising the old ways. That said, we have reached a new age of enlightenment where religious, racial, and sexual tolerance is growing. Who knows, maybe one day we can coexist with humans openly again.'

They reached the club. 'Well, here is the first stop on our tour. The place won't be busy yet, though, 'cause it's still early.' As they stepped inside, a decent number of fae were already enjoying a drink at the bar. They all turned and gasped. 'Oh right. The glamour spell only works on humans—these folk can see you for who you are.'

'It is of no consequence.'

Brendan was inclined to disagree. Set was a God to these people and the Gods were not known to walk among them and drop into the local watering hole on a whim. *But who am I to argue?*

With a lustful eye, Set made his way over to one of the endarkened sitting in the lounge area. Her eyes widened with shock at the monstrous God standing above her. 'I will start with you,' he announced.

'Excuse me?' she replied with an air of sass.

But Set ignored her words as he grabbed her, eliciting a scream from the helpless woman.

Brendan cringed, but for his plan to work, he needed to keep Set occupied. So, he jumped on the bar and hollered, 'Okay, listen up people. I am Lord Jet, Dark Syndicate Boss, and I bring a God before you. That's right, a literal God. May I present Set, the Egyptian God of Chaos.' He thrust his arm out toward Set for dramatic effect. 'Tonight, I am declaring this bar to be Set's breeding ground. Think of it like a dark Beltane where an actual God will honour the lucky babes. So, ladies, you have two options: either line up to become a willing recipient of Set's lovin' and let him rock your world like only a God can. Or cower in the corner and pray like hell he doesn't turn his attentions on you, but I don't fancy those odds. Either way, none of you can leave here before he finishes with you.'

Caleb stood near the door, shaking his head as he thought, *'I don't like this plan much, Winters.'*

'Well it's the best I've got,' Brendan replied telepathically. *'Would you rather I unleash him upon the unsuspecting masses at a regular nightclub to keep him busy while the warlocks hatch their plan?'*

'Of course not, but I still don't like forcing him upon anyone. Plus, this won't go down well for you in the Syndicate ranks.'

'I couldn't give a shit about the Syndicate ranks. Right now, my priority is saving the world at large from the horrors this God can unleash upon them.'

Five drinks into the night and Brendan decided he better not go back for more else he become too inebriated to banish Set to hell. Surprisingly, over half the women in the unseelie bar had willingly offered themselves up to Set. Brendan could not help but think Set owed much success with the ladies to his own speech, and he felt a sense of pride in his oratory skills.

But as the night wore on and the consenting partners stopped lining up, things took a turn for the worse, and the heavy drinking commenced.

Caleb slumped over the bar next to Brendan, nursing his seventh or eighth drink. 'I know Set's old-school, but this shit is sick and twisted. I could never treat a woman like that.'

Brendan snorted. 'No, but you let *our* woman treat *you* like that.'

'Not cool, man.' Caleb tried to hold Brendan's eyes in a death glare, but his gaze was too unsteady.

'Hey, I'm as pitiful as you. Bridey may not have used magic compulsion on me, but she coerced me in other ways. She did a lot of wrong shit to us and yet we both encouraged it and now we can't imagine living without her.'

'Yep, we're one big fucked up family. Maybe you should change your surname to Hawthorn.'

With a smirk, Brendan leaned in closer to Caleb. 'Are you proposing to me, Thornsy?'

A few laughs erupted from Caleb. 'I'm sorry, but the thought of you legally married to anyone is too funny; although, I could totally imagine the three of us in a hand fasting, but good luck finding an acolyte willing to sanctify our union.'

A moment later, Set stepped up behind them, slapping them both on their shoulders. 'Have another drink with me, men!'

'Gladly,' replied Caleb as he pushed his empty glass forward and threw another fifty down on the bar.

'I'll pass. I've had enough tonight,' explained Brendan.

'What? The night is young, and the alcohol has barely touched your system. You promised to have an enjoyable time with me tonight.'

'Fine.' Brendan groaned as he pushed his own glass forward. 'I never thought I'd still succumb to peer pressure at the age of twenty-one.'

As they clinked their freshly filled glasses together, the phone in Caleb's pocket beeped.

'What was that?' Set's eyes darted from Caleb to Brendan.

'What was what?' Brendan asked nonchalantly.

'The peculiar noise.'

Brendan shrugged. 'Must be one of the machines behind the bar. How are you going with the ladies out there, Set? Have you had your fill already?'

His big burly chest rumbled with a deep chuckle. 'I am far from satisfied, but there is only one damsel left for me to ravish.'

'Why don't you go violate her while Caleb and I work out where to take you next?'

Excitement radiated in orange sunbursts from Set's uber aura. 'You are a better servant than any of those stuffy old dark elves. They never took me drinking and whoring at the taverns like this.' Turning away, Set stalked his last victim.

'Please tell me that's a newsworthy update,' Brendan pleaded as he turned back to Caleb.

Caleb's eyes lit up as he read the message, but his brow furrowed toward the end.

'What is it? What's wrong?'

'They have a place setup, but they don't have enough mages attuned to Aether.'

'Shit! How many more do they need?'

'Two.'

'Wait, did they include you in their numbers?'

'No, but I'm pretty plastered. I don't know if I can do much magic.'

Brendan waved his hand dismissively. 'Shouldn't matter. All you need to do is channel the mana. Tell them you'll do it and get them to ask the bookshop owner in Darlinghurst. They will also need to make sure Tyler is there.'

'Will do.'

'So where are we doing it?'

'High Magus O'Grady's house.'

Brendan gave him an impish grin as he replied, 'Kinky.'

'Your ability to shamelessly flirt in such dire times amazes me.'

'So sue me for feeling horny after the free porn show Set put on for us.'

Caleb was gobsmacked. 'Please tell me you haven't enjoyed the sight of him raping women.'

'Not the raping part. I'm talking about the women who threw themselves at him. As if you didn't enjoy watching that.'

'Maybe.'

'You know, I kinda feel like I've bonded with the bastard. If it weren't for his propensity to take without asking, I'd say it's a shame to send him away.'

Shock spread across Caleb's face. 'You aren't reconsidering, are you?'

'Reconsidering what?' Set had snuck up behind them.

Brendan startled, but swiftly regained his composure. 'Caleb worried I would reconsider his suggestion for our next party destination. But I'm all in.'

Set's eyes gleamed with devilish delight. 'You have another venue arranged?'

'Yes, we do,' Caleb replied. 'We should get going now if we want to make the most of the night.'

'Good thinking,' agreed Set.

They took a taxi to O'Grady's harbour view mansion in Cremorne Point.

'This does not look like a tavern,' Set observed.

The driver cast a wary glance at Set.

Brendan paid for their fare and beckoned Set out the car. 'Because it's not. We are going to a private party. In this day and age, a lot of people have wild parties in their homes, and they are often a lot more fun than nights out at pubs and clubs. The drinking works out a lot cheaper too.'

'Is this your house?' Set eyed the place warily.

'No. It belongs to a friend of ours. Come on.' Brendan tugged on Set's arm to encourage him inside.

As soon as they passed through the wards, Set stiffened. 'This place feels wrong. I don't like it.'

'You are probably reacting to the wards. All mages put those up around their homes. It's nothing to worry about.' Brendan tried to sound as calm as possible, but a sliver of anxiety slipped through the cracks.

Set stood firm. 'You are not being straight with me, Brendan. Why is that?'

'I'm nervous about introducing you to my friends, okay? Some of them can be aloof or even hostile with strangers. Hopefully your divinity will help break the ice.'

After a moment of hesitation, Set nodded and followed them. 'If this is a party, where is everyone?'

'Downstairs, in the basement,' Caleb replied.

Bemused, Set shook his head. 'Modern people are strange.' When Brendan flung open the door to the cellar, Set froze. 'You tricked me; this is no party!' His voice roared at a near-deafening volume. He attempted to back out of the doorway, but Caleb wrapped his arms around Set and Aether flowed from his hands, effectively trapping them together in a forcefield.

'So much for being too drunk, Thornsy!'

With a smug grin, Caleb steered Set into the middle of the pentagram.

The Hierophant cast the circle and invited High Magus O'Grady, Acolyte Carran, Brendan, Caleb, and Tyler to join. After working together to bring the devil to Earth, it made sense for Brendan and his doppelganger to join once more and send Set back to hell.

As the four Aether users worked together to bind Set in celestial shackles, Brendan visualised the fiery pits, pulling the stygian element into his mana conduits. He could also feel the power flowing into him from Tyler—like he had in the summoning ritual earlier—only this time, the connection was stronger. It was as though Tyler's willingness to help intensified their doppelganger bond.

When the time came for Brendan to perform his part, he closed his eyes and spoke the mantra, 'We banish thee Set. You are no longer welcome on Earth. Return to the fiery pits.' After a minute of chanting, Brendan began to tire and Set was still resisting, crying out in pain as he did so.

Set snarled in his mind. *'You will pay for your betrayal, puny mage!'*

Guilt tugged at Brendan's heart, and he felt the need to explain. *'The world has changed too much, and it is no longer acceptable to treat women the way you do.'*

'Bah! Men have grown soft. I should take you with me and toughen you up.'

'Not gonna happen, Set.' Brendan reached into the last of his reserves as he sent a blast of hellfire at Set.

The God retaliated, using the fire to burn the flesh above Brendan's heart.

Brendan yelped and doubled over in pain. As it eased, everyone else fell silent, and he opened his eyes. The middle of the circle was empty, which meant they had successfully vanquished Set. He expelled a large breath and grinned as he glanced around the room. But the others wore apprehensive looks, and when he could not see Caleb, fear and understanding clenched his chest. 'Where is he? *Where is Caleb?'*

True remorse showed in Tyler's expression as he spoke, 'I'm sorry, Brendan. Set took Caleb with him.'

With those five words, Brendan felt the world cave in around him.

Chapter Twenty

Feeling wrecked, Tyler dragged his feet up the basement stairs and into O'Grady's living room. The sight of Samantha sobbing against Shane's chest cut to the bone. The memory of her suffering would live with him forever, along with the guilt he felt for allowing it to happen. 'It's done. Set has returned to the Underworld,' he announced to the room at large.

Jaxon looked up from comforting Tanya. 'Good. You should get some rest. O'Grady is happy to put us all up for the night.' His attention shifted behind Tyler.

Turning, Tyler watched as the others emerged from the basement. O'Grady was conversing in hushed voices with the Hierophant and Acolyte Carran as he led them away, but Brendan had not yet shown his face.

Still wrapped in a blanket, Bridey stood up from her armchair. 'What about Brendan and Caleb?' When Tyler looked at her with silent remorse, her eyes widened. 'No!' Dropping the blanket, she dashed past Tyler and ran down the stairs to the cellar.

'What happened?' Jaxon asked.

'We lost Caleb,' Tyler replied solemnly.

'Oh.'

After crossing the room, Tyler sat on the couch next to Samantha. He needed to touch her, to comfort her. But when he attempted to pull her into his arms, she resisted. 'Sam?'

She shook her head.

'Sam, please. I need to hold you.'

'No.' Her voice sounded aloof.

'I'm sorry, baby. I didn't want any of that.'

Her muffled voice came between sobs. 'I thought you were different, but you are as depraved as the rest of them, as evil as Kek.'

'What? Sam—'

Shane glared at him. 'Quirky, please. I think you should give her some time. She's had an extremely traumatic experience.'

With intense pain piercing his heart, Tyler stormed out of the house, slamming the door behind him as he stepped out into the back garden. When he found a wooden bench a decent distance from the house, he collapsed on it and let out a furious scream. He was not angry with Samantha. It was those Cultists and their Dark Lord who boiled his blood. But he directed most of the rage inward at himself.

After the frenzy wore off, sorrow kicked in and Tyler let the tears come. He cried for the terror Samantha must have felt; for the soul-destroying way that monster had used her; for the betrayal she must have felt knowing Tyler had enabled it all. And he wept for his own loss, because things would never be the same between them. Even if Alannah's life had not been on the line, Tyler's selfish side would not have allowed them to take Samantha's life, no matter how much she pleaded for the sweet release of death.

Shit! Alannah! In all the chaos of the night's events, he had almost forgotten about the assassin sent to watch her. He grabbed the burner phone in his pocket and dialled her number.

'Hello?'

Relief washed over him at hearing her voice, at knowing she was alive. 'Hi Lana. It's Tyler. Are you okay?'

'Have you been channelling cosmic mana? Because I swear you must be psychic. I was thinking of calling you because honestly, I feel like shit.'

'But are you physically okay? Has anyone harmed you?'

Her tone became riddled with anxiety. 'No, why? What's going on?'

'I've had a totally fucked up night. Can I see you? I'd rather talk about this stuff in person.'

'Yeah, okay. I was hoping to see you anyway. Meet at our hotel in an hour?'

'Yes please.' When he signed off, Tyler tuned in to the ley lines. As he suspected, the High Magus had bought property with intersecting lines of power, one of which led south and straight across the harbour bridge. He arrived hastily and made use of the shower in the meantime. When he walked out of the bathroom, wearing nothing but a towel, Alannah was waiting for him on the bed. Her sudden appearance made him jump. 'That was quick.'

'I guess I'm getting better at magiporting.'

'I'd say! Plus, I can see you didn't bother changing first.' His eyes scanned her scantily clad body, dressed in nothing more than a black satin slip.

A sly smile tugged at one side of her lips. 'I put a coat on before stepping out.' She pointed at the black overcoat she had draped across the back of a chair before standing to embrace him. 'What's going on, Tyler? Why did you worry about me? And why have you been crying?'

Clinging tightly to her, another wave of sorrow hit him. But rather than drown in it, Tyler let Alannah carry it away as their lips crashed together and their bodies merged.

A sense of calm set in as Tyler's breathing settled, and he used it to tell Alannah everything about the night.

'Poor Sam,' Alannah said in a soft voice.

Tears threatened Tyler's eyes again. 'It was horrible, Lana. And Damien wouldn't let me look away. It kills me knowing she suffered all that because of me. I desperately need her forgiveness, even though I know I don't deserve it.'

Alannah straddled Tyler, pressing all her weight into him as she brought her face close to his. 'Hey, what happened wasn't your fault. The Cult used you too, Tyler. Sam will come around to see it, but she needs time. I never told you this, but I kind of know what she's going through.'

Tyler's lidded eyes flew open. 'What do you mean?'

'Remember my trip to the big house?'

Nodding, Tyler felt his stomach stir.

'One of the Council's warlocks raped me in prison. The incident turned me into an emotional wreck for a while and I misdirected a lot of my rage toward Liam. Logically, I knew it wasn't his fault, but emotionally it took a while to forgive him, not only for the way he dumped me in the first place, but for the imaginary part he played in letting Clayton defile me.'

'But you did forgive him?'

'Yeah, I did.'

'Yet things won't ever be the same for the two of you, will they?'

Alannah sighed. 'No. But that has more to do with my feelings for Brendan. Speaking of which….'

Tyler brought his hands up from her hips to encircle her back with his arms. 'Is this what you wanted to call me about?'

'Yeah. I need someone I can confide in because the truth of the matter is quietly killing me.'

'Hey, you can always talk to me, and you know I will never betray your secrets.'

'I know. Thank you, Tyler.' She took a deep breath. 'This baby I'm carrying… it's Brendan's.'

'Oh, hell. But didn't your uncle say it was a blessed baby?'

'It is, but Brendan was my only partner at Beltane.'

'I see.' He fell silent for a minute.

'Does this upset you, Tyler?'

'Yeah, but not in the way you might think. I'm sad for you, Lana. I know how much your separation from Brendan has hurt you, and now you're carrying his child. It's gonna make it much harder to get over him.'

'Exactly. And that's where I'm going to need your help a lot in the coming years.'

'Fuck!' Tyler rolled Alannah over, pinning her down as he looked into her eyes. 'What are you saying, Lana?'

'I'm saying I don't want these therapy sessions to end.'

Those were the sweetest words Tyler had heard all day... possibly all his life.

An ominous red glow filled the ritual room as Bridey entered, fearing the worst. The sight of Brendan's hunched form sent her heart lurching into her throat. 'Oh Gods!' She ran to his unmoving body and knelt beside him. 'Oh, Brendan.'

Turning, his gaze lumbered toward her, and she felt a moment of relief knowing he was alive.

That was until she saw his red, puffy eyes. 'W-what happened?'

His expression was almost blank as he blinked at her. Shock. He was in shock. The symptoms were obvious even without reading his aura. The mere fact he was letting her read him should have been the first clue.

'Brendan, sweetie, what happened?'

'He's gone.' The coarse, scratchy voice sounded almost alien.

Panicked, Bridey looked up and scanned the room, looking for Caleb's body, but there was no sign of him. 'Gone where? Where did Caleb go?'

'Hell.' Brendan choked up as waves of hysteria set in.

She could not quite make out what he was saying, but she heard something about hell and whatever he meant was clearly the cause of his distress. She tried to subdue her own fears and focussed on calming him. With her attunements, Bridey placed her hand on Brendan's back and whispered soothing words as she poured a sense of calm into him. 'It's okay, handsome. Everything will be okay.'

After gulping a lungful of air, he sat up and focussed on her. 'I'm sorry, Bry. I didn't realise there was a risk of banishing Caleb when I sent Set back to the Underworld. The dark lord dragged Caleb down with him!'

With a sinking heart, Bridey understood what Brendan meant. If they had sent Set to hell and Set took Caleb with him, her beloved boy was currently in the Volcanic Pits, the lowest level of the Underworld, where nether formed. It was where the most wicked souls went. *Poor Caleb must feel terrified.* 'Listen to me, handsome. If you were able to release Set in the first place, surely you can get Caleb out?'

'That was the first thing I thought of, but it's not likely.'

'Why not?'

'Summoning Set took a lot of power, more than I have. I would need to find others willing to help despite the risk.'

'What risk?'

'Releasing Set again.' He leaned into her and brushed a hand along the side of her face. 'I can't believe how close things got for you, Bry. If he'd defiled you, I never would have forgiven myself. And poor Samantha and Tyler. I can only begin to imagine what they are going through right now. I don't think I could ask Tyler to take the risk again.'

'It's okay, sweetness, we will find a way.'

Brendan shook his head defiantly. 'You're forgetting one major complicating factor here: Set is an immortal Celestial, but Caleb's not. What if Caleb can't survive conditions in the Volcanic Pits?'

'We can't afford to think like that, Brendan. Let's try to stay positive so we can focus on rescuing Caleb. Can you keep your hopes up for me?'

He still looked defeated when he nodded, but it was a start.

'Come on. Let's go home and get some rest.' She began to rise.

But Brendan tugged at her hand, pulling her into his lap. 'Wait a sec. I need to hold you.'

'Of course, handsome. Whatever you need.' The warm comfort of his arms was more than welcome.

Pressing into the crook of her neck, he inhaled her scent and traced his fingers along her side. 'Where did this tracksuit come from? I don't recall you owning anything like this.'

'O'Grady's wife gave me these clothes. I lost my own at the Mara building.'

'That was nice of her,' he replied absently, shifting back enough to look at Bridey. Something dark flashed in Brendan's gaze and his eyes filled with hunger. With a swift movement he pinned her down on the floor, right in the middle of the pentagram. 'Although you look much better without any clothes.'

Bridey gasped from the sudden movement. 'Brendan! What are you doing?'

Tearing her pants down, he grinned wickedly. 'What does it look like I'm doing?' When he rose to his feet, Bridey tried to sit up, but he pushed her back down with a bare foot placed on her chest.

'Brendan, have you forgotten where we are?'

'Not at all.' To prove his point, he removed his ritual robe and threw it across the room. When he looked down at her a moment later, lust burned red in his eyes and aura. 'I've always wanted to fuck someone in a ritual circle. Looks like you're the lucky someone.'

Bridey's body flooded with desire at the sight of him standing over her in nothing but a pair of red silk boxers that did nothing to hide his erection. A moment later, the red silk dropped to the ground.

'Remove your top,' he commanded.

With expert deftness, she stripped herself naked.

'On your hands and knees.'

The authoritative tone he adopted sent a thrilling rush to her core. Damien had been right. This was exactly what she wanted from Brendan. Assuming the position, Bridey relished the feel of cool, hard stone pressing into her knees and palms.

Brendan dropped to the floor behind her and without any warning, he grabbed a handful of hair and pulled her head back as he thrust deep inside her. Holding his position, Brendan brushed his lips against her ear. 'You thought you could own me, but you need to understand no one *owns* Brendan Winters. I am the one who *owns* you, Bridey Hawthorn.'

Amazement did not even begin to describe how Brendan felt when Tyler rang, inviting him to visit his home. 'Why?' He laced his tone with scepticism.

'I have a surprise for you. Get over here.'

Brendan accepted the invitation. Bridey had been busy working in her study, so he gave her a quick kiss and took off. It had been two weeks since the whole mess with Set and they had yet to find a safe way to bring Caleb back. But she refused to give up on him, devoting hours every day to studies into the arcane.

After ringing the doorbell of the large Darlinghurst townhouse, he stepped back and waited anxiously.

Within seconds, the door flung open, and Tyler grinned back at him. 'Come in.'

It was odd how Tyler had recently taken to styling his hair the same as Brendan's. *Should it flatter me or creep me out?*

When they stepped into the living room, a fiery redhead looked up at him and gasped. Samantha looked much healthier and happier than the last time he had seen her, and it did wonders for her sex appeal. Her eyes darted between Brendan and Tyler. 'Babe?'

Tyler laughed. 'That'd be me, Firecracker. So, yeah, this is the first opportunity I've had to formally introduce you. Brendan, this is my girlfriend, Samantha.'

Reaching forward, Brendan clasped Samantha's hand and shook it. 'A pleasure to meet you.'

'Likewise,' she replied with eyes fixed on his.

A throat-clearing noise from Tyler broke her gaze. 'So, uh, before I show you the surprise, I need you to promise you won't ask any questions like how, or why etc.'

Brendan cast his dubious glance over Tyler. 'O-kay.'

'Promise?'

'Fine. I promise.'

'Right. Follow me.' He led Brendan up a flight of stairs and onto the first floor. They stopped outside a door. 'I would suggest bracing yourself though. This won't be a pretty sight.'

Vague curiosity shifted to full intrigue as Brendan prepared himself for something grotesque.

'Go in when you're ready.'

With a deep breath, Brendan entered the room. Tanya sat on the far edge of a large bed, and she was in a trance with her hand resting on the crown of a man's head. The heart beating in Brendan's chest became the only thing he could hear. Three long strides brought him close enough to see who lay in the bed. His skin as red as a lobster, blistered from third degree burns, but there was no mistaking the slender body and well-defined face.

A few tears trickled from Brendan's eyes as he perched on the nearest edge of the bed. 'Thornsy?'

Caleb's eyes fluttered open. 'Winters?' he asked with a hoarse voice.

'Christ, Thornsy! You look like shit. And you sound even worse,' Brendan jested as the tears flowed more freely. He grabbed a glass of water from the bedside table. 'Here, have a drink. Sorry it's not the good stuff, but I wasn't able to sneak the whiskey past Dr. Tanya.'

Tanya opened her eyes long enough to roll them, then resumed the meditation in which she was channelling the mana needed to heal Caleb.

With Brendan's help, Caleb shuffled up the bed enough to prop himself up against the pillows. He took a few sips of water using the straw Brendan held for him. 'I guess I'm not the pretty one anymore,' he whispered.

'I'm sure Bridey will happily wear that crown until you get better,' Brendan gave him an impish grin. 'Seriously, it's great to have you back, Thornsy. Bridey and I have missed you something fierce. Can I kiss you if I'm gentle?'

'Yes.'

Reclining on his side, Brendan leaned in carefully to press his lips against Caleb's. He kept the touch feather soft. But Caleb's hand jolted up from his side and grabbed the back of Brendan's neck, pulling him in closer. After wincing from the increased pressure, Caleb deepened the kiss. Even when dry and cracked, Caleb's lips felt incredible against his own, especially when moaning.

'Okay, that's enough excitement for my patient,' Tanya interjected.

Brendan smirked at the tent between Caleb's legs. 'Indeed. I'll let you get some more rest, Thornsy. But I'll return soon.'

''Kay. Love you,' Caleb whispered.

'Love you too.' Brendan rose and left the room. After shutting the door, he leaned against it to find his bearings. *Caleb is alive!* Questions about how Caleb got home and what he'd endured filled Brendan's head. He jogged down the stairs and found Tyler curled up with Samantha, watching television in the living room.

Tyler looked up and gestured toward an armchair. 'Take a seat.' He paused the show they were watching to focus on Brendan.

'Thank you,' said Brendan once he had settled in his seat. 'You didn't have to do this for him, and I know you Council folk aren't usually fond of unseelie.'

'You and he are welcome. It was the least we could do. Unseelie folk aren't usually known to help the Council combat the forces of evil.'

'Yeah, Caleb's pretty special.'

Tyler studied Brendan a moment. 'Are you really in love with him?'

'I am.'

'And his sister, Bridey?'

'Yup. In love with her too.'

Another moment of awkward silence.

'What about Lana? Do you still love her?'

Why the hell is he interrogating me on my love life? With careful consideration, Brendan opted for the truth. 'Even after severing the soul link and trying everything in her power, Bridey could not shake my feelings for Lana. That love runs deeper than any other emotion.'

Tyler did not even appear surprised. 'So why aren't you trying to win her back?'

'Because I can't. There are greater forces at work here, Tyler. Lana's better off keeping me at a distance.'

'I doubt that. Not when—'

'Tyler, please. It hurts me as much to stay away from her, but would you risk the life of the woman you love for your own selfish gain? If being with her put her life in danger, would you continue to see her?'

Tyler stared at him in stunned silence, then shook his head. 'What aren't you telling me, Brendan?'

'I'm not telling you anything that will put your own life at risk. I suggest you stop this line of inquiry before it's too late.'

'Is your life in danger?'

'I'm the boss of a criminal syndicate, Tyler. My life is always on the line.'

With a nod of understanding, Tyler quit his questioning.

'I'd better get going. Bridey doesn't know the wonderful news yet and she will want to see Caleb.'

Brendan had reached the door when Tyler stopped him, 'Oh and Brendan?'

'What?'

'Lana sends her regards.'

The penny dropped and Brendan understood how Tyler was able to bring Caleb back from the Volcanic Pits. 'For her own sake, please don't send her mine.'

Chapter Twenty-One

Five years and six months later.

Sweat poured from every inch of Brendan and Liam's bodies as their swords clashed blow for blow. The duel had been intense, lasting for at least one hour, if not two. But what Liam failed to realise was Brendan had not even attempted mind reading yet.

The moment Brendan dove into his brother's mind, it was easy to anticipate Liam's next move. Liam may have had spent years learning to block Brendan from his mind, but that was before Brendan had mastered his attunement to the stygian element. Bypassing Liam's defences had become a cakewalk.

Seizing the moment, Brendan plunged his blade deep into Liam's heart. He watched with delight as daddy's golden boy fell backwards with a look of pure horror on his face. Leaning over Liam's dying form, Brendan scowled bitterly. 'Good riddance, *Brother.*'

Brendan's forehead was dripping with perspiration as he woke from the vivid dream. Sitting up in bed, he rubbed the throbbing brand on his chest: Set had given him the cartouche shaped scar as a parting gift. Brendan cursed the clock for showing how little sleep he had gotten so far. Not wanting to disturb his lovers who slept on either side of him, he carefully slid down to the bottom of the bed and made his way to the bathroom.

After wiping his face with a cold, damp cloth, he headed into his study to continue working on the latest translation. With all the volumes from the Obsidian Cult's library he had been working through, his Arabic literacy was exceeding that of his Celtic. What he found strange, however, was his ability to read ancient hieroglyphics without need of a reference book.

The subject of Brendan's study was a fascinating analysis of the original *Book of the Dead*, better known to the original elves as *Spells for Coming Forth by Day*. Several spells contained within related to various forms of immortality, including paths to the Celestial Realm. *I would love to get my hands on the original tome!* He wondered where the Egyptians had hidden such a book.

Sensing movement at the door, he looked up from his desk. Caleb slouched against the doorframe, arms crossed against his firm chest, a hint of muscle bulging in his biceps. Every inch of his silver skin shimmered in the dim lamplight. *Fuck! He grows more beautiful every day!* Thankfully, Tanya's healing magic had worked miracles all those years ago, so there was not a single scar or blemish left on Caleb's perfect complexion.

'Hey, what are you doing out of bed?' Caleb crossed the room and moved around behind Brendan, where his hands got to work on the tension in Brendan's shoulders.

'I couldn't sleep.'

'Was it another one of those vengeance dreams?'

Brendan dropped his work and leaned back into the massage. 'Yeah.'

'They're getting more frequent of late. Maybe you should give the Egyptology a rest for a while.'

'You think it's related?'

'I'm almost certain. You must come across the name Set often in your reading. It's gotta be like a big subconscious trigger.'

'Maybe. But if that were the case, why am I not dreaming about the shit Set did?'

'I dunno. I'm not an expert in dreams. It seems likely, considering Set's M.O. along with your own resentment towards Liam.'

'You're probably right. Once I finish working on this book, I'll move on to something different.'

Caleb's hand trailed down Brendan's chest as he leaned forward. 'Did you realise it's after midnight?'

Brendan huffed. 'And?'

'And, happy birthday, Winters.'

'Ah damn. I was hoping you'd forget it was today.'

'Not gonna happen.' His fingernails skirted around Brendan's nipples. 'Why don't you come back to bed and let Bridey and me spoil you?'

'Mm, now that's an idea I can get behind.' Brendan let Caleb pull him up from his chair and take him back to their room.

The scent of violets filled the air as he approached the bed. And Bridey knelt on the mattress, waiting for him with a mischievous glint to her eyes. 'Happy birthday, handsome. I have the perfect gift for you.'

'Is that so?'

Nodding, she handed him a purple box with a silver ribbon. 'This is from both of us.'

Making quick work of the ribbon, Brendan opened the box. But he took a full minute to recover from the shock after peering inside. When words became possible, he looked up at Bridey. 'Are you sure this is what you want?'

'Yes.'

Brendan turned to Caleb.

'You shouldn't even need to ask me. You know I've wanted this for years.'

'I want you both on the floor.'

Once Caleb and Bridey were both kneeling before him, he retrieved the two collars from the box. He inspected them. The rings of delicate silver thorn embellishments suggested a custom job. Brendan fastened the grey collar around Caleb's neck and stooped to kiss him on the head before doing the same with the violet collar on Bridey. Taking a step back, Brendan admired the incredible view. *What a gorgeous pair of subs. And they are mine!*

Unable to contain his excitement any longer, Brendan climbed into bed. 'Get up here and make me feel good.'

Brendan's pair of Hawthorns obeyed his command to the letter, bringing him pleasures beyond his wildest dreams.

To be continued…

What's Next?

Thank you for reading *Winter's Thrall*. I would be most grateful if you could show your support by leaving a rating or even a review.

Alannah and Brendan's stories continue in *Winter's Mother 1*, due for release Nov 2022.

Keep reading for a sample…

Bonus Content

Winter's Magic: Trouble in Paradise
(Winters Wedding)

Lord and Lady Ross Winters cordially invite you to attend the nuptials of Alannah Winters and their son Liam Winters...

Things have never been easy for Alannah and Liam, and their wedding day is no exception. All the chaos, calamity, and cold feet leaves their restless guests wondering if the ceremony will even go ahead. Will Liam and Alannah successfully tie the knot?

If you are keen to read this bonus content, you can access it on the 'Freebies' page of my website: www.starlaarts.com

Acknowledgements

Oh what fun! I thoroughly enjoyed writing this book. It also pushed my limits as far as erotic content goes. I hope you enjoyed the sex scenes because I popped my explicit writing cherry on them.

This story holds a special place in my heart because Brendan Winters is still my favourite book boyfriend, even as I write this note years after the first draft. This novel was much darker than the main entries in the series because it needed to be. This was Brendan's opportunity to grow up and become the man you will see in future books.

I would like to acknowledge my editor—Felix Staica—and cover artist—Jana Hoffmann—for the amazing work they provided.

A special thanks to my beta readers for volunteering such helpful feedback on this book: Ariel Mareroa, Amanda Mashburn, Breen Rodriguez, Elli Morgan, Hayley McKenna, and Joshua Wake.

And a huge shout out to all my street team and ARC readers for your reviews and social media support.

Winter's Mother 1

Most mistakes have consequences.
This one has a legacy.

Alannah

Following the birth of her daughter, Alannah slipped into a deep depression. Many blamed it on the hormones, but they did not know the truth: this precious baby girl was the spitting image of her father, a man who broke Alannah's heart and shattered her soul.

After years of escaping her grief, either at the bottom of a whiskey bottle or in the arms of Brendan's doppelganger, Alannah is finally sober and on the road to recovery when the devil himself walks back into her life. Will his return spell her ultimate destruction, or will they find a way to reconciliation and a second chance at love?

Brendan

Having escaped sexual slavery, Brendan has become the master of his own universe and Boss of the unseelie underground. Everything is good until work takes him back to Gaeilge Shores where he discovers the daughter he never knew existed.

Old wounds reopen and priorities change when he throws himself back into Alannah's life. And all this family drama takes place amidst an apocalyptic threat. Can Brendan help the Council save the world, and reunite with his soulmate?

Warning: This book contains coarse language, adultery in a crumbling marriage, and explicit scenes, including steamy m/f/f romance, that may upset or offend some readers. It also ends on a cliff-hanger, with the sequel launching in May 2023.

AVAILABLE NOVEMBER 2022
Keep reading for a sample…

Chapter One

Sixteen years following the events of Winter's Maiden 2

Glancing at her reflection in the bedroom mirror, Alannah cringed. She studied her cotton unicorn pyjamas and felt the beginnings of a mid-life crisis set in. *When did I trade in the black satin slips for these pyjamas? How am I only noticing how frumpy I look these days?* With a bamboo brush and some concerted effort, she managed to tame her wild bed hair. It had been another restless night.

The house was quiet when she made her way to the kitchen. The silence was unusual, but not alarming. Being a summer Saturday meant Liam was likely at the beach already, making the most of the surf. She turned on the coffee machine and looked across the open plan living space. Her daughter sat at the dining table, watching something on her laptop.

Neve was using headphones which explained the lack of noise. But the sound of grinding coffee beans got her attention. 'Morning, Mum.'

'Morning, hun. I didn't expect to see you up before me on a Saturday.'

'You do realise it's nearly midday, right?'

'Oh shit! Really?' Alannah looked at the old grandfather clock. She had recently acquired the timepiece from an antique auction for a bargain price. 'Damn. I guess I overslept. Did you get yourself some breakfast?'

Returning her attention to whatever YouTube had to offer, Neve shook her head.

Alannah took her fresh brew to the table and sat next to Neve. 'You know, if you want your father and I to show more lenience, you are gonna have to start behaving responsibly. That means looking after yourself more.'

'Spare me the lectures, Mum. I get enough of those from Dad. Besides, I remembered to feed the cat.' Neve gestured at the ball of white fluff sleeping on the couch.

Sighing, Alannah returned to the kitchen. She threw together some avocado and cheese toasted sandwiches. 'Here, eat this.' She put one of the plates beside Neve's laptop, then sat in front of her own computer.

Sipping her coffee, she scrolled through her social feed. Not much engaged her foggy brain beyond some cat memes. She clicked like on a few and went to close her laptop when a news bulletin caught her attention.

'Mum, can—'

'Wait a sec, hun. Come look at this.' She opened the live video feed and gasped at the aerial footage.

'The Victorian Government has declared a state of emergency. Melbourne residents flock from their homes amidst the City's collapse.'

'Oh wow! Is that a volcano erupting?' Neve asked. 'It looks awesome!'

'The dormant volcanoes erupting form part of the Newer Volcanic Province. This disaster follows a series of earth tremors. Experts claim the odds—'

Alannah muted the sound. 'It's devastating is what it is. Don't forget I spent nine years of my life living in that city. I have friends there.'

Remorse filled Neve's bright green eyes. 'Shit! Sorry, Mum. Can you call to check if they're okay?'

'Now's not a good time to be clogging up the phone towers over there. I hope they've marked themselves as safe.' Alannah's hands trembled as she clicked over to Melissa's profile. Nothing. She looked at Emma's and Cole's next. *Damnit!* None of them had checked in.

'Mum?'

'Mm?' Alannah was too distracted to give Neve her full attention.

'Is it okay if Cat and Fi come over for a bit?'

'Yeah.'

Neve disappeared down the hall. Alannah switched between face-stalking her friends and watching updates on the disaster. The more she watched, the more uneasy she felt about the whole thing. The reports coming from the scientists only fed her suspicions. *Why is a dormant volcano with such low odds of current activity erupting in such a prominent place? Could this be the work of dark mages?*

The issue warranted some investigation, so she sent a quick email to Kieran Lane, the High Magus of her state. She included a link to the newsflash with the question: *Could this be dark magic?*

When Kieran did not reply within an hour, she grew impatient and rang him.

'Yes, Councillor Winters?' His curt tone was typical even after years of working with her.

'Did you get my email, Your Honour?'

'I did.'

'And?'

A loud sigh crackled through the line. 'Why are you asking me about the goings on in another state? You know I don't have any jurisdiction over there.'

'Are you not the least bit concerned for them?'

'I sympathise, sure, but it's not like I can do anything. If High Magus Hanigan has need of us, I'm sure he'll be in touch. Now if you don't mind, I am in the middle of something.'

'Of course. Sorry to bother you.' Alannah hung up and flung her phone at the couch out of frustration. *Sixteen years on and I still haven't earned enough respect from the man.* Then it struck her. *If this volcano business is a dark magic conspiracy, they could hit South Australia. What if I can uncover such a plot and prevent devastation at our doorstep?* Surely *doing so would raise Kieran's esteem.*

With newfound enthusiasm, Alannah dialled her friend Monique.

'Hey girl, what's up? I hope Caitlin isn't causing you any grief.'

'What?' Alannah remembered the girls were over and hanging out in Neve's room. 'Oh right. No, she's fine. Have you seen the news?'

'No. Why? What happened?' Monique's cheerful tone plummeted.

'A volcano in Melbourne. It's all-over social media, so you should check it out. But listen, I was hoping you could hack into your dad's work files. I need some contact details for the magic community in rural Victoria.'

'You thinking foul play?' Monique was always more astute than her father, the High Magus.

'Yeah. Your dad's too stubborn to look into it, so I need to use some back channels to check it out.'

'I'll see what I can do.'

'Thanks.' After signing off, Alannah returned to checking on her friends. A little relief washed over her when she found Emma's update declaring she was fine and out of the danger zone. She continued to wait for news from the other two.

'Well, there's go my plan to fly under the radar.' Brendan huffed as he stuffed his phone back in his pocket. Zipping his small carry-on case closed, he became thankful for the decision to pack light.

'What do you mean?' asked Caleb.

'My flight got cancelled, something about a volcano in Melbourne spewing too much ash into the air. Now I need to magiport there, which sucks 'cause I'm not keen for High Magus Kieran to know I'm in town.'

Caleb's big, dark, soulful eyes looked so pretty when they grew wide with surprise. 'A volcano in Melbourne? Are you for real?'

'Yup.'

Grabbing his own phone, Caleb became engrossed in footage of the volcano erupting. 'I didn't even know we had active volcanos in Australia, let alone under cities.'

'Hmph. We should have paid more attention in school.'

Sardonic eyes peered over the small screen in Caleb's hands. 'You were the one playing hooky all the time. I kept my head down and got the work done.'

'That's right.' Brendan cast wistful thoughts back to their youth. Stalking around the bed, he backed Caleb up against the wall. 'I'd almost forgotten you were a nerd back then. Hm, I wonder... Would I have noticed your beauty sooner if your hadn't buried your head head in books so often.' He brought a hand up to Caleb's face, tucking a strand of long, black hair behind one of his pointy ears. The proximity aroused them both, their dicks tenting against each other.

The pitch of Caleb's voice lowered. 'Perhaps, but then I would have been nothing more than a distraction. A passing fad like all the girls you used back then.'

'Touché. Instead, your timing was perfect. You were like my life raft in a sea of despair.' Brendan drew Caleb's lips into a deep, passionate kiss. When the calendar alarm on his phone sounded, he groaned as he pulled back. After silencing the damn thing, his gaze returned to Caleb's mouth. Subconsciously, Brendan grazed the pad of his thumb along the bottom lip. 'Gods I'm gonna miss these sweet lips.'

Caleb's mouth curled into a mischievous smile. 'Jacob has pretty soft lips.'

'You sly fox.' Brendan laughed. 'You never told me the pair of you hooked up.'

'Sure I did. I told you about all the times I partied with him whenever I paid our hometown a visit.'

'You told me about the gang bangs, but you never related the details of being intimate with *him*.'

'My bad,' Caleb replied with a wry smile. 'I figured you'd assume we fucked.'

Brendan drilled into Caleb's soul with a stern expression. 'You know I don't like it when you leave me guessing. When I ask for details, I want *everything*. The who, the where, and most definitely the how. I am going to have to punish you for such insubordination.'

A slight moan escaped Caleb's lips as his eyes darkened with lust.

With a wicked grin, Brendan stepped back, breaking all body contact. 'I can see how much you want me right now, Thornsy. But you see, punishment is never about what *you* want.'

Caleb's eyes lowered. 'Of course. I'm sorry for offending you, Sir. What is my punishment?'

Seeing his submissive stance sent signals southward and tested Brendan's willpower. It would have been too easy to dish out a few lashings and take him then and there. But what he had in mind would be more fun in the long run, and it would give Caleb time to reflect upon his actions. 'No intentional sexual release until I return home. You will not touch yourself and you will not initiate intimate contact with anyone else while I am away. I'll let Bridey know the deal too, so she won't let you get off.'

Caleb gasped.

'What's wrong, Thornsy? Are you afraid of a little celibacy?'

'Not afraid, more… frustrated. I can't remember the last time I went so long.'

Closing the distance, Brendan reached inside Caleb's pants and gripped his erection. Then he leaned in to press his lips to Caleb's ear. 'If you think this is frustration, how do you think you will feel in two weeks?'

'Ah Gods!' Caleb gritted his teeth against the torture of Brendan's teasing touch.

'Will you be good for me Caleb?'

'Y-yes Sir,' he replied with a shaky voice.

'Good man. Now I want my goodbye kiss.' Embracing Caleb, Brendan kissed him with ardent fervour. Their passion rivalled anything Hollywood ever put on the big screen. He walked out sporting a massive smile and the boner to match. At least he could use magic to control the latter. Although he didn't have time to hide it before finding Bridey in the parlour.

She glanced at his situation and grinned. 'Oh dear. Has my brother left you unsatisfied?'

'Quite the reverse, I assure you.' He dropped his case beside the chaise longue and straddled her lap. 'At least I can do something about mine, unlike Caleb. I forbid him from seeking relief for the next two weeks. Can I rely on you to police him for me?'

'Certainly, Sir.'

'Thank you, Bry.' The farewell kiss he shared with Bridey was much more savage, like a pride lion with his lioness. By the time he left, Brendan considered the merit of Caleb's suggestion. Seeking out Jacob might prove necessary. The pickings in Gaeilge Shores were slimmer after the Council had exiled him. He was not even sure if Bianca would welcome him back in her bed.

EDM blared from Neve's speakers as she sat on her bed with the girls. Clicking next on the photo slideshow, she gasped at the fine specimen on her laptop.

Fiona squealed with delight, 'Oh. My. God. Dorian Pearce is so hot!'

'I know right! And you know what they say about vampire bites.' Neve licked her lips.

'Your parents would have a fit if they heard the two of you lusting after a vampire,' Caitlin scoffed. 'Especially your mum, Neve.'

Neve shot Caitlin a suspicious look. 'Why do you say that? I know my dad can be an arrogant arse, but Mum is more tolerant than most bloodline mages.'

'Didn't she ever tell you about her vampire ex?'

After scooping her jaw up off the floor, Neve questioned her blonde friend, 'My mum dated a vampire? I can't imagine her doing something so sordid.' A giggle slipped out as she thought of her mother letting a vampire bite her.

'She did. He was Dorian's late uncle, in fact. Austin was working for your great-grandmother who was a Lich. Under her orders, he tried to talk your mum into becoming cursed, which freaked her out, so she dumped his arse. But he went crazy and tried to force the curse on her. A big battle ensued where your mum killed the lich, and your dad killed the vampire.'

'Wow! How did you know all this and how have I never heard anything?' Neve asked.

'My mum told me. She was there. I guess the memory is too traumatic for your mum to retell.'

'Hm, I guess.' Neve continued looking at the photos she had downloaded from her phone. She paused when one of the Rowan family filled the screen.

'Mm, Jasper!' Neve and Fiona chimed in perfect unison.

'At least our folks can't complain about his bloodline status,' added Fiona.

'No, but he is a massive slut. I heard he's already slept with half the girls at Gaeilge High,' explained Caitlin. 'And he is a senior! Good luck pinning him down for more than one night.'

Neve laughed. 'I'd gladly pin him down for a night.'

As if on cue, her phone buzzed with a message from Jasper: END OF SUMMER HOLIDAYS PARTY AT MY HOUSE TONIGHT. OPEN INVITATION.

Screaming, she threw the phone at her friends. Then using the breathing exercises Mum had taught her, Neve tried to calm her excitement.

Jasper messaged me! The hottest boy in town sent me personal invitation!

Fiona gave her a wicked grin. 'Looks like you might get your wish.'

'Will you give up your V-card to the rat? Don't you want your first time to be special?' Caitlin asked.

Neve frowned at Caitlin for throwing a wet blanket over the elation she felt. 'With Jasper, it will be special.'

Caitlin sighed. 'To you sure, but not to him.'

'So?'

'So, you should hold out for someone who will treat you with respect. Someone who appreciates you.'

'Ugh, why are you being such a drag, Caitlin?'

'Because I care about you, and I don't want to see you get hurt. What about Lorcán Ó Máille or Kane Sheridan? They are both hotties and they're nicer boys.' Caitlin grabbed one of the carrot sticks from the snack plate on the bedside table.

'They are in our year level, so they're way too young. Boys mature slower than we do, so you need to pick one at least one year older, two years is even better. Besides, I doubt they even look at girls that way yet.'

A loud crunch filled the air, then Caitlin grinned. 'Trust me, hun, they've noticed us. Don't forget mages grow up quicker than humans.'

Neve gasped. 'You like one of them, don't you? Alright, spit it out, who are you crushing on?'

Caitlin blushed, but kept her mouth shut.

'Oh, come on, Cat. You know we won't tell anyone. Your secrets are safe with us, right Fi?'

'Of course,' replied Fiona with an eager tone to equal Neve's.

'Okay. It's Lorcán. He is so… dreamy.'

Fiona cupped her mouth in her hands to hide the big smile on her face. But the joyous expression was still there when she pulled them away. 'Are you in love?'

Caitlin bit her lip. 'Hardly,' she scoffed. 'I don't even know how he feels about me. The attraction is purely physical at this stage.'

Fiona shrugged. 'Let's go to this party. Then you can both find out what the guys think of you. Plus, it would be a great ice breaker before we start senior high school on Tuesday.'

'True,' agreed Neve. 'So, the big question is, what should I wear?'

Liam hung up his surfboard beside the outdoor shower affixed to the back of his house. Peeling off his wetsuit, he slipped under the warm water. He closed his eyes and basked in the feel of the stream cascading over his skin and seeping into his tight muscles. It was his favourite form of meditation. Then a scream, followed by fits of giggles coming from an upper floor window broke his reverie. 'Curse that girl,' he muttered as he stepped out and grabbed a towel.

Wrapping the Egyptian cotton bath sheet around his waist, Liam stepped inside. He spotted Alannah curled up on the sofa with Luna the cat purring beside her.

She was texting someone, tension swirling around her like storm clouds.

Is she oblivious to my presence, or choosing to ignore me? 'Who are you messaging?'

'Hm, what?' Alannah's attention remained on her phone.

Meanwhile his own attention shifted to the sight of her curvaceous body in a skimpy summer dress. He had not seen her wear anything so revealing for years, and the design looked new. 'Who you are chatting to and why do they have you so worried?'

'Oh. It's Emma from Melbourne.' Alannah finally glanced at him, but she took little heed of his partial nudity, or his growing arousal. 'Have you seen or heard the news at all?'

'No. I've been out at sea all day. What happened?' He sat next to her, adjusting himself in a none too subtle way, although she did notice.

Alannah showed him the footage of the volcano erupting in Melbourne.

'Christ! That's horrible. I'm so sorry, babe.' Leaning in, Liam kissed the crown of her head. At least she did not flinch when he did so. 'Are your friends okay?'

'Emma is. But we can't get hold of Mel or Cole.'

When his hand moved to her back, she stiffened. But he refused to pull away from his wife when she needed comforting.

'Neve's friends are here, by the way, so you should put some clothes on.'

So she did notice. Liam dismissed the thought as soon as it occurred. *Doesn't mean she cares.* 'Explains the squeals coming from upstairs.' He rose and headed into his room, closing the door with a little too much force. The last thing he wanted was for Alannah to feel pressured, especially at a time like this. *But what was she thinking when she put that damn dress on?*

Slumping onto the bed, he eased the towel free. He used it to contain the mess he made when thoughts of his last time with Alannah brought him over the edge. Then he threw it in the laundry hamper and fetched some clean clothes. Dressed in black cargo shorts and a tight, white surf brand t-shirt, he returned to the living room.

'Can I get you something to eat?' he asked as he fixed himself a snack in the kitchen.

'Just a coffee, thanks.'

Concern furrowed his brow. 'Have you eaten much today?'

Alannah glared at him. 'I'm not hungry, okay? What do you expect me to do? I can't exactly conjure up an appetite.'

'Jesus, Lana. I'm worried about you. I can tell you're not sleeping properly, and you've been losing weight again. Why won't you let me help you?'

'Because you can't. Let me work through my own shit, okay?'

'You could see your therapist again,' he suggested, trying to be supportive.

She snorted. 'You have no idea what my therapy entails, do you?'

'Not exactly, no. I know you said he uses unconventional methods. You tend to feel better but after a weekend of therapy, and it's those results I care about.'

Neve chose the moment to interrupt. 'Mum, can I go to Naomi's house tonight?'

'Yeah I—'

'Wait,' Liam cut Alannah off. 'Will her parents be there?'

Neve shrugged. 'I dunno. Probably.'

'Unless you can get me confirmation from her parents the answer is no.'

'But Dad—'

'I won't hear it, Neve. I don't trust Jasper anywhere near you. Rowan boys don't exactly have the best reputation for respecting girls.'

Noticing Alannah's shiver, Liam kicked himself for reminding her of Clayton.

'*You're so unfair, Dad!* All my other friends will be there.'

'So not only are Naomi's parents unlikely to be there, but it sounds like a party. You are most definitely *not* going.'

She gaped at him. 'I hate you, Dad!' Storming off to her room, she slammed the door behind her.

'Fucking brat,' he cursed under his breath.

'Do you have to be so hard on her?' Alannah asked.

'Do you have to be so soft on her?' he retorted. 'She's only fifteen, Lana. Far too young to be going to parties and hooking up with boys.'

'She turns sixteen in July. Have you forgotten what we were like at her age?'

Recalling Alannah's reckless past, Liam paled. He dreaded the thought of Neve following in her mother's footsteps. 'I remember. That's the problem. Especially if she's anything like you.'

Thunder rumbled from inside Alannah as those storm clouds burst around her. 'How. Dare. You.'

Startled, Luna sprang from the couch and skidded along the floor in her attempt to flee the room.

Shit! 'Lana, I didn't mean it like that. I'm concerned about her is all.'

'Right. Like you're worried about me. But there's nothing wrong with *you*, is there?'

Liam froze. 'What do you mean?'

Alannah sighed. 'Never mind.'

'No. I want to know what's on your mind. If I've done something wrong. If I've upset you somehow, I need you to tell me.'

'Do you really want to know what's wrong?'

'Yes. I do.'

A tense moment passed as Alannah studied him. 'You're a lousy lay, Liam. Sex with you is boring. It's why I stopped putting out for you. You don't do it for me.' Her words floored him.

Anger simmered away inside his nerves. 'So what, no sex is better than any sex with me? Is that it?'

A malicious grin formed on her perfect face. 'Who said I wasn't getting any?'

Liam's heartbeat kicked up a notch.

'Would have been so quick to suggest therapy sessions if you knew what they involved?'

Shaking his head, he denied what he was hearing, 'No.'

'Oh, yes, Liam. My therapist fucks me the way I like it because you can't.'

With his blood boiling, Liam took off in a mad dash for the gym where he pummelled the punching bag with his fists. 'Fuuuuck!'

Also By L. Starla

The Phoebe Braddock Books
(Taboo Romance & Forbidden Love)

I Heart Mr. Collins
From Prying Eyes
Crystal's Crucible
Undeniably Wrong

Winter's Magic Series
(Magical Realism / Paranormal Romance)

Winter's Maiden 1
Winter's Maiden 2
Winter's Thrall
Winter's Mother 1
Winter's Mother 2
Winter's Bride (TBA)
Winter's Crone 1 (TBA)
Winter's Crone 2 (TBA)

Serial Fiction Boxsets

Well I'll Be Damned Season 1
The Dark Matter Between Our Hearts Season 1

About the Author

Laelia Starla is an Australian author who often raided her mother's shelves for any form of fiction she could get her hands on. Her first love was the horror genre, but she owes her love affair with the romance novel to her high-school English teacher, who started her on the classics. Given her earlier reading, magical realism and paranormal romance were a natural progression. Along with steamy romance, these are the genres she writes.

Laelia also loves spending her spare time playing tabletop and video games, paper crafting, singing, dancing, and watching anime.

Access Exclusive Content

Join my newsletter to access free stuff like short stories, deleted scenes, fan art, and invitations to future launch events.

Newsletter: www.starlaarts.com>freebies

Follow me Online:
Website & Blog: www.starlaarts.com
Goodreads: 19660804.L_Starla
BookBub: www.bookbub.com/profile/l-starla
Amazon Author Profile: author/l.starla
Instagram: lstarlaauthor
Facebook: StarlaArts